# SISTERS AND STRANGERS

Nina Lambert was born in London and gained an honours degree at Kings College after studying at the Sorbonne. In 1986 she won the Romantic Novelists' Association's New Writers' Award for a first novel, the year she also began writing full-time. As well as novels, she has also written several short stories and magazine serials. Nina Lambert lives in Fulham with her husband, a Fleet Street photographer.

By the same author

PLAYERS

# SISTERS AND STRANGERS

## Nina Lambert

ARROW

Published by Arrow Books in 1995

1 3 5 7 9 10 8 6 4 2

© Nina Lambert 1994

Nina Lambert has asserted her right under the Copyright,
Designs and Patents Act, 1988 to be identified as the
author of this work

First published in the United Kingdom by Century in 1994

Arrow Books Limited
20 Vauxhall Bridge Road, London, SW1V 2SA

Random House Australia (Pty) Limited
20 Alfred Street, Milsons Point, Sydney,
New South Wales 2061, Australia

Random House New Zealand Limited
18 Poland Road, Glenfield
Auckland 10, New Zealand

Random House, South Africa (Pty) Limited
PO Box 337, Bergvlei, South Africa

A CIP catalogue record for this book is available from the
British Library

Random House UK Limited Reg. No. 954009

Papers used by Random House UK are natural, recyclable
products made from wood grown in sustainable forests. The
manufacturing processes conform to the environmental
regulations of the country of origin.

ISBN 0 09 9414015

Printed and bound in the United Kingdom by
BPC Paperbacks, a member of The British Printing Company Ltd

*For Mike, as always, with love and thanks.*

# PROLOGUE

HARRIET COLLINGTON WAS five months pregnant before anyone found out.

Collington Hall, the family seat in Sussex, lent itself to secrets, with its excess of rooms and insufficiency of occupants; Harriet was well used to being ignored. And for once in her discontented life she was glad of it. Glad that no one paid her sufficient heed to notice her swelling girth, or her wan complexion at breakfast or her sudden disinclination to ride – once her favourite recreation. One which had led to her present condition, thanks to a brief encounter with a stable hand during her Easter holidays. He had disappeared without giving notice, scared off by the letter Harriet had written from school telling him of her pregnancy. Not that she should have expected any better of him. Which made the baby all the more precious, all the more important. The baby, unlike everyone else in the world, would love her back.

With luck, her secret would be safe till she left for finishing school in Geneva in the autumn. Her parents would hear the news from a scandalised principal, who would expel her on the spot. Desperate to hush things up they would allow – no, force – her to remain abroad, which suited Harriet very well. She had no desire to return home ever again.

There was no one she would miss, except her Uncle John, an affable Cambridge don whom she saw only rarely, and poor old Aunt Rose, a polio victim who lived in a nursing home in Chichester, kept alive by an iron lung. She certainly wouldn't miss her ill-tempered old despot of a grandmother, or Aunt Emily, her father's widowed, childless sister, who was too wrapped up in Good Works to pay her niece much attention, other than by way of routine nagging.

As for her parents, she had never seen much of either of them; they spent most of their time in London. Charles Collington, as a rising Tory MP, had returned to his constituency home in Norfolk, where Harriet had grown up, only at weekends – even less frequently during the war, when he had been a junior minister in the coalition government, his reward for a leg injury sustained at Dunkirk which had spared him further active service. The unforeseen loss of his safe seat in the 1945 general election was conveniently offset by the death of his father, enabling him to take over control of *The Courier*, the family-owned newspaper, and pursue a less precarious route to power.

Harriet had always hated Collington Hall, a gloomy Victorian pile she associated with duty visits to her grandparents. And now that she had to live in it she hated it more than ever. She had no friends nearby, and the family cook, her much-loved surrogate mother, had found other work in Norfolk, near her family, depriving Harriet of a watchful eye and a listening ear, leaving her with the familiar, recurring sense of rejection and betrayal.

'The country's so much healthier for children,' Pamela Collington would declare, whilst indulging her own preference for a child-free life in Chelsea. Whenever she favoured Harriet with her perfumed presence, it was always with a party of braying weekend guests in tow, none of whom showed the slightest interest in her sullen, charmless, painfully plain daughter, what a disappointment that girl must be, and poor Pamela such a beauty.

But it wasn't just Harriet's ugly-duckling looks that failed to endear her to her parents. She had been made well aware, from an early age, that her birth had left her mother incapable of bearing any more children – specifically the son and heir Harriet should have been – a transgression for which her father would never forgive her. Divorcing Pamela, the better to beget a son, would have been political suicide, and now that a knighthood seemed well within his grasp, and in due course the peerage which had eluded his jumped-up tradesman of a father, his public image as a solid family man remained vital to his ambitions. He had married Lady Pamela Blakeney, the daughter of an impoverished earl, for her snob value, not for love, while she had married him for his

2

inheritance – a contract which still held good, despite their indifference to each other and their child.

They were both hypocrites, thought Harriet, both obsessed with keeping up appearances. And now she would turn that to her advantage. This child would be her passport to blessed independence – a flat of her own in Paris, where she would disport herself on the Left Bank at her father's expense, the price she would exact for concealing the existence of his bastard grandchild. It would be sweet revenge for all these years of being written off as 'only a girl' because only a girl, after all, could get into this particular type of trouble. Which didn't stop Harriet hoping for a son. She wouldn't have wished her own sex on an innocent baby.

If she could only have held out till October, till she was safely out of the country, everything would have gone according to plan. But in September her belly began swelling at an alarming rate, attracting the evil eye of Maureen Brady, the housekeeper, who promptly reported her suspicions to Aunt Emily. Confronted and forced to confess, Harriet waited, trembling, for her father to arrive from London.

She remembered making her defiant speech, remembered the look of loathing on his face, remembered the first savage blow to the side of her head. Remembered running away from him, and then being knocked down, on the landing. And the next thing she knew she was in bed, unable to move, with Maureen Brady keeping watch by her side.

She was told that she had tripped and fallen down the stairs, knocking herself unconscious. But Harriet knew very well that her father had pushed her, in an attempt to kill the baby and probably her as well. One which had failed, thank God, but one which condemned her, thanks to a broken leg, to remain locked in her room for the remainder of her pregnancy, well away from public view.

Pamela Collington tried every incentive to persuade her errant daughter to have a simple little operation, nothing to it, or at least give the child up for adoption. But Harriet remained adamant, repeating her threats that if they tried to force her into anything, she would broadcast her story from the rooftops; they would never be able to hold up their heads in polite society again. Likewise if they failed to meet her list of demands. For the first time in her life, she felt powerful. But she also had the sense to feel afraid.

Her father never once visited her during her imprisonment, unable to stand the sight of her, he said. But she could feel his hatred from afar. Powerless against her threats to disgrace and humiliate him, he put a curse on her unborn child. A curse which trapped it inside her, through endless agonising hours of premature labour, while she struggled in vain to set it free. A curse which consigned her to sudden, terrifying oblivion, while the doctor cut it out of her. A curse which delivered a tiny, stillborn girl into her arms, not the strong, healthy boy she had dreamed of.

Her parents and grandmother weren't there to witness their moment of triumph; they were spending Christmas in the South of France. So Aunt Emily said. But Harriet knew better. She knew that her father had been there, in the house, in spirit if not in person. That her baby hadn't been born dead at all. That he had stifled the life out of her or got someone else to do it for him – the doctor or that witch Maureen Brady or even Aunt Em herself – rather than risk a scandal. Because no matter what anyone told her, no matter how much they all denied it, Harriet was sure of one thing.

She had heard her daughter cry.

# PART ONE

*Now hatred is by far the longest pleasure;*
*Men love in haste, but they detest at leisure.*

Lord Byron

*Spring 1983*

VIVI WAS LATE for her father's funeral.

For once in her life she had stuck to the speed limit, she hadn't jumped a single red light, she had even stopped, sensibly enough, in a lay-by when a sudden spurt of tears reduced visibility to zero. And even then, half an hour behind schedule, she hadn't hurried, Vivi who hurried everywhere, who prided herself on her punctuality. For once she couldn't bear to be on time, as if by delaying the event she could deny its reality. So much so that she had almost turned round and gone home again, in a futile attempt to stop it happening altogether.

But she didn't, because They would be there – Vivi had never been one to shirk a confrontation. Especially a confrontation with her two sworn enemies – the Other Woman who had stolen her father, and more importantly the Other Woman's daughter, Dad's daughter, Vivi's half-sister, whether she liked it or not. And she didn't like it, or rather her, Gemma, Gemma who was everything Vivi wasn't – sweet-tempered, sensible, modest, nice, a good little daddy's girl. An unworthy rival who wasn't worth hating, except on principle.

She was twenty minutes late by the time she drove through the gates of the crematorium in the battered VW Beetle she had bought two years, one endorsement and several minor prangs ago. Quelling another bout of nausea – she had been sick twice that morning already – she joined the ranks of parked cars outside the soulless municipal chapel. Standing by the door, watching for her arrival, was a tall, slim, fair-haired girl of twenty wearing a navy raincoat – a sober contrast to Vivi in her blood red suit and matching broad-brimmed hat, accessorised by outsize gypsy earrings. Black tights were her only concession to mourning.

'Vivienne?' queried Gemma, tilting her head. And then, with provocative politeness, 'Of course it is. You haven't changed a bit.'

'You have,' drawled Vivi, feeling infuriatingly short and squat despite her customary three-inch heels. 'Last time I saw you you were only up to here.' She indicated somewhere well beneath her.

Gemma had grown to a perfectly proportioned five-foot-nine against her sister's top-heavy five-four. In a perfect world Vivi would have cut a few inches off her bust and added them to her legs, but in an imperfect one, largely populated by tit-men, she had learned to make the most of what she had – unlike Gemma, who was wearing not a scrap of make-up, and as for that shapeless gaberdine mac, it looked like a leftover from her school uniform.

None of which stopped her being pretty, damn her. Looking at her, Vivi felt like a child again, a sturdy, graceless tomboy of seven confronted with a cute little three-year-old moppet, a creature she hadn't known existed until her mother had broken the news of Dad's second, secret family through a haze of gin.

'Daddy's not coming back,' Harriet had told her, in a high, cracked voice. 'He's left us for a horrible, wicked woman he loves more than Mummy. He's gone to live with her, and his other little girl.' A little girl he obviously loved more than Vivi. And when Vivi first saw Gemma she could understand why, which made the pain even harder to bear. She would have scratched out those innocent grey eyes on the spot if she hadn't been too proud to admit to being jealous, too afraid of losing Dad altogether.

He had wanted her to get to know and love her little sister, so he claimed, displaying his journalistic knack for dressing up malice as morality. And so from that day on Vivi had had to share him with a boring brat, a blight on the precious Sundays when he drove to London to see her, an even worse blight on the weekends he took Vivi back to his new home in Wiltshire.

It had taken Vivi eight years to pluck up the courage to refuse to see him except on her own territory, and without her sister's presence. A decision in which her mother had supported her wholeheartedly – which was why it had taken Vivi so long to make it. In Dad's presence she might be fiercely loyal to her mother, but at home she insisted on siding with the enemy. Harriet thought that Vivi blamed her for the split, Dad that she blamed him. The truth was that Vivi had always blamed herself.

Dad had visited less frequently after Vivi's ultimatum, but she had got her own back on him later. She had been too busy forging her career to make much time for him. Even when he had had heart surgery, three years ago, she had visited the hospital only once, taken in by his false reassurances that the operation had been a complete success . . .

'We'd better go in, everybody's waiting,' said Gemma. Vivi followed her numbly to the front pew, where they had kept a seat for her. The place was packed, the numbers boosted by a few old colleagues from the Street, plus the entire staff of the *Alchester Weekly Post* looking for a free piss-up – the usual local rag assortment of young indentured cheap labour and ageing plodders, peppered with the odd burned-out case like Dad. Dad who had risen to editorship of *The Courier*, once Britain's best-selling national daily, and then thrown it all away in a fit of mid-life crisis.

Gemma's mother, the second Mrs Chambers – whom Harriet still referred to as 'that scrubber' – was just as Vivi remembered her, a blowsy, heavily made-up, brainless blonde reeking of too much perfume. She was wearing a mock-ocelot coat over her tight black dress, and dark glasses over eyes that were leaking into a naff lace-trimmed hanky.

Vivi sat stiffly while some all-purpose cleric who had never met Dad in his life delivered a fulsome eulogy, referring frequently to his notes. She had to suppress a twitchy urge to take down his words in shorthand, as if to distance herself from the proceedings. She had never understood how Dad had borne it, living in this backwater, presiding over pages of church fetes, weddings, baby shows and amateur dramatics. He had grown to hate Fleet Street, so he claimed, warned Vivi repeatedly not to let it destroy her, the way it had nearly destroyed him. Transparent self-justification for running away. If his second marriage, and this tinpot editor's job, had been a success, of sorts, it was only because they had been too easy to fail at.

Vivi herself had never worked for a local paper; she had served her three years' apprenticeship on a big provincial daily, moved on to a London news agency, and thence to casual shifts on *The Echo*,

*The Courier*'s much more successful mid-market competitor, where she had finally landed a staff reporter job, having declined a better offer from her grandfather. She couldn't have borne to work for the old sod, better known as Viscount Collington, proprietor of *The Courier* and Dad's erstwhile boss and father-in-law. Too bad this wasn't his funeral instead.

Never having been to a cremation before, Vivi wasn't prepared for the swish of a curtain and the creaking disappearance of the coffin. Collington family funerals — Vivi's maternal grandmother had died the previous year — were of the old-fashioned six-feet-under variety, with everybody standing round the grave in the fifteenth-century churchyard in Little Moldingham. Cremation was an awful lot cheaper, of course, which was presumably why Barbara had chosen it, although the coffin had been a polished mahogany brass-handled model. Bit of a waste, really, in the circumstances. Vivi found herself wondering if they really incinerated it with the body, or whether they were in cahoots with the undertakers to recycle it. Could be a story in that. FURORE OVER FUNERAL FIDDLES. CREMATORIUM CON-MEN BOX CLEVER. A burning issue, ha ha. Oh God. She was going to cry . . .

Vivi cried often. Stormily, angrily, copiously, but always in private, determined not to appear soft, the way most women were. Although a self-styled feminist, she had little respect for her own sex, most of whom were just the kind of weak, weepy creatures who got women a bad name. And now here she was, being weak and weepy, blubbering her heart out over someone she wasn't supposed to love. For the first time since Gemma's bald, matter-of-fact telephone call, it hit her that her father was really gone. He had deserted her a second time, only this time it was for ever.

Blowing her nose to stifle another sob, she stumbled out into the daylight, as if reaching for wakefulness after a bad dream. It was a bright, clear March day, the kind that ushered in a killer frost, threatening the early buds lured out of hiding by a mild winter. Fearing another bout of tears she took refuge in the privacy of the Beetle, amid the usual detritus of empty cigarette packets, sweet wrappers, old newspapers and used polystyrene cups, struggling to pull herself together, envying Gemma her dry-eyed composure. Even as a small child, Gemma had been infuriatingly self-contained; it took a hell of a lot to make her cry. She had had plenty of time, of course, to prepare herself for Dad's death. She had known all along that it was only a matter of time before his heart gave out altogether. Knowledge he had chosen to share with her, his favourite, but not with Vivi – presumably to make her feel guilty for neglecting and rejecting him, after he had gone. Well, she didn't. Why should she, when he had done the same to her?

There was a tap on the driver's window. Swallowing hard, Vivi wound it down.

'Mum says she hopes you'll come back to the house,' said Gemma. 'There are a few things of Dad's she'd like you to choose from. He wanted you to have his watch.'

Vivi would have liked to tell her to poke the watch, she wasn't about to be paid off with some cheapskate memento for all those years without a father. But fear that her voice would break, and make her sound hysterical, forced her to settle for a craven nod.

'Are you all right to drive? You don't look well.'

'I've just got a filthy hangover,' croaked Vivi, quite untruthfully. Alcohol gave her vicious migraines. When imbibing at *The Echo*'s local she would stick to bottled Guinness, which she detested, thereby making it impossible for her to drink too much of it, and feign varying degrees of inebriation as the occasion warranted, so as to seem like one of the gang. Not that she would ever be one of the gang. How could you be, when your grandfather was proprietor of a rival paper? Not that she cared one way or the other; she despised people who needed to be liked.

Vivi had no desire to go to the wake, just a perverse compulsion to revisit that hated house one last time. She had always dreaded coming here as a child, despite Barbara's stubborn efforts to make her welcome – efforts designed, to Vivi's mind, to put her in the wrong.

Thirty-nine Chipstead Close was a far cry from Trevor Chambers' first matrimonial home, a listed Georgian house in Holland Park, a place where he had never fitted in. He had adjusted more easily to life in a nondescript semi, much like the one he had grown up in. An only child born to middle-aged parents, both of them dead long before Vivi was born, he had got into journalism in the war, editing a forces newsletter, and done time on *The Mail*, *The Sketch*, *The Express* and the news desk of *The Courier* before his surprise elevation to the editor's chair at the age of thirty-five. He had met Vivi's mother at the old man's annual birthday party, unluckily for both of them. They had fallen madly in love on sight, so Harriet said, a cautionary tale which had not been lost on her daughter.

Faced with a sea of unknown faces, Vivi latched on to the first person she recognised, Reg Beatty, a veteran Fleet Street snapper, who homed in on the booze like a fly on a dungheap and dispensed her chosen poison of gin and tonic. She listened patiently to the well-worn story of how Reg and Trev had scuppered a *Mirror* buy-up by rumbling their hotel hide-out in Brighton and posing as room service waiters. Recognised by their rivals as soon as they entered the room, Reg had nonetheless managed to fire off a few frames, while Dad had milked yards of copy out of their twenty-second sortie.

Ah yes, those were the days, agreed Vivi, knocking back her drink in one gulp to loosen the prickly tightness in her throat. Recklessly she accepted another, cursing herself for being stupid enough to come here. She might have known she would see things she hadn't seen – or allowed herself to see – before. Since her last visit she had been trained to observe, to pick up on little details. And this house told her what she had always suspected, always denied. If you looked beyond its mass-market decor, its neat-as-a-new-pin ordinariness, you saw, or rather felt, something else – that Dad had been happy here, or at least as happy as he was capable of being. And once you acknowledged that unpalatable fact, every-thing else made perfect, obvious, utterly depressing sense.


'Poor lamb,' clucked Barbara Chambers, shutting the door of the spare room. It wasn't the first time Vivi had disgraced herself in this house. 'She looks terrible.'

'She's drunk, that's all,' said Gemma, who had had to scrub the sick out of the bathroom carpet.

'Perhaps we should phone her mother.'

'She'll be all right in the morning,' said Gemma, well aware that the task of phoning Harriet would fall to her. 'Just leave her to sleep it off . . . oh Mum.'

Gemma put a weary arm around her while she wept anew. Now that everyone had gone Mum would go back to bed, where she had spent the last seven days, and continue to nurse her grief while Gemma emptied the ashtrays and cleared up the debris and did the washing-up before returning to the mountain of worrying paperwork death had left in its wake. Dad had elected her executor of his will, to save on legal fees, thus subjecting her to a nightmare of form-filling and letter-writing, as if she hadn't had enough to do, organising the funeral and cutting sandwiches into the small hours of last night, while her mother slept in the arms of Mogadon.

'Promise me you'll look after her after I'm gone,' Dad had said, three years ago, when he had received his death sentence. 'She can't manage on her own.' Mum was a delicate flower to be cherished in a hothouse, Gemma a hardy evergreen shrub who could weather any storm. It was as if she had been preparing for this moment all her life, learning to be strong and capable and uncomplaining and unselfish, if only to compensate for all the things she could never be, all the things Vivi was without even trying – clever, witty, talented, outgoing and, above all, lovable.

Much as Gemma had dreaded meeting her again, she was determined not to let it show; Vivi had always been good at smelling and exploiting fear. Dad had made a point of turning a blind eye to the torments Vivi inflicted on her, and once the twice-monthly ordeal was over he would scold a sullen Gemma for 'spoiling things'.

'What a misery you are,' he would bark, followed by variations on the eternal theme of 'why can't you be more like Vivi?' even though it must have suited him very well, in the end, that she wasn't. What she wouldn't have given to be like Vivi, her bright, brave, brilliant sister! But it was like trying to fly. And so she had fallen, almost gratefully, into the alternative role life had offered her, striven to be good instead, even though she wasn't the least bit good inside, in the hope of pleasing him, as Vivi did, as her little-woman of a mother did, a mother who always followed Dad's example by taking Vivi's part against her, because poor Vivi was the victim of a broken home. Lucky thing. A child was bound to have more power in the wake of a divorce, with both parties courting its allegiance. But in a love match, a united front, a third party didn't get a look-in.

Just as Gemma was preparing to take the dog for his bedtime

walk, her final job of the day, she noticed a whey-faced Vivi at the top of the stairs, watching her.

'I'll do it,' she said, descending and taking hold of the lead. 'I feel like some air.' She crouched down and nuzzled the dog. 'Hello there, Snatcher,' she murmured. Dad must have told her his name, thought Gemma. Snatcher, Dad's faithful companion, had ostensibly been bought as a birthday present for twelve-year-old Gemma, who would have much preferred a cat. 'Are you dying for a crap, old boy? Come on, let's go and do it on somebody's front path.'

'You'd better take my coat,' began Gemma automatically, but Vivi, normally a chilly mortal, waved aside the offer, stepping out into the cold night in her thin suit with an ecstatic Snatcher bounding after her like a rat in thrall to the Pied Piper.

Glad as she was to be spared the chore of supervising Snatcher's bowel movements, Gemma felt duly spurned and couldn't suppress a frisson of satisfaction when it began to rain, never mind the muddy pawprints she would have to clean up. She expected a hurried return, but it was a good half hour before Vivi reappeared, soaked to the skin. Snatcher shook himself messily before retiring to his basket in the kitchen; Vivi had evidently exhausted him.

Her normally fat, glossy curls had gone frizzy, her red jacket was soaked through, her silver hoop earrings adorned with crystal droplets, her face gleaming with a sheen of rain. The mascara which had withstood her fit of weeping still hadn't run, her huge dark kohl-ringed eyes looked more houri-like than ever.

'You'll catch cold,' scolded Gemma. 'You'd better take those wet things off. There's hot water for a bath, if you want one.'

She hadn't intended to be hospitable, let alone so boringly mumsy, but looking after people was second nature. Ignoring these overtures, Vivi picked up her handbag, rummaged for a fag, and sat down damply on the floor, removing her wet jacket to expose a white jumper through which her large breasts (which Gemma envied like mad) bulged explicitly. 'I don't suppose you smoke, do you?' she asked, shivering, offering her the crumpled pack.

Gemma didn't, but she took one anyway while Vivi struck a Swan Vesta, even though she must surely possess a gold lighter or three. Gemma thought smoking a filthy habit, but she was well used to inhaling fumes willy nilly; Dad had never been without a cigarette in his hand, polluting every room in the house, flouting his doctor's orders to cut down. Gemma had resented him for not taking better care of himself, for the years of weak-willed self-indulgence which had hastened his death and left her to cope with Mum alone. She envied Vivi her ability to weep for him; so far Gemma had wept only for herself.

'Is there any coffee on the go?' said Vivi, excavating the contents of her outsize handbag, disgorging a spare pair of tights, a toothbrush, a dog-eared shorthand notebook, two odd earrings, a whiskery comb, a phial of Opium, a can of Mace, and a wad of parking tickets before finally locating an elusive packet of Anadin.

'No milk, three sugars,' she called after Gemma, who was already in the kitchen. And then, as an afterthought, 'Thanks.' Thanks rather than please, acknowledging the service rather than soliciting it. Vivi, unlike Gemma, was used to people doing things for her. Gemma returned with two mugs of instant and a plate of biscuits, and re-lit the gas fire.

'Ginger nuts,' approved Vivi, dunking one. They had always been her favourite. 'So, what are you doing these days? Still working for the *Post*?' As if she didn't know.

Gemma nodded uncomfortably, well aware that Vivi despised her for being only a secretary.

'You must have been there going on for three years now. Time you moved on.'

'I like the job,' lied Gemma.

'So Dad kept telling me. Following in your mother's footsteps, he said.' As if Gemma needed reminding that Mum had once been Dad's secretary on *The Courier* – until she had got pregnant and been set up in what Harriet would have called a love nest in North Ken, a stone's throw from his legitimate family home. 'Terribly efficient and unflappable, a real little treasure. That's a big mistake, you know. Good secretaries never get promoted.'

A 'little treasure', eh? Patronising bitch. It wasn't even true. Dad had never missed a chance to find fault. Gemma hadn't wanted to work for the paper at all, except that he had set it all up for her, as if doing her a big favour, and she had bottled out of rebelling, as always, telling herself that one boring job was much like another. Even though she knew that this was just his way of keeping her at home, of making sure she would still be around to look after Mum when he died.

If she'd gone to art school, as she'd longed to do, instead of taking that shorthand and typing course, she would no doubt have ended up unemployed and unemployable. Or worse, discovered a world full of promise and possibilities, only to be forced to forsake it, out of duty. As it was, the one abiding passion of her life had been dismissed as an adolescent infatuation, her one talent confined to a harmless little hobby which threatened no one but herself.

'Perhaps I don't want to be promoted,' said Gemma, puffing ineffectually on her cigarette. 'We can't all be clever like you.'

'You don't need to be clever if you're blonde and pretty,' observed Vivi, with what seemed, to Gemma, like contempt. 'Specially if you've got good legs. There are a couple of hackettes at *The Echo* who are thick as shit.'

Like me, you mean, thought Gemma. Dad had certainly thought so. Three O levels from Alchester Comprehensive, one of them in art, which didn't count, was no match for Vivi's four A levels from St Paul's, or the place at Somerville she had turned down to make an early start on her career. As for 'blonde and pretty', Gemma's vanity had been knocked out of her at an early age. Dad had been a great one for yelling at her to 'wipe that muck off your face, you look like a tart' – something he would never have dared to say to Vivi. And Mum, who plastered on make-up with a trowel herself, was obsessed with Gemma 'not getting herself into trouble', which was great, coming from her. When Gemma looked in the mirror she saw someone colourless and ordinary, someone who wasn't brave enough to be anything else.

'So what was he like to work for?' said Vivi suddenly.

'Impatient,' shrugged Gemma. 'Intolerant. Tactless. A bit of a bully.' Just like you, she thought. 'He didn't suffer fools gladly. People were pretty scared of him.'

'Including you? Or did you get special treatment?'

'In a way. That is, if I slipped up I got bawled out twice as loud as anyone else.' If he had done it in front of other people, Gemma would have minded less. But he treated her as teacher's pet at the office, much to her discomfiture, saving his criticisms for the dinner table.

'Typical macho management technique,' snorted Vivi. 'Can you imagine a woman editor behaving like that? All the men would be sniggering about her time of the month and saying what she needed was a bloody good gangbang.' She drowned another biscuit. 'Talking of which, got a man at the moment?'

'No one special,' said Gemma evasively. It had become easier to turn dates down than endure the humiliation of having her misguided admirers vetted and found wanting by her parents. 'You?'

'No time. Too busy. Just the odd one-night stand here and there.' She dropped her stub into the remains of her coffee, making it hiss, and helped herself to the last biscuit. 'Sorry to be such a pig, but I'm eating for two.'

'Oh,' said Gemma, trying not to sound shocked. It was hard to imagine Vivi with a baby, even one of those deliberate single-parent jobs that proved how liberated and independent you were. Vivi had always despised Gemma's collection of immaculately cared-for dolls.

'Till two o'clock on Saturday afternoon, that is,' added Vivi. 'Then it's bye-bye, baby.' She made a pulling gesture and a whooshing noise to indicate the flushing of a loo. 'So there's no need for you to start knitting bootees just yet.'

Typical, thought Gemma. A routine abortion had been predictable, a compulsory rite of passage for someone like her sister. She had always been a conspicuous consumer with a low boredom threshold, the type of person who threw away an ice cream or an apple before she had finished it, who left food on her plate, unlike Gemma who had been brought up to waste not, want not. She hadn't even bothered to smoke her cigarette down to the tip, and half her coffee had cooled in the mug, mushy with bits of disintegrated biscuit. And at two o'clock on Saturday she would discard her baby too. Easy come, easy go . . .

No, not easy. If it was easy, she wouldn't be crying again. Unable to hide her face behind the crumbling remains of a tissue, she had turned away, shoulders heaving in time to her silent sobs. Dad's grandchild, thought Gemma. His favourite grandchild, had he lived, had it been allowed to live, never mind who its father was. At least her own children, assuming she ever had any, wouldn't find themselves competing for his favour with Vivi's.

'Here,' said Gemma, handing her a clean cloth hanky. She had never seen her sister cry before, and now it had happened twice in one day. Weeping for Dad was one thing but she wouldn't have expected her to shed a single tear over her right to choose. And yet she was obviously deeply distressed, so much so that Gemma blurted out, 'Are you sure you don't want to have the baby?' because there were other solutions, after all.

'It's not a baby!' snapped Vivi. 'Just because I'm pregnant doesn't mean it's a baby! Stop trying to make me feel guilty, will you?'

'I wasn't trying to make you feel guilty,' protested Gemma. 'It's just that you seemed so upset that I – '

'I'm not upset! My fucking hormones are up the creek, that's all. I suppose you think it's murder, you would do. Well, I won't be forced into doing anything I don't want to do, by you, by anybody.'

'Since when have I ever forced you to do anything? You're the one who used to force me to do things, not the other way round.'

Vivi's scowl erupted, with startling suddenness, into that familiar, sinister, wide, wicked grin. Odd that Vivi was so attractive when she didn't ought to be. Her nose was too resplendently Roman, her jaw too square, her mouth too big, features she had inherited from her mother. But somehow they conspired, in her as in Harriet, to create an illusion of beauty.

'Like that time I dared you to drop Dad's keys down the drain?' she goaded.

Dad had left the car parked on a yellow line while he went to buy some cigarettes. Gemma couldn't remember the exact wording of the taunts Vivi had used to coerce her into removing the keys from the ignition and doing the dreadful deed, but no doubt she had called her a goody-goody and a cowardy-custard. What she did remember, very clearly, was the thrill it had given her, the heady mixture of triumph and terror. And then, just as she was quaking at the prospect of having to own up to her crime, Vivi had blithely beaten her to it by making a false confession, claiming that she had been jingling the bunch of keys through the open window and dropped them, tee hee.

Dad had laughed, called her a walking disaster area, and produced a spare set from the glove compartment, leaving Gemma feeling strangely cheated. In a fit of kamikaze pique she had tried to tell him the truth, but he hadn't believed her, and later he had told her off for attention-seeking and telling lies.

'I can't remember,' said Gemma.

'No, I don't suppose you would. You were only six or seven at the time. Time I got moving.' She stood up, showering biscuit crumbs everywhere.

'Are you sure you don't want a bed for the night?' Gemma felt bound to say.

'No. Got to work tomorrow.'

'Mum wanted you to have a look at these.' Gemma fetched a box of keepsakes from the sideboard; besides the watch she had mentioned there was a silver fountain pen, a pair of cuff links and a signet ring. Vivi fingered them absently.

'He's left you a load of books in his will,' added Gemma. 'I haven't had time to sort them out yet. There's been so much else to do. But I'll get them to you in the next couple of weeks.'

Vivi slipped the pen into her bag and left the rest.

'This'll do,' she said. 'I'm not much of a one for souvenirs. And anyway, it's sheer hypocrisy, given that I've spent most of my life hating his guts.'

Gemma stifled the reckless urge to say 'You too?', muzzled by long practice of keeping her feelings to herself. Or rather, from herself. So effectively that she hadn't realised until that moment how close love was to hate.

Or hate to love, come to that, she thought, as she saw her sister out.

IT WAS THREE in the morning by the time Vivi arrived at her flat in Clapham Junction. She had felt horribly middle-aged, sinking her legacy from her great-aunt Rose (which had been kept in trust until her twenty-first birthday) into bricks and mortar, instead of blowing it all on something wild and wicked, but it was better than enriching yet another rip-off merchant of a landlord or having to share with other people. Vivi had a low tolerance level to other people. She didn't mind mess, as long as it was her mess. Woe betide anyone else who neglected the washing-up or left pubic hairs on the soap. Or who dared object when Vivi did the same.

She didn't like the area much, or the flat, but that was part of her policy of not getting too attached to places or things. Or people, come to that. She had never got round to redecorating and had purchased the furniture with a studied lack of interest; it was just a place to sleep. Sleep meaning sleep – she only ever had sex at the man's place, where she was the one who got up and walked away afterwards, not him.

And besides, she couldn't afford anywhere better; Rose, like her brother John, had died before she had the chance to inherit her share of the Collington millions, which had remained locked up until the death of their mother who had outlived them. Vivi might be technically rich, thanks to the nine per cent holding in *The Courier* Rose had left her, but those were paper assets she had no intention of converting into cash. Not even if Gramps carried out his oft-repeated threat to sell to an outsider – his way of keeping Gerald, Vivi's half-brother, in line, Gerald who lived for the day when he would sit in the proprietor's chair, and transform the ailing, pompous right-wing broadsheet into a politically indepen-dent, classless bastion of integrity and truth.

Gerald and Daniel were the issue of Harriet's first marriage to

Toby Lawrence, an impecunious English artist she had met in Paris whilst attending a cordon bleu cookery course; much as her father had opposed the match he had had no choice but to give his consent to legitimise the child she was carrying. Two years later Toby had left her with a pile of debts, one small son, and another one on the way.

Vivi adored both her brothers – Gerald, the elder, for his unfailing good nature, and Daniel because he was a selfish, cold-hearted swine. Daniel had made his name in the early seventies, as a freelance war photographer in Vietnam, since when he had secured assignments in the pick of the world's trouble spots, from Northern Ireland to Afghanistan; he was currently somewhere in the wilds of El Salvador. Vivi worried about him almost as much as Harriet did, the stupid macho bastard.

Gerald, now aged thirty-two, was the prospective heir to the Collington empire. He had started on a regional daily straight from Oxford, having taken a first in PPE, and spent several years as *The Courier*'s lobby correspondent before taking up his current post of leader writer, expounding his grandfather's views to one point four million readers – less than half as many as there had been when Dad resigned, a situation which Gramps blamed on everyone but himself.

Charles Collington (commonly referred to as CC) spent more and more of his time at his villa in Cannes, but he continued to keep a tight telephonic hold on the running of the paper, becoming more unreasonable and dogmatic with every year that passed – at least as far as his staff and his family were concerned. The rest of the world knew only his public face, a very charming one when it suited him; having been a politician in his time, CC was an accomplished actor, best known for his roles as staunch defender of family values and old-fashioned aristocrat.

In fact there was no blue blood in his veins; his only pretensions to class were via his wife, a penniless society beauty whose expensive tastes had driven her to marry beneath her. Arthur Collington, Charles' father, who had died in 1945, was a builder's son, who had got rich out of the First World War, thanks to his investments in coal, iron, steel and shipping. His profits had served to expand the thriving family construction business which had funded the purchase of *The Courier* in 1928

21

and secured, however indirectly, a safe parliamentary seat for his eldest son.

There was never any question that Charles would succeed him as proprietor. John, his younger brother, a history don, had no interest in running a newspaper, Emily had got religion after her husband was killed in the war, and poor Rose, an invalid, was living on borrowed time. And at least Charles had a child to pass his heritage on to; only a girl, unfortunately, but one who might go on to bear sons.

Rose had succumbed to pneumonia in 1962, leaving her estate to Vivi. John's will had divided his property and shares equally between his two nephews. He had shot himself in 1964 in the wake of a homosexual scandal involving one of his students, an event which had given his mother the seizure which led to her own death a few months later, thus releasing the bulk of the Collington fortune, which passed to Charles in its entirety. Emily, although still alive at the time, had converted to Catholicism and joined a closed order of nuns; Charles had had the foresight to buy out both her shares in the paper and her claim on her mother's estate, an offer which had been snapped up by her superiors, who were both greedy and unworldly enough not to realise they were being cheated.

It was no coincidence, in Vivi's view, that Dad had resigned soon after the old man became mega-rich. CC had always been autocratic, but now he became megalomaniacal. No editor since Trevor Chambers had lasted longer than three years, while the board consisted of a bunch of self-seeking yes-men, hanging on in hope of a takeover and a golden handshake. Fiercely protective of Gerald, Vivi had staunchly resisted the old man's attempts to turn brother and sister into rivals for his throne, suppressing the one inadmissible ambition which had haunted her all her life. Gerald, touched by her loyalty, had promised to appoint her his right hand if and when he inherited. Daniel, meanwhile, wanted nothing to do with the paper. As a reluctant and largely absentee shareholder, he retained his holding only because he would have been obliged, under the terms of the company articles, to offer them for internal sale first, which effectively meant offering them to CC – the only one who could have afforded to buy them.

Vivi let herself in, switched on the light, and received a winking welcome from her answering machine. Yawning, she pressed the playback button.

'Vivi, it's Harriet. Why aren't you back yet?' (Harriet, ahead of her time, had reared all her children to call her by her Christian name; 'mother' and all its diminutives made her feel old.) 'Ring me when you get in.' Beep. 'Vivi, it's Nick Ferris.'

It had been a waste of time refusing to give him her home number. Nick Ferris of *The Torch* had been known to call up public figures on their private, unlisted lines and write up long and detailed interviews on the basis of a single expletive. He and Vivi had been stuck on an all-day doorstep together the previous week and she'd made it clear, despite his gift for making her laugh, that there was nothing doing.

'I was wondering about dinner one night next week,' went on the cheerful cockney voice. Dream on, thought Vivi, annoyed to find herself smiling. 'I'll ring you again.' Beep. 'This is the Carlton Clinic. Can you kindly check in at eight a.m. on Saturday instead of twelve noon? Please confirm.' Beep. 'Vivi, it's Daniel. All right if I crash at your place tonight?' Beep, beep, beep.

Stifling a yelp of glee Vivi opened the door of the second bedroom to see her brother fast asleep. She had given him a set of keys when he had moved to Paris, following the break-up of his marriage, so that he could use her flat as a London base. But this was the first time he had visited in months; working for a big French news agency kept him constantly on the move.

The divorce had been inevitable. Daniel had never been husband material. In theory, he had married Natasha, a Russian exchange student he had met at a party, to enable her to stay in the country. In practice, he had fallen in love with her. Something he had only admitted after their split, when Vivi had succeeded in getting him very drunk. He had certainly never admitted it to his wife.

After two years Natasha had packed her bags and gone back to her old boyfriend in Moscow. Perhaps because Daniel was never at home, or because she couldn't cope with the dangerous job he did, or because she knew he wasn't faithful to her, or because life in the West wasn't all it was cracked up to be. Daniel had been too proud to lift a finger to stop her, professing himself relieved to be free again.

The shaft of light from the hallway woke him instantly, his blue eyes opening wide in alarm; years of working under fire had left him alert even in his sleep.

'Vivi,' he said, his face relaxing. It was brown and weather-beaten; his dark hair was long and shaggy, and he had grown a beard which softened the line of his jaw, making him look uncharacteristically benevolent.

'How are you?' said Vivi, jumping on the bed and hugging him, thankful that he was still in one piece. 'How long are you home for?'

'Just a few days, between jobs. Where have you been all night, you dirty stop-out?'

'At my father's funeral.'

'God. I had no idea. I'm sorry.'

'Don't start being sympathetic. It doesn't suit you.'

'What did he die of?'

'Terminal boredom. So, did you get some good pictures?'

'Average.' Daniel lacked the self-congratulation endemic to his trade. 'You've been crying,' he added, matter of factly, reaching for his cigarettes. 'Want to talk?'

'Not really,' said Vivi, before sitting down on the side of the bed and giving him a spirited take-off of the funeral and the wake. Odd how she couldn't bear to tell him about the baby when she had told bloody Gemma, of all people. But Daniel, unlike Gemma, would demand to know whose it was, and she would end up telling him, and she didn't want to do that, because if nobody else knew she could pretend, afterwards, that it had never happened.

'I can't understand,' said Daniel finally, 'why you've still got this childish hang-up about Gemma after all these years. Your father's dead now. There's nothing to be jealous of any more.'

'I'm not jealous. I can't help it if I don't like her. She doesn't like me either, except that she's always been too pious to tell me so to my face.'

'Too clever more like. Learn from it. If someone gets under your skin, for whatever reason, you shouldn't give them the satisfaction of knowing it.'

'Like you didn't give Natasha the satisfaction of knowing it?' countered Vivi, hitting back. Daniel had a knack for making her feel over-emotional, even when she thought she was being ultra-cool.

'Bitch.'

'You asked for it.'

'And now you're asking for it. Shut up and go to bed, I want to sleep.'

Vivi did so, well used to such curt dismissals. This one she had invited, to cut their discussion short. She could feel another bout of tears coming on and she didn't want Daniel to see them.

That evening found Vivi and Daniel at their mother's dinner table. Harriet had rung again first thing and Vivi had used the news of Daniel's visit to evade an interrogation on the funeral.

The Honourable Harriet Driscoll (even after three marriages she was still entitled to use the handle, her only legacy, so far, for being the daughter of a viscount) still occupied the house in Holland Park bought on her marriage to Vivi's father. Keeping up the mortgage on two homes had kept him poor until she had found another husband to take it over. But within two years of her divorcing Simon Driscoll, another adulterer, his antique business had gone spectacularly bust, leaving her with no maintenance, a large overdraft, and an expensive drink problem. Her father had refused to bale her out, saying that she should sell up and move into his country home in Little Moldingham, as she had been forced to do once before when her first husband had deserted her.

It was Gerald who had come to her rescue. Like Vivi, he had sunk his inheritance into buying a modest property (Daniel had frittered all his away); trading up from a bachelor flat to Harriet's four-bedroomed house, even at a bargain price, had meant taking on a hefty mortgage which gobbled up most of his salary, but it had enabled Harriet to clear her debts, realise some capital, and keep her home. An act of defiance, as well as charity, on Gerald's part; he couldn't bear, by his own account, to deliver her into the old man's clutches. Exiled to Collington Hall, she would undoubtedly have drunk herself to death.

Thanks to Gerald's supervision, Harriet was now on the wagon, most of the time, if dependent on other non-alcoholic palliatives – shopping, prolonged holidays, Valium, alternative medicine, and sex, in the shape of a succession of biddable, beddable young men – all of which made inexorable inroads into her nest egg, making it ever more vital that Gerald secure his birthright. Harriet's mission in life was to marry him off to a nice girl who would provide him with a son – or rather provide the old man with a great-grandson, thereby giving him an incentive to keep the paper in the family. But so far Gerald had remained stubbornly single, much to Lord Collington's disgust.

'What's the matter with you, boy?' he would demand at regular intervals. 'If you carry on like this, folks will take you for a queer like my brother, God rot him.' An innuendo which Gerald bore with his usual stoical composure.

'Are you?' Vivi had asked him once, wanting only to tell him that it didn't matter, she was on his side.

'Sometimes I wish I was. It would make life a lot simpler.'

Since when she had concluded that he was simply shy, or ultra-fussy, or a frustrated romantic, or a combination of all three.

'Well?' Harriet challenged Vivi, having fussed at length over Daniel, who bore her attentions with his usual steely indifference. 'How was the Scrubber?' Thank God she hadn't come to the funeral, thought Vivi; the news of Dad's death had knocked her sideways, propelling her into a three-day binge from which she was still recovering.

'I barely spoke to her,' said Vivi, pouring Daniel a Scotch and water and herself a glass of tonic. Harriet wasn't a scrubber, of course, any more than a man could be. The last few years of pleasing herself had elevated her to the status of honorary male. Luigi, her current escort, returned from the kitchen at that moment bearing a glass of mud-coloured juice, some vile health-giving concoction from the blender, which he handed to Harriet with all the deference of a geisha. She had discovered him waiting tables in a trattoria in Covent Garden, and was making the most of him while Gramps was out of the country.

It infuriated Vivi how a grown woman of fifty could be so under her father's thumb. It was hard to believe that Harriet had once had the guts to defy him by getting herself knocked up at the age of fifteen. Vivi was regularly regaled with maudlin reminiscences of her dead elder sister, the original Vivienne, who had allegedly been strangled at birth, an accusation which Harriet was careful never to repeat in CC's presence. As she so often said, she had to keep the old bugger sweet, whatever the cost to herself, for Gerald's sake. A mother's life was one long sacrifice.

'Gerald's been held up at the paper again,' said Harriet. 'He said to start dinner without him. Daniel, you've lost an awful lot of weight. You're not still moping over that wretched girl, are you?'

Not deigning to answer, Daniel took another swallow of whisky and fell to intent perusal of the *Evening Standard*. He had an automatic cut-out in his mother's presence, a technique akin to meditation.

'Why don't you stay at home while you're in London?' persisted Harriet. 'I can't understand why you want to camp out at Vivi's place when it's so much more comfortable here.'

'Thanks,' said Daniel. 'But I'll be spending the next few days with a friend.'

The 'friend' was an old flame called Sally Archer. Daniel had only got as far as 'A' in his little black book before he struck lucky. Vivi had sat there and listened to him chat up the silly bitch with a callousness that defied belief. Still, at least this way he wouldn't see her in her post-abortive state. By the time he got back from his dirty weekend she would be over it.

Harriet was a brilliant cook; she adored feeding people, especially her family. High days and holidays apart, she had abandoned traditional French cuisine in favour of poly-unsaturated, high-fibre, low-cholesterol recipes, but the lentil soup, steamed lemon sole and poached pears were delicious nonetheless. Even Daniel roused himself to issue a compliment, while Luigi delighted her by identifying the hint of chervil she had chopped into the salad.

Vivi moved her food around her plate listlessly while Harriet rattled on about her plans to replace the curtains in the living room, and what the tree surgeon had said about the magnolia and how her manicurist had told her she was short of trace elements and recommended this little Chinese herbalist in Dalston, of all places, and how she and Luigi had been to see that new play at the Barbican, the one recommended by *The Courier*'s fool of a theatre critic, and it was so deathly dull they hadn't even waited for the interval . . .

It was a relief when Gerald arrived, interrupting her relentless monologue. As fair as his mother and siblings were dark, he took after his father, although the late Toby Lawrence would never have worn a Savile Row pin-stripe suit, a Harvie & Hudson shirt or the perennially anxious expression Gerald hid behind heavy hornrimmed spectacles.

'Sorry I'm late, had the old man on the blower from France for the best part of an hour. Daniel, old boy.' He shook his brother's hand. 'Good to see you. How did it go, Vivi?' Luigi he ignored. Unable to reconcile himself to his mother's taste in juveniles, he compromised by pretending they didn't exist.

'It went,' shrugged Vivi.

'Must have been an ordeal. Poor darling, you don't look at all well.'

'You should take Vitamin E, Vivi,' said Harriet. 'Though nothing compensates for an unhealthy diet. All that horrible fried canteen food and those eternal bacon sandwiches. What you need is a complete colonic irrigation, followed by a – '

Vivi just made it to the bathroom in time.

Gemma finally got the books sorted out on Friday evening. There were over fifty volumes in all, mostly about journalism – Dad had been unable, in his Fleet Street days, to walk past Simmonds without adding to his collection. There were far too many to post; she would have to take them to London by car, which would have to be this weekend – Dad's company Cortina was due to be returned on Monday – and would therefore entail the risk of finding her sister at home.

Meeting her here, on her own ground, had given Gemma the upper hand; intruding on hostile territory would reduce her to the timid, tongue-tied child of long ago. She would feel like a delivery boy, especially if Vivi had company, in front of whom she would either disown her or worse, acknowledge her, asking her in and introducing her and putting her through her paces for their amusement.

And then she remembered that Vivi definitely wouldn't be home on Saturday afternoon. She would be busy getting rid of her baby. If she timed her visit for then, she could simply leave the books outside her door and flee, her duty done.

As it happened, some visitors arrived just as she was preparing

28

to leave for London – Fred Palmer, the *Post*'s advertising manager, and his elderly mother, the Chambers' next-door neighbour. Fred, sixtyish, florid and balding, was a widower of ten years' standing who had worked on the *Post* man and boy. Dad had thought him an old fool, an opinion which Gemma shared, discreetly editing his ill-dictated letters and fending off his clumsy attempts at sexual harassment. Just the sight of him made her flesh creep, but she was glad enough to see his mother, relieved that Mum would have some company while she was out.

Gemma served them all tea and then made her escape, glad of the pretext to have some time to herself. She enjoyed driving. It was one of the few things that made her feel in control. Even Dad hadn't been able to fault her technique, which was far superior to his. Warned that he might collapse suddenly at the wheel, he had been glad enough to pay for her lessons and appoint her as his chauffeur. And Mum's, of course. She had never managed to pass her test, a failure which she blamed on her nerves.

Gemma was curious to see where Vivi lived, but Bamber Court, SW11, turned out to be an uninteresting, characterless modern block. Gemma hauled the two heavy suitcases out of the boot and set them atop the luggage trolley used for the annual family package holiday. The front door was guarded by an entryphone. Ignoring the bell for Vivi's flat, Gemma pressed others randomly until someone answered.

'I have a delivery for Miss Chambers but she's not in,' she told the occupant of flat five. 'Can you buzz the door open for me please?' Reassured by her polite, feminine tones number five complied.

Gemma pushed the trolley into the lift, alighting at the fourth floor. She had expected Vivi to live somewhere classy, but there was no carpet on the stairs or landing, and no shade on the light bulb that lit it. It wasn't sordid, exactly, but it was very far from smart. She began unpacking the books into piles outside number fifteen, which adjoined the narrow stone stairwell. In the middle of her labours an elderly woman emerged from the flat next door to find her way out barred by an open suitcase.

'You in my way,' she accused Gemma, in a thick Eastern European accent. She was small and aggressively bony, with heavily plucked startled-looking eyebrows and a small mouth painted into a grotesque red Cupid's bow.

'I'm sorry,' said Gemma, turning to remove the obstruction and knocking over a pile of books as she did so, sending several volumes cascading down the stairs.

'What you doing here?' enquired the woman suspiciously, as Gemma began gathering them up.

'I'm leaving these for Miss Chambers, she's not in.'

'She in. I hear her go out early this morning and I hear her come back, she slams door so loud everybody hear her.' And then, as Gemma returned with her arms full of recalcitrant books, 'If Miss Chambers don't let you in, who answer bell?'

'Um . . . a neighbour. I – '

'Is wrong. You could be rapist or murderer. I say at residents' committee meeting, we must not – '

The door of number fifteen flew open, curtailing her harangue.

'Something wrong *again*, Mrs Pulowska?' enquired Vivi sweetly. She looked wild and witch-like standing there, dressed in a baggy black jumper and a long black skirt, her normally tawny complexion pale against her dark clothes and the mass of uncombed curls. Mrs Pulowska shrivelled visibly.

'You have visitor,' she informed Vivi briefly before scuttling off down the staircase, as if fleeing a bad fairy.

'Old bag,' muttered Vivi. 'I'll swing for her one day. What are you doing here?'

I might ask you the same question, thought Gemma, caught in the act. Had Vivi decided to have the baby after all?

'I would have thought it was obvious. I've brought the books Dad left you.'

'I never realised there were that many. You didn't come specially, did you?'

'No, I had to come up to town today in any case. Actually, I must be going, I – '

'You couldn't help me get them inside, could you? I'm feeling a bit rough.' Vivi pointed at her stomach and pulled a face.

'Oh, you mean you – '

'Had it done this morning. They brought my appointment forward. Only takes a jiffy, they use this vacuum cleaner thing, you don't even have to stay in overnight. I worked out they were charging about a hundred quid a minute, I thought I might do a story on it . . .'

She tailed off, leaning dizzily against the door jamb.

'Are you all right?' said Gemma. 'You look about to faint.'

'I've never fainted in my life.' She threw open a large broom cupboard. 'Shove them in there, will you? I've just bunged some more caffeine in the filter, you may as well have a cup before you go.'

'Oughtn't you to be in bed?'

'I'm not ill,' snapped Vivi, over her shoulder, as she headed for the kitchen. 'It's no worse than the curse.'

Having stacked the books neatly inside the cupboard, Gemma followed the smell of fresh coffee. It would be a dark, strong, continental kind bought from an expensive specialist shop that roasted it on the premises, not the insipid own-label instant Gemma had served the other night, for lack of any alternative. Now that she was here, she might as well indulge her inferiority complex to the full, gather fuel to keep the fires of her resentment burning bright.

But not everything was as predictable as Vivi's taste in coffee. Gemma had imagined her flat as loud and flamboyant, like Vivi herself, but its predominantly beige colour scheme was safe, inoffensive and boring. The living room was equipped with two oatmeal-coloured settees and a glass coffee table; there was no other furniture, apart from built-in bookshelves, no ornaments or knick-knacks or framed photographs, nothing which bore the stamp of personality, unless you counted the jungle of luxuriantly healthy pot plants which jostled for space amid the used cups, discarded clothes, books and assorted newspapers. Gemma wouldn't have expected Vivi to have the time or patience to nurture so much rampant greenery, although she would have expected there to be a large, undisciplined dog bounding around; Vivi had always preferred animals to people. If it hadn't been for a striking oil painting of a much younger Vivi, hanging over the mantelpiece, the place could have belonged to almost anyone but her sister.

'Sorry about the mess,' said Vivi, returning from the kitchen with a tray. 'The place is overdue for a blitz.' And then, following Gemma's gaze, 'Daniel painted it, years ago.'

'It's very good.'

'Not according to him. I only keep it there to annoy him.' Daniel had won a scholarship to the Slade, but never taken it up. Something Dad had quoted at Gemma when she had wanted to apply to art schools. Daniel had real talent, he conceded (implying that Gemma didn't), but even he had the sense to know that he couldn't make a living as an artist, any more than his father had done before him.

'I was covered in spots in those days,' went on Vivi. 'He left them out, bless him.' She sat down and poured fragrant jet black liquid into thick green bistro cups. The settee was spattered with coffee stains, giving it a piebald appearance.

'I think it's brilliant,' repeated Gemma unguardedly, admiring the way he had captured Vivi's elusive personality, the potent mixture of menace and charm. He had caught the wicked glint in the almost-black eyes, the self-mocking quality of the smile; he made you look twice, the way people looked twice at Vivi in real life.

'Do you think so?' said Vivi, brightening. 'I'm no judge of a painting, especially one of myself. But then you were always good at art, Dad said, so I suppose you'd know what to look for.' She knocked back a couple of Anadin, the last two in the packet, lit a cigarette, took one puff, abandoned it, and made a bolt for the loo. There was a sound of retching, the lavatory flushing, a tap running . . . and then a bloodcurdling scream. Gemma jumped up, alarmed.

'What is it?' she called.

'I can't get out. There's a fucking s-spider hanging over the bloody door. It's not locked,' she added, by way of a plea.

Gemma swallowed a snort of childish mirth. Vivi's arachnophobia was the one chink in her armour. Dad had been regularly required to scour the Chipstead Close bathroom for lurking octopods before Vivi would venture inside. And once, in their shared bedroom, Gemma had been called upon to play knight errant when an intruder was spotted scurrying along a window sill. Had Gemma been the one with the affliction, of course, Vivi would have exploited it mercilessly, collected the creatures in matchboxes, put them down Gemma's neck, encouraged them to nest in her undies drawer. But Gemma hadn't dared behave in similar sadistic fashion, knowing that Vivi would exact a terrible revenge.

'Keep still,' ordered Gemma, composing her features. 'I'm coming in.' She opened the door to find a scowling, petrified Vivi, back against the washbasin, staring intently into thin air, tracking the enemy's movements.

'Where is it?' said Gemma, looking round.

'What's the matter with you, are you blind? There!'

Gemma followed the line of her finger. A microscopic spider was suspended, at head height, from the centre shade. Gemma detached it from its mooring, catching it in her cupped hand.

'Don't kill it!' implored Vivi. 'It's bad luck.'

She jumped convulsively to one side as Gemma reached over the bath and opened the window, releasing the hapless trespasser into the void.

'That was the smallest spider I've ever seen,' she commented. 'The poor thing was just a baby . . .' She bit her tongue too late, heard the strangled sob and turned to see Vivi sitting on the floor, face hidden behind her hands.

'Sorry. I didn't mean – '

'Piss off,' growled Vivi, blowing her nose on a towel. 'Trust you to show up when you're not wanted.'

'Pardon me for interfering. I'll just go and fetch the spider and hang it up again before I go.' She perched on the rim of the bath, looking down on Vivi. 'You're awfully pale,' she added, softening. 'You really ought to lie down.'

'There's no point being nice to me, you know. I haven't changed. If I'd changed, I'd have some soppy best friend seeing me through this, pitching in with tea and blankets, all girls together. Perish the thought.'

'Well, I'm not your friend,' said Gemma, wishing, despite herself, that she was. 'And I'm as keen to get out of here as you are to get rid of me. So do me a favour and go to bed, so I can leave with a clear conscience. You can get up again as soon as I've gone.'

After some hesitation Vivi got to her feet, brushing aside Gemma's supporting arm, and led the way, shoulders hunched, into her room. Gemma was surprised to find that it contained a single bed, occupied by a battered teddy bear she had never seen before. Like the rest of the flat it was underfurnished and done out in the same muted shade of beige. She was like some exotic bird, thought Gemma, taking refuge in a well-camouflaged nest, hiding her bright plumage from predators and the light.

'I'm cold,' muttered Vivi petulantly, even though the central heating was on full blast. She kicked off her shoes, flipped out her contact lenses, tore off her harem-sized earrings and wriggled out of her tights. 'The bloody electric blanket's on the blink.'

'Do you have a hot-water bottle?' Vivi raised her eyes to heaven at the question. 'I'll go out to the chemist's and get one. Give me your keys so I can get back in.'

Gemma bought some more Anadin while she was about it, plus a packet of sanitary towels, a carton of orange juice, a supply of ginger nuts and a bunch of daffodils. By the time she got back Vivi was asleep, or more probably feigning sleep, her head buried beneath the covers, the teddy bear languishing on the floor. Gemma boiled a kettle for the hot-water bottle, which she wrapped in a teatowel before slipping it under the duvet at the foot of the bed. This done she put the flowers in a jug – Vivi didn't seem to possess any vases – and left them by the bedside table, together with the rest of her purchases and the keys.

Poor baby, she thought as she let herself out.

## 3

RETURNING FROM HER early morning run armed with the morning papers, Vivi flicked through *The Courier* first, established that her piece – a grotty industrial tribunal job – hadn't made it past the first edition and threw it down in disgust. She was sick of her efforts being spiked, sick of never seeing her by-line – or worse, having her work credited to a more senior hack – sick of being subbed out of existence, sick of standing on doorsteps in all weathers, sick of not getting any foreigns, sick of having her expenses queried, and sick of being bawled out by Attila (alias Tony Tiller, news editor of *The Echo*, also known as the Hun) either for not coming up with a story or not checking her facts carefully enough, as if the two things were always compatible.

The competitive atmosphere on the paper – management fostered a frenetic sense of insecurity to keep everyone on their toes – encouraged its hard-pressed reporters to make a story out of nothing, adding a bit of top-spin for good measure, rather than fail to deliver, even though it was always the hack who carried the can when things backfired. Attila, who had never been on the road himself, was one of those non-flying wing-clippers who had taken the subbing route to power and who had all your copy rewritten on principle, just to remind you who was boss. Vivi hated the foul-mouthed bastard.

But she had set her sights on *The Echo* precisely because it was known to be a tough billet; if you survived it, so everybody said, anywhere else would seem a breeze. She had told herself things would improve, once she stopped doing casual shifts and joined the permanent staff. But she had been an anonymous 'staff reporter' for nearly a year now, flogging her gut day after day and getting nowhere fast; her one dubious claim to fame was holding the office record for getting rid of front-of-house callers – mostly cranks who came in with far-fetched stories – despite her well-concealed terror of turning away the scoop of the century.

Every time she came up with one of her bright ideas – like going undercover at Greenham Common – it was either ruled out of hand, or someone above her in the pecking order got the benefit of it. Every time she took a flyer – pretending she had a lead to get herself assigned to the story she wanted – Attila either smelt that she was conning him, or couldn't bear to see her shine and rewarded her with some rubbish rookie job instead.

So far she had managed not to walk out or get herself fired, if only because either course of action would have been too easy to give her any satisfaction. And if she started looking elsewhere with next to no track record, Tony would soon put the word about that she couldn't cut it.

Vivi knew that he was making things deliberately hard for her because of who she was; living up to Dad was bad enough, without having to live Gramps down. There was always the unspoken suspicion that she might leak *Echo* secrets to *The Courier*. And the underlying hope, on Tony's part, that she might start coming on to him to give herself an easier ride, an option she refused to consider. She had no moral objection to sleeping her way to the top – women got accused of it anyway, if they were successful, whether they were guilty or not – but unfortunately there was no one in the upper echelons of *The Echo* who wasn't either bald or fat or old or ugly or married, or, as in Tony's case, all five. Vivi might be promiscuous, but she was also fastidious, especially when it came to other women's husbands.

Still brooding over her first cup of coffee she tuned into the seven o'clock news, which reported a story which had broken too late to make the final editions – the explosion of a car bomb in the West End, killing both the driver and his female passenger. Almost immediately the phone rang; it was Steve, Attila's number two, despatching her to an early start. Police had traced the two victims to a semi in Kilburn, where an arms cache and a large supply of Semtex had been found, identifying them as IRA terrorists who had blown themselves up by mistake. It was a case of 'Talk to the neighbours and see what you can find out'.

Some of the neighbours would be only too willing to talk, revelling in all the attention, but that type seldom knew anything beyond the inevitable 'they were a quiet couple who kept themselves to themselves'. Others would take a superior delight in slamming the door in her face; journalists – who ranked even lower in public opinion polls than politicians, vying for bottom place with estate agents and used-car salesmen – were generally deemed unworthy of common courtesy. Attila would keep her hanging about all day, long after everybody else had gone home, and then use copy someone else had written from the agency bulletins without stirring from the office.

By the time Vivi arrived the road was already lined with parked cars and TV crews, with the pack busy carving up the territory between them, devising an information-pooling system and working towards an agreed knock-off time, when they would each ring in and tell their respective desks that all the other papers were pulling their people off the job, there was no point in hanging around here any longer. Photographers were taking identical snaps of a nondescript house, front and rear, and knocking on doors in search of a 'collect' – a private snapshot of the guilty couple.

'Hi, Vivi.'

It was Nick Ferris of *The Torch*, with his cheeky Jack-the-lad grin, hailing her as if she hadn't failed to return his phone calls and invented a dozen excuses not to go out with him. But Nick was famous – or rather notorious – for never giving up on a case.

Vivi had decided that she didn't fancy him, despite a certain off-beat sex appeal which she was loath to analyse or even acknowledge. With his stocky build and nondescript mid-brown hair, his only attractive feature was his eyes, clever, hazel, mischievous eyes that seemed to engage her in some unspoken private joke, to assume an instant intimacy. Presumably it was a variant on the technique he used on the unsuspecting public to lull them into trusting him. Originally Nick had been destined for the print – his father was a linotype man on *The Courier* – until he had jacked in his apprenticeship, on the grounds that being a hack was cushier. A hardened foot-in-the-door artist, he would carve anybody up to get a story, and yet, however much people slagged him off behind his back, everyone was glad to share a joke or a drink with him, because face to face he was impossible to dislike, and at one time or another he had done most of them a favour.

'Fancy pairing up on this one?' he said. A lot of unofficial teaming up went on between non-competing papers. *The Torch* was well downmarket of *The Echo* with its shock-horror headlines, scurrilous splashes and topless pin-ups. Nick assumed a gangsteresque undertone. 'I think I've got a hot lead.'

'So why share it?' said Vivi. The information-pooling system only applied to the kind of routine facts that no one would get any credit for anyway. If you got hold of anything special, you kept it to yourself.

'So that you'd owe me one, of course.' He smiled that untidy smile again. It made her want to touch his face and rearrange it, the way she might have tweaked an ill-knotted tie. 'We've got a meet in Rosa's caff in the High Road. Greasy spoon opposite the bingo hall.'

'When did you set this up?'

'About half an hour before anyone else got here. I used to live in the area, and my tame copper at the local nick tipped me off nice and early, so I was first on the scene.'

Somehow Nick was always first on the scene; in ten years on the job he had built up a formidable network of contacts. *The Torch* might be a comic but Nick was a bloody good writer; Vivi had never underestimated the art of telling a story in tabloidese.

'I got hold of a Mrs Fisher in number twenty-six just as she was leaving the house,' he went on. 'Turns out that her and her old man were guests at the couple's wedding, before the two men fell out over some fight in a pub. She showed me a wedding photo. Wouldn't part with it without her husband's say-so, he drives a meat delivery truck, started work at the crack of dawn. She says he has breakfast at Rosa's before he knocks off, we can talk to him there.'

'So it's basically a collect? Aren't you bringing your snapper in on it?'

'Never mind about that now. Wait five minutes or so. No need for the others to know we're working together.'

He drove off, with everyone else wondering where he was off to, and pondering the advisability, or folly, of following him. People who had tailed Nick in the past had tended not to try it twice.

Once, with a rival hack sitting on his bumper, he had stopped his car in the middle of the road, tapped smilingly on the driver's window, thrust his hand through it as soon as it opened, whisked the keys out of the ignition and pocketed them. On another occasion, on his way to a *Torch* hide-out (where they were guarding a kiss-and-tell call-girl), he had lured a posse of pursuing vehicles to a pub, made his exit through the window of the gents' and let their tyres down before making his getaway.

Just as Vivi was getting into her car she was hailed by Reg Beatty, Dad's old crony, who had been at the funeral back in the spring.

'Packing it in already?' he said.

'I've just rung in and been diverted to another job.'

'All right for some. Waste of time, this lot is. What did you make of the news about your stepma, then?'

'What news?' Vivi never thought of Barbara as her stepmother, only as her father's wife.

'I thought your little sister would have told you.'

'I'm not in contact with my sister,' said Vivi, with an annoying pang of conscience, remembering Gemma's stubborn kindness that dreadful Saturday. 'What's happened?'

'Seems Babs remarried, some bloke who works on the *Post*, and young Gemma took it pretty badly, packed in her job and left home. I was on a job down Alchester way and bumped into a local hack in the pub.'

'She's remarried? Already?' Dad hadn't been dead a year.

'Last week, he said.'

'Well, fancy that,' said Vivi, affecting a languid lack of interest. 'Look, I have to go. See you.'

Vivi remembered how she had felt when her father had finally married Barbara, thwarting her childish hopes that he would come back home. Remembered how she had felt when her mother had married slimy Simon. And felt a stab of fellow-feeling which she hastily disguised as a glow of triumph. What a piece of poetic justice . . .

The windows of Rosa's Café were steamed up, affording its clients a fuggy privacy. Nick was sitting deep in conversation with a big bruiser of a bloke dressed in blue overalls.

'I can't let it go for less than a grand,' the man was saying as he tucked into sausage, egg, bacon and two slices, which would be clocked up to Nick's expenses, with bells on, whether he had paid for them or not. 'I mean, if they're IRA, it's a case of sticking my neck out, innit? I'm talking danger money here.'

'Don't know if I can get you that much, mate,' said Nick, shaking his head.

'Any less and you can poke it. I can always ring *The Sun*.' He wrapped two large paws around a tankard of tea.

'You won't get much change from *The Sun*, mate. As for ringing them . . . well, whatever they say on the phone, my advice to you is to get it in writing. Isn't that right, Viv?'

'Definitely,' said Vivi, sitting down at the Formica-topped table. She hated being called Viv. It suggested a fat woman in curlers with a fag behind her ear.

'We can get you two hundred within an hour,' Nick went on. 'More's going to take longer, and someone else might come up with a better picture in the meantime . . .'

Vivi sat there, feeling superfluous, while Nick wore his quarry down, demonstrating, for Vivi's benefit, what a good operator he was, as if she didn't know that already. He was just showing off, damn him. If he was going to pay out *Torch* money for this picture, it would be more than his job was worth to share the goods with her. Eventually they shook hands on five hundred quid, in cash.

'Viv, you'd better ring the Hun,' said Nick, 'while I'll drive Mr Fisher round to where his wife works, to collect the picture. We'll see you back here, okay?'

It took a moment for the penny – or rather the five hundred quid – to drop.

'You'll be glad you stuck with *The Echo*, mate,' added Nick, to make sure she got the point. So he was giving her his exclusive, on a plate, no prizes for guessing why. But the chance to impress Attila was too good to pass up. If Nick thought that was all it took to get her into bed, thought Vivi, she would take a delight in proving him wrong.

She rang in from the nearest unvandalised phone box.

'Have you seen this effing picture?' demanded Attila.

'Of course. I beat him down from a thousand.' God, if she couldn't get him to agree this, Nick would despise her for evermore. 'I can write a good story round it. They've known the couple for years.'

'Hang about.' She hung about while some woman waiting to use the phone graduated from pointing at her watch to shaking her fist to hammering on the glass. By the time Tony came back a five-deep lynch mob of a queue had formed outside.

'I've got the picture desk to go halves with us. Three hundred in all.'

'Only three hundred?'

'And the effing picture had better be worth it, or I'll never hear the effing end of it.'

Vivi queued interminably at the bank and arrived back at the café breathless from running, to find Nick and Mr Fisher talking football. She began counting out notes.

'Only two hundred?' growled Fisher, pocketing the money nonetheless.

'I can make it three if I come up with a decent story,' said Vivi, whipping out her notebook. 'Now, what exactly was this fight in the pub about?'

'I saw your by-line,' said Nick, when he phoned her next morning, a Saturday. The whole story, complete with creative embellishments, had been copied from the first edition by the rest of the popular press, but that gave it credibility; Attila would have got quite jumpy if *The Echo* had ended up running it alone. The point of an exclusive – apart from the big, expensive ones you saved for the third edition – was that you had got it first, whether the public realised it or not.

'And now I suppose you're looking for your pay-off as well,' said Vivi, wishing she didn't like him so much.

'You mean, do you have to take pity on me tonight, at long last?'

'I don't have to do anything. I owe you a story, and that's all. I never promised you anything else.'

'Even if you had, I wouldn't have believed you. It takes one con-man to recognise another. Come on, Vivi. Pretend that you like me. Let me take you out to dinner.'

'No. I'll take you out to dinner,' said Vivi, who never let a man buy her a meal on principle. 'I'll book a table in my name for nine o'clock at Langan's,' she added, determined to pay her debt in style. 'And I'll be bringing my own car so you won't have to take me home.'

She rang off and sat for a moment scowling at the phone. And not just because she had finally been tricked into going out with Nick. Ever since she had heard about Barbara's remarriage, she had been toying with the notion of contacting Gemma and finding out more. It would be a pity to pass up the chance of a good old gloat.

She looked up the number in her address book – she had only ever rung Dad at work – and dialled.

'Hello?'

'Hello Barbara, it's me, Vivienne.'

'Oh. Hello dear.'

'Can I speak to Gemma please?' she said, playing it dumb.

A sound somewhere between a sniff and a sigh.

'Gemma moved out last weekend.'

'Oh really? Where can I get hold of her? It's just that I'm throwing a little party tonight, and thought she might like to come.' A likely story. But Barbara was too thick not to swallow it.

'She's at some horrible hotel in Bayswater,' she said, aggrieved, 'till she finds a place of her own. *If* she finds a place of her own. If you see her, you can tell her from me not to be too proud to come home . . .'

'Do you have a number for her?' said Vivi, cutting through the maternal crap. Having noted it down, she bid Barbara a curt goodbye and re-dialled, smelling a good story, if only she could persuade Gemma to tell it. There was a long delay while a churlish receptionist went to knock on Gemma's door; evidently it wasn't the sort of place that ran to phones in the rooms.

When her voice came on the line, it was bored, weary, unrecognisably harsh.

'Mum, I wish you wouldn't keep ringing me here. I told you before, I'm all right . . .'

'You don't sound it,' said Vivi.

There was an audibly tense silence.

'How did you know I was here?' snapped Gemma.

'It's my job to know things. Is it true that your ma threw you out?'

Even people who didn't want to talk to you couldn't resist denying wrong information.

'If you think that, then you don't know much,' said Gemma. 'Three was a crowd, that's all.'

'Have you got another job yet?'

'I'm temping. Look, I've got a lot to do, and – '

'Fancy a spot of lunch? My treat. I owe you for all the stuff you bought that day.'

'Forget it. It was only a few quid.'

'A very cheap lunch then. I'll be there around noon. 'Bye.'

Vivi arrived early as always, discovering a fire-trap of a so-called hotel. It was the type of place that catered for backpackers on a budget, with a tackily flash reception area fronting the dingy shared rooms above. Gemma didn't appear in the lobby till ten past twelve. The cool, composed ice queen of the funeral had reverted, gratifyingly, to the wary, mistrustful child of long ago.

'This is a bit of a dump,' said Vivi, stubbing out her cigarette.

'Yes, well the Ritz was fully booked.'

'Italian all right for you? There's a place across the road.'

'I don't mind.'

Vivi jaywalked her way across four lanes of moving traffic and into the restaurant, where she selected a table by the window, lit up, and asked for a bottle of the house white while Gemma was still waiting for the lights to change. Predictably, Gemma refused a starter and selected the cheapest entrée on the menu. Amused, Vivi ordered the most expensive one for herself.

'So, what's your new daddy like?' she goaded, swallowing two Anadin with her wine as a prophylactic. It was worth a headache to try and get Gemma mildly pissed, in the hope of loosening that buttoned-up tongue of hers.

'He's the office lech,' said Gemma shortly. 'Fred Palmer, his mother lives next door to us. I don't know how Mum can bear him to touch her, after Dad. I couldn't stand them pawing each other any longer. Dad made me promise to look after her, but she's got a new husband now, so he can do it instead. And that's all I'm going to say about it,' she finished, glaring, as if she hadn't been dying to get it off her chest to someone, anyone, even her sister. 'I only agreed to have lunch to pick your brains. Do you happen to know of any places for rent, or people looking for a flatmate?'

She made ravenous inroads into her plate of ravioli while Vivi toyed with a large steak she didn't want. The story was a lot less interesting than she had hoped.

'Sorry, I don't.'

'I've been to see a few bedsitters, but the landlords all want an employer's reference, and employers all want you to have a permanent address. It's a vicious circle.'

You're breaking my heart, thought Vivi. Poor little Gemma, alone in the big bad city, discovering belatedly that the world didn't revolve around her after all, a world that no longer included her doting father, one in which she would have to rely on herself for a change, as Vivi had done all her life . . .

Her conscience was pricking again, dammit. She knew she ought to offer to put Gemma up until she found somewhere else, rather than leave her to rot in that scummy hotel. But what if she didn't find somewhere else, what if she couldn't be got rid of? Worse, what if she started feeling responsible for her? She liked her life just the way it was, with no one to consider but herself. She didn't need anyone to look after her, so why should she look after anyone else?

'Is it better to go through an agency?' went on Gemma. 'What about housing associations? Is it worth putting my name on the council list, do you think?'

She sounded like a market researcher with a clipboard. She had always been methodical and cautious and practical. As a child she would never touch the interesting bits of a jigsaw until she had found all the straight pieces and assembled the frame – unlike Vivi who preferred to work the other way round. Once Vivi had given her a puzzle with half the straight pieces missing, and watched with evil delight while she tried in vain to piece them together.

Oh to hell with it. If she didn't help her out, Dad would probably start haunting her. 'Can't you be kinder to your little sister?' he had berated her, time and again, gratifying her need for his disapproval. 'What harm has she ever done to you?' And she could have replied, 'It's you that's done me the harm. But you're untouchable, you smug bastard, so I'm taking it out on her instead . . .'

'Okay, I get the message,' said Vivi irritably. 'You can stop hinting.'

'Hinting at what?'

'Oh, don't give me that innocent look of yours.' The look that said please can I have a bite of your apple or a lick of your lolly, a request she would never put into words, manipulative little beast that she was. She could turn any treat to dust and ashes in your mouth if you didn't offer, however grudgingly, to share it.

'Oh. I see. You think I want to move in on you. Well, you can stop worrying. I'll find my own accommodation, thank you very much.'

'Are you trying to make me feel like a perfect bitch?'

'No more than you're trying to make me feel like the poor relation.'

'You are the poor relation. And I'm a perfect bitch, come to that. But I was going to offer you a stop-gap anyway, that's why I asked you to lunch. No skin off my nose, I'm hardly ever in. And you don't need to be grateful, if that's what's worrying you. I'm doing it for Dad's sake, not yours.'

'Even though you hated his guts?' Gemma reminded her.

'No. Because I hated his guts. And because it'll annoy the hell out of my mother.' Vivi could never resist winding Harriet up; in a perennially vexed relationship, it was the nearest she came to communicating with her, creating a warped but compulsive intimacy.

'I can believe that,' said Gemma, with feeling.

'So don't start playing hard to get.' Vivi swapped plates abruptly. 'And get your teeth into that, you look as if you haven't eaten for a week.'

Gemma sat for a minute with her fork in the air while Vivi ate the last few ravioli.

'You're still the same rotten bully you always were,' she said, picking up her knife by way of assent. But it takes two, thought Vivi . . .

A dormant maggot of a migraine uncurled itself, woken by more than the wine, and began burrowing busily behind her right eye. She knew already that she would live to regret this, that she would get more than she bargained for, that her life would never be the same again. She felt the way she had felt when she had gone to bed with Max Kellerman, the last time she had kidded herself that she was acting of her own free will . . .

She had met him at Gramps' house in Little Moldingham, six weeks before Dad died, at the old man's seventy-third birthday party – an annual ritual to which he had invited over two hundred guests, including other press barons, politicians, media movers and shakers, senior staff of *The Courier*, sundry business associates and the usual assortment of hangers-on. Daniel was the only one of the family spared an invitation, to deprive him of the pleasure of turning it down – an academic omission, given that he was in El Salvador at the time.

Vivi had obeyed the summons as usual, if only to give Gerald moral support. And besides, this birthday might prove to be the old bastard's last . . . with a bit of luck. Harriet, who knew better than to turn up with Luigi, was escorted to the party by Gerald; mother and son were staying overnight, while Vivi was planning to make an early getaway, on the grounds that she had a hard appointment next morning.

'On his own again, I see,' muttered Gramps, to Vivi, scowling at Gerald's immaculately tailored back. A big, tall, heavy man with a full head of white hair and bushy white eyebrows, he was still an imposing if slightly stooped figure, oozing the smug self-importance that came from undeserved power and privilege. The only visible sign of frailty was his limp, a relic of a war injury, which had become more pronounced in recent years, forcing him to use a stick and to spend most of the cold winter months in the South of France, which gave him, unlike more exotic retreats, quick and easy access to London. He had been known to make a day trip of it, usually unheralded, in the hope of tripping somebody up, preferably Gerald.

'I'm on my own as well,' pointed out Vivi, who preferred to be unaccompanied on such occasions despite no lack of willing escorts. She hated being seen as half of a couple, even for an evening.

'By the time I was his age,' complained Gramps, 'your mother was nine years old. I should have half a dozen great-grandchildren by now. You work all your life to build up a business . . .'

'To run it down, more like,' Vivi corrected him, with her usual lack of reverence.

'That's enough of your cheek, young woman,' he barked. Vivi was the only person on earth who got away with being rude to him. 'All right, so I've lost heart for the struggle. But can you blame me? I might as well not have a family, what with Gerald getting more like his uncle every day, and you working for the bloody *Echo*, and Daniel marrying that little Commie tart, not that it lasted five minutes, and your mother running about with one gigolo after another, making a perfect fool of herself and thinking I don't know what she's up to. If the paper's going to end up outside the family, sooner or later, I might as well be the one to choose who it goes to.'

'You're bluffing, you old bully,' snorted Vivi. 'Nobody's going to want to buy *The Courier*, except for peanuts, and you know it. What would they be getting? A bunch of disgruntled hacks, an army of print heavies looking for a fight, a building that's falling to pieces, machinery that's on its last legs, and a fall-happy circulation. You're lucky that Gerald's prepared to take on a can of worms like that. If you had any sense you'd retire early and let him take over . . .'

She broke off as a new arrival approached, catching her eye over the old man's shoulder. Following her gaze, CC turned round.

'Max,' he boomed, extending a horny hand. 'Glad you could make it. Vivi, meet Max Kellerman. Max, this is my grand-daughter Vivienne.'

Vivi felt the instant hammer-blow of lust at first sight – less a physical response, in her case, than a psychological one. She could tell, instinctively, that Max Kellerman was a first-class bastard. He said that he was glad to know her, Vivienne, in a warm Californian drawl, shook her hand firmly enough for her to feel its imprint for several minutes afterwards, and used his smile to touch the rest of her without moving his eyes from her face, heavy-lidded eyes the colour of dark, bitter chocolate, eyes that were a good ten years older than the rest of him, as was his hair, which was prematurely grey. The rest of him looked just the right side of forty, old enough to be interesting, young enough not to be running to seed.

'Max Kellerman of Kellerman International?' queried Vivi, making the connection. Kellerman's was an up-and-coming Silicon Valley computer firm, specialising in new technology for the newspaper industry. Abroad, at least, and in the provinces,

47

where such innovations weren't blocked by the powerful Fleet Street print chapels.

Max Kellerman acknowledged his identity with a modest nod. He was well known, thanks to an efficient PR machine, as a rags-to-riches success story, who had made a fortune by devising his own revolutionary brand of software, using the proceeds to branch out into hardware manufacture.

'Max and I had an interesting meeting the other day,' said Gramps. 'He's been telling me how we could halve our production costs, with electronic typesetting.' He tried to sound as if he were actively considering the proposition, not that Vivi was fooled.

How impotent he must feel, being offered goods he couldn't buy without inviting a mass walk-out. *The Courier* had lost more than its share of issues to strike action in recent years, despite escalating wages and ever more outrageous Spanish practices. The print workers had far more power over the paper than its proprietor, and abused it without mercy. Gramps might bully his editor and despise journalists as being two a penny, but the men who controlled the presses made a coward of him, of everyone.

'Chance would be a fine thing,' commented Vivi, still looking at Max.

'Give it time,' said Max, still looking at Vivi.

'Have you met Lord Matthews?' said Gramps, curse him, striding forward to greet his fellow-proprietor and making the introductions – hoping, perhaps, that one of his competitors would blaze the trail for him.

Thwarted, Vivi drifted off, covertly watching as Max Kellerman worked the room, striking up an immediate shallow rapport with men and women alike. Vivi was forced to admire his skill at networking, one she was still trying to master; she might cultivate people assiduously when she had an immediate, specific use for them, but she lacked the patience, or the pretence, to ingratiate herself with all and sundry, just in case. Weary of feigning fascination with the arid chit-chat these functions generated – VIPs weren't nearly as interesting as outsiders assumed them to be – she assuaged her boredom by eating more than her fair share of fat Colchester oysters from the sumptuous buffet. She was just raising her twentieth half-shell to her lips

when she saw Max Kellerman heading her way, and eschewing th
slow, sensual pleasure of chewing, swallowed her prey whole.

'Are you enjoying the party?' he enquired.

'Not as much as you seem to be.'

'I'm keen to meet as many Fleet Street people as possible.
Specially as I'm flying out tomorrow. Unfortunately,' he added,
smiling. He had a cruel, determined mouth, one that only smiled to
get what it wanted, one that was designed to devour. 'CC was
telling me you should have been a boy,' he went on, taking in the
spectacular cleavage revealed by her low neckline (courtesy of an
uplift bra that was killing her), the sensual mass of thick dark curly
hair, the dramatic look-at-me kohl and blood red lipstick. 'But I
have to disagree with him on that.'

'That was his idea of a compliment,' said Vivi. 'And a back-
handed one at that. In his book all women are fit for is producing
babies.'

'Don't you want children?'

'Not for another ten years or so,' said Vivi, because nobody
believed you if you said you didn't want them at all. If she couldn't
even commit to a man – who could easily be got rid of if things
didn't work out – how could she hope to commit to a child, who
couldn't? How enviably casual procreation was for men! No
threat to their career, or their independence, not to mention their
figures, and they could walk out on the child any time they liked, as
Dad had done, and no one thought any the worse of them. But if a
woman did the same, she was a monster.

'Do you have kids?' she asked, seizing her chance to find out his
marital status and put her principles to the test.

'None that I know of.' And then, seeing through her question, 'I
don't have a wife either.'

'You mean you're divorced?' Probably more than once. He was
too attractive not to be.

'I mean I've never married. I like my freedom. Same as you.'

Encouraged, Vivi returned his candid stare, because, after all, if
he was leaving next day, there was no time to waste. She liked
things to be sudden, urgent, and above all transitory. He would be
here tonight and gone tomorrow, the perfect disposable man.

But Harriet descended on them at that moment, forcing Vivi to
introduce her, whereupon she bore Max off to meet some

American guests and stuck to him like a limpet for the rest of the evening, never mind that he was much too young, or rather too old for her. She was still talking intently at him well after most of the other guests had gone home and Gramps had retired to bed. Vivi, who would have left long ago, in normal circumstances, engaged a yawning Gerald in an endless and quite pointless conversation, reassured by the way Max kept catching her eye, hating herself for deigning to compete with her own mother.

'Won't you stay the night, Max?' cooed Harriet, as he finally managed to take his leave of her. 'I can drive you to the airport in the morning.' Vivi could just imagine her tripping along to Max's bedroom while Gramps snored.

'Thank you, but I couldn't ask you to get up that early. I'm catching the seven-thirty flight to Frankfurt for a meeting before I fly home. If I could just ring for a cab – '

'A cab?' trilled Harriet. 'But it's nearly fifty miles!'

As if Max Kellerman would think twice about a taxi fare.

'I can give Max a lift back to town,' interrupted Vivi, seizing her chance, before Harriet had time to volunteer Gerald's services. 'But perhaps I ought to warn Max that I'm the world's worst driver. So if you want to play safe, take a cab.'

Max Kellerman gave her a look that left her panties damp with desire.

'I never play safe,' he said, smiling.


'So did you find any takers?' said Vivi, as she steered the Beetle down the long curving drive and out into the unlit lane beyond. Now that she was alone with him at last she felt exposed, self-conscious, horribly transparent.

'Oh, I wasn't expecting to just yet. This trip was just a fact-finding mission. Your Fleet Street proprietors are one bunch of frightened people.'

'No one wants to take on the unions single-handed. Everyone's hoping someone else will do it first. Specially my grandfather. Look what happened to *The Times*. Something like that would finish *The Courier* off for good and all.'

*The Times*' battle with the print unions had kept it off the streets for the best part of a year, cost it millions of pounds and ended up with the paper being sold.

'Not if it was handled right. You'd lose money, sure, but in the long run you'd recoup your losses. It's crazy that they have new technology somewhere like Kuala Lumpur and not in London, the newspaper capital of the world.'

'You underestimate the power of our unions,' said Vivi. 'For one thing, the print would never let new machinery through their picket lines, and for another the NUJ would forbid the hacks to undermine their action. My grandfather's all talk, he's too old to take on that kind of conflict. And when my brother takes over, he'd have too much of a conscience to put all those men on the dole.'

Gerald wasn't anywhere near tough enough to face the battles that lay ahead, thought Vivi. Not without her help, anyway. When the time came she would have her hands full keeping him on the right track. Especially as he had a stubborn streak, as far as his principles were concerned. A failing, or quality, which had done him no favours with the old man. Gramps might enjoy arguing with Vivi, but he loathed Gerald quietly disagreeing with him, loathed the way he refused either to creep or to rebel.

On reflection it was just as well that power mattered more to Gramps than money. Having sold the Collington building business for a vast sum back in the sixties, he could afford to sustain the paper's losses as the price of hanging on to his biggest status symbol, one he would never let go of, in Vivi's opinion, no matter how much he blustered. Without it he would be just another rich old fart. With it he was a shaper of public opinion, one of the unelected politicians who really ran the country.

Max was staying at the Savoy, he told Vivi, he hoped it wasn't too far out of her way. As they got nearer to London she battled against the fear that had become, in her case, synonymous with desire. She had spent most of her life forcing herself to take risks, trying to become the sort of person she wasn't – brave, decisive, forceful, ruthless, independent, thick-skinned. She wished she had the nerve to proposition him, as Harriet would no doubt have done in her place, instead of hoping, like some shrinking virgin, that he would make the first move. She knew how to be obvious, but she hated to be too obvious, and she had never mastered the in-between tactics of fascinated flattery and coy innuendo. Such feminine wiles would look ridiculous on her, it would be like dressing up in pink chiffon or painting her bitten-down nails. Usually men didn't take much encouragement. But Max Kellerman had a cool that she found unnerving.

'Thanks for the ride,' he said finally, as Vivi drew up in front of the hotel.

'Don't mention it.'

'Too bad I'm going home tomorrow.'

'Oh, I expect we'll run into each other next time you're in London,' said Vivi airily, hiding her will-he, won't-he impatience. 'Specially if you're trying to do business with my grandfather.'

'That's why I'm trying not to come on to you,' he said. 'I wouldn't like you to think I was using you.'

'I'll bet you use people all the time.'

'True. But you seem like a nice kid, underneath that *femme fatale* number of yours.'

Much to her chagrin, Vivi found herself blushing. Her *femme fatale* number, as he called it, had always passed muster in the past.

'Wrong,' she said curtly. 'I use people as well. And I'm not the least bit nice. Ask me up to your room and I'll prove it,' she added boldly, before the moment cooled. 'Unless you'd rather play safe, for once.'

His eyes glittered in the gloom. 'Give them your keys,' he said, 'so they can park the car.'

Living in the dog days of the permissive era, before Aids was to cast its long shadow, Vivi still relied blithely on the Pill and antibiotics to protect her from her own sporadic promiscuity. Nonetheless she was gripped by an indistinct fear on the way up in the lift, as if aware that this time she would pay the price, a feeling she dismissed as a variant on her usual pre-coital nerves. She knew from experience that once the sexual fever had run its hectic course it would leave her purged and lethargic and indifferent with no desire to see the man in question ever again. But at this stage of the game there was always a tiny seed of inadmissible, shameful hope, hope that was bound to result in disappointment and a kind of perverse relief, thereby thickening the carapace she was building around herself, reinforcing the fortress of her cynicism.

Max showed her into a vast suite.

'What can I get you to drink? Coffee, cognac . . .'

'Nothing, thanks,' said Vivi, slipping off her coat. She couldn't bear the ritual of sitting around marking time, waiting for the room service trolley to come and go before they got down to business. He stood looking at her for a long slow moment, making her twitch with frustration. She didn't want to waste time talking or getting to know each other. This kind of thing worked best when it was impersonal. Unable to bear the suspense any longer, she reached for his flies, closed her hand around the biggest erection she had ever encountered in her life, and let him know, wordlessly but very clearly, that she had done this kind of thing many times before, that one-night stands, preferably with a stranger, were her preferred form of congress.

Too late to wish otherwise. Too late to regret all the soulless encounters she'd had in pursuit of sexual liberation. Too late to want to believe in the pathetic romantic myths women had conned themselves with since time began. This was an exchange of pleasure, nothing more, with both of them on equal terms, not a conquest for him nor a surrender for her, with no messy emotions to get in the way, no scope for pain or loss or betrayal. It worked for men, it had always worked for men, which was why men ruled the world. So why shouldn't it work for women too?

At least this way she was in control, and if she felt cheap and degraded afterwards, that was just conditioning, a throwback to some ancestral memory of shame, shame that was inculcated to keep women from exercising the power men feared in them. And she could feel her power over Max Kellerman as he responded, suddenly and savagely, with a force that took her breath away, giving her what she wanted of him, and taking from her only what she chose to give, which was her body, not her soul and most definitely not her heart . . .

Until she realised, fractionally too late, that something had gone wrong. Somewhere or other along the line she must have lost her concentration, let down her guard, allowed him to seize the advantage. It was the kind of accident that experts fall prey to through overconfidence, one which tore her out of the self-induced fantasy she used to distance herself and plunged her, rudderless, into the here and now, leaving her defenceless and at his mercy.

Or his lack of it. There was no getting away from him, no pretending that he didn't exist, no reducing him to a mere instrument of her pleasure. He gave her no quarter, he drained her dry, he dominated her absolutely, the first man ever to have turned the tables on her and beaten her at her own cold-blooded game. And yet she wouldn't admit defeat, she fought through to the bitter end and lost, wallowing in her own subjugation, letting him exhaust her into staying all night, something she never, ever did . . .

When she woke, sore with too much sex, there was a note on the pad by the telephone saying, 'Didn't want to wake you. Sign for breakfast if you want it. I'll call you. Max.'

She didn't want breakfast. As soon as she was vertical, she was horribly ill, the result, she assumed, of a bad oyster the previous night, and carried on being horribly ill for the next three days, unable to keep anything down except water and the Pill. Which must have gone straight through her, not that she realised it at the time.

By the time she did realise, Max still hadn't called her, not that she had thought for one minute that he would. Which didn't stop her ringing her answering machine a dozen times a day and repeatedly checking her message book at the office. But not to worry. Gemma phoned instead. Gemma phoned her one evening at home, while she was staring at a blue blob in a test tube, to tell her that Dad was dead.

Which made two lots of bad news in one day, on top of everything else. Too much to cope with at once. Otherwise she surely wouldn't have stooped to ringing Max, long-distance, let alone left a message with a secretary for him to call her back, it was urgent.

She knew as soon as she heard his voice on the line that she had made a crass error of judgement. That to him she was just another piece of ass he had picked up at a party, something to be fucked and forgotten. That he was treating her as she had intended to treat him.

'I got your message,' he said guardedly. 'How can I help you?'

'Why didn't you phone me?' demanded Vivi, trying and failing to sound casual.

'I'm sorry about what happened, Vivi. Like I said, you're a nice kid. It was wrong of me to take advantage.'

What a bloody hypocrite he was. How many women had he said that to, to spare their feelings? How many women had made a nuisance of themselves, wanting to see him again? How unthinkable that she should be humiliating herself like this. It was all she could do not to weep and plead and tell him that she had never wanted anyone this badly before, that she couldn't get him out of her mind, that he had spoiled her for sex with anyone else, even though she hated him, hated him more than he could possibly imagine. No one since Dad had managed to hurt her this much.

'I told you before, I'm not a nice kid. I would have thought that was obvious by now.' Nice kid was adding insult to injury. She had behaved like a demented whore.

'I didn't mean to jerk you around. I shouldn't have said I would call you.'

It didn't sound like an apology. His voice was hard, cold, leaving no room for hope. Yielding to a spurt of uncontrollable rage, Vivi heard herself hissing, 'The only reason I'm calling *you*, you conceited prick, is to let you know you got me bloody pregnant!'

For a moment he didn't say anything, spurring Vivi to add, 'And before you ask, yes, I'm sure, and yes, it's definitely yours.' She wished she couldn't be so certain of that. It would have made things so much easier.

Another pause, even longer this time.

'I assumed you were on the Pill.'

'Of course I was on the Pill! What kind of idiot do you take me for? It's not infallible, obviously.'

'Presumably you're going to have a termination?' How she despised that prissy euphemism.

'I'm having an abortion, if that's what you mean.'

'I'm very sorry you have to go through that,' he said levelly. 'I'll get a cheque off to you right away.'

A cheque. A lousy hand-out. But what had she expected? Congratulations? A proposal? God. How could she have been stupid enough to degrade herself by telling him? Not that she had told him the half of it. No one would believe that a tough bitch like her would think twice about getting rid of a baby . . .

She had been eight years old when a drunken, deserted Harriet had told her about her little sister. The adult Vivi had doubted her

55

lurid version of events; Harriet was prone to dramatise everything. But her younger self had had nightmares about it, on and off, for years; she would wake up fighting for breath, thinking that someone had a pillow over her head. And in the last few days the old dreams had started up again with a vengeance. Even though having an abortion wasn't the same as suffocating a helpless newborn baby . . . was it?

'I'll dispose of it at my own expense,' said Vivi, slamming the phone down before she compounded her folly by bursting into tears.

Next day she received a bank draft for a thousand pounds drawn on Max Kellerman's personal London account. She tore it up into tiny pieces and air mailed it back to him. She had never heard from him again. Good bloody riddance.

But she hadn't got rid of the baby, not really. It still lived inside a part of her head, growing a bit larger every day.

# 4

VIVI HAD MEANT it, about hardly ever being in. Which explained why she didn't keep a dog; it was cruel, she said, to leave one cooped up in a flat all day, or to let it roam the streets like a stray until it got itself run over.

Gemma hardly saw her, other than over a hideously early breakfast; she found it impossible to get back to sleep once Vivi, with much slamming of doors, went off for her six a.m. run (no wonder Mrs Pulowska hated her). Even on her days off, or when she was on a late shift, she was up with the lark and off for her morning jog, however inclement the weather, while a thick-headed Gemma was still easing herself into the day.

Vivi was at her most talkative in the mornings, as she rustled her way through half a dozen papers, punctuating her criticism of their coverage of the news with the odd 'What do you think?' – a question that caught Gemma unawares, the first time, given that no one had ever solicited her opinion on anything before. Reluctant to appear opinionless, she would hazard a tentative comment, trying to sound better-informed than she felt, bracing herself for a withering Dad-style put-down. But much to her surprise Vivi actually listened, if only to argue robustly against her, even when she agreed with her, on the grounds that she enjoyed playing devil's advocate.

And then, having ministered to her forest of plants with casual but touching care, pinching them out and dispensing Baby Bio and Volvic from a brass watering can, she would dash off to either work or leisure with the same unstoppable urgency. And that would be the last Gemma saw of her till she returned late that evening.

Gemma was used to preparing a solitary supper and eating it in front of the television, ignoring the periodic ring of the telephone.

She always let the answering machine cut in, knowing that she could pick up in the unlikely event of the call being for her, and enjoying being an involuntary — if avid — eavesdropper. Mostly the messages were from men suggesting drinks or dinner, or from Harriet ('If you're not too busy entertaining That Girl, could you possibly find the time to ring me?') or occasionally from the *Echo* news desk — the only call Vivi bothered to return. She wasted the people in her life the way she wasted everything, she didn't seem to appreciate or value her own popularity — with men, at least. Vivi had no female friends that Gemma knew of. She took some cold comfort from that. It made her feel she wasn't the only woman in the world to feel the chill of Vivi's indifference.

Gemma hadn't intended to stay at Bamber Court this long, but with Christmas coming up, no one seemed to be letting rooms, or recruiting permanent staff, till the holidays were over. Meanwhile she phoned her mother dutifully, twice a week, anxious to mend fences. She had been stupid, on reflection, to object to Fred, given that Fred had set her free. Nevertheless it had come as a blow to her ego to discover that she wasn't as indispensable as she, or Dad, had thought. And now she was labelled 'ungrateful' and accused of being 'in a huff', and all because she had spoken her mind, for once, seized her chance of escape before she got cold feet.

At some stage during the phone call Mum would dissolve into tears and pass the receiver to Fred, who had been primed to say things like 'Your mum's pining for you, Gem' and to imply that she wasn't at all well, he was very worried about her. So much so that if Gemma wasn't going to come home for Christmas, then he was thinking of taking her off to Tenerife for some sun, he had an option on a cancellation. Gemma had never implied that she wasn't coming home for Christmas — she wouldn't have been so hard-hearted — but she took the hint and agreed that the break would do her mother good, miserably aware that she had been set up.

Unfortunately she was out when Fred rang to give her their holiday details 'just in case you want to phone your mum to wish her a merry Christmas'. It was Vivi who relayed the message he had left on the answering machine, thwarting Gemma's plan to check into a hotel under pretence of going home.

'You can't sit here moping on your own on Christmas Day,'

she decreed. 'You'd better join in the family revels, if you can bear it.'

'I couldn't possibly. I haven't been invited.'

'I'm inviting you now, aren't I? What's the matter? Still scared of my mother, are you?'

'Of course not,' lied Gemma. Harriet was still rooted in her mind as the wicked witch of her childhood visits to London. She had sensed and feared her dislike long before she was old enough to understand what she had done to deserve it. And yet, despite the evil eye Harriet had given her at every opportunity, Gemma had always found her strangely fascinating. She was so elegant, her house was so beautiful, she radiated glamour and sophistication, she was part of the charmed world Vivi inhabited, a world that would always exclude Gemma to a hinterland of envy.

'Well, then. I'll ring her up and tell her to lay an extra place.'

'But —'

'Gerald would have my guts if I didn't bring you along. He's a great one for doing the Right Thing. Don't worry, the old man won't be there, he's spending Christmas in Cannes as usual. And we won't be staying the night. Harriet's flying to Miami on Boxing Day to find herself a new fucktotem, she's staying with one of her rich-widow cronies. And Gerald has to go into work. And I'm off skiing for a fortnight, with Nick Ferris.'

It was the first time Vivi had mentioned Nick Ferris, or her intended skiing trip. Vivi never talked about her love life, which Gemma imagined to be highly active and adventurous, à la Cosmo woman. Anxious to remedy her own sexual ignorance, Gemma had spent many a lunch hour in W H Smith, furtively reading endless variations on 'How to Please Your Man in Bed'.

'Nick Ferris?' she echoed, forming an instant image of the kind of carefully tanned and tousled hunks they used to illustrate such articles.

'A mate of mine, on *The Torch*,' said Vivi casually. 'It's a last-minute freebie he wangled from some half-witted tour company. He's conned them into thinking he's going to give them a big write-up, lying sod.'

'I hope I'm not the reason you've never brought him back here,' Gemma felt bound to say.

'I never bring men home. This is my space, and I like to keep it that way.' Another hint, thought Gemma, that the sooner she moved on the better.

'By the time you get back I should have found a job and somewhere else to stay.' Damn. She hadn't meant to say that. Just to do it.

'Stop making like I'm breathing down your neck, will you? If I've left you to your own devices, it's so as you can do your own thing. And besides, I need someone to water the plants while I'm away, it'll save me tipping the porter.'

Vivi told her not to buy anybody presents, it wasn't expected, so Gemma settled for a peace-offering of a poinsettia for Harriet and a bottle of port for Gerald recommended by the man in Thresher's. She didn't get anything for Vivi, for fear it would look as if she was soliciting something in return.

'Don't look so stricken,' Vivi told her, as she drove Gemma to Holland Park on Christmas morning. 'The worse my mother behaves, the nicer I'll be to you, just to stir things up. So make the most of it.'

Twenty-four Lansdowne Gardens was a tall, narrow town house rendered in white stucco, set well back from the road. Gemma had never been further inside than the hall before. She remembered cowering by the telephone table as a child while Vivi put on her coat and outdoor shoes, admiring the high moulded ceilings, the polished wood floor and the splendid grandfather clock, looking longingly up the curved staircase, wondering what Vivi's bedroom was like, and catching the occasional tantalising glimpse of the living room through the open door, with its exquisite flower arrangements and gleaming baby grand piano. Chipstead Close seemed so squat and ugly by comparison, devoid of mystery or style, boring. Gemma's early drawings of houses at school had never depicted her own home, always Vivi's.

Vivi loaded herself with parcels from the boot, including a huge, heavy oblong box tied with silver ribbon.

'Looks like Gerald's had another prang,' she commented, indicating the dark blue Peugeot saloon in the driveway, sporting a smashed tail light and a scrape all along one wing. 'We're all useless drivers in our family,' she added, having already demonstrated her own ineptitude on the journey from Battersea, riding the clutch, steering with one hand, forgetting to indicate, ignoring the driving mirror, and leaving her braking till the very last minute, turning every red light into an emergency stop.

As they climbed the front steps Gemma caught a strong aroma of garlic overlaid by the smell of meat cooking, but it wasn't turkey, or beef, or anything else she could readily identify. Gerald answered the door, a tall, sandy-haired man with a high forehead and kind blue eyes hidden behind thick hornrimmed glasses. Gemma wouldn't have recognised him; she had encountered Vivi's brothers only rarely, and briefly, a long time ago now. He shook Gemma's hand firmly and said in a deep, donnish voice, 'Gemma. How nice to see you again after all these years.'

He had the kind of bashful good looks that aspired, like Gemma's own, to invisibility. His line in rather fussy small talk as he took her coat – was there much traffic about, no chance of a white Christmas this year, and so on – had an apologetic ring to it; he seemed over-anxious to make her feel welcome.

'How very sweet of you,' he exclaimed, with apparently genuine pleasure, as Gemma handed him the bottle of port, unwrapped, so it wouldn't seem like a very inadequate gift.

'New togs,' said Vivi, squinting at his Aran sweater, worn over a pair of grey flannels.

'Harriet's Christmas present.'

'Hardly recognised you without a suit and tie. You look like a knitting pattern out of *Happy Housewife*.' She gave him a playful jab in the ribs. Vivi herself was wearing distressed jeans, trainers and an old jumper; Gemma was in her Sunday best, courtesy of Marks and Spencer, a frilly white blouse and a plain black velvet skirt.

'Harriet will be up in a minute,' said Gerald. 'She's still thrashing about in the kitchen.'

There was a big vase of beautifully arranged hothouse roses standing atop the piano in the living room. A coal fire was burning in the grate and a huge, real Christmas tree (Barbara trotted out a tinsel job each year to save Hoovering up the needles) stood by the front window, next to a magnificent antique walnut bureau. The cream silk-lined walls were hung with good-quality reproductions, mostly lesser-known Impressionists, which Gemma recognised as Caillebotte and Berthe Morisot, but it was the portrait, presumably by Daniel, of his mother, which caught her eye first; Harriet

61

had given it pride of place above the fireplace. God, what she wouldn't give to be able to paint like that . . .

The alcoves either side of the marble mantelpiece were lined with bookshelves; Gemma scanned the titles while Gerald and Vivi heaped the parcels round the tree, longing to look through all those big fat volumes on art, the kind you were never allowed to take away from the library. The furniture was a skilfully eclectic mix of antique and modern, blending glass, brass, wood and leather; everywhere she looked was some beautiful object or other, placed exactly right, without ostentation; even the threadbare carpet seemed classy. Imagine living in a house like this, surrounded by so much good taste. It must have been wasted on Dad, who had always been a Philistine and proud of it. She sat down gingerly on a green button-backed chair, still clutching the pot plant for Harriet, head bowed, face hidden behind the curtain of her long fair hair.

'What can I offer you to drink?' said Gerald.

Gemma asked for a dry sherry, which she knew to be socially okay, even though she would have much preferred sweet.

'You're lucky there is any,' commented Vivi. 'Booze is banned in this house, except when there are guests. On account of Harriet being an alky. That's why he's hiding your bottle of port.'

Gerald, caught in the act of shutting it into a drawer, looked embarrassed. It was typical of Vivi not to warn her about Harriet's drink problem, something she had presumably kept from Dad, unless Dad had kept it from Gemma. Vivi asked for a straight tonic, making Gemma wish she had done the same. Gerald joined her in a sherry, as if to reassure her of her choice. It must be a really superior brand, she thought, because it tasted horrible. She struggled to like it and to listen intelligently, while Gerald and Vivi discussed the goings-on in Warrington, where Eddy Shah, the owner of the *Messenger* group, was fighting a pitched battle against the NGA in his bid to print his free sheet with non-union labour. Well informed though she was about the dispute, thanks to Vivi's breakfast dissertations and a new compulsion to educate herself, she didn't like to join in, especially as Gerald seemed to be an expert on the two recent employment acts which outlawed secondary picketing. Most of what he said went over her head while she waited, distracted, for the moment when Harriet would appear and treat her with her usual scorn, which Gemma would meet with her customary false composure.

A moment later Harriet swanned into the room, still as glacially elegant as Gemma remembered her, or rather more so, with age affording her extra dignity. The extra years showed, despite her immaculately applied make-up and the lack of grey in her hair, which was now its original colour, a glossy burnt caramel like Vivi's, though Harriet had been both a blonde and a redhead in the past. Although not a tall woman, she carried herself like a model; she had the kind of dramatic, strong-featured looks that wore well, even though she was far from conventionally beautiful. In one hand she was carrying a provençal pottery bowl of shiny, crinkly black olives, in the other one of pistachio nuts – a far cry from the crisps and Twiglets Mum would have served.

Gemma proffered the poinsettia with a mumbled 'Happy Christmas'. Harriet smiled thinly and managed a stiff 'How nice. But Vivi had better look after it, it's bound to die on me. Gerald darling, can you pour me a Shloer with lots of ice?' She sat down in the armchair next to the fire and slotted a cigarillo into the end of a long holder.

'Too much to hope that Daniel would ring,' she remarked, flicking her lighter. 'I tried to get through to Beirut, a few minutes ago, to thank him for his cheque, but all the lines were down again. Trust him to make me worry at Christmas, God knows he's used up his nine lives already. Bloody testosterone. And they say that women are slaves to their hormones.'

'I'm sure he's quite all right,' said Gerald. 'If he wasn't we'd have heard.'

'I expect he's having a better Christmas than we are,' added Vivi. 'You can just imagine all those dedicated hacks and snappers, holed up at the Commodore, pissed out of their skulls. Sorry to rub it in,' she added, as Gerald handed his mother a glass of teetotal apple juice.

'Did the old bastard send you anything?' demanded Harriet.

'Yes,' admitted Vivi, rather uncomfortably. 'A grand.'

'I got a miserable five hundred,' sniffed Harriet. 'Which is better than the fifty he deigned to give Gerald. What an insult.'

'Don't worry, you're getting most of mine as a Christmas present,' Vivi reassured her.

'Thank you darling,' said Harriet, brightening. 'But it's not the money. It's the principle of the thing. When you think what a party planner would charge him for organising his putrid birthday bash . . . he's got no idea how much work's involved. And that so-called secretary of his is no help at all, snooty bitch. No wonder *The Courier*'s losing money, carrying people like her. One can only assume she provides other services.'

'An old boot like that?' snorted Vivi. 'If he wants that kind of thing, he can afford a pro. Don't suppose he can get it up any other way, at his age.'

'Really Vivi,' remonstrated Gerald, with surprising sharpness. 'We have a guest.'

'Oh, I've already been filling Gemma in about the family,' said Vivi. An exaggeration, as usual. Gemma knew about the old man's threats to sell *The Courier*, but not much else, except that he was a power-mad, machiavellian old swine.

'Like I told you,' said Vivi, turning to Gemma, even though she hadn't, 'ever since Grammie died last year Harriet's been terrified that the old bugger will marry again and sire a son at last.'

'Such things have been known,' said Harriet, flinging Gerald a meaningful look. 'There are plenty of little slags out there who'd be happy to oblige him.'

'Except that he's past it,' said Vivi. 'Even if he did produce a so-called heir, everyone would wonder if it was really his, including him. He knows very well he'd be a laughing stock. There's nothing more pathetic than an impotent old fool with a gold-digging wife half his age.'

'That's enough, Vivi,' said Gerald. 'Let's not talk about CC at Christmas. So tell me, Gemma, how's the job hunting going?'

'Fine, thank you. I've got several interviews lined up for the New Year.'

'Who with?' asked Vivi ungrammatically, helping herself to pistachios.

'One with a merchant bank,' admitted Gemma unhappily. 'One with a firm of chartered accountants. And one with a marine insurance company.'

'God,' commented Harriet, throwing an olive stone into the fire. 'How boring.'

Like me, thought Gemma, stung. She found herself driven to

explain how all the ads for interesting-sounding jobs in advertising, publishing, and the like – places with art departments she might work her way into sideways, not that she owned up to this ambition – were bogus ones, placed by agencies, designed to lure you on to their books, only to be told that particular vacancy had just been filled and offered a 'boring' one instead.

'Good jobs are never advertised,' commented Vivi discouragingly. 'Except by word of mouth. It's a question of who you know.'

'Talking of which,' put in Gerald diffidently, 'I might be able to help. There are usually a few vacancies knocking around at *The Courier*.'

'Only because it's the worst payer in the Street,' said Vivi. 'Except when it comes to the bloody print, that is.'

'That's terribly nice of you,' said Gemma, afraid that Gerald had thought she was fishing and noting the filthy look Harriet was casting in his direction. 'But I wouldn't like to put you to any trouble . . .'

'No trouble at all,' said Gerald, avoiding his mother's eye. 'I'll make some enquiries and give you a ring.'

'Well . . . thank you,' said Gemma. She had always been curious about *The Courier*, Dad's old domain. However beleaguered it might be, it had to be more interesting than working for the *Alchester Post*, or any of the other jobs she was likely to get off her own bat. Less admissibly, it would give her another toehold in the family, a family she had always wanted to be part of, just as she had wanted to escape her own.

'What a super idea, Gerald darling,' put in Harriet, determined to get her son's attention. She took a languid puff at her cigarette holder. 'If you can possibly get the editor to run off with you, Gemma, my father will be eternally grateful to you. He's been trying to get rid of him for the last six months.'

Gemma blushed scarlet, Gerald gave his mother a freezing look, and Vivi said brutally, 'Ignore her.'

'For heaven's sake,' said Harriet, glad to have provoked an effect, even a hostile one. 'Can't anyone around here take a joke? Lunch is ready when you are.'

She got up and went downstairs.

'Don't let her faze you,' said Gerald quietly. 'Christmas is always a bad time for her. She didn't mean any harm.' He exchanged glances with Vivi.

Had Dad left her at Christmas? Gemma had been too young to remember. But it was hardly the kind of thing she could ask about. Abandoning her half-finished sherry, she followed Gerald down the narrow picture-lined staircase into the cooking-and-eating area below. The open kitchen door revealed a quarry-tiled floor, an Aga, open shelves laden with glass apothecary jars, an old-fashioned pulley from which copper saucepans and kitchen implements were suspended from meat hooks, and a row of gleaming knives on a magnetic rack. The small, square dining room adjoining it was centred by an oval mahogany table, its polished wood left bare, with a plain cork mat at every place and tall white candles in a centrepiece of festive greenery. The cutlery was old, chased silver, the napkins of cream-coloured damask, the glasses of heavy crystal. Like the delicate china sideplates, these were chipped, an indication of their age and irreplaceability. Mum would have thrown them out years ago and bought new ones.

Harriet came in with a large tray, bearing four brown steaming earthenware dishes. Mushrooms, thought Gemma, inspecting the brown blobs swimming in garlic butter.

'I do hope you like escargots?' said Harriet sweetly.

'She loves them,' put in Vivi quickly. 'We had snails when we went out to dinner the other night, didn't we Gem?'

Gerald looked relieved at this comment. Evidently he had had no idea what his mother was cooking for lunch. At least they weren't in their shells, thought Gemma, which spared her the ordeal of battling with unfamiliar implements, but in a way that made it more difficult, because once you knew what they were you had to look at them, little horns and all, while you ate, instead of making a quick, blind stab and stuffing them into your mouth. They tasted of earth, but the texture wasn't so different from whelks, not that she cared for whelks either. She chewed with stolid determination, and, imitating everyone else, mopped up the last vestiges of butter, conscious of Harriet watching her. The garlic didn't taste nearly as strong as it smelt, and the bread was the best she had ever eaten.

'Thank you,' she smiled, as Vivi helped Harriet clear away the plates. 'That was lovely.' Whereupon Vivi hissed in her ear, 'Not bad. You almost had me fooled.'

A few minutes later Harriet brought in the main course – not a roast, as Gemma had expected, but something in a large cast-iron casserole belching pungent fumes.

'I thought it would make a change from pheasant this year,' said Harriet. 'The butcher promised me it was very well hung.'

'Good God. You mean we're eating Luigi?' gasped Vivi, with mock horror. Gerald snorted into his napkin. 'I was wondering what had happened to him . . .' Gemma had never heard of Luigi, but she got the general drift and found herself swopping furtive smiles with Gerald across the table.

'I do hope you like jugged hare, Gemma,' went on Harriet, ignoring this dig, as she ladled out a generous portion. 'I always use the blood to thicken the gravy. It makes for a richer flavour. And of course, it's all one hundred per cent organic.'

Feeling like a vampire, Gemma helped herself stolidly to forcemeat balls, redcurrant jelly, something which she later discovered to be celeriac purée, glazed baby onions and carrots, and boiled potatoes. The meat was indeed sky high, but like the snails it tasted better than it smelt. Even if it hadn't done she would have eaten every morsel, going so far as to accept Harriet's hostessy offer of a second helping.

'Better than fish pie?' queried Vivi, flashing her a mocking grin, a remark which was lost on everyone else but which hurtled Gemma back to a memory from their shared past, when Vivi had come to Alchester for the weekend. Gemma had been forced, not for the first time, to stay at table after everyone else had finished their meal until she had cleared her plate; Dad had always been fanatically strict about not wasting food, at least as far as Gemma was concerned. Vivi, as a guest, was allowed to leave anything she didn't like, and Vivi obviously didn't like fish pie – Dad's favourite – any more than Gemma did, abandoning her own barely touched portion with impunity.

Gemma had sat there alone and miserable, listening to the sound of the television next door – she was missing *Doctor Who* – gagging on the watery fish and lumpy mashed potato and hating Vivi for not having to suffer as she did. And then Vivi had appeared, with a finger to her lips, taken her fork from her and bolted the disgusting mess in half a dozen rapid swallows. She hadn't been sympathetic, quite the reverse, she had abused her between mouthfuls for being a wet little git, but she had freed her nonetheless from unspeakable torment and seven-year-old Gemma had been hard put not to love her for it. A few minutes later, having rejoined the rest of the family in front of the TV set, Gemma had watched, transfixed, while Vivi was spectacularly, maliciously sick all over her mum's brand new loose covers, after which she had announced piteously that it 'must have been something she ate'.

'Much better,' confirmed Gemma. It was also better than the soggy frozen prawn cocktail, overcooked turkey and packet stuffing Dad had always proclaimed as delicious; even the most unadventurous eater would have been seduced by Harriet's culinary skill. By the time the Christmas pudding was brought in, Harriet was being almost civil to her, mollified by her clean plate; or perhaps, like all bullies, she backed off if you didn't show you were afraid. Gemma felt as if she had just executed one of Vivi's diabolical dares.

At last they rose from the table and returned to the living room with a tray of coffee. The fire had perked up in their absence, and soon it was blazing fiercely with discarded wrapping paper, as they set about opening presents.

Gemma was disconcerted to find Vivi's large parcel set before her, together with a small one, bearing the legend 'Happy Christmas from Gerald'. She opened the latter first, uncovering a bottle of Miss Dior.

'You really shouldn't have,' began Gemma, wishing that she'd brought him a proper present, instead of the port.

'Not very imaginative, I'm afraid,' said Gerald. 'But Vivi didn't know what perfume you used, so I had to guess what would suit you.'

The perfume Gemma used was the olfactory equivalent of plonk, and not one she would care to admit to wearing in present company. This was real vintage stuff. After sniffing it appreciatively, she put it to one side and turned her attention to Vivi's parcel, which was dauntingly huge and heavy. Gemma began untying the silver ribbon. How typical of Vivi to tell her not to buy her anything and then to put her in the wrong like this . . .

Vivi had given Gerald a new recommended recording of the *Ring* cycle, begging him please not to play it now, bloody Wagner always gave her a migraine. Gerald had bought her an antique edition of Keats sonnets, which would have surprised Gemma more if she hadn't already inspected the well-thumbed volumes on Vivi's bookcases and discovered her unlikely weakness for the romantic poets. Both she and Gerald appeared to have given their mother cheques, large ones judging by the tearful way she hugged them both; Vivi had mentioned that Harriet was perennially short of cash.

Gerald's present from Harriet was the sweater he was wearing, Vivi's a pair of delicate silver filigree earrings – she never wore gold – which Gemma was reluctant to admire openly, assailed by another memory from long ago when she had once exclaimed at the beauty of Vivi's Victorian silver locket. Vivi had promptly taken if off and tossed it at her, saying, 'Keep it. I don't even like it,' overwhelming her with the unexpected enormity of the gift, even one Vivi herself affected to despise. But then Dad had made Gemma return it because it turned out to be valuable, an heirloom from the Blakeney side of the family; Vivi had never worn it in her presence again.

'Well?' said Vivi, tossing more screwed-up paper on to the fire which despatched red hot floating embers up the chimney. 'Aren't you going to open your prezzie from Santa?'

'We agreed not to give each other presents,' said Gemma, still fiddling with the silver twine.

'Stop bleating and unwrap it,' said Vivi, poking at the coals and making the sparks spin. Gemma did so to find a collapsible easel, several large sheets of ready-primed canvas board, and a box fitted with oil paints, a palette, a bottle of turpentine and a selection of brushes.

'I asked the shop to bung in everything you'd need to start off with,' said Vivi casually. 'Couldn't think what else to get you.'

It was all Gemma could do not to burst into tears. She had never possessed anything beyond a sketch pad and water colours before, and she had left the latter at home, along with most of her belongings, till she found a place of her own. Vivi must have spent a small fortune, but that wasn't the point, the point was that she had bothered to choose something appropriate, unlike Mum who had sent her the usual gift token, signed 'Mum and Fred' this year instead of 'Mum and Dad'.

'It's lovely,' said Gemma stiffly. 'Thank you.'

'Forget it,' shrugged Vivi, more embarrassed, if anything, than Gemma. It wasn't the first time Vivi had mortified her with unexpected, unnecessary kindness which Gemma couldn't acknowledge without inviting a curt rebuff. She fought against a tidal wave of sentimentality, recognising the gesture as the symptom of a guilty conscience. The occasional act of self-inflicted penance didn't cancel out all the callous contempt and downright spite to which Vivi had subjected her over the years, let alone her final crushing rejection. 'Vivi doesn't want to see you any more,' Dad had told her at the anxious age of eleven. 'She's fed up with you whining. And I can't say I blame her.' It wasn't fair. She hadn't whined, not for years and years. If anything, she had been too compliant. You couldn't win, with Vivi – or with Dad, come to that.

Nonetheless, she wished now that she had gone ahead and bought her that new electric blanket for Christmas; Vivi had never got around to replacing her old one. She would get her one while she was away skiing and make up the bed with it, as a surprise for her return. The quest for her approval, however futile, was a hard habit to break.

# 5

VIVI LEFT AT the crack of dawn next morning to catch an early flight to Innsbruck. Gemma spent the day doused in Miss Dior, writing a bread-and-butter letter to Harriet and playing with her new toys. She was just cleaning out her brushes when the telephone rang. As always, she let the machine answer it.

'Gemma, it's Gerald. Can you ring me back on . . .'

'I'm here,' she said, picking up. 'Thank you so much for yesterday.'

'I do hope it wasn't too much of an ordeal.' He sounded apologetic, as usual. 'Listen, there's a vacancy here that might be of interest to you, but I'm afraid it's a bit of a tricky billet. That is, it's a reasonable job, in Features, but Myra Shaw, their number one, is a bit of a tartar.'

'That's all right. I'm used to working for a tartar.'

'I know the feeling,' quipped Gerald, rather heavily. 'Well, in that case, can you come in at about half twelve tomorrow, after morning conference? Then I can introduce you to Myra myself. And then perhaps . . . perhaps we can grab a spot of lunch afterwards, if you haven't got to rush off, that is.'

'No, I'm free all day tomorrow.' The agency had warned her there would be no work in the fallow week between Christmas and New Year. 'Thank you for putting in a word for me.'

'My pleasure. I'll see you tomorrow then. Goodbye.'

He's such a perfect gentleman, thought Gemma. So polite, and old-fashioned, and unassuming, and kind. He was almost too good to be true.


Vivi was an accomplished skier. No one watching her would have guessed the anguish she had put herself through to reach her present stage of proficiency – both the physical discomforts of sore shins, bruises and the occasional sprain or fracture, and the additional mental torment of a fear of heights. But she had learned to enjoy it. Just as she had done with swimming, despite a fear of water, and riding, despite a fear of horses, just as she had done with sex, despite a fear of men. Adrenaline was addictive.

Nick freely admitted she was out of his class, and amused himself on the nursery slopes while she tackled the black pistes and the moguls and went off the beaten track in search of deep powder. By the time fading light drove her back to the hotel, euphoric with an excess of endorphins, he would be lounging in the heated indoor swimming pool or propping up the bar, striking up conversations with strangers, chatting up pretty girls, having an annoyingly good time without her.

As for her intended refusal to sleep with him, he had been one jump ahead of her. 'Let's get one thing straight,' he had said, that very first evening. 'I'm not going to try anything on, okay? Not yet, anyway. So relax.'

Vivi rarely relaxed, even when she was roaring with laughter in the pub (whether she was amused or not), or being ultra-cool (and twitching with boredom), or sleeping (lightly and fitfully). Relaxing was something she had never mastered, only the art of appearing to do so. From the moment she woke in the morning, seething with nervous energy, to her perennially late bedtime, with her mind still buzzing, she never stopped pushing herself.

But Nick had an inner calm that was infectious. With Nick, what you saw was what you got. He was at ease with himself, and with her. His brash, combative professional persona seemed all of a piece with his sunny off-duty serenity; he reminded her of a boxer who was a killer in the ring and a pussy-cat outside it. Nick was . . . nice.

She had seen a lot of him after that first dinner together, in so far as their long and erratic working hours allowed – although Nick, unlike Vivi, was a fearless skiver; *The Torch*, ever wary that he would defect to a rival paper, accepted that he was a law unto himself. Reluctantly, Vivi had come to regard him as a friend. She had never been any good at making friends, only acquaintances, unable to trust anybody enough to let down her guard. But it was hard to hold out against someone as open and unthreatening as Nick.

'Sex would spoil everything, you know,' she had warned him, knowing that things couldn't carry on like this for ever. He might have let her off the hook as a softly-softly ploy, to wear down her defences, but he had never pretended the reprieve was permanent. 'For one thing I . . . I like you too much.'

She squirmed as she said it, as if making some absurd declaration of love. And then, knowing that wanting to be friends was the ultimate put-down, and overcome by a quite unprecedented fear of damaging a man's self-esteem, she added, 'The truth is, I'm right off sex. Not just with you, with everybody.'

It was the first time she had admitted it, even to herself. She had been telling herself ever since the abortion that she was simply too busy, and so she was, because being busy kept her mind off Max Kellerman and the gross humiliation of having wanted anyone that badly, let alone someone who didn't want her, who had made a weak and emotional woman out of her, stolen a part of herself, and left her with a part of himself in return, a part she had wilfully destroyed, doubling her sense of loss.

'You mean somebody hurt you?' He sounded as if he had known all along.

'No. I allowed myself to be hurt.' There had been something self-destructive about the whole dream-like episode, something akin to Daniel's death wish. 'That's why I don't want to hurt you.'

Which was odd, because men (with the honourable exception of her brothers) were fair game. Get them into bed, enslave them sexually – which was pathetically easy to do, or had been, until Max – and then drop them like a stone, thereby moving a few more of the abacus beads of pain and anger over to the credit side of the equation. She had it in her power to hurt Nick very easily. That she didn't want to was to his credit rather than her own.

'Then I'll just have to tie a knot in it, won't I?' he had said, with that cheeky grin of his, and a moment later he had her laughing again, with Vivi wondering how many women he had laughed into bed, and how long it would be before his patience gave out, and how sorry she would be to lose him.

But he clearly wasn't ready to give up on her yet. God knows how he had wangled this skiing trip, assuming he had, it wouldn't surprise her if that wasn't just a cover story. Two single rooms, he had promised, with both of them free to do as they pleased when they got there, not necessarily together – though he always found an excuse to accompany her in the evenings, out of some misplaced notion of gallantry. He would pretend, with difficulty, not to watch while she drove other men wild with her low necklines and frenzied disco-dancing, lured them into making a confident pass and then told them to get lost with her best ball-shrivelling stare.

'I don't need a chaperon, you know,' she goaded him.

'Don't you just. One night you'll tease the wrong guy and get yourself raped. That's not what happened to you, is it?'

'Do me a favour. I can look after myself.'

'Famous last words.' He put a casual arm around her, where-upon Vivi spun round and twisted it behind his back, eliciting a yelp of pain.

'Now do you believe me?'

'Jesus Christ. Leggo, you're hurting me. What are you, a black belt or something?'

'Brown. So don't worry your pretty little head about me.' She released him. 'You can go off on the pick-up tonight with a clear conscience.'

'A clear conscience? What about all those poor defenceless men I'm leaving to your tender mercies?'

He looked mildly emasculated, the way men always did when she pulled her favourite party trick. Or the way Simon Driscoll, her stepfather, had looked, when fifteen-year-old Vivi had kneed him in the groin. She hadn't waited for him to try to touch her up again before enrolling for judo classes, thereby giving herself a false sense of security, a secret weapon, so she thought. One which had proved useless against a much more subtle threat to her well-being. If Max Kellerman had taught her anything, it was to recognise and fear the shameful lure of surrender. She would never connive at her own downfall again.

*The Courier* occupied a dingy grey building in Whitefriars Street; the 'C' on the replica of its masthead was slightly crooked, giving it a tired, dilapidated air. Gemma had been here before, though not with Dad, who had kept well away from Fleet Street on his visits to London, claiming that he had been glad to see the back of it and pooh-poohing the much-vaunted romance of a place which reeked of wrecked relationships, cirrhotic livers and overblown egos. But a curious Gemma had explored the area herself, roamed the cobbled alleyways linking its squares and narrow streets, jumped out of the way of delivery vans driven at manic speed, sensed the frenzied collective struggle against time. There was no putting off news till tomorrow. News was the here and now, it wouldn't wait. There was nothing more dead than yesterday's paper.

Dad had found it hard to slow down, at first, Mum said. When she first met him he had been working a sixteen-hour day, living on his nerves, drinking too much and nursing a stomach ulcer, squeezed between a demanding wife and an even more demanding proprietor. If he'd stayed on his heart would have given out years ago. Mum had never had a good word to say about *The Courier*, or Lord Collington. If she were here now, thought Gemma, she would undoubtedly try to talk her out of this job, which only made it seem all the more desirable.

The front hall was manned by two security guards and a receptionist who rang through to Gerald to announce her arrival and directed her up to the second floor. Gemma emerged from the lift into an ill-lit landing and walked through the double doors into a vast, open-plan room with dingy brown walls and barely space to move between the battered old desks. The pillars and low ceilings added to the sense of claustrophobia; it seemed overcrowded even though there were few staff about, the next day's paper being a skeleton affair largely composed of pre-written features. There was seldom any hard news at Christmas.

Gerald was sitting at a surprisingly untidy desk, hunched over an ancient typewriter with a phone to his ear. Catching sight of Gemma, he waved an acknowledgement and gestured her towards a nearby chair. His rather raffish spotted red bow tie didn't match his otherwise sober attire.

'I'd rather you spoke to the editor direct, CC,' he was saying. 'You appreciate that he and I have already discussed this at length, and . . . Then why not tell him so yourself? . . . But you're putting me in an impossible position . . . Yes, I know you're the proprietor, but going below his head like this . . . Very well then. Yes, I'll tell him. Goodbye.'

He held a hand across the desk to Gemma.

'I'm sorry about this,' he said, brow furrowed. 'Can you bear with me just one more minute?'

He crossed the room, tapped on a door marked 'E. Fowler. Editor', and disappeared inside. Gemma was just wondering if that was where Dad used to sit when she heard a snigger somewhere behind her.

'Did you clock the Herald on the blower just now?' one male voice snorted to another. He assumed Gerald's rather plummy voice. 'CC Señor, no no Señor, three bags full of shit, Señor.'

'I feel sorry for the poor bastard. The word is the Howler's using him to try to get himself sacked. And CC's setting him up as well, to try and force the Howler to resign.'

'If I were in his shoes I'd tell them both to take a running jump . . .'

Their conversation was interrupted by a ringing telephone. Gemma sat uncomfortably waiting for Gerald to return, trying to make sense of what she had heard. It sounded as if Gerald, as leader writer, was being given conflicting briefs by his editor and his grandfather, in furtherance of some war of attrition between them. Being sacked was an honourable, almost inevitable fate sustained by most Fleet Street editors at some point in their careers, the blow softened by a hefty pay-off in line with their contracts. Resigning voluntarily, however – as Dad had done – was generally seen as a triumph for the wily proprietor who had driven you to leave empty-handed.

It must be wretched for Gerald, having to work in such an atmosphere. And 'the Herald' was a horrible, cruel nickname. Gemma hated the two men for their snide comments, she would have liked to have turned round and confronted them, as Vivi would no doubt have done in her place, assuming that they would have dared to utter such remarks in Vivi's hearing. They had no idea who Gemma was, of course, not that they would have been impressed if they had. She was only a secretary, after all. And not even that, yet.

Gerald emerged a few minutes later, looking harassed.

'I'm sorry to have kept you waiting,' he said. 'Let me introduce you to Myra Shaw.'

He led the way towards a partitioned-off corner of the room, where a bleached-blonde (Gemma, as a real one, could always tell) hard-faced shoulder-padded woman in her mid thirties was drawling into a telephone about the pictures being unusable, not what she wanted at all, and could they arrange a re-shoot for tomorrow, yes tomorrow, and no of course it wasn't coming out of her budget, what did they take her for?

'Gerald,' she cooed, replacing the receiver and treating him to a brilliant smile.

'Myra, this is Gemma Chambers. Can I leave her with you? Got a spot of bother to sort out. I'll see you when you've finished, Gemma.'

He left her with Myra Shaw, who switched off the smile instantly, handed her a form to fill in 'for the record', quizzed her about her experiences at the *Post* and briefly scrutinised her shorthand and typing certificates. Evidently the previous incumbent, who was sullenly bashing a typewriter nearby, was working out her notice; Myra sounded off at length about her multiple shortcomings, heedless of whether she could overhear or not, breaking off several times to answer the phone and altering her tone of voice from a purr to a bark according to who was on the other end of the line.

The job involved servicing Myra, her two deputies, and a team of a dozen writers – typing letters, memos, filing, photocopying, answering phones, making travel arrangements, and so on. The usual routine stuff, thought Gemma. Features was a popular billet, Myra told her, but as a favour to Gerald she would square things with Personnel. Finally she said that she had a lunch appointment, Gemma should report to Room 209 at nine-thirty on Monday morning, see you then.

'How did you get on?' said Gerald, when Gemma rejoined him.

'I start on Monday. It was awfully nice of you to pull strings for me.'

'Tell me that again when you've been here a month. Have you got time for a sandwich and a drink at the pub?'

'If you have, yes.'

'Then let's get out of here before the old man rings again. Come on.'

*The Courier*'s local – all the papers had their own watering holes – was situated further down Whitefriars Street; like the office it was having a quiet day. Gemma sat looking at the yellowing prints of Old Fleet Street on the dark panelled walls while Gerald fetched a pint for himself, a half of lemonade shandy for her, and two rounds of chicken sandwiches.

'Money all right for you, was it?' he said.

'Yes thank you.' It was less than she would have got at the merchant bank, but working, however indirectly, for Gerald, would make up for that. Obviously he needed all the allies he could get. 'It'll make it much easier for me to find a flat, now that I'm on a permanent payroll.'

'Bit hectic, sharing with Vivi, I imagine.'

'Oh, I didn't mean that. But I don't like to be in the way.'

'I felt dreadful about the way my mother treated you the other day. But you know how it is. A woman scorned and all that.'

'Don't apologise. I can't expect her to like me, in the circumstances.'

'Well, I thought you handled her extremely well.'

'Oh, I'm used to humouring people,' said Gemma, sensing that he was used to it too, recognising another beleaguered soul like herself. She longed to say 'Don't worry. You'll win through in the end,' to erase that permanently worried look he wore, to defend him against his detractors and his despot of a grandfather.

Instead she said, 'I wish you'd fill me in about *The Courier* before I start work. I feel so ignorant.'

'I'm surprised Vivi hasn't already told you all about it. Or rather, about the things that are wrong with it.'

'Not really,' said Gemma. 'What's wrong with it? Or rather, how would you put them right?'

She knew what he was going to say, because she had heard it all before, not just from Vivi but from Dad. The paper had to get rid of its stuffy image, attract younger readers to replace the ones who were dying off, and above all change its format – better to be an upmarket tabloid than a downmarket broadsheet. More ABC1s read the popular press than the heavies, and their earning power was what attracted vital advertising revenue. It needed bigger headlines, more pictures, more appeal to women, it needed to invest in higher-calibre staff, streamline its unwieldy administration, and get rid of a lot of dead wood, especially on the management side . . .

But it all sounded new and different coming from Gerald. It was like opening up a box of treasure, glittering with intelligence and creativity and idealism, and yet tarnished with self-doubt, a self-doubt Gemma made it her mission, from that day forward, to chase away.

It was sleeting when she got back to the flat. Mrs Pulowska was lying in wait for her at the top of the stairs.

'Your sister back,' she informed her grimly. She had evidently been looking forward to missing reveille for the next two weeks.

'But she's only just left! Did she say anything?' Had she and Nick had a tiff?

'I don't see her. Only hear her. No one else slams door that way. Here. For you. Happy Christmas.' She extended a loaf-shaped object wrapped in foil. 'Poppy-seed cake. My muzzer's recipe.'

'Oh Mrs Pulowska, thank you. That's awfully sweet of you.'

'Is nussink. You good girl.'

She said it in an accusatory tone, but then an accusatory tone was the only one Mrs Pulowska possessed, in English, at least. After their uneasy initial meeting, Gemma had made a point of smiling at her, offering to take down her rubbish, and listening patiently to her long-winded reminiscences about prewar Poland.

Compromised by the cake, she stood listening while Mrs Pulowska recounted her Christmas with some relatives in Ealing; Gemma reciprocated by mentioning that she had found a permanent job at last and would be looking for a bedsitter. Luckily the old woman's phone began to ring at this point, summoning her back inside and freeing Gemma to solve the mystery of Vivi's premature return.

'Vivi?' called a male voice, from within, as she let herself in. A dark, bearded man with his arm in a sling was sprawled on the settee in the living room. So that was why they were back so soon, thought Gemma. Nick must have had a skiing accident . . .

'Hello,' she said. 'You must be Nick.'

He wasn't as good-looking as she had imagined him, not that you could tell what he looked like underneath the beard. But he was attractive, in the same unconventional way that Vivi was attractive, with eyes even bluer than Gerald's, but harder, colder, full of mockery and malice.

'Not the last time I looked I wasn't.' He rose lazily to his feet and extended his left hand. A beautiful hand with long tapering fingers. 'I'm Daniel Lawrence. Vivi's brother. Who are you?'

'Her sister,' said Gemma, feeling absurd. She shook the hand warily. So this was Daniel. The artist, the cynic, the danger-freak, the womanising divorcé. A man who didn't bother to shut doors quietly. Coming in from the cold outside she felt suddenly hot and sticky.

'Haven't you grown?' he said, looking her up and down with a mixture of surprise and amusement. It must be more than ten years since they had last met, Gemma realised, retrieving an elusive memory of Daniel as a long-haired hippy, of herself in ankle socks. 'Sorry I didn't recognise you, but you're the last person I'd expect to find in Vivi's flat. Does this mean you two have buried the hatchet at last?'

Gemma could guess the kind of things Vivi had said about her over the years. Gemma the wimp, the coward, the pain in the neck. Gemma the bore.

'You'd better ask Vivi, the hatchet belongs to her, not me. I'm afraid she's not here at the moment,' she added. 'She's gone skiing for a couple of weeks. Did the caretaker let you in?'

'I've got my own key. Vivi said I could crash here any time. I hope that's all right with you.' He tapped the damaged arm. 'A Druze grenade went off too close for comfort, two days before Christmas. I copped some shrapnel and broke a wrist. So I won't be taking any more snaps for a while.' The prospect didn't seem to trouble him.

Harriet would have had hysterics, thought Gemma. Which was presumably why he hadn't phoned to tell her before she left for Florida.

'That was bad luck,' said Gemma.

'Bad judgement, actually. I was careless. I've just made some coffee. How do you take it?'

He strolled into the kitchen to fetch it, seeming perfectly at home, while Gemma hung up her coat and scarf, disconcerted at the prospect of sharing the flat with a man, Vivi's brother or not. Perhaps he would go and stay with Gerald instead. Not that she could very well suggest it; he had more right to be here than she did, after all. Rejoining him in the living room, she remembered her painting, still on the easel by the window. Too late to hide it now.

'Er . . . would you like some of Mrs Pulowska's poppy-seed cake?' she said, by way of a diversion, fetching a knife and a couple of plates. She dispensed two slices, feeling clumsy and self-conscious.

'I take it you're the mystery painter,' he said, jerking his head towards the easel. His voice was harsher than Gerald's, roughened by too many cigarettes. The coffee he had made was even stronger than Vivi's.

'Yes,' admitted Gemma, mortified.

'I'm amazed you got Vivi to sit for you.'

'I didn't. That is, I'd started to copy the picture you did of her, for practice. I haven't worked with oils since I was at school . . .'

'That's obvious.' Gemma wished that the floor would swallow her up. 'Did you make a sketch first?'

'Yes.'

'Let's see.'

'I'm afraid it's very rough . . .'

Spotting her pad of cartridge paper, he parked his cigarette and began flicking through it. Gemma cringed.

'Please don't look,' she said. 'It's full of all sorts of rubbish.' Her request ignored, she sat miserably while he worked his way through the pencil drawings she had made since coming to London – one of the flower seller at Clapham Junction station, another of children playing on the Common, another of weary commuters strap-hanging in the tube, and finally, her preliminary sketch of his painting.

'False modesty doesn't become you,' he said.

'It isn't false. There isn't a single thing in there I'm happy with . . .'

'I'm glad to hear it. But you're still too good to waste any more time copying my mistakes. You want to forget this and start on something of your own.' He fell to inspection of the paints Vivi had bought her. 'A lot of the ready-made stuff in tubes is crap. Wrinkles and darkens as soon as you look at it. You were right not to economise, this range is the best on the market.'

'I didn't buy them,' Gemma felt bound to admit. 'They were a Christmas present from Vivi.'

'Well, give her her due, she's not mean. She's bought you far too many colours, in fact, mind you don't get carried away. Best to work with a limited palette. This canvas board stuff isn't ideal, but it's okay for practising on.'

'I intend to enrol for evening classes,' said Gemma, defending her ignorance. 'And to buy some books.'

'There's a stack of them at Lansdowne Gardens you can have,' he said casually. 'Learning how to use the materials is the easy part, I can give you a few lessons if you like.'

'Oh, that's very nice of you, but – '

'I've got time on my hands at the moment,' he said curtly. 'Or rather, on my hand. And the left one at that. Those who can't, teach.'

That the offer was less than gracious was oddly reassuring; at least he wasn't just being polite. Gemma had never had much in the way of individual tuition; as the best pupil in the class she had been left largely to her own devices, especially once Dad had made it clear to her teacher that art school was not an option to be considered or encouraged.

'Well . . . if you haven't got anything better to do . . .'

'Just promise me you won't burst into tears on me, I'm even less tactful than Vivi. How about if I sit for you?' he added, retrieving his cigarette, a French brand that smelt of burning rope. 'That should straighten out your tendency to prettify things. Don't worry, I'm not going to take my clothes off. Head and shoulders will do.'

He was even more irresistible than Vivi. Except that Vivi was a woman, however much she might chafe at it. It was unnerving to experience, first hand, the effect that Vivi must have on men.

'If you like,' said Gemma, rising to the challenge. Hearing the phone ring, she made a move to answer it, but Daniel beat her to it, saying that he was expecting a call.

'Sally!' Suddenly he was all sweetness and light. 'You got my message . . . Tonight?'

Shit, thought Gemma.

'I'd love to, sweetheart, but I'm lumbered with my mother this evening. You can just imagine the paddy she's in, won't believe I'm in one piece until she sees me.' He sounded utterly convincing. 'How about dinner tomorrow? Can't wait. 'Bye Sal.'

'You didn't have to put her off on my account,' said Gemma stiffly.

'Nothing to do with you,' he replied. 'I'm tired after the flight and I could do with a good night's sleep.'

'Then why not say so?'

'Because she would have suggested a good night's sleep at her place. And then kept me hard at it till dawn.' Gemma flushed, wishing she hadn't asked, hating this Sally, whoever she was, suddenly hating Daniel. 'Better make a sketch before you start,' he said, getting back to business. 'Where do you want me to sit?'

Gemma positioned him by the window and got down to work, her interest in her subject gradually overcoming her fear of it. His was a difficult face to master, there was something peek-a-boo about his eyes, one moment staring back at her with arrogant candour, the next shuttered, evasive.

'So are you working in London?' he said, as her pencil flew over the paper.

'As from next Monday.' Briefly, she explained about Gerald finding her a job on *The Courier*.

'First you seduce Vivi into sharing her flat with you. Then you get my mother to cook you Christmas lunch. Then Gerald puts you on the payroll. And to cap it all that dragon Pulowska gives you poppy-seed cake. Not bad going so far.'

'Everyone's been very kind,' said Gemma.

'Harriet didn't eat you, then?'

'No. She's a gourmet. Luckily for me.'

'Myra Shaw's a first-class bitch, you realise.'

'So Gerald warned me.'

'Do you enjoy being a secretary?'

'No.' It seemed pointless to lie; she could sense that he wouldn't have believed her.

'Did the parents talk you out of it?' he said, not needing to clarify what 'it' was.

'Yes.'

'I suppose I was lucky with Harriet. Or unlucky. She was convinced I was some kind of genius and of course I reacted against it. Especially once she got round to showing me the stuff my father left her when he did a runner. She'd held on to it, in case it ever became valuable, which says all there is to say about her artistic judgement. I told her to bung it on the nearest skip. That's when I decided there was no point in being second rate at anything.'

Being driven to succeed must be worse, in a way, than being programmed not to, thought Gemma. All three of Harriet's children were compulsive achievers, of one sort or another. Perhaps she ought to be glad to be plodding along in the slow lane, brooding over what might have been, rather than having to prove herself, as they did.

Except that now, belatedly, the achievement bug was getting to her as well. Daniel turned out to be a merciless critic, he noticed all the bad, lazy habits she had got into, he made her want to try harder, for fear of being labelled 'second rate'. She had never tried hard enough in the past, deliberately so, because what was the point? But now there was a point. She wanted to impress him. She wanted him to take her seriously. And most of all she wanted to immortalise him on canvas, because that was surely the only way she would ever capture a man like him.

Next day, after the luxury of a nice long lie-in – Daniel wasn't an early bird like Vivi, thank God – Gemma learned the right way to choose and lay out her palette, to mix her paints and vary their texture. Daniel demonstrated how colours changed according to how they were applied. Yellow ochre spread thickly looked dull and brown; as a glaze it conferred a golden glow; used in conjunction with blue it made white seem whiter. He stood near enough for her to feel his heat, making her painfully aware of her own, and glad that she was wearing her new perfume, and annoyed with herself for caring. But at least she didn't let it show; not letting things show was automatic.

Which was just as well, given that he not only spent that night with this ex-girlfriend of his but the one after that as well. Evidently she had indeed kept him 'hard at it' because he dozed off twice in his chair, his head lolling forward, his thick, dark hair flopping over his closed eyes, his cigarette falling to the floor. Gemma stared her fill, enjoying the luxury of watching him unobserved, fighting an almost overpowering temptation to reach out and touch him. He seemed to exude a smell of sleep, as infectious as a yawn, one that made her want to curl up next to him and hibernate in a cocoon of sensual warmth.

When he was awake, they talked. Mostly about art, the one subject on which she regarded herself as reasonably well informed. Daniel's knowledge was encyclopedic, his passionate views on the subject stripping away the veneer of studied cynicism.

'Do you do much painting these days?' she said.

'Now and again. Just to remind myself that I made the right decision to pack it in.'

'I thought that portrait of Harriet in Lansdowne Gardens was brilliant,' ventured Gemma boldly.

'Which just shows what a little ignoramus you are. So shut up and concentrate on what you're doing.'

He was uncannily like Vivi. And different from Gerald in every way. Like Vivi he was arrogant, brusque to the point of rudeness, and wore his misanthropy like armour, a loner who deployed his sex appeal with all the callousness of a serial killer. He had none of Gerald's gentleness or sensitivity, none of his beautiful manners. And yet Gemma was bewitched by him. Hardly surprising, really, given that she had been hopelessly, if unwillingly, in love with Vivi for as long as she could remember.

'If you want to invite Sally over here,' she said, provocatively, 'I can easily make myself scarce.'

'You must be kidding. I'd never get rid of her.'

'That's a remarkably big-headed thing to say.'

'Not really. Sally's not fussy, believe me.'

'Neither are you, by the sound of it. Will you please sit still?'

Ignoring her request, he jumped up yet again to inspect her work and took the brush from her hand impatiently to illustrate a comment, his left arm stretching around her body, his chest against her back, his breath caressing her ear, his mind on what he was saying, unlike Gemma's mind which was focused on the hot, dark pulse between her legs and the way her nipples were standing to attention underneath the blessed camouflage of a thick jumper . . .

Suddenly he stepped back, gave the brush back to her and sat down again, and she thought, oh God, he knows, he can smell it. A suspicion which was reinforced when he took pains not to touch her again, even accidentally. To him she was just Vivi's kid sister, a pathetic juvenile he felt sorry for . . . The thought of it made her work harder than ever, if more cautiously, fearful that her feelings would find their way on to the canvas.

He spent that night with Sally again. Rather her than me, thought Gemma, as she tossed and turned. Next morning – he never got back before noon – Mrs Pulowska knocked at the door just as Gemma was setting off to buy the first edition of the *Evening Standard*, intending to work her way through the flats to let. There wouldn't be room for three of them in the flat once Vivi returned – not that Daniel slept there anyway, but his presence, however peripheral, made finding a place of her own all the more urgent, in more ways than one.

'I speak to my friend Mr Kuron,' announced Pulowska. 'He own property in Balham. I tell him you good girl.' She handed over a scrap of paper bearing an address and phone number. 'He has nice clean room available. You ring him straight away.'

Thanking her profusely, Gemma did so and arranged to view later that morning. The nice clean room turned out to be a large mansarded bedsitter on the top floor of a Victorian house off Wandsworth Common, with a shared bathroom on the landing below. The present tenant was still in occupation, but was moving out at the end of next week. Mr Kuron, a male version of Mrs Pulowska, explained that he intended to redecorate the room before reletting it, so it wouldn't be ready till the end of the month.

'I'd rather move in as soon as possible and decorate myself,' said Gemma, hoping to pre-empt renewal of the ubiquitous woodgrain vinyl wallpaper; he had even covered the doors with it. 'At my own expense, of course,' she added, by way of an incentive. 'I'd check the colours with you first.' This agreed, she wrote a cheque for the deposit, relieved that she would be able to move before Vivi got back.

On her return she phoned Gerald to let him know that she had given his name as an employer's reference, she hoped he didn't mind.

'Heavens no,' he said. 'I had a call from Daniel, by the way. I do hope he isn't the reason you're moving. I did offer him a bed at Lansdowne Gardens, of course, but I gather he's been spending most of his time with one of his old flames.'

'Er . . . yes. But I was already looking, before he arrived. I think I've tried Vivi's patience long enough.'

'Or the other way round,' he observed wryly. 'You must let me help you with the move, when the time comes. Well, I'll look forward to seeing you on Monday, then.'

'Me too. Goodbye.'

Daniel rolled up at one o'clock, looking haggard. He seemed in a bad mood, switched on the television, and spent the afternoon channel-hopping from his seat by the window, glaring balefully at the screen over Gemma's shoulder. Perhaps he and Sally had had a row, she thought, pleased.

'If I sit still much longer I'll get piles,' he announced finally, giving the painting no more than a cursory glance for her pains. 'I'm hungry. How about getting a takeaway?'

'Won't that spoil your appetite for dinner with Sally?'

'I'm not having dinner with Sally. She thinks I'm spending an evening with the boys.'

Which he could have done, thought Gemma. And instead he was suggesting eating in, with her . . .

'There's plenty of food in the fridge. I was going to cook supper anyway, I can easily make enough for two.'

'Vivi would have my guts if she thought I'd let you skivvy for me. Come on, let's see what we can find.'

There was a Chinese place nearby, whence they emerged laden with foil dishes, picking up a couple of bottles of chilled white wine at the off-licence on the way back. They spread the food out on the coffee table and helped themselves, sitting on the floor. Assessing Gemma's tastes correctly, Daniel had chosen an innocuous-tasting German Riesling, as quaffable as water, which she drank more of than she realised, thanks to him keeping her glass topped up. Otherwise she surely wouldn't have talked, self-pityingly, about the last few anxious years of keeping Dad's condition a secret from her mother, and incidentally from Vivi, whom he hadn't wanted to worry, preferring to leave all the worrying to Gemma. Neither would she have mentioned the horror of coming home early from work one day to find Mum and Fred copulating grotesquely on, or rather over, the kitchen table, less than six months after Dad had died, or the even worse horror of their subsequent marriage.

'Which just goes to show,' said Daniel, spearing the last sweet-and-sour prawn and depositing it on her plate, 'that you should have left home long ago, instead of giving in to emotional blackmail.'

'It's easy to be wise with hindsight.'

'Then at least learn by your mistakes instead of repeating them. You said you hated being the boss's daughter and how bored you were being a secretary. So what do you do? You take a job bashing a typewriter at the bloody *Courier*, courtesy of the proprietor's grandson.'

'*The Courier*'s different.' *The Courier* represented everything Dad had left behind him, *The Courier* was part of the exotic Collington world she had always longed to inhabit.

'Only if you treat it as a temporary job, till you take up a place at art school, which is where you really want to be.'

'Not any more I don't,' said Gemma perversely. 'I can't afford it. I've got a living to earn.'

'You can get a grant. There's nobody to tell you what you can and can't do any longer. Except yourself.'

But that was what made it so hard. Doing what you wanted to do was a terrible responsibility. There was nobody else to blame if you failed.

'Time you took a few risks for a change,' went on Daniel, sharing out the remainder of the second bottle. 'You can't go through the rest of your life repressed and frustrated, hiding behind that placid front of yours.'

'What makes you think it's just a front?' It was unsettling, but thrilling as well, to know that he had seen through it when everybody else was so easily taken in. He leaned back on his hands and looked at her till she couldn't hold his gaze any longer.

'What's wrong with your work is that you hold back. You're afraid of showing what's really there, inside and outside you. You want things to be tidy, orderly, pleasing to the eye. You're looking for approval all the time.' He stood up, pulled her to her feet, and dragged her over to her picture.

'See what I mean? It's clever, it's competent, it's safe, but it's not honest.'

But surely he knew why she had held back, why she hadn't shown what was really inside her? She was woozy with too much wine, the hand pressing into her shoulder made her feel faint, breathless, reckless . . . honest.

She didn't say anything. She simply turned and looked at him, and somehow found the courage to let her feelings show in her eyes, to let him see the longing and fear that went with it, to stay very still, in an agony of expectation, instinctively sure that he was going to kiss her, every nerve in her body vibrating in readiness, wanting much more than a kiss. His head bent towards hers until they were sharing each other's breath, Gemma's eyes closing as if to heighten her other senses . . .

'We've both had too much to drink,' he said curtly, bringing her back to earth with a jolt. 'Go to bed. I'll clear up in here.'

Gemma fled to her bedroom, crimson with humiliation. She had done what he had exhorted her to do, given him more than he bargained for, revealed her absurd adolescent infatuation, scared him off. How typical of her to want something she couldn't possibly have! Learn by your mistakes, he had said. She should have learned, long ago, the futility of hankering after things that were beyond her reach. Thank God she had had too much to drink. That would at least give her an excuse. Please God he didn't say anything to Vivi . . .

Pupils fell in love with teachers the way patients fell in love with nurses, the way ingénues fell in love with rakes. The most hackneyed scenario in the world. It would have been only too easy for him to seduce her, if he had wanted to. Obviously he couldn't be bothered. Why should he take the time and trouble to instruct a novice when he had access to experts like Sally?

Blonde and pretty, she thought, glowering at her flushed face in the mirror, hating her large, grey eyes with their pale lashes, her cute little upturned nose, her small, neat mouth and her Alice-in-Wonderland haircut. Blonde and pretty but not sexy. And now she wished she was. Wished she was an experienced woman of the world, like Vivi, instead of a socially inept twenty-one-year-old virgin. Wished she had what it took to give Daniel a run for his money. But it was too late now to transform herself into a would-be vamp. He must find her ridiculous enough already.

Feelings were like dynamite, she thought, packing them carefully away. Quite safe, as long as you didn't light the fuse.

# 6

TWO DAYS BEFORE the end of their fortnight's holiday Nick and Vivi had dinner at a restaurant situated at the top of a narrow mountain track. The only way up was by ski-lift, the only way back down, in the dark, by two-man toboggans provided by the management – the reason Nick had chosen it, no doubt, because they managed to fall off every few yards, thanks to his avowed incompetence at steering, or rather his skill at engineering their collective tumbles into the snow. Though in fact they fared no better when Vivi took over the driving seat, innocently blaming her unwieldy passenger.

They returned to the hotel late, glowing with laughter, limp with over-exertion, to find a message waiting with Nick's room key for him to ring his father urgently. The desk clerk explained that the gentleman had telephoned several times in the course of the evening. Which meant that it must be bad news.

Vivi sat on Nick's bed while he made the call, watching his face drain of colour. At least her father had died in his early sixties, of a largely self-inflicted disease. But Nick's mother had been mown down by a hit-and-run, probably drunken driver, at the age of forty-nine, when she had gone to the trouble to use a zebra crossing.

There was nothing Vivi could say or do except put her arms around him and hold him while he wept. She should have felt awkward and embarrassed; the men in her family never cried and she had always striven to emulate them, in public at least. But she was touched that Nick felt able to let her see him like this, that he was willing to let her look after him.

Looking after people didn't come naturally, but she did her best.

While Nick sat brooding over the triple brandy she had fetched unbidden from the bar, she got busy on the phone, securing two seats on a fully booked flight next day – sometimes the Collington name came in pretty useful – and arranging for a car to drive them to the airport.

'Try to get some sleep now,' she said, having packed his suitcase for him. 'See you in the morning.'

'Don't go,' he said, coming out of his trance. 'Stay with me tonight. I won't try anything on, I promise.'

It would have seemed coy, and cruel, to refuse at a time like this. Even if he did try anything on, she wouldn't have had the heart to stop him. Anything to make him feel better; it was only sex, after all, the cheapest thing in the world. Vivi went back to her room to change and returned, feeling rather self-conscious, in her dressing gown and slip; she would have hated Nick to see the winceyette pyjamas she wore for warmth rather than allure. Vivi possessed no glamorous night attire, because nobody ever saw it, after all, except Gemma. Gemma who wore pretty-pretty sleeveless sprigged nighties with broderie anglaise and lace trimming, who looked stunning first thing in the morning with her perfect, naked complexion, unlike Vivi, who wouldn't even go jogging without full war paint.

She was still wearing it now, even though she knew she would wake up with itchy skin and gritty eyes. Nick had stripped down to his boxer shorts, another of those lucky people, like her sister, who didn't feel the cold. The thermostat at Chipstead Close had always been kept down low, except when Vivi came to stay; Gemma was probably saving her gas at this very minute.

He pulled back the covers for her, and Vivi slid off her dressing gown, wondering why she should feel so shy, they had seen each other in the swimming pool, after all. Nick was one of those men who looked bigger with his shirt off, with well-muscled arms and shoulders. There were an awful lot of weeds, Vivi had discovered, hiding their puniness behind well-cut clothes.

'Thanks for coming back,' he said, snuggling up close to her, tucking his head under the arm she put uncertainly around his shoulders. Vivi was amazed at how comfortable it was, how everything seemed to fit. And he was wonderfully warm and dry to the touch, not sweaty as men invariably were after sex, when Vivi preferred to avoid a sticky slumberous embrace in favour of a quick shower and a speedy exit. She had only ever broken that rule once before, if for completely different reasons . . .

His warmth seemed to penetrate her, drugging her into an uncharacteristically deep sleep. When she awoke, long before the alarm, she was lying on her side, facing away from him, with Nick's arm around her waist and a rampant erection pressing into the small of her back. For a moment she felt panic-stricken, despite her resolution to go through with it for the first time in nearly a year, until she realised, to her relief, that he was still asleep and slipped quickly out of bed before he woke up.

The danger past, she stood looking at him, resisting the urge to kiss him. Not a sexual urge, an emotional one. At the time it seemed harmless enough, as harmless as those innocent comforting cuddles that had soothed them both to sleep. Vivi hadn't been cuddled since childhood. Dad had stopped doing it, abruptly, when she reached puberty, and Vivi had rebuffed Harriet's come-to-mummy embraces long before that. As for sex, that had always been a denial of intimacy rather than a celebration of it. She had never been as intimate with any man as she had been with Nick, last night. Least of all Max bloody Kellerman.

Nick said little on the two-hour drive to the airport, or during the flight, but he held her hand tightly throughout, the one point of contact between them, as if to apologise for the rest of him being so far away. Vivi found herself morbidly substituting her own mother's death for his, and ended up having to shut herself in the loo at the rear of the plane for a furtive weep. God, what a burden it was, loving people, even though she would have denied loving Harriet, the embodiment of everything Vivi feared to become.

'Any chance of another lift?' Nick said bleakly, on arrival at Gatwick. Vivi had driven him to the airport and left her car in the long-term car park.

'Better than letting you get ripped off by a cab,' she said tactlessly, momentarily forgetting that Ferris senior, in common with many print workers, had a second job as a taxi driver. Or rather a third job. Sixteen hours a week on *The Courier* (for which he picked up the best part of £1000 – more if a story broke late, or demanded a bigger print run) left him plenty of time to fit in a few shifts for *The Mail* as well, albeit under a false name, to supplement his meagre wages.

'Thanks,' said Nick. 'My dad did offer to pick me up but I didn't want him driving all that way, he sounded pretty rough on the phone.'

'Er . . . do you want to go to the hospital first?'

'God no. I'd rather remember her alive. Let's go straight to the house.'

The house turned out to be a large, detached affair on a new estate in Barking; the Ferrises had long since moved upmarket from the East Ham council flat where Nick had grown up. Before he had time to press the bell a girl opened the door and flung herself at him, simultaneously with a large black labrador.

Vivi knew from what Nick had told her that this must be his sister, Jackie, aged seventeen, who had been knocked up while still at school by some lout of a boyfriend. A moment later a big, burly bear of a man appeared and encircled his son with two beefy arms. Jackie began crying; Ferris senior wiped his eyes with the back of his hand; Nick blew his nose and said in a cracked voice, 'Dad, Jackie, this is Vivi.'

Dad and Jackie responded to this introduction by ignoring her, while Vivi, feeling distinctly *de trop*, concentrated on making friends with the dog, which had better manners. They passed into a large L-shaped living room, where a grinning baby dressed in a little sugar-pink dress shouted incomprehensible greetings from her playpen. Nick picked her up and kissed her, eliciting a gurgle of delight, before depositing her back in her toy-strewn cage.

The room was expensively if tastelessly furnished, all highly polished repro and shag-pile carpet and shelves full of gold-tooled classics, the kind non-readers bought from a book club for show. Vivi wondered how soon she could politely leave. Nick would no doubt wish to stay here until the funeral, and besides, his family surely didn't want a stranger intruding on their private grief. But the Ferrises proceeded to speak as freely as if she wasn't there, as uninhibited as aristocrats in the presence of a parlour maid.

Jackie was a thin, pale, freckled girl wearing teeshirt, jeans, nose stud and three pairs of pierced earrings, collectively heavy enough to distort her lobes. Her hair was cropped in a spiky style which made her look hard-faced, especially as she had dyed it black, which looked all wrong with her pale brows and lashes. She was telling Nick, between sniffs, that Mum had called the doctor out, on account of Casey running a temperature, and she'd gone to that all-night chemist to get the prescription made up . . .

'While your sister here was at a disco, so she said,' put in Ferris senior. ''Cept that she wasn't where she was supposed to be. Didn't roll up till three this morning –'

'Tell him to lay off me!' wailed Jackie, turning to Nick. 'It weren't my fault!'

'She cons her poor mother into looking after her bastard for her while she goes out on the tiles every night . . .'

'Don't you call Casey a bastard!'

'. . . and she won't be happy till that tea leaf of a boyfriend of hers gives her another one . . .' Whereupon Jackie stomped off upstairs with much slamming of doors.

'What's the point in taking it out on her?' Nick challenged his father. 'It won't bring Mum back.'

'That's right. Jump to her defence, same as usual. Now you're here, she'll be laying it on thick, both of you ganging up against me . . .'

The baby, alarmed by the raised voices, began grizzling, her cries drowned out by the sound of very heavy metal music emanating from above.

'See what I mean?' bellowed Ferris senior. 'Jackie! You come down here this minute and see to Case!'

He marched off, elephant-footed, up the stairs.

'I'd better go up there, stop them killing each other,' said Nick. 'Do something with the baby, will you, love?'

Vivi, who had no idea what to do with a baby, picked Casey up like a squirming kitten and sat her on her lap.

'It's all right,' she murmured helplessly, adopting the same technique as she would have used with a hostile stray. 'They're not angry with you.' She remembered her own childhood experience of raised voices, the miserable feeling that it must be her fault. Spying a glove puppet lying on the floor of the playpen, she played ventriloquist for a while in an attempt to distract the poor little brat from the sounds of discord above, with Nick trying in vain to play peacemaker above the din. The fight was mercifully broken up by a ring on the doorbell, heralding the

94

arrival of a couple of family friends who had come to offer their condolences.

'Brew up some tea, will you, love?' said Ferris senior, offending all Vivi's feminist principles. But she did as asked rather than look like some toffee-nosed bitch who thought such tasks beneath her. Waiting for the kettle to boil, she noticed the framed photograph of Nick and Jackie, arm in arm, on the window sill by the kitchen sink. Vivi could just imagine Nick's mother gazing at it fondly while she went about her chores, trying to convince herself, Harriet-style, that her children made up for an otherwise wasted life.

'Are you all right, doll?' said Nick, putting his head round the door.

For once Vivi didn't rebuke him for calling her doll.

'Yes. But I really ought to go in a minute. I – '

'Do us a favour and wait another hour and then I can leave with you. Otherwise I'll get lumbered with staying the night. You can see what it's like. Dad and Jackie at each other's throats, me as referee. I'll end up falling out with both of them.' He put his arms around her and kissed the top of her head. 'Thanks for everything. Don't know what I would have done without you.'

The hour proved to be nearer two, thanks to a fresh batch of visitors and the need to brew more tea, but by that time the house was quiet again, the guests departed, the baby asleep and Nick's father and sister reconciled in an uneasy truce. There were more tearful family embraces on the doorstep, making Vivi feel excluded again.

"Bye then, love,' said Dad, acknowledging her departure, 'love' being easier than trying to remember her name. Just as well he hadn't registered who she was; as a union militant he had been a thorn in Gramps' side for years and would no doubt regard Vivi as a class enemy. As it was she was just some new bit of skirt Nick had been shagging on holiday.

'You don't have to rush off home yet, do you?' said Nick, on the drive to his place in Stockwell. 'Let's dump our stuff and find somewhere to eat.'

It wasn't as if she could go home and be alone, thought Vivi. Gemma wouldn't be able to resist cooking her something, or putting her dirty clothes in the machine along with hers, or ironing them tomorrow because she had the board out anyway and it didn't take a jiffy, or generally making Vivi feel like a slut, in more ways than one.

'Oh, all right. Might as well.'

She should have realised by this time that she was getting in too deep. That Nick had used his mother's death to take their relationship one stage further. That he had wept in front of her, slept beside her, and taken her home to meet his family to make it impossible for him to be anonymous, like all the others. He had risked scaring her off as the price of sucking her in.

But the warning bells rang to stubbornly deaf ears. Otherwise she would surely have run for cover before she committed the ultimate folly of falling in love with him.


Gemma had learned, on her very first day, that no secretary in Features had ever lasted longer than six months and that there hadn't been a single internal candidate for her job, thanks to Myra's reputation as a snake. She was the type of journalist who was popular with no one but the editor, but she treated Gemma civilly enough, which Gemma put down to her obvious desire to stay on the right side of Gerald. She found herself wondering, protectively, if Myra liked him for himself, or simply because of who he was.

The work was easy, and came in fits and starts. Every section demanded its own secretary to type its vital last-minute lists for conference at the same times of day, which meant that the rest of the time they were underoccupied, despite the mass of bureau-cratic paperwork generated by Room 149, the mysterious administrative core of the building. Overmanning seemed to be endemic; no wonder *The Courier* was losing money. Myra, like every other departmental head, was neurotic about her budget; if she didn't use it all up, or preferably exceed it, it would be cut next year, which did little to encourage good housekeeping.

There were two main categories of *Courier* employee, Vivi had told her. Those who were using it as a stepping stone to something better and had no long-term commitment to the paper, and those who had worked there for donkey's years and were hanging on either for their pay-offs or their pensions. Any would-be reformers in between were doomed to be outnumbered and demoralised. The cynicism of the younger staff was balanced by the complacency of the old stagers who held the key positions. Many of these belonged to CC's unofficial army of informers, and all of them shared the same objectives as the sycophants on the board – to protect their own jobs and resist any threats to the status quo. Chief among them was CC's dragon of a secretary, a fiercely loyal shrivelled-up stick of a woman who was hated even by her fellow-spies.

But the real power was wielded in *The Courier*'s composing and machine rooms. The first time Gemma heard, or rather felt the locomotive-like roar of the presses starting up, sending a rumbling tremor through the whole building, she had asked Gerald if he would show her round, curious about the huge and heaving creature giving birth below them. She had never seen the hot-metal system in action. At the *Alchester Post*, in common with many local and regional papers, it had been abandoned some years before in favour of web offset, but here in Fleet Street the old time-honoured methods still held immutable sway, with the Chapel Fathers presiding over their domains with all the solemnity of high priests guarding their temples.

The 'stone' or composing room had a mystique all its own; its operatives, members of the NGA, considered themselves to be several cuts above the rest of the profession. They set the type and assembled it into a metal forme from which the printing plates would be made, skilled work carried out amid the rhythmic hammering of the compositor's mallet and the clatter of the linotype machines, each with its own pot of molten lead suspended above a heater. Extinguishing those heaters, in the course of a dispute, effectively cut off the paper's blood supply, because once the lead was allowed to set hard, it took a long time to melt again, meaning lost editions, lost readers, lost revenue. Hence the perennial pressure on management to keep it flowing at all costs.

The machine hall, a SOGAT stronghold containing the presses and the foundry, was a factory by any other name, an inferno of heat and noise. It was here that the plates were made and bolted on to the presses, which swallowed up huge rolls of newsprint and disgorged them as finished copies, ready to be bundled up by the warehousemen and loaded into the waiting vans which would rush them to the railway stations.

The machinery was old and unsafe and the working conditions dickensian. It was impossible to see from one end of the hall to the other, thanks to the dense mist of vaporised ink and paper dust. Inadequate ventilation made the temperature unbearable, even more so in the summer months, and the decibel level regularly exceeded the legal limit. It would have cost a fortune to restore the dilapidated building, which was plagued by rising damp and rats, to modern health and safety standards; it was only a matter of time before the factory inspectors shut the place down altogether.

Small wonder that the men who worked there were permanently disgruntled, if reluctant to see the building condemned, given that some of them earned more than the editor. And all of them earned more than the journalists, a source of much unspoken resentment – no one dared to criticise the print out loud, for fear of having his work blacked, or butchered by deliberate typos. To hell with it, was the general attitude. Do what they do. Clock on, clock off, take the money and run.

'All ready for your move?' Gerald asked Gemma, following his guided tour.

'There's nothing much to get ready. Just a couple of suitcases to pack.'

'I was supposed to be meeting Daniel for a drink tonight. But he hasn't shown up yet. Care to join me instead?'

'I'd love to,' said Gemma, annoyed with Daniel for letting his brother down. Ever since she had nearly made an idiot of herself, the previous week, her attitude towards him had hardened, as purposefully and bloody-mindedly as those all-important pots of lead. No longer did she allow herself to nurture romantic fantasies about restoring his faith in women (Vivi had made his ex-wife Natasha sound like a calculating bitch) or blame the Sallys of this world for leading him astray. Daniel was an aggressor, not a victim – selfish, arrogant, irresponsible and heartless, one minute sarcastic and aloof, the next oozing lethal cold-blooded charm to stun his prey into surrender. Rejected or not, she had had a lucky escape.

There had been no more painting lessons since that night; the 'dishonest' portrait of him remained unfinished by mutual unspoken agreement. As a sop he had taken her on a gallery crawl last Sunday, an invitation which she couldn't turn down without looking as if she was sulking. They had worked their way round the National, the Tate and the Courtauld, arguing over the respective merits of painters and paintings, taking refuge in the equivalent of shop talk, steering clear of personal topics, if you could call art an impersonal topic, given that it aroused such strong passions in both of them. But at least one passion served as camouflage for another, with Gemma busily digging a nice deep grave for a body that would have to be buried alive if it refused to do the decent thing and die.

Just to make sure she got the message, he had spent the last few nights God knows where – certainly not chez Sally Archer, who had rung up in his absence, sounding neglected and demanding that he ring her back, a request which Gemma had conveyed two days later in her best deadpan voice.

'That woman can't take a hint,' he had said, which Gemma took as an if-the-cap-fits warning. As if to reinforce it, he had phoned Sally in Gemma's hearing to say that he had just got back from the doctor's, it turned out that he had the clap, he was terribly sorry, but she ought to get herself checked out . . . He held the phone at arm's length to spare himself an ear-bashing, which terminated in a hysterical Sally hanging up.

'It never fails,' he said, as Gemma glared her disgust. 'What's the matter? Would you rather I'd given her a dose for real?'

'It's a wonder you didn't, the way you carry on.'

'Don't worry, somebody else'll do it for me.'

What a swine, seethed Gemma. But not enough of a swine to have taken advantage of her pathetic willingness to provide him with yet another scalp. Not that she gave him any credit for either scruples or self-control. He just didn't fancy her, thank God. At least this way Vivi wouldn't have the satisfaction of hearing from Daniel what a lousy lay she was.

Gerald took her to El Vino's, saying that if Daniel turned up later, it was one of the places he would look for him. He ushered her past the crowded bar, with its huge butts of sherry and crated wines on the wall and nicotine-enriched yellow ceiling, through to a quieter area at the rear where drinks were brought to the table. Gemma knew from Dad that this was a management watering hole, which served wines and spirits only. Evidently Gerald was a regular client, because he asked for his 'usual claret', before remembering belatedly that Gemma was with him and asking her if she would prefer white. Seeing through her disclaimers he changed his order to a bottle of Gewürztraminer.

'So tell me about this flat you've found.'

'It's just a room,' admitted Gemma. 'It looks pretty dingy at the moment. But it won't be once I've spruced it up. Luckily I'm a wonderful little housewife, as Vivi keeps telling me.'

'Yes, I gathered you'd been keeping the place in good order and feeding her the odd square meal. Believe it or not, I think she appreciates having you there. She finds it lonely, living on her own, but she recognises that she's an impossible person to live with. Except for you, evidently.'

Gemma shrugged dismissively, gratified nonetheless.

'I know she can be unkind sometimes,' went on Gerald, demonstrating his mastery of euphemism. 'But it's only because she's so insecure. Especially as far as you're concerned. With you being your father's favourite, I mean.'

'That's nonsense,' said Gemma. 'She was his favourite, not me.'

'That's not the way it seemed to her. But then Vivi's notoriously hard to satisfy.'

'She takes after him then.'

'Really? I always found him very easy-going. But then, I was comparing him with CC. When he first came along we were living back at Collington Hall. Or Colditz, as we used to call it. We never knew when the old man was going to turn up from London and start laying down the law. School holidays never seemed so long.'

'What about your grandmother?'

'Oh, she doted on us in short sharp bursts, but we hardly ever saw her. She was a dedicated socialite in her day, made Bubbles Rothermere seem like a recluse. She hated Little Moldingham, it was strictly the old man's domain. We were so glad to get away from there that Trevor seemed like a knight in shining armour.'

Especially to Harriet, thought Gemma, desperate for a home of her own.

'Were you close to him?'

'No, we were both away at boarding school most of the time, at CC's insistence, one of those spartan places that's supposed to make a man out of you. To stop Harriet spoiling us, he said.'

'She must have missed you terribly.' Whatever Harriet's other failings, she was obviously devoted to her children.

'Oh yes. But she went along with it. It was all part of her master plan to suck up to CC and make sure we inherited. But it meant she was on her own a lot of the time. She resented the long hours an editor has to put in, it caused no end of trouble in the marriage.'

'And yet she wants to see you take over as proprietor? Surely that's equally demanding, in its way?'

'Oh yes,' smiled Gerald. 'Specially as I'd want to be a hands-on proprietor. Which is different, I hope, from an interfering one, like CC, barking orders from his ivory tower. And of course Harriet would expect my wife to make all the allowances she didn't. She's always coming up with what she considers suitable candidates. Namely, girls who couldn't care less if they hardly ever saw me or not.'

He made it sound like a joke, but it rang too true to be funny. Vivi had mentioned Harriet wanting to 'put poor old Gerald out to stud', and Gemma admired him for not giving in to the pressure. It would have been easy enough, surely, to contract a loveless marriage of mutual exploitation.

'I can't deny that turning the paper around, when the time comes, will be a labour of Hercules,' went on Gerald, warming to his favourite theme. 'Of course, a lot will depend on how much money we have to play with . . . Sorry. I must sound as if I'm wishing the old man dead.'

Gemma wouldn't have blamed him if he did. It must be intolerable to have CC forever threatening to disinherit him and undermining his position at the paper.

'Of course you don't,' she said, not wanting him to clam up on her. 'Go on.'

'What the paper needs is a massive injection of cash, instead of this drip-feed method he employs at the moment. Understandably he's unwilling to liquidise his other assets and put all his eggs in one basket, and even more unwilling to attract outside investment, which would mean a loss of overall control. When he sold the family construction business, twenty-odd years ago, he was worth over five million, and it's reasonable to assume he's increased that at least tenfold, given the rate of inflation since then.'

Fifty million pounds, thought Gemma, stunned. No wonder

Harriet was so neurotic about keeping Gerald in the will. And no wonder Myra Shaw was so keen on Gerald.

'I'm certainly not interested in a millionaire life style,' continued Gerald. 'One has to keep up appearances, of course, and I'd have to take care of my mother, but apart from that every penny of the old man's estate, if need be, will be invested in getting *The Courier* straight again. I want to get rid of the them-and-us attitude, specially with the print. Give everybody a stake in the paper, by way of a profit-sharing scheme and productivity bonuses . . .'

'You can't share profits if there aren't any,' put in Daniel, appearing from nowhere. 'Or pay bonuses if there's no productivity. As for a stake in the paper, just make sure it goes through the heart. Only way to kill a vampire.'

'Thank you for that vote of confidence,' said Gerald wearily. Gemma bristled.

'If you want to spoil the old bastard's fun,' said Daniel, signalling for another glass, 'you'll tell him to stuff his bloody paper.'

'Telling him to stuff the paper wouldn't be spoiling his fun,' said Gerald. 'It would be letting him think he'd beaten me. I wouldn't give him that satisfaction.' He turned to Gemma. 'As you can see, my little brother has touching faith in me.'

'So I do,' said Daniel. 'Unlike Harriet and Vivi, I happen to believe you don't need *The Courier*. In your shoes I'd go back to Oxford, take a doctorate or two, and settle down to a nice quiet life as an academic, which is what you would have been if Harriet hadn't brainwashed you from birth.'

'When you decide to have a nice quiet life,' said Gerald testily, 'perhaps I'll do the same. As it is, I'm not about to throw away the last eleven years.'

'What about the rest of your life? What if he sells over your head, one, two, five years from now?'

'You take risks for a living, why shouldn't I?'

'That's not the same thing at all.'

'Why not? Because you're a winner and I'm a loser?'

'I never said you were a loser. I just don't trust the old bastard not to stab you in the back. Even if you do inherit, *The Courier*'s a poisoned chalice if ever there was one.'

'Well, nobody's asking you to drink it. You opted out nice and early, as I recall.'

'I refused to toe the line, if that's what you mean.'

'Spare me your sixties philosophy of life, will you? Ignore us, Gemma,' he added, embarrassed. 'The only way we can communicate with each other is by squabbling like a pair of toddlers.'

'More like one toddler and one grown-up,' said Gemma.

'Well, that's put me firmly in my place,' said Daniel. And then, getting his own back, 'Have some more wine, Gemma. It might improve your opinion of me.'

Gemma coloured as he refilled her glass. Luckily Gerald didn't seem to notice. But Daniel did, damn him. She hated him for the way he put Gerald down, even though Gerald himself seemed to take it in his stride; a moment later they were discussing Australia's chances against the West Indies in the third Test, their spat apparently forgotten. Feeling superfluous, Gemma made an excuse to go, at which Gerald insisted on driving her home. Daniel declined to share the lift, saying he had other plans for the rest of the evening. I'll bet you do, fumed Gemma.

'I'm sorry about that little set-to,' said Gerald, in the car. 'We're chalk and cheese, as you'll have gathered.' Like me and Vivi, thought Gemma. 'We've always traded insults, as a matter of course. But it's all water off a duck's back.'

Not to Gemma it wasn't. She couldn't bear for Daniel to patronise Gerald, the way Vivi patronised her. It wasn't that she trusted CC, or underestimated the problems facing the paper. But if Vivi and Harriet could have faith in Gerald, then so could she.

'I didn't realise you owned the place,' said Vivi, as Nick fished for his keys. When she had arrived to drive him to the airport, she had hooted from the street without going in, and assumed that the dilapidated multi-doorbell house was divided into rented flats. 'What do you want with all this space?'

'It's an investment,' shrugged Nick. 'It's already put on ten grand since I bought it. And once I put in new plumbing and wiring and central heating, and the rest, I can sell it at a big profit . . . Bloody hell,' he groaned, as he opened the door. 'This is all I need.'

The ground floor was flooded. Investigation revealed that two ceilings had come down, and a steady stream of icy water, under mains pressure, was still leaking from the burst pipe feeding the tank in the loft. Just as well, thought Vivi, paddling through the mess, that the place was almost bare of furniture and as yet uncarpeted and undecorated.

While she got down to work piling sodden plaster into a dustbin liner Nick rang for an emergency plumber and did his best to stanch the flow till he arrived. Vivi was called upon yet again to brew tea while Nick acted as plumber's mate, which at least gave her an opportunity to have a snoop while they were busy in the loft.

There was fresh linen on the one and only bed, a double, evidently put there on the morning of his departure. Vivi wasn't sure whether to be flattered that he had gone to the trouble or affronted that he had assumed too much. But he had failed to take such care underneath it, where Vivi spied two dusty socks, an empty condom wrapper, and a discarded bra. She fished it out and inspected it. A 32A. Which was presumably why its owner hadn't missed it. Vivi could have no more gone out without a bra than without her knickers.

She replaced it quickly as she heard the loft ladder creaking and returned to her post in the bathroom, from which she could hear Nick haggling over the bill and saying you must be joking mate, what do you take me for, some middle-class wanker of a stockbroker or what? A loud altercation ensued, with Vivi fearful that it would come to blows, especially as the plumber was much bigger than Nick.

'All right, in that case you can have a bloody cheque, and I'll want a VAT receipt,' conceded Nick finally, before settling on twenty quid off for cash, only to find that he didn't have enough money on him. Vivi, who would have paid up no questions asked, middle-class wanker that she was, had to lend it to him, with Nick hissing in her ear, 'Make out you're down to your last tenner,' which secured a further discount, reducing Vivi to a fit of quite untypical giggles.

'How are you ever going to get this place dried out?' she asked, teeth chattering, when the plumber had gone. Nick's one and only fan heater had been on the ground floor and become waterlogged. 'You'll freeze to death if you stay here tonight.'

'Is that an invitation?'

It was almost as if he'd rigged the whole thing.

'I haven't got a spare room at the moment, I've got my sister staying. And before you ask, no you can't share with me. Last night was a one-off. So you'd better go back home and stay with your dad.'

'Spare me, Viv, you've seen what it's like back there. Your settee will do me fine. Better than catching pneumonia, on top of everything else.' He managed a plaintive sneeze.

Nick didn't look the least bit cold, despite stripping down to his shirt-sleeves to help the plumber. It was Vivi who was shivering through a thermal vest, a long-sleeved teeshirt, thick polo-necked sweater and ski jacket.

'Or you catching it first,' he added, putting his arms around her to warm her. He radiated heat like a furnace. 'Poor love. Your feet are sopping wet.'

'So are yours.'

'Save me washing them tonight. You're a real life-saver, Vivi.'

'No I'm not,' said Vivi, rather crossly. 'I just happened to be around, that's all.'

'That's what people always say when they've rescued someone from drowning.'

'No. That's what the papers say they say.'

'But you just said it, didn't you?'

'Then perhaps I've started to think in journalese.'

'Like that bit about us being "just good friends"? Now there's a cliché and a half.'

'Don't push your luck, will you?'

'I'm not feeling very lucky at the moment,' he reminded her. 'So feel sorry for me, there's a love. Come on, let's go.'

Vivi's discomfiture was less the result of having Nick as an unexpected house guest than at the prospect of him meeting Gemma, whom she had depicted, by implication, as a frump. Which she was, as far as her clothes and make-up went, but she was still a blonde and pretty frump, with terrific legs. Whenever Vivi had found Nick chatting up a girl, she was invariably blonde with terrific legs. As the owner of that tiny-tit bra had probably been.

The door opened as she was putting her key in the lock. Her delight at seeing Daniel, albeit a Daniel with his arm in plaster, was quickly superseded by a perverse annoyance that Gemma had already moved out to a flat procured for her by that old witch Pulowska and underwritten by a reference provided by Gerald, who was helping her move in at this very moment.

'If you ask me,' said Daniel, casually, 'our big brother is pretty taken with your little sister. You should have seen his face when I offered to lend them a hand.'

'You're kidding,' said Vivi.

'While the cat's away,' he mocked, enjoying himself. 'I was just about to go out for a curry. You two coming with me?'

Nick took him up on the invitation. Vivi, who could no longer feel her feet, declined in favour of a hot bath, if only to deprive Daniel of the fun of winding her up in front of Nick. Gemma and Gerald. It was too bloody appalling not to be true . . .

She lay in the bath for a long time, making a meal of the titbit Daniel had thrown her. Gemma's presence still seemed to hover everywhere. The bathroom smelt of that sandalwood soap she used. She had dyed the water in the cistern blue and bought peach-coloured loo paper, to match the towels, which felt soft and fluffy, the result of using a fabric softener, something Vivi never bothered to buy. The mirror hadn't fogged, as it usually did, Gemma must have polished it with some wonder product she had seen advertised on the telly. Another few weeks and she would have taken over the place completely.

And now she was manipulating Gerald the way she had manipulated Dad, Gerald who belonged indisputably to her, Vivi. That was part of the attraction, of course. Gemma had always coveted her possessions, made her feel as if she didn't deserve them, even driven her, on occasion, to hand them over just to fend off the curse of her envy. Vivi didn't mind sharing her things, or even her flat, if need be, but she hadn't bargained for sharing someone she loved, not that she would have embarrassed Gerald by telling him so. Both her brothers were even less demonstrative than she was, all of them reacting against an over-emotional mother.

So the lame duck had turned out to be a crafty little cow, not that she should have been surprised. Gemma had never been as weak and pathetic as she liked to pretend. Or, more honestly, as Vivi liked to pretend. It had always been easier to dismiss her as feeble than acknowledge that curious inner strength of hers, as stubborn and bolshie, in its way, as Gerald's. The more Vivi thought, or rather stewed, about it, the more ideally suited they seemed. A sweet, shy, innocent little virgin, tailor-made for her pernickety brother. And she, Vivi, was the one who had brought them together . . .

Stop jumping to conclusions, she told herself, climbing out of the bath. The unfogged mirror mocked her, reminding her that she would have to take off her make-up tonight, Nick or no Nick, otherwise her eyes would be too sore to put in her lenses tomorrow. Her reflected scowl deepened as she stripped herself of eyeliner and blusher and lipstick, ceased to be 'striking' – the nearest to pretty she would ever be – and reverted to heavy-jawed, large-nosed, sallow-skinned, unmitigated reality. Oh the misery of those childhood years before she was allowed to hide herself behind a mask of paint! Oh for the smug modesty of a Gemma, who couldn't be bothered to improve on nature . . .

Which didn't mean she envied Gemma, of course. She was merely responding, like ninety-nine per cent of the female population, to the distorted perceptions promulgated by the media, which bombarded women with false images of perfection. But it didn't help to know that, it just made her feel worse for lacking the moral fibre not to care. She might despise the soft option of plastic surgery, but that didn't mean she had come to terms with her looks. Given her time again she would have traded in her brains, instantly, for beauty. If you were beautiful and brainless you didn't need to struggle or strive, some man would willingly do it all for you, and in your ignorance you would be more than happy to let him. Life must be so simple for women like that, damn them all to hell.

Hungry now, Vivi padded into the kitchen in her pyjamas and dressing gown and inspected the contents of the fridge, which Gemma – it couldn't possibly be Daniel – had stocked up with eggs, cheese, bacon and salad stuff before she moved out. If she had still been here, supper would have appeared as if by magic; Vivi, who often forgot to eat, let alone shop, had already been corrupted by Gemma's habit of cooking enough for two and passing off the spare helping as leftovers. In her absence she made herself a boring cheese sandwich which she ate moodily, without relish, staring sightlessly at the television. Such a lot had happened in the last twenty-four hours, and all of it beyond her control . . .

She must have fallen asleep in the chair, because the next thing she heard was Daniel's key in the lock. She made a bolt for the bedroom before Nick spotted her in her hideously unadorned state, jumped into bed, and buried her head under the covers. She could hear the men laughing and joking raucously in the kitchen, and then the sound of some breaking crockery. They were obviously both as pissed as rats . . .

It was then that she noticed the switch for a new electric blanket, with a gift tag dangling from it saying 'Happy New Year. Gemma.' Vivi turned it on, shivering, and lay hugging her moth-eaten teddy till the heat warmed her through, resenting Gemma for being so bloody thoughtful. It worked a lot quicker than the old blanket she had had to throw away. But it still worked an awful lot slower than Nick.

## 7

*February–March* 1984

GEMMA HEARD NOTHING from Vivi over the next few weeks. According to Gerald she was doing a lot of extra shifts, thanks to a flu epidemic at the *Echo*, his way of excusing her failure to respond to the message Gemma had left on her machine giving her new address and phone number. As for Daniel, he had apparently gone off 'in search of some sun', though not before he had asked half a dozen London art schools to send Gemma their prospectuses, a gesture which fell somewhere between the provocative and the placatory. Like Vivi, he had been thrown on her company briefly and reluctantly and was now glad to be shot of her.

Well, to hell with both of them, thought Gemma. Gerald seemed more than happy to fill the breach. The drink after work led to dinner out, which she repaid by cooking him a meal. He seemed impressed by the transformation in her little bedsit, and the speed with which she had wrought it; the imitation woodgrain walls were now stripped and painted white, the mock-parquet lino floor concealed beneath rush matting, and the tan vinyl armchairs camouflaged by loose covers in the same red-and-black striped Indian cotton as her new curtains (both run up on an ancient sewing machine borrowed from Mrs Pulowska).

'I knew that arrangement with Vivi wouldn't last,' Mum had sniffed, calling round to inspect her new abode, a visit she had combined with an expedition to the Sales. 'And now you're stuck in this poky little room. What your father would say I just don't know. Just as well Gerald rigged that job for you, I hope you thanked him properly for his trouble . . .'

Compare that with Gerald's 'You've done wonders with this

place. It must be a relief not to have Vivi thundering about.' And 'You seem to be coping with Myra brilliantly.'

'I hope I haven't been boring you,' said Gerald, over coffee and a post-prandial pipe, lit only after repeated assurances that Gemma didn't mind the smell. 'You must get fed up with me droning on about work all the time. It's your own fault, you know, for being so easy to talk to.'

'So are you.' Especially when compared with Daniel and Vivi, who forced her to keep all her wits about her. With Gerald she could relax and do what she was best at – listening. 'And I'm not bored. I love hearing about all your plans for the paper.'

'Dreams might be a more accurate word. Sometimes I think Daniel's right, you know. That I'm fooling myself.'

'I don't agree. Why would Lord Collington have subsidised the paper all these years just to sell up to an outsider at his time of life? You know its workings inside out, you're committed to it heart and soul, and you're his grandson, after all. What more does he want?'

'It's more a case of what he doesn't want,' said Gerald, taking refuge behind a cloud of smoke. 'CC's always been a man's man. He was pretty disgusted when I didn't take to riding or shooting and turned out to be hopeless at games. I was too like his brother John for his taste, he was another short-sighted swot who always had his nose in a book. Daniel was his favourite, at the beginning. Outgoing, good at sports, with the cheek of the devil. But once he got older they soon fell out. Partly because he was never interested in the paper, but mostly because he was always sticking up for me. When CC found that he couldn't drive a wedge between us, he started work on Vivi instead, he's spent years trying to bribe her into ganging up with him against me. But she wouldn't give an inch, bless her. Which leaves him stuck with me. Or, as he would say, with a namby-pamby intellectual, a mummy's boy, a closet poof . . . now do you get the picture?'

'Then all the more credit to you for not letting him grind you down,' said Gemma staunchly.

'Be careful what you're giving me credit for. Not patience or forbearance or tolerance, that's for sure. No, the only thing that keeps me going is hatred. If I thought I could get away with it, I'd help him on his way to hell.' He met her eyes, letting her catch a glimpse of the anger buried deep within him. 'Does that shock you?'

Coming from Vivi, it wouldn't have done. 'I wish the miserable old sod would get a move on and die,' she had said, more than once, unashamed of her flamboyant hostility. But Gerald, a natural lover of peace and harmony, clearly found it hard to cope with the depth of his own ill will. Gemma knew what it was to bottle things up. Like him, she feared her own capacity for rage.

'A bit. But only because it's you.'

'And I'm the quiet, harmless, long-suffering type, right?' He sighed, wishing no doubt that he wasn't.

'It takes one to know one.'

He reached for her hand and squeezed it shyly. 'Tell me now if I'm overstepping the mark. But I'm getting very fond of you, Gemma.'

'I'm fond of you too, Gerald.' And so she was. Gerald was a good person, who treated her with courtesy and respect. Which was more than she could say for either of his siblings. He might not make her heart beat any faster, but that was all to the good. What she had felt for Daniel was dangerous and painful; with Gerald she felt safe, comfortable. She closed her fingers round his, not wanting him to feel spurned, as she had been.

Encouraged, he leaned towards her and kissed her. A gentle, tidy kiss that she found charming; Gemma's only experience to date was of eager, callow youths who attacked her mouth like pigs at a trough. It was nice not to have to engage in a session of soulless tongue-wrestling in the hope that suddenly, miraculously, she would start to enjoy it, the way you were supposed to do. There was nothing to not enjoy about Gerald's kiss.

'Don't ever change, will you Gemma?' he said. 'Girls like you are a dying breed.'

For someone who had spent her entire life wishing that she was different, being told not to change was the biggest compliment she could have wished for.

It annoyed Vivi to get the gossip second hand. Not only had Gerald chosen not to confide in her – she couldn't bring herself to question him on the subject – but the world at large assumed she knew more than she did, making it difficult for her to admit otherwise by soliciting information. Instead she was obliged to keep up a show of discretion to hide her own ignorance.

'Harriet will be apoplectic when she finds out,' she predicted darkly, seeking cold comfort.

'You don't seem exactly delighted yourself,' said Nick.

'It's all the same to me,' shrugged Vivi. If she had wanted to know more, she should have rung Gemma back, instead of ignoring her invitation to 'come over and have supper one evening'. But she had no wish to see this grotty bedsitter; just the thought of it made her feel guilty as hell. Gerald, having moved her in, had confirmed that it was a dump, as if to say, 'Couldn't you have made her feel a bit more welcome? Did you have to drive her away?' which was exactly what Dad would have said. More annoying still, Vivi found that she missed having Gemma around, if only to dispose of the occasional spider. After all these weeks of resenting her presence, she resented her absence even more.

But if she carried on avoiding her, Gemma was bound to feel slighted; more importantly Gerald would feel slighted on her behalf. At least she was an improvement on the vapid Sloanes Harriet had procured for Gerald's benefit, or on predators like Myra Shaw. Which didn't mean that Gemma wasn't a predator, in her own quiet, unassuming way, but at least Gemma was the devil she knew.

Anxious to be one jump ahead of Harriet, who was due back from Florida next week, Vivi returned Gemma's call at last, and was duly invited for a meal. She arrived armed with a pound of Bendicks chocolates from the shop near the office, in the hope that they would bring that perfect English-rose complexion out in spots.

'This is nice,' Vivi felt bound to say, looking round the room. She had always found Harriet's obsession with decor tiresome, and reacted against it when she found a place of her own. Nonetheless, she was forced to admire the way Gemma had made a silk purse out of a sow's ear.

'Cheap and cheerful,' Gemma shrugged, but the accent was on the cheerful; the predominance of red surprised Vivi, given Gemma's pastel personality.

'So how are things going with Myra?' she prompted, as Gemma

served up a succulent lamb stew, cooked on a single gas ring, no doubt some miraculous transformation of bargain-buy scrag end of neck. She could just see her flitting from stall to stall in Leather Lane market in her lunch hour, intent on value for money, unlike Vivi, who invariably ended up paying Fortnum's prices at her local late-night mini-mart.

'Oh, not too bad.'

'She's been trying to get her claws into Gerald for years. Must be a bit galling for her, watching a harmless little thing like you help yourself from under her nose.'

'I wondered if that was why you deigned to come round at last,' said Gemma levelly. 'I'm not about to discuss Gerald behind his back, so don't fish. If there's anything you want to know, ask him.'

'Mmm. Sounds like it's getting serious.'

'I didn't say that.'

She didn't need to say it. Vivi knew her brother. If it wasn't serious, he'd have told her about it.

'So what's Gerald going to tell Harriet?'

'Just that he's taking me to the old man's birthday party at Little Moldingham.'

When Gemma was scared she didn't flap or squawk or flee. She stayed stock still, daring you to do your worst. If you threatened to thump her, as a child, she didn't give you the satisfaction of running away; she simply braced herself for the blow, rather than endure the humiliation of chase and capture. And she was doing the same thing now, inviting Vivi to knock her down, denying her any triumph in doing so.

'I don't kid myself that she'll be pleased at him taking up with That Girl,' continued Gemma. 'Any more than you are. You think I'm not good enough for him. And you're right. I'm not intelligent or educated or classy enough. If you want to know what he sees in me, I honestly don't know.'

'Oh, look in the mirror for God's sake. Men don't care if you've got any brains. They prefer it if you don't, it makes them feel superior. As for class, what about good old Cinderella? No one thought any the worse of her. And you can cook. What more can a man ask? If you can make him happy, good luck to you. I mean it. But if you hurt him, I will personally tear you limb from limb. Got that?'

It was a hollow threat. Gemma wasn't capable of hurting anyone, any more than Gerald was. Which made them both sitting targets for the hurters of this world. At least they would be safe together.

Whatever Gerald had said to Harriet, the effect was miraculous. Gemma was quite winded by her sudden Gemma-darling good-will. Perhaps, like Vivi, she thought that opposition would prove counter-productive. Gerald, like a lot of quiet people, was very stubborn.

'So Gerald's talked you into coming to this wretched party,' sighed Harriet, over dinner at Holland Park, two days after her return. There were no snails or game on the menu this time. Just an exquisite cheese soufflé, followed by veal escalopes and an orange sorbet. 'Such a bore, but one has to be there. Tell me, what are you going to wear?'

'I was going to buy something new,' said Gemma, well aware that her present wardrobe was not up to the occasion.

'So am I. We'll go shopping together.' She eyed Gemma critically. 'And perhaps do something about your hair. That long, straggly style does absolutely nothing for you. You want something that shows off the shape of your face instead of hiding it. And even a natural blonde like you looks better with a few highlights. I'll ring Michaeljohn and fix up an appointment.'

'Harriet,' put in Gerald, 'Gemma's hair is fine just the way it is.'

'Of course it is, darling. But it could be even better.'

Oh God, thought Gemma, this is some kind of trick. She's going to turn me into a peroxide tart, force me into a low-cut dress, make me look common. She can't be being nice to me for real . . .

'Thank you,' said Gemma. 'It's very kind of you. I'm never quite sure what suits me, so I'll leave it all to you.'

That way Gerald would know that the end result wasn't her choice. Gerald was no fool. Gerald was the cleverest man she had ever met, and an unexpectedly romantic one at that, a great one for flowers and chocolates and opening doors. Gerald made her feel special, important, needed rather than used, for the first time in her life.

'Well, that went very well, I thought,' he said, when he delivered her back to Balham that night.

'Too well,' said Gemma, making coffee. She had bought one of those little Italian pots that made espresso over the stove, and invested in a small electric grinder. 'I can't believe she's suddenly taken a liking to me. What on earth did you say to her?'

'That I wasn't going to stand any nonsense. And the only way to convince her of that was to tell her . . .' He hesitated for a moment. '. . . that I was going to ask you to marry me.'

It still came as a surprise, even though Gemma had imagined this happening often enough. How could she help but fantasise about how different her life would be if she married a man like Gerald? And yet she had been enjoying the journey too much to be in any hurry to reach her destination. And now suddenly she had arrived, too soon, having missed all the stops along the way. She felt disoriented, lost, bewildered, ill prepared for what should have been her moment of glory.

'I know I'm putting you on the spot,' said Gerald anxiously, when she didn't respond. 'I realise we haven't known each other very long. I planned to wait a few months before saying anything. But I had to let Harriet know I meant business. And then I felt I shouldn't have told her before I'd asked you. So I'm asking you now.'

No, thought Gemma panicking, not yet. I'm not ready for this yet . . .

'I'm afraid it would mean Harriet living with us,' went on Gerald, misinterpreting her hesitation. 'But the house is big enough to convert the top floor into a separate flat for her. I've impressed on her that we need our privacy, and she's promised to respect that. She's pleased, really she is.'

Only because the chance of marrying Gerald off at last, even to such a lowly creature as herself, was too good to miss, thought Gemma. To Harriet, she was just a means to an end. An unambitious, homely, malleable sort of girl who wouldn't mind having a baby right away, the key, as she saw it, to securing Gerald's inheritance. Was that how Gerald saw her too?

'Why?' she said, not daring to put the question more directly. 'Why do you want to marry me?'

'Because you're not like other women. Because you're genuine and unspoilt. Because we have a lot in common. Because . . . because I love you, Gemma.'

He sounded heartbreakingly sincere. Gerald wasn't a liar by nature, and if he'd wanted to marry out of self-interest he could have done so long ago. Why couldn't she just bless her good fortune instead of looking for the catch?

'But . . . what about your grandfather? He's bound to take a dim view of you marrying me. My father didn't just walk out on Harriet, he walked out on him as well . . .'

'If he doesn't approve, that's just too bad. Some things are more important than the paper.'

'But I can't let you risk losing *The Courier* . . .'

'I've risked losing it every day, borne every kind of insult, rather than marry a woman I didn't love. But perhaps it's not fair to expect you to take that risk with me . . .'

'I was thinking of you, not of myself,' said Gemma quickly, afraid that she had given the wrong impression. You could love without being 'in love', surely? Being 'in love' was a transitory state, like drunkenness, one which clouded your judgement and lured you into folly. Affection and admiration and respect were the kind of sane, sober feelings you could trust, more enduring than crude physical attraction and a much better basis for marriage . . .

'Yes,' she heard herself saying, before she had time to think herself out of it. 'Yes, I'll marry you.' She would be mad not to. She would never get another chance like this.

In a rare gesture of ebullience, Gerald lifted her up in the air and swung her round and round in delight.

'I was worried you'd say it was too soon. You're usually such a cautious, sensible little thing.'

Which she was. No matter that it had been the proverbial whirlwind romance, there were no risks entailed in marrying a man like Gerald, one who would look after her and be faithful to her, who claimed, incredibly, to love her just the way she was. All her life she had been an outsider, even in her own home. And now she had the chance to be the most important person in Gerald's life, to join the family she had always wanted to be part of – better still, to create one of her own, one of which she would be the undisputed centre . . .

He kissed her with a new proprietorial candour and Gemma responded eagerly, wanting to inflame herself and him, to prove that this wasn't a cold-blooded decision on either side. And she succeeded, at least as far as Gerald was concerned, until he pulled away from her, saying, 'No, Gemma. Please don't tempt me. We've waited this long, a few more months won't do any harm.'

She knew she ought to appreciate his restraint and respect, respect she would lose if she revealed too much of herself. He thought that she was a virgin in mind as well as body, he had no idea of the shameful longings that plagued her lonely bed, longings she had learned to quell, if not satisfy, with her own hands, longings inspired by thoughts of another man. All that furtive self-indulgence would stop, once she was married. Once she had experienced the real thing she would feel like a proper woman at last.

'Rather than tell people individually,' said Gerald, 'let's announce it at the party next week. That way it'll get on the society page and everyone will know at once. And it gives us time to choose the ring.'

Once everybody knew, thought Gemma, there would be no going back. And if she felt another frisson of killjoy doubt and fear, she dismissed it as a sign of cowardice. The sooner she burned her bridges the better. There was nothing behind them but an undistinguished past.


'Are you sure you want me to come to this do?' said Nick. He and Vivi were perched on twin stepladders, scrubbing distemper off the living room ceiling of the Stockwell house and getting soaked in the process. Two fan heaters were blasting away at Vivi's insistence, turning the room into a sauna.

'Why shouldn't I?'

She couldn't face Gramps' birthday party unaccompanied this year. Not with Max Kellerman on the guest list. There was always the danger that he might turn up, if only in the hope of doing business.

'Want to show me off as your bit of rough, do you?'

'Naturally. Us posh bitches love slumming it with the proles.'

Harriet had been duly appalled at Vivi's choice of escort. Not that she had ever met Nick, but she knew his father, a horrible, vulgar rabble-rouser of a man who diminished the family fortune every time he opened his mouth. Luckily she had plenty else to worry about at the moment.

'I shall have to take That Girl in hand if she's going to be a credit to Gerald,' she had told Vivi. 'No one will ever take him seriously with a wife who looks and behaves like a typist, least of all the old man.' She might be less than delighted at the prospect of having Gemma as a daughter-in-law, but better half a loaf, as Vivi reminded her, than no bride. Ironically, it should work in Gemma's favour that CC had always blamed Harriet for the divorce, or rather for Dad's resignation, a much more serious matter. He might have had little regard for Gemma's scrubber of a mother, complete with three-year-old bastard, but he had even less for Harriet, for losing her husband to such an unworthy rival. And besides, he almost certainly already knew about Gerald's romance from his winter retreat in Cannes; nothing that went on at *The Courier* escaped the old man's attention. If he had wanted to express disapproval, he would have done so by now.

Another dribble of white water landed on Nick's bare chest and trickled down towards the tell-tale bulge in his jeans, provoked by the sight of Vivi in a wet teeshirt. She stretched artfully, making his torment worse.

'I suppose it'll give me a chance to get off with your sister,' he said, getting a bit of his own back. 'Daniel said she was a real looker. And you know how I've always had this thing about blondes . . .'

Vivi got down from her ladder, climbed up behind him and attacked him with her wet scrubbing brush, producing a roar of protest and a general loss of balance, with both of them landing in a sodden heap on the *Torch*-strewn floor.

Now, thought Vivi, rolling on top of him. Things couldn't go on like this. No matter that she was still off sex, she couldn't bear to deprive him any longer.

'You're hurting me,' he panted, as she pinned him down with one of her judo holds. 'For Chrissake, Vivi, I can't breathe . . .'

Kissing him for the first time was like burrowing into a warm, soft pillow, but only briefly. After a moment of passive, startled response, he pushed her away and growled, 'What the hell are you playing at?'

It wasn't the reaction she had expected.

'I don't know what you mean. I just kissed you, that's all, without even thinking.'

'You never do anything without thinking. I've been waiting for something like this to happen. You've been teasing me half to death ever since we got back from Austria. What are you trying to prove? That I want you? I've never pretended not to want you. You're the one who made the speech about how going to bed together would wreck everything. And now that's what you want, isn't it? To wreck everything. If you want to dump me, do it honestly. Just say, I can't cope with being this close to anyone, so piss off.'

'All right then!' exploded Vivi. 'Piss off, then. I'm fed up with you being so bloody patient and making me feel like a selfish bitch. If you don't want sex, what the hell do you want?'

'The same thing as you, if you'd only admit it.' He took hold of her scowling face and forced her to look at him. 'I love you, Vivi.'

I love you, Vivi. It wasn't the first time she had heard those words. But it was the first time she hadn't despised a man for saying them. 'I love you, Vivi' was a bribe or a reward, according to its timing, the ultimate insult to her intelligence. And now Nick had taken that worthless coinage and turned it into gold, reminding her that she was a pauper.

'More fool you, then. Because I don't love you. I'm no good at loving people.'

'You're too good at loving people. You give one hundred per cent, and when you don't get it back you feel cheated.'

In other words, she was jealous and demanding and possessive, like her mother. She drove people away, the same as she had done with her father, the same as she was desperately trying not to do with Gerald, over bloody Gemma. And Nick knew it. Quite how he had wormed her hang-ups out of her she wasn't sure; he was too good an operator to ask obvious questions. That she hadn't gone the whole hog and told him about Max too was a measure of her shame.

'Well, I never give a hundred per cent to men,' countered Vivi.

'Which is why you're trying to pay me off with a tuppenny fuck, same as all the rest of them. Well, you can keep it. It's not enough. So just forget that I'm a man and I'll carry on being your friend because God knows you need one.'

He put his arms around her to soften his words, a comforting, asexual embrace that took her back to those distant pre-Gemma days when she had still been naïve enough to think herself worth loving.

'I wasn't trying to dump you,' she mumbled into his chest. 'I just wanted to give you something back, that's all. I know it's not what you want, but it's the best I can do.'

Sooner or later, he would give up on her, once he realised that he couldn't change her. Or she would feel trapped and run away. But not yet. She couldn't bear to lose him just yet. At least she was good at sex. That would hold him for a little while longer.

Almost shyly, for her, she pulled off her teeshirt and bra, fighting the fear that he would say no again. Despite all the evidence to the contrary, Vivi could never quite believe that men found her top-heavy body attractive.

'Vivi, I just explained that you don't have to –'

She silenced him with another kiss, and this time he didn't have the will power to resist her, this time he returned it with a clumsy urgency she found strangely touching. Likewise the painful erection that wouldn't last two minutes, if he was lucky, not after nearly three months of foreplay, and then he would feel bad about coming too soon. She tugged at his zip, released the poor frustrated creature fighting to get out, and bent down, taking it between her breasts and coaxing it towards a quick, merciful death before cleaning it up, very gently, with her tongue, until it lay at pampered peace.

And so did she, for once. She wanted only to lie there, with her head on his chest, feeling his warmth, being lazy. She would have liked to go to sleep like that. But Nick said softly, 'First round to you. Now it's my turn. Let's go to bed and do it properly.'

He needn't have bothered to say 'I love you' again because it showed in the way he looked at her, a look which swamped her with its intensity. It should have made her feel powerful, but it was weakening, humbling. And so was the way he made love. No one had ever made love to her before.

He was generous, unselfish, tender, which explained why nothing happened for her, not that she let him know that. It didn't feel like lying when she faked it – something she never, ever did on principle, men were quite big-headed enough already. She was able to tell him it was good for her with perfect honesty, because it was, affording her the first emotional orgasm of her life. Sex was best with a bastard like Max Kellerman. But love was only safe with a friend.

'You look beautiful,' said Gerald, staring at Gemma, as if looking at her for the first time. And for once, Gemma felt it, thanks to Harriet, who had supervised an expensive new hair-do, a make-over at Elizabeth Arden, and the purchase of a stunningly simple white crepe dress, its modest neckline nicely offset by a thigh-high slit in the ankle-length skirt, revealing tantalising glimpses of long slim leg. The overall effect was one of effortless, natural, if totally false sophistication.

'It's absolutely vital that you come across as a suitable wife for a future Fleet Street proprietor,' Harriet had lectured her. 'Gerald's whole future is in the balance. Your job from now on is to keep the old bastard happy at all costs. Smile a lot, flirt a little, agree with everything he says. Gerald's always refused to curry favour for himself, until now I've had to swallow my pride and do it for him. And now, if you love him, you have to learn to do the same.'

Suddenly Gemma was up there with Gerald on his tightrope. One false move and she could send them both toppling. The responsibility was awesome.

'A man's wife can make or break his career,' went on Harriet, ramming her point home. 'When you're alone, with Gerald, you can be as sincere and spontaneous as you please. But out there, in the jungle he has to survive in, you have to learn to charm and manipulate and pretend. For his sake. At least until he's home and dry.'

Gemma was used to pretending. This was only a question of adapting her familiar role – that of a good, polite little girl who never answered back or put herself in the wrong. Only this time it wouldn't feel like a cop-out, because she would be doing it for Gerald, not herself. And so she had allowed Harriet to play fairy godmother, half expecting her finery to turn to tatters at midnight.

'If I saw you for the first time today,' said Gerald, 'I don't think I would dare to speak to you.'

'I haven't really changed. It's still me inside.' Unfortunately. It would be nice to be like this all the way through.

'I shall have to keep reminding myself of that. I knew I was lucky, but I didn't realise how lucky.'

I'm the lucky one, Gemma reminded herself. She imagined the hush when Gerald announced their engagement, her mother's astonishment when she told her the news, the reaction of people at the office. She pictured herself giving up her lowly job, living in that beautiful house, filling it with children, consigning boring, insignificant Gemma Chambers to oblivion and becoming Mrs Gerald Lawrence, a different person altogether. One who would be able to forgive her father for all those years of preferring Vivi to her. Who would charm the old man into giving Gerald everything he wanted. Who would be Vivi's true sister, at last.

'Looks like something out of a Hammer horror movie,' commented Nick as they drew up outside Collington Hall. Vivi, like Harriet, had always thought it ugly, a gloomy grey Victorian mock-Gothic pile with vaulted windows and overhanging gables covered with creeper. It was occupied only at weekends, and not even then when Gramps was in Cannes, costing him a fortune in upkeep, but he was too much of a show-off and a snob to trade down to something smaller, or make do without the cachet of a country home.

'I'll bet it's got a west wing, and a Chinese room, and a secret passage hidden behind the bookcase . . .'

Vivi wasn't listening. Claiming that she was dying for a pee, she ran up the gravel drive ahead of him, dumped her coat on a uniformed maid, and took refuge in the suite of rooms upstairs set aside as the ladies' cloakroom, where she shut herself in the old-fashioned loo, pulled the chain to drown out the sound effects, and threw up everything she had eaten that day. Fear always went straight to her stomach.

She knew now that Max was going to be here. A bouquet of red roses had arrived while she was getting dressed, with a note saying simply, 'See you tonight, I hope. Max.' Fair warning. All she had had to do was stay at home. Bugger that. She was damned if she was going to let him think she was afraid, or upset, or sulking. But she certainly wasn't so cheap that he could buy her with a lousy bunch of flowers.

She emerged, feeling like death, to see Gemma's reflection in the full-length, gilt-framed mirror.

'Dig that crazy war paint,' she said, trying not to stare. God, but she was beautiful. Her newly short hair gleamed gold, showing off skilfully contoured cheekbones, and her grey eyes looked twice their normal size.

'Am I wearing too much? Harriet made me have it done professionally.'

'That's obvious. The dress must have cost you a bomb.'

'Harriet gave it to me for a . . .' She tailed off, thinking it was still a secret.

'For an engagement present,' said Vivi. 'You didn't seriously think she'd be capable of keeping it to herself, did you? Congratulations, by the way. Good men are hard to find.' She couldn't bring herself to offer a warmer response, afraid of sounding false.

'I'm aware of that,' said Gemma, hiding her hurt at Vivi's lack of enthusiasm.

'Is Harriet here yet?'

'She's been here for hours, supervising the catering.' Gemma hadn't seen her yet. She had wanted a few minutes up here on her own, before she had to face the old man, in front of Harriet's critical eye, but facing Vivi was an even bigger ordeal, in its way.

'God. I look like shit,' muttered Vivi, tugging a comb through her fat, glossy curls and renewing her lipstick, a scarlet-woman shade that accentuated her full, sensual lips. 'Talk about Beauty and the Beast.'

'You look fine. Just a bit pale, that's all. I heard you being sick.'

'No, I am not pregnant again,' snapped Vivi. 'I just can't shift this bloody migraine. I've had a hell of a week. The Hun's been working me like a dog.'

'I've seen your by-line a lot lately.'

'Yes, well, the chief sub's hoping to get lucky. Your bra strap's showing. Hold still. I've got a safety pin.' She withdrew one of the dozen which were holding up the unravelled hem of her little black dress – a high-necked, long-sleeved number chosen in a futile attempt at invisibility. 'Sorry,' she added, as Gemma winced. 'You moved. Or rather you're shaking like a leaf.'

'I'm a bit nervous about meeting CC,' admitted Gemma.

'Just flutter your eyelashes and hang on his every boring word and you'll do okay. If he gives you any shit, tell me and I'll sort him out for you. I'm the only one who's not afraid of him.'

Which was more than could be said for Gemma, poor little cow. If the old man took to her, Harriet would claim all the credit for having turned the flower girl into a duchess. And if he didn't Gemma would get all the blame.

'You've tarted yourself up long enough,' said Vivi. 'Come on. Let's beard the bastard in his den. He won't bite you while I'm around.'

As they reached the bottom of the wide, curved staircase, lined with pretentious family portraits, some new arrivals were being ushered through the heavy front door into the oak-panelled hallway. One of them was Max.

'Hi, Vivi.' Neither the hooded eyes nor the bland smile gave anything away. Seeing him again was like thrusting a poker into a sluggish fire, exposing the hidden heat within.

'Hello Max,' said Vivi casually. 'Meet my sister, Gemma. Gemma, this is Max Kellerman of Kellerman International . . . and you've already met my brother, Gerald,' she added, as he approached in search of his bride-to-be.

'Vivi. You're looking lovely as usual. Max.' He held out a hand. 'We weren't sure if you were going to make it. Are you going to be in London long?'

'On and off. I'm here to set up a new warehousing operation, to improve our UK distribution. I'm looking at suitable sites at the moment.'

'Well, I'm sure I can get you a plug in the business pages, once it's up and running,' said Gerald helpfully. 'Keep me posted, won't you? Excuse us.' He led Gemma away. Vivi tried to follow, but Max put out an arm to stop her.

'Is there somewhere private we can talk?'

Vivi restrained an urge to lunge at him and beat him to a pulp.

'You said all you had to say last time we spoke. And don't waste flowers on me in future, they make me sneeze.'

'The flowers were to give you fair warning that I'd be here. I need to speak to you, Vivi. But if you insist, I can do it here, in front of other people. What I wanted to say was that I –'

'Will you keep your voice down?' hissed Vivi, as two more guests passed within earshot. She couldn't face him embarrassing her in public, couldn't bear for Nick – or worse, Harriet – to guess there had been anything between them. 'This way.' She turned and walked very fast down the corridor leading to the morning room, on the opposite side of the house, Max following at a leisurely pace. He shut the door behind him and leaned against it as if to prevent her escape.

'I wanted to say that I was sorry. About everything. Particularly the abortion. It's been preying on my mind.'

Preying on his mind? He wasn't the one who had had to go through with it, who had been haunted, since early childhood, by the spectre of a murdered baby.

'Forget it,' shrugged Vivi. Not that she would ever forget it. 'I led you on, I knew the score. It wasn't your fault I got pregnant. If I lost my cool, that day I phoned, it was because my father had just died.'

'I heard. I understand how you must have felt. I lost my mother, a few months later.'

What did he expect her to do, sympathise?

'I know I hurt you, Vivi. But only because I was afraid of hurting you even more. I didn't want to get involved and so I tried to end it quickly. But it didn't end. I've spent the last year trying to keep away from you. And here I am.'

It was like a statement of intent. What Max Kellerman wanted, Max Kellerman got. Well, not any more, vowed Vivi. Now she had a chance to take him down a peg.

'I'd like to make things up to you,' he went on. 'I want to put the past behind us and start again.'

God, the nerve of the man. He was back in London, so he fancied having a girl on tap, one he had already broken in. And yet for one reckless moment she was tempted to go along with it. A few wild weeks with Max Kellerman, and the affair would burn itself out. It was the only sure way to exorcise the demon.

But if she did, she would either have to lie to Nick – not an easy thing to pull off – or invite the certain consequences of telling him the truth: she would lose him. She succumbed to a dizzying vision of the two of them fighting over her, pistols at dawn, and Max going down with a bullet in his skull. Except that it wouldn't

125

happen like that. In real life Max would win. So there mustn't be any contest.

'I don't want to start again. Last year I was still screwing around, you were one of many, believe me. Now I'm in a stable relationship' – she winced as she said it – 'with a man who cares about me, and I'm not about to cheat on him with someone who only wants me for sex.'

And yet she wanted Max for the very same reason. As an enemy to be captured and conquered, turning her previous defeat into victory. She wished he would make a grab for her, so that she could fight him off, or not, test her own strength or weakness. But he just said, 'You're still angry with me. Which is fair enough. All the while you're happy with him, I guess I'll have to wait.'

It was as if he knew that she was incapable of being happy for long, incapable of monogamy or commitment. It was discontent and self-loathing that had propelled her towards him last time. He had smelt it, like blood.

'Good. I'll hold you to it.'

'Does that mean we have a truce?'

'For what it's worth.' She held out a hand and he passed the test, shaking it, not holding it, and letting go immediately. But it still provoked a treacherous tremor of remembered lust. Thank God for Nick. She might be a bitch but she wasn't that much of a bitch.

'I guess it's time we got back to the party,' said Max. Now that he had said his piece, he seemed anxious to prove his good faith by not detaining her. 'Before you're missed.'

She already had been. Nick intercepted them on their way back to the ballroom.

'I've been looking for you,' he greeted Vivi. 'Are you okay? You don't look well.'

'I'm fine. Max Kellerman, Nick Ferris.'

Seeing them together, she was forced to compare and contrast them. Max, tall, suave, grey-haired, distinguished, with his perfect American teeth and his year-round tan, ostensibly open and friendly and relaxed, but calculating, cold. And Nick, a bare five-ten, nothing much to look at, a strange mixture of cockiness and vulnerability, radiating a natural, infectious, seductive warmth. She could sense Max writing him off as no competition. It made her want to shout 'Don't kid yourself, he's worth twenty of you!' And of her. Knowing that was already a burden.

'Kellerman the computer king?' said Nick.

'I wouldn't say king. I'm still a relatively small outfit, globally speaking. But the market's expanding fast, and so are we, so I'm hoping for more than my fair share of it. Particularly as far as the newspaper industry is concerned.'

'And how many people do you reckon to put on the dole in the process? Or is that not something you worry about?'

'The dole?' echoed Max politely, affecting not to understand.

'Unemployment benefit,' translated Vivi. 'Nick's father is a linotype man,' she added, by way of explanation.

'A machine imported from America in 1889,' said Max. 'One which the compositors of the day fought tooth and nail. If they'd had their way your father would still be hand-picking type, letter by letter. Well, it was nice meeting you, Nick, Vivi. Will you excuse me?' And with this polite dismissal he left them.

'Smug bastard,' muttered Nick. 'Are you sure you're all right?'

'I had a bit of an upset stomach, that's all. But I'm feeling much better now.' And so she ought. She had headed off the danger, for the moment. But the headache she had invented for Gemma's benefit now smote her for real. A post-tension migraine with a vengeance.

'Vivi,' boomed CC, as they entered the ballroom.

'Gramps, meet Nick Ferris. Son of Bert.'

'Pleased to meecha, your lordship,' said Nick, without a trace of deference, touching a satirical forelock and laying on an exaggerated barrow boy accent. ''Course, I feel as if I've known you all me life. Me dad talks about you all the time. Like he was saying only yesterday . . .'

Vivi looked on in glee while he forced the old man to listen to a résumé of the current yard-long list of Chapel grievances; to add to the fun she slipped her arm through Nick's and laid an adoring head on his shoulder, attracting a baleful glance from Harriet, who was busy introducing Gemma all round the room. Before Gramps could find an excuse to move on to more important guests, Nick delivered the ultimate put-down by beating him to it, with a mocking 'Sorry to interrupt, your excellence, but I've just spotted a mate of mine', leaving his host in mid-sentence.

'I take it that object is just another attempt to annoy your mother?' said CC, unamused. The old man had absolutely no sense of humour.

'Actually, I promised I'd pass him on to her when I'd finished with him,' said Vivi. 'Cheer up. I may be a lost cause, but Gerald's making up for it, don't you think?'

'She's turned out quite a little glamour-puss, your sister,' growled Gramps. 'Good figure too. Just the right amount on top, not too narrow in the hip.' Vivi loathed his habit of describing women like livestock, but at least he was thinking along the right lines, weighing up Gemma's breeding potential. 'None too bright, mind, but then that's not a bad thing in a woman. As gold-diggers go, he could do worse. Not that anything will come of it, I daresay, knowing your brother.' Vivi bit her tongue again. 'I liked that piece you did on teenage runaways,' he went on, still watching Gemma.

'Thanks. Attila lent me out to Features for a week.'

'There's a features vacancy coming up on *The Courier*.'

'Isn't there always. Obviously I'm not the only one who can't stand Myra Shaw.'

'Your little sister seems to get on all right with her.'

'My little sister gets on with everyone. And besides, I've told you before, I've no intention of joining the paper until you put Gerald in charge . . .'

The music stopped and there was a clash of cymbals as Gerald stepped up on to the bandstand, looking self-conscious and determined with a flushed Gemma at his side, head bowed. Harriet's eyes were fixed on the old man, watching anxiously for his reaction to the news.

'My lords, ladies and gentlemen, I have an announcement to make. Miss Gemma Chambers' – he took Gemma's hand – 'has done me the honour of consenting to be my wife.' And with that he slipped a ring on her finger and kissed her.

There was a burst of applause and a series of flashes as a *Courier* snapper, always present on such occasions, recorded the moment for the archives.

'Bloody hell,' said Gramps, impressed. 'I would never have thought he had it in him.' He strode forward to congratulate them, his face wreathed in benevolent smiles.

'Did you know?' said Nick.

'Of course.'

'Are you pleased?'

'I'm doing my best.'

She went forward to embrace her brother, but Gemma got to her first, throwing her arms around her, the first time she had ever done such a thing, and saying, 'Oh Vivi. Please try not to mind. I'll make him happy, I promise.'

Not an easy task, thought Vivi, inspecting the extravagant diamond and sapphire cluster on her finger; it must have cost Gerald a packet. Happiness didn't run in the family, it was something that would have to be created, patiently, from scratch.

'You'd better,' said Vivi thickly, returning her hug. 'Or else.'

# 8

*Spring 1984*

THE WEDDING WAS fixed for the first week in May, the earliest Harriet could contemplate, given the extent of the preparations. (There had never been any question of the bride's mother hosting the occasion, much to Gemma's relief.) It was to be a top-hat-and-tails affair at the village church in Little Moldingham, followed by a reception in the grounds of Collington Hall, where a huge marquee was to be set up to cater for nearly five hundred guests. Gemma was fitted for a hand-made dress based on her own roughly sketched design, with a scooped neckline, a tight bodice shimmering with tiny beads and a full skirt in heavy ivory satin. She didn't dare ask how much it was all going to cost. Harriet, who was never happier than when spending money, told her not to worry.

'The old hypocrite may be as mean as they come,' she said, 'but he likes to look good in public. So we may as well screw him for every penny we can get.'

CC, like Harriet, had evidently decided to make the best of a bad job. He had taken the newly betrothed couple to a celebration dinner at Le Caprice, at which he had treated Gemma – wearing one of the many new outfits Harriet had put down to 'wedding expenses' – with the utmost gallantry, and Gerald with newfound respect, listening to his views without interrupting him, and even agreeing with him occasionally, which Gerald assured her was most unusual.

'I hear you had the old fool eating out of your hand,' said Harriet, with self-congratulatory glee. 'He always was a sucker for a pretty face. Mind you keep it up.'

Keeping it up would mean producing a baby, or rather a son,

within a year of the wedding, to convince Lord Collington of the long-term worth of keeping the paper in the family. Gemma didn't flatter herself that he liked her for herself, any more than Harriet did. As Mum had been quick to point out to her, it wouldn't take much to turn her fancy new relatives against her.

Gemma had hoped that Mum would be pleased at the news of her engagement, especially once she took Gerald home to meet her. A superficially successful, if embarrassing, event, with Gerald displaying his usual immaculate manners and Barbara at her most genteel and gushing . . . to his face. But the encounter didn't change her view that Gemma was rushing into this, she hardly knew Gerald, after all, and if she wasn't 'in trouble', what was all the hurry?

'What's the point in waiting?' said Gemma. 'It's not as if we need to save up to get married. Gerald's already got a house.'

'Odd that you're happy to live with his mother when you couldn't wait to get away from your own.'

'We won't be living with her. Gerald's going to convert the top floor into a granny flat . . .'

'And what if he didn't have a big posh house? What if he wasn't the boss's grandson? Would you still be so keen to marry him then?'

'Are you saying I'm after his money?'

'You won't want to know me and Fred in future, I daresay. You'll be too grand for us.'

'Oh Mum. Don't start . . .'

'If only Dad was alive. He could tell you what it was like, being part of that set-up. They're not like us, Gem.'

Of course they're not, thought Gemma stubbornly, stifling another qualm. That was the whole point.

Harriet more than made up for Barbara's huffiness, hauling Gemma off to Harrods, where they drew up a wedding list of staggering magnitude, giving her a crash course in the social skills she would need for her future role, and teaching her the names, relationships, histories and foibles of all the people she must invite to dinner once she was married. The message underlying all this unstinting tutelage was always the same: she mustn't let Gerald down.

For this reason it was deemed quite unacceptable for her to

continue to live in a humble bedsitter or be seen to man a typewriter at *The Courier*. At CC's insistence, and at his expense, Gemma was installed in a one-bedroomed furnished service flat overlooking Regent's Park, her temporary home until the wedding. It was small, but very plush, more like a hotel suite than a flat; she dreaded to think what the rent must be. Gerald opened a joint account at the bank so that a newly jobless Gemma wouldn't have to ask for money, but Gemma was reluctant to draw on it, given that she wasn't performing any wifely duties. Having looked forward, in principle, to giving up work, she found it hard to adjust to the sudden loss of her independence. Sometimes she found herself harking back, absurdly, to her little room in Balham, only to rebuke herself for not knowing when she was well off.

Harriet was naturally garrulous, especially when she allowed herself the odd glass or three of wine with lunch. Gemma listened attentively to the stream of verbiage, greedy for every crumb of knowledge about her new family. Harriet's abrasive personality was as much of a shield, she realised, as her own docile one; for all her surface polish, she was profoundly lacking in confidence, something which Gemma could readily identify with. It turned out that she had been labelled stupid from an early age, thanks to undiagnosed dyslexia, a condition which CC had been quick to ascribe to the inferiority of the female brain.

Gradually the whole life story came out. Gemma heard, piecemeal, about Harriet's unhappy, lonely childhood, her ill-fated schoolgirl pregnancy, the alleged murder of her baby and her subsequent exile to cookery school in Paris, where she had met her first husband and given birth to Gerald, the happiest period, she claimed, of her life. At least until Toby Lawrence had deserted her while she was expecting Daniel, leaving her with nothing but a dozen unsaleable paintings. He hadn't set eyes on his sons, or paid a penny in maintenance, from the day he had left her till his death from heroin addiction ten years later.

Tactfully – or perhaps because it was too painful – Harriet glossed over her second marriage except to say that she had been unable to play the docile, submissive wife a man like Trevor needed, adding that Vivi would be the first to admit that her father was the original male chauvinist pig, a point of view with which

Gemma could hardly disagree. Not that that had stopped Vivi turning against Harriet after the divorce.

'It's not that she doesn't love me, in her own way,' sighed Harriet. 'She just can't bring herself to show it, that's all. She made up her mind, at seven years old, that she wasn't going to need me any more, the way she'd needed her father, in case I left her too. I did my best to make her feel secure, but then she'd felt secure once before, poor darling. I'd always vowed that my children would never feel unwanted and unloved, the way I did, and I suppose that's why I tend to be over-protective of them. I've made such a mess of my own life, I can't bear to see them do the same.'

Making a mess of her life had gone on to include twelve years of putting up with Simon Driscoll's drinking and womanising before finally finding the courage to throw him out and be alone again. It should have been yet another chapter in an unremitting tale of woe, but Harriet chose to relate her saga with a satirical, and endearing, lack of self-pity, as if mocking the misfortunes of a third party with whom she had little patience. Underlying her narrative, however, was one powerful, unifying theme — a sense of how different her life would have been if she had been born a boy. Harriet was a seething mass of thwarted ambitions which Gerald had been groomed to achieve on her behalf. If she couldn't reign in her own right, the role of Queen Mother was the next best thing. The parallel with her own situation was not lost on Gemma. She knew what it felt like to be passed over, understood the lure of second-hand power.

Unaware of his mother's remorseless proselytising, Gerald was relieved that she had taken Gemma under her wing. Despite all the wedding preparations, however, Gemma still found herself with time on her hands. She fell back on her painting, ignoring Daniel's advice and sticking to pretty, chocolate box representations of fruit and flowers with never a bruise or a blemish to spoil the illusion of perfection. She was working at her easel one evening when she heard the doorbell, an hour sooner than she had expected. Gerald must have got away early for a change. Pleased, she went to let him in.

Lord Collington was standing there. Gemma hadn't realised he was back in the country; he had returned to Cannes shortly after the party. He must have a key to the outer door, she thought, as

Gerald did, which explained why he hadn't used the entryphone. A liberty she could hardly object to. He was paying her rent, after all.

'Good evening,' said Gemma. 'Er . . . do come in. I'm afraid Gerald's not here yet, I'm expecting him shortly . . .'

'I wouldn't have come if I didn't know he was busy working. Wouldn't like to risk interrupting anything, knowing what you young folk get up to these days. And besides, it's you I want to see.' He hobbled in as if he owned the place. Which he did, more or less. 'Comfortable here, are you?'

'Very, thank you. It was very kind of you to – '

'Kindness nothing. Couldn't have my future granddaughter-in-law living in a slum.' He made himself comfortable on one of the two settees and lit a large cigar.

'Can I offer you a drink? I'm afraid there's only whisky.' Gerald was partial to Glenfiddich, a precise amount poured over two ice cubes.

'If you'll join me. Straight, no ice. Ice ruins good Scotch, I've told Gerald time and again.'

Gemma poured the drinks, a large one for him and a very small one for herself, wondering what he wanted to say to her. Was he displeased with her in some way?

'Will you excuse me one moment?' she said, realising that she was still wearing her paint-smeared overalls. She didn't want him thinking that she was another 'arty' type like Gerald's feckless father; if she'd known he was coming she would have hidden her painting away. She disappeared into the bedroom where she changed out of her old jeans and touched up her hair and make-up with all the urgency of an imposter donning a disguise. She rejoined the old man to find him puffing cigar smoke all over her canvas, making her feel like a criminal caught in the act.

'Gerald's been telling me how talented you are,' he said, with apparent approval. 'Seems like we're going to have another artist in the family.'

'Oh, I wouldn't compare myself with Daniel . . .'

'I should hope not. At your age he was running around with a bunch of beatniks with his hair down to here, smoking dope, sleeping in a different bed every night, squandering all his uncle's money, getting the family a bad name . . .'

At least he was having a go at Daniel, rather than Gerald, thought Gemma.

'He takes after his father, of course,' continued CC. 'He ended up in the gutter, you know. Bad blood. Once bad blood gets into a family, there's no getting rid of it. You don't go in for any of that modern art rubbish, I hope?'

'Oh, I wouldn't presume to try.'

'Thank the Lord for that. I don't want to end up with three noses and an eyeball coming out of my ear. I'm an old man, Gemma, and I'm not as strong as I was. I could die tomorrow. I want something my great-grandchildren can remember me by. And if it's painted by their mother, then so much the better, eh?'

'You mean . . . you want me to paint your portrait?'

'May as well keep these things in the family.'

'But . . . but I'm not nearly experienced enough. It's just a hobby . . .'

'I thought you wouldn't object to doing me a little favour.' He looked round the room, as if to remind her of her indebtedness to him.

'Of course I don't. But –'

'It'll give you something to do while Gerald's at work, apart from helping Harriet spend my money.' Gemma blushed, mortified. 'I'll be round at three on Monday. That should give you time to get your materials together. I want a nice big canvas, to match the other pictures at Collington Hall. So the sooner we get down to work the better.' He drained his whisky in one gulp. 'You're my hope for the future now, Gemma. And Gerald's. Remember that.'

He stood up to go, leaning on his stick, a tall, broad, still-powerful figure, with his shock of white hair. Despite his claims to be not as strong as he was he seemed remarkably fit for his age. Harriet often bemoaned the fact that the old bugger was healthy as a horse apart from his limp and his rheumatism, proof that the devil looked after his own.

'I hope I'll live up to your expectations,' said Gemma prettily. 'Are you sure you wouldn't like to wait for Gerald?'

'I see more than enough of Gerald as it is. Well, goodnight, my dear.' He kissed her on the cheek, leaving behind a cold clammy imprint. 'Till next week, then.'

It sounded like a threat.

'I had a call from Daniel,' said Gerald, a couple of days later.

'Oh really?' said Gemma vaguely. 'Where is he?' Nobody had heard from him for weeks.

'Back at Vivi's place. He's been sunning himself in Martinique, apparently. Some French friends of his gave him the run of their flat there while his arm healed. He kept it quiet in case Harriet invited herself to join him.' Harriet's brazen talent for wangling free holidays was a family joke. 'He wasn't to know that she was much too busy arranging the wedding. I've asked him to be best man, of course. He's out of plaster now, due to start work any day. He wants to take us out to dinner, before he flies back to Paris. I suggested we meet up here for a drink first.'

'That'll be nice.'

Ridiculous to feel self-conscious about seeing Daniel in her new role as Gerald's fiancée. She didn't have to feel guilty about her brief infatuation. It pre-dated her involvement with Gerald, and besides, nothing had actually happened. But the memory of that moment still clung, his grip on her arm as he raged at her to be less inhibited, the insane urge to take him at his word, the fleeting sense that something extraordinary was about to happen to her . . . Thank God it hadn't. It would only have ended in tears.

Gerald rang the following evening to say that he might be late, the old man wanted to see him at seven. They were to go on to the restaurant without him, if necessary, and he'd join them there. Daniel arrived at eight; Gemma buzzed him up. Catching sight of herself in the hall mirror as she went to let him in, she stopped to admire her new self for a moment and found herself thinking, too late now, you bastard.

'Daniel!' she greeted him gaily. 'How nice to see you again. I'm afraid Gerald's been held up at the paper . . .'

'God almighty. What have you done to yourself?'

Gemma longed to slap his face.

'I've had my hair cut, that's all.'

'And the rest.' He walked past her into the living room and flopped into an armchair, treating her with the instant familiarity which was still a world away from Gerald's studious reserve. 'You seem . . . unreal.'

'I take it that's not a compliment.'

'Don't fish. You look a bloody knockout and you know it. But it's still unreal. It's too perfect, too plastic, it doesn't suit you.'

'Well, everyone else seems to like it.'

'Including the old bastard, I hear. What's all this about you painting his portrait?'

'Spare me. I know perfectly well I'm not qualified to do it. But he insisted.'

'You're eminently well qualified to produce a polite flattering likeness, which is what he'll want.'

'Thank you. What can I get you to drink?'

'Nothing. I had some booster shots this morning, I'm on the wagon. But congratulations anyway.' He raised an imaginary glass. 'To Gemma and Gerald.'

'You might try to sound as if you mean it.'

'Why shouldn't I mean it?' He met her eyes for a minute, succeeded in making her look away, and then rose to his feet. 'Sorry. I'm being my usual boorish self.' He took hold of both her hands, and kissed the top of her head. 'I'm delighted for you both, cross my heart. You're a gem, Gemma. Exactly the kind of girl Gerald needs.'

'Don't patronise me.'

'There you go again. Butter wouldn't melt in your mouth with everybody else, why are you always so prickly with me? I'm trying to be nice to you, for once.'

'Well, don't bother.' And then, throwing his words back at him, 'It's unreal. It doesn't suit you.'

She released her hands and moved away, shaken by the effect his touch had on her, hating herself for being so fickle, hating him for unwittingly feeding the doubts and fears she thought she had starved into submission.

'In that case, what have you done about getting into art school? You don't have to worry about earning your living any more, after all.'

'There's no point in starting something I can't finish,' said Gemma, ignoring the dig. 'We intend to start a family right away.'

'Whose idea was that? Harriet's?'

'Mine!'

'She didn't waste much time giving you your orders, did she?

For God's sake Gemma, live a little first, you're still a baby yourself . . .'

'I knew it! I knew you'd pour cold water on everything. Why do you always have to –'

She broke off as Gerald rang the bell; relieved, she ran to answer it. She didn't need Daniel to rub it in that Harriet was using her, that the goodwill she was currently enjoying was conditional, self-interested, essentially false. Except for Gerald's. All the more reason to earn his love, love she didn't yet deserve.

'Double celebration,' said Gerald, with rather forced heartiness, embracing Gemma and shaking his brother's hand. 'I bring good tidings for a change.'

'You mean the old man's suddenly snuffed it?' said Daniel.

'The next best thing. He's just appointed me vice-chairman, pending ratification by the board later this week. For a six-month trial period, he says. I'm to be acting proprietor while he takes a back seat. With a view to him retiring altogether and me taking over permanently.'

'Oh Gerald!' Gemma hugged him. 'That's wonderful news!'

'Is it?' said Daniel. 'What exactly will you be taking over, apart from falling advertising revenues, a shrinking readership, and the current NUJ pay demand?'

'As you predicted, there's some poison in the chalice,' said Gerald lightly. 'But not a lethal dose, I hope. Meanwhile, champagne seems like a good antidote. Shall we go to dinner?'


Vivi saw Daniel off next day, a Saturday. He remained sceptical about Gerald's sudden elevation, suspecting that the old man was setting him up to fail. Apparently he and Gemma had ended up having words over dinner last night, with Gemma accusing him of running Gerald down and being a Jeremiah. Hard to imagine Gemma saying boo to a goose, let alone a sarcastic swine like Daniel. Evidently her metamorphosis was more than skin deep.

But Vivi had taken Gemma's part, preferring to believe that the old man had experienced a late-flowering surge of patriarchal benevolence, much as it pained her to side with Harriet, the Svengali to Gemma's Trilby. As for Gemma painting CC's portrait, she would find her talents as a good listener tested to their limits. The old bore was never happier than when talking about himself.

Having dropped Daniel at the airport, Vivi drove on to Stockwell, where she was supposed to be helping Nick rewire the house. But no sooner was she inside the door than he had her panties down to her feet and his head under her skirt, the prelude to yet another bout of inexhaustible lovemaking. Vivi wasn't really in the mood, but she could never bring herself to refuse him, for fear of feeding his sexual insecurities. It still troubled him that she had had so many other lovers – for want of a better word – to compare him with, that she was so much more experienced, by her own admission, than he was.

'I can't do it unless I like the girl,' he had explained artlessly. The reverse problem to her own. If she'd hung on for a man she liked, Nick would have been the first, the one and only.

'Are you sure it was good for you?' he said afterwards, not totally convinced by her performance.

'Of course.' If only she could stop herself caring so much, everything would be fine. 'Couldn't you tell?'

'You wouldn't put it on, just to please me, would you?'

'I never put it on. When I'm not getting what I want, I complain loudly, believe me. I'm one of those ballbreakers who shouts instructions. Faster, slower, higher, lower. Start slipping and you'll see.' She couldn't bear for him to think it was his fault.

'You're still shutting me out. I can't get inside your head.'

'You could have fooled me,' said Vivi dryly, reaching for her jeans as the doorbell rang below.

'Leave it. It'll be somebody selling something.'

There was another ring, longer than the first, supplemented by a rap on the knocker.

'I'll get it,' said Vivi, anxious to avoid another heart-to-heart. Nick wasn't content with her body. He wanted her mind as well, stripped bare. And when it came to her mind, Vivi was the world's worst prude. Pulling her sweater over her head, she ran downstairs to open the door.

'Hi, Viv,' Jackie greeted her sullenly, trundling the pushchair into the hall. At least this time she didn't have Spike, the baby's father, with her (his real name was Maurice, would you believe), a thuggish-looking lad whom Vivi had hated on sight. Ferris senior had recently banned him from the house, following a major row; a pity Nick couldn't bring himself to do the same.

'Who is it?' shouted Nick, from above, whereupon Jackie ran up the stairs, bleating about another fight with Dad and how she wasn't going home no more ever again.

Reluctantly responding to a signal from Nick, Vivi set about making the inevitable tea, and filled Casey's little spouted beaker with diluted orange juice, a courtesy she accepted with a disarming toothy grin which a stony-faced Vivi found impossible not to return. As usual she was neat and clean, plump and healthy-looking, wearing a sunshine yellow dress and little white shoes and socks.

'I hate being at home,' Jackie was wailing. 'I hate him treating me like a kid. Can't Spike'n'me come and live here, with you?'

Nick caught Vivi's eye, sensing, no doubt, that if Spike'n'me came to live here with him he would be sleeping alone in future.

'No, love. This place isn't suitable for Casey. We've got no central heating yet, and no carpets, a kid her age falls over all the time, she'd be bound to hurt herself. And besides, it'd only make things worse between you and Dad. Just keep your nose clean for a year or so and he'll set you up in your own little flat, you'll see . . .'

Vivi kept well out of it, while Nick continued to listen, with infuriating patience, to Jackie's catalogue of woes. He loves her more than he loves me, she thought, despising herself for thinking it. But she couldn't help it. All the people who had ever loved her ended up loving someone else more . . .

Nick compromised, in the end, by giving Jackie a spare key, so that Spike'n'me had 'somewhere to go', on condition that she went back home tonight and made her peace with Dad.

'You shouldn't be encouraging them,' said Vivi, after she had gone, conveniently forgetting her own rampant behaviour at a similar age with a succession of undesirable boyfriends.

'You're never going to stop them having sex,' shrugged Nick. 'Spike's got nowhere to take her, he's been sleeping rough ever since his stepdad threw him out. At least they can bring Casey with them, instead of dumping her on God knows who.'

'Casey ought to be in care,' asserted Vivi. What chance did the poor little bastard have with parents like that? 'Jackie ought to be in care, come to that.'

'Don't be so self-righteous. Jackie loves that kid, she loved her from the day she knew she was pregnant. She could have had an abortion and she didn't, even when everybody tried to force her into it. That took guts, at her age.'

He's not getting at me, thought Vivi, stifling a wave of paranoia. He doesn't know he's being tactless. Seeing Casey again had set her wondering, not for the first time, what her baby would have looked like, smelt like, felt like, had she allowed it to live. It didn't help to think of Gemma queening it over her, in a year or so's time, with Harriet drooling over her first grandchild . . .

Vivi, like Nick, had to work next day, a Sunday. Attila was more than usually rabid at the moment because a big exclusive was breaking, one so cast iron and red hot that they were saving it for a late edition, to prevent routine copying by the opposition. It was the kind of story that was labelled merely 'special assignment' on the conference list, to keep it confidential, and Vivi was gratified to find herself roped in on it, even in a back-up capacity. Her role was to cobble together the cuttings on the previous wives and girlfriends of an ageing but still active sixties pop idol who was marrying for the fifth time – supposedly in secret – in Bermuda.

*The Echo*'s showbiz hack having rumbled the wedding plans, the news desk had been detailed to take over, and a deal had been done with the unhappy couple, granting *The Echo* exclusive coverage of the event, in return for keeping the other papers out of it. (Threatening to spill the beans to all and sundry was standard technique for persuading reluctant celebs to co-operate.) The ceremony was taking place the following evening – late Monday night, GMT – with an *Echo* reporter and snapper in attendance; the lucky bastards were already sunning themselves on expenses while Vivi did the donkey work back at the office, ready for the Tuesday morning splash. An extra hundred thousand copies were due to be printed, to meet expected demand – even though, as always in such cases, the bonus payments to the print would all but wipe out any potential profit. But some of the readers, having bought *The Echo* once, would stay with it. Many of them at *The Courier*'s expense, thought Vivi ruefully, thinking of Gerald.

She got home on Sunday night to find a message from Nick on her machine. Vivi phoned him back, but he wasn't home yet; like her he must be working late. She caught him at *The Torch* just as he was knocking off, and let him work her up to such a pitch – Nick had a gift for verbal foreplay – that she gave in and agreed that he could spend the night. By the time he arrived, she had already made love to him in his absence, unhampered by the compulsion to please him; when he got into bed beside her she was too tired and sleepy to be more than compliant, passive, lazy . . .

'That's more like it,' he whispered triumphantly. 'That's the real thing, for a change.' And then Vivi realised, with something like dismay, that she had reached a turning point, that she would never be able to deceive him again, that feelings and sensations, love and sex, had finally escaped their separate compartments, coalesced into a force so powerful it scared her half to death.

She lay awake for a long time, while Nick slept peacefully in her arms. She had no experience of being happy, if happy was the right word to describe such an anxious state. She felt as if she had found a priceless diamond in the dirt, something she had no right to, which would surely be taken from her if she dared to flaunt it openly. Her only hope of keeping it safe was to deny possession of it, hide it away from view . . .

She waited for Nick to roll over naturally in his sleep before creeping out of bed to make herself a mug of Horlicks. She was foraging for ginger nuts when the telephone rang, only to stop before she could reach it, a groggy Nick having automatically picked up the bedroom extension.

'It's the Hun,' he hissed, as she rejoined him, keeping his hand over the mouthpiece. He must be ringing from home, thought Vivi; he had handed over to the night news editor hours ago. Which meant that the night news editor had rung him from the office. Which meant trouble.

'Tony?' said Vivi. 'Something wrong?'

'Ask your boyfriend to tell you what's in today's *Torch*,' barked Attila. 'Like you told him what was in tomorrow's *Echo*.'

'What?'

'They're running a front-page spoiler. Jake weds Sandy today in paradise isle. Full effing story inside.'

Shit.

'Are you accusing me of leaking it?'

'Well, it wasn't Father bloody Christmas who answered the phone just now, was it?'

'You don't seriously think I'd blow an exclusive?'

'What exclusive? Either the whole of the world's effing press will be there, or more likely they'll call the wedding off, if they've got any effing sense. We'll be knee deep in bloody memos by tomorrow.'

'This is ridiculous. I never said a word to Nick, and even if I had, he would never . . .' Damn. She shouldn't have said that. Hearing his name, Nick put his ear to the phone.

'Even if you had, eh?' snarled Tony, pouncing on her slip. 'How much other pillow talk has he been getting?'

'None! Nick had nothing to do with it . . .'

'Oh no? Then why is his bloody by-line all over their splash?' God. No wonder he didn't believe her. 'Be in early tomorrow. I'll see you at nine sharp.'

He's enjoying this, thought Vivi. He's been waiting all this time for a chance to nail me . . .

'No you won't be seeing me!' she heard herself yelling, incensed, ignoring Nick's signals to cool it. 'Not tomorrow, or ever again. I'm fucked if I'll work any longer for someone who doesn't trust me . . .'

'You're fucked, all right,' said Tony. 'And we all know who by . . .' Vivi slammed the phone down.

'Bastard,' she hissed, trembling with rage. And then, turning to Nick, 'Why didn't you tell me you were running a spoiler on the Jake Jackson wedding?'

'Because it was top secret, we were holding it back for the third edition. How was I to know you were involved? You never said anything.'

'Of course I didn't bloody well say anything! But somebody did, obviously. Who told you?'

Nick didn't answer.

'Oh, I get it. You're not going to reveal your sources. Even to me.'

'All right, all right. It was my dad. He got it from a mate of his at *The Echo*. I had no idea that they'd put you on the story, or I wouldn't have touched it. I'm sorry, doll. I'll go round and see Attila tomorrow, put you in the clear.'

'What's the point? He won't believe you. Not unless you name names.' It wasn't fair to ask him to drop his father's contact in the shit.

'We'll get the NUJ rep involved . . .'

'Forget it. I'm pissed off with *The Echo* anyway.'

'If you walk out, people will see it as an admission of guilt. Whenever something like this happens, management looks for a sacrificial lamb. Why do you think he accused you like that? Because he knew how you'd react. He dug a hole for you and you fell right into it.'

'That's not the only reason I'm leaving!' snapped Vivi. 'I'm fed up with apologising for who I am and trying to do things the hard way. If I'm not going to get any credit for it, why bother? I'm going to phone Gerald in the morning, ask him for a job.'

'But you swore you'd never work for *The Courier*!'

'I swore I'd never work for the old man. People can scream unfair advantage all they like, I'm past caring. Gerald's only got six months to show results. If he's going to succeed, I want to help him do it. And if he fails, then I may as well fail with him.'

'Sleep on it. You're all wound up . . .'

But Vivi didn't need or want to sleep on it. This was just the excuse she had been waiting for.


'If you hadn't sacked yourself already,' said Gerald, 'I'd have a conscience about taking you on. We could both be out of work by October.'

'Then I won't be any worse off than I am now, will I? Why so glum all of a sudden? Last time I spoke to you, you were full of the joys of spring.'

'So much for the power of positive thinking. The old man had Gemma and me to dinner last night, at the Albany flat. After all that stuff about giving me my big break, we're back to the old cat and mouse games again. Lots of heavy-handed stuff, in front of Gemma of course, about having to sell up if I don't deliver.'

Typical, thought Vivi.

'Then at least let me do my bit to help. We always said we would sink or swim together, remember? Or have you decided you don't need me any more?' He had Gemma now, of course.

'You know very well it's not that,' said Gerald wearily. 'Would you settle for a freelance job? I'd feel easier in my mind if you had other irons in the fire.'

'What kind of freelance job?' said Vivi, disappointed.

'I was thinking of a twice-weekly column. Opinions on the news stories of the moment, with the accent on the outspoken and the controversial and the witty. Brewster's contract is up in June and he's top of my hit list.'

Sebastian Brewster, an ancient crony of the old man, wrote an unreadable column of stultifying pomposity which the subs were not allowed to touch under the terms of his contract.

'In other words, you can't afford Jean Rook, so will I write brilliant copy for peanuts?'

'That's about it. The more outrageous you are the better. I want to generate readers' letters by the sackful. It's just the kind of shot in the arm the paper needs, to get rid of its fuddy-duddy image.'

Vivi felt a flutter of excitement. Her own column!

'Have you told the old man? About getting rid of Brewster, I mean?'

'Not yet. But if he thinks I'm going to spend the next six months pussyfooting around, he'll be disappointed. I may as well be hanged for a sheep as a lamb.'

'What will the Howler have to say about it?' said Vivi, referring to Ted Fowler, the editor, with whom Gerald had never seen eye to eye, thanks to endless divisive stirring by CC.

'It won't matter what he says,' said Gerald, showing his teeth again. 'He's going to get what he wants at last. I'm going to fire him.'

'Gerald's a lucky man,' CC told Gemma, for the umpteenth time. 'You're a very pretty girl, Gemma.'

Gemma had begun to wish that she wasn't.

'Thank you, CC. It's very nice of you to say so.'

I hate you, she was thinking. After all that phoney bonhomie he had shown her what he was really like, the other night, demonstrating his power over Gerald in some warped attempt to impress her. The whole point of giving something, in CC's book, was the fun of threatening to take it away.

Gerald had been very quiet on the drive home, and she had hardly seen him since. He had spent the first week of his stewardship briefing his newly appointed editor and ploughing through reams of paperwork, staying at the office till late every night. Vivi had already fired off her opening column, declaring her dedication to the slaughter of sacred cows, and a dozen other new projects were already in the pipeline.

'And a very influential young woman,' continued CC. 'I've given Gerald this chance for your sake, you realise.'

'Well, I'm sure he'll repay your trust in him.'

'It's you I'm putting my trust in. You could be the making of Gerald. Or the ruin of him . . .'

It took Gemma longer than it should have done to realise what he was driving at. He was seventy-four, after all. When she did realise, she told herself that he was just flirting with her, he didn't actually mean anything by it. Then, when the remarks became more explicit, she tried to rebuff them by saying coyly, 'Please don't, CC. You're embarrassing me.' But clearly it delighted him to embarrass her.

'Come now,' he said. 'You can't really be as innocent as you pretend to be. Not unless my grandson's even less of a man than I think he is. Tell me, does he satisfy you?'

What was she supposed to say? Actually, I'm still a virgin? Far from respecting her, he would merely despise Gerald.

'Yes, thank you,' said Gemma, blushing. 'Can you please not move your head? I need you to stay perfectly still for the moment.'

'There are parts of me that can't stay still, looking at you.'

'Keep looking very slightly to the right, will you?'

'A girl like you makes a man feel young again. I dreamed about you last night, Gemma.' He proceeded to relate the dream in all its lurid detail.

'Would you mind if we didn't speak for a while?' said Gemma, cutting him short. 'I need to concentrate.'

Mercifully, he fell silent. Or not quite silent. She kept her eyes resolutely on the canvas, but she couldn't help hearing his heavy breathing, and next time she looked, to her horror, he was masturbating, with a filthy grin all over his face. She debated whether to leave the room, or pretend not to notice, or pluck up the courage to rebuke him, settling finally for the latter.

'If you're going to do that kind of thing, CC, I'm afraid I'll have to abandon this commission. I can't possibly paint your portrait if . . .'

'You'll do as you're told,' he said coldly. 'You don't want to cost Gerald his inheritance, do you? Specially one you stand to gain by . . .' He closed his eyes, grunted, and shuddered. 'Aah. That's better.' He put his soiled handkerchief back in his pocket. 'Thank you, Gemma. I'm very grateful to you. Haven't I already shown you how grateful I can be?'

Gemma felt sick. She had no idea how to handle a situation like this. What would Vivi do, if she were in her shoes? Call him a disgusting old pervert and dare him to do his worst. And Vivi would get away with it. But she, Gemma, wouldn't. Gerald had nothing in writing to protect his position, the old man could simply remove him from office tomorrow, without so much as an explanation. She couldn't bear for that to be her fault.

Which was why she took the coward's way out and carried on working. When the session was over he thanked her politely, and reminded her that he would see her again on Monday, behaving just as she had done, as if nothing had happened. At least he hadn't tried to touch her, thought Gemma, her blood running cold at the thought of it. But what if he did try?

If she spoke to Gerald, masculine pride would demand that he confront the old man and tell him to stop harassing her. With predictable and dire consequences. It was equally unthinkable to confide in Harriet. She was so pleased with her at the moment, in her own gruff way, this would ruin everything. Vivi would go up in feminist smoke and provoke a huge family row, despising her all the while for not being able to cope on her own. As for Mum, Gemma could just imagine her reaction. 'I warned you about that family, Gem. I told you so . . .'

On the Saturday evening they went out in a foursome, with Nick and Vivi. Vivi and Gerald talked shop solidly all through the meal, while Nick did his best to entertain a neglected Gemma by regaling her with his bottomless repertoire of shaggy dog stories.

'The hacks have got a case,' Vivi was saying emphatically. 'God knows they're underpaid, and we've lost enough good people already.'

'I don't disagree with you. I'm just saying that I want to contain the situation until my trial period's over. That way I'll be able to get them a better deal.'

Not that anyone would appreciate it, thought Gemma. The old

'Herald' label, however unjust, took a lot of living down, and there would be plenty of people ready to accuse him of selling his soul for a chance of power. She was in much the same position herself. Caught between the devil and the deep blue sea . . .

'So how's your magnum opus going?' said Nick, attempting to refill her glass. Gemma covered it with her hand, fearful that wine might loosen her tongue.

'All right, thanks.'

'I expect you're having to creep to the old boy something chronic.'

'Oh, inevitably.' She smiled, making light of it.

'You want to watch him,' said Nick. 'Half these nobs are dirty old men on the quiet. You wouldn't believe the stuff we pull in at *The Torch* that never gets into print, I mean there's just too much of it, it would get ridiculous . . .'

Whereupon he named a cabinet minister, claiming that he had been visiting an S & M parlour in Soho for years, they had the pictures to prove it.

'Haven't you got anything better to do,' put in Gerald suddenly, 'than rake up dirt and destroy reputations?'

'You mean this geezer's reputation as a solid family man, who never misses a chance to sound off about declining moral values? Do me a favour. Politicians, aristos, celebs, they're all out to use the press to peddle their opinions and keep their public profile nice and high. And if they're really what they pretend to be, then they've got no worries, have they? Like I said, we only expose the tip of the iceberg. Otherwise we'd have brought down every government that was ever elected.'

'Well, assuming you haven't got anything on my grandfather yet, I'd be glad if you wouldn't cast aspersions on his character in front of my future wife.'

Considering that Gerald hated the old man, by his own admission, it surprised Gemma that he should spring to his defence. On the other hand, Nick wasn't family, and Gerald had never washed his dirty linen in public.

'I only said . . . sorry, mate. My big mouth. Sorry, Gem.'

'You haven't got anything on him, have you?' said Vivi, her eyes lighting up.

'Nope. Newspaper proprietors are off limits, worse luck. Dog

148

doesn't eat dog, and all that. But if he ever sells up, he'd better watch out.'

'Have you quite finished?' said Gerald coldly.

'Oh, don't be so touchy,' put in Vivi. 'The family honour is quite safe. Whatever CC's got up to in the past, the old fart's obviously well past it now . . .'

Gemma could only hope that she was right.


On Monday she was careful to position CC's chair so as to give herself a clear route to the door. She put a tape in her cassette player – she was trying hard to share Gerald's passion for Wagnerian opera – in an attempt to preclude conversation and give her mind something else to focus on besides the hated image taking shape on her canvas. For the first half hour or so, CC behaved with perfect civility, saying what a good job Gerald seemed to be doing so far and how Gemma had made a man of him. She had almost allowed herself to accept these fulsome comments at face value, when Dr Jekyll turned swiftly and suddenly into Mr Hyde.

'Take off that overall,' he said. 'It hides your figure.'

'I need it to protect my clothes.'

'I'll buy you new clothes, dammit. Don't make me repeat myself, Gemma. I don't ask for much. And I give a lot in return. Too much, I'm beginning to think.'

Uncertainly, Gemma took off her overall, revealing a sweatshirt and jeans.

'That's better. I love a nice tight bottom. But I like nice long legs even more. Put on a dress.'

'CC . . .'

'How would you like it if I said no to you, Gemma? If I said no to Gerald? Put on that blue thing you wore at Le Caprice. But without the tights. Bare legs are so much more attractive.' And then, when she didn't move, in a tone midway between menace and pathos, 'Go on, humour me, like a good girl. Otherwise I'm going to feel very hurt. And you wouldn't want to hurt my feelings, Gemma, now would you?'

He's getting senile, Gemma told herself as she fetched the blue dress and locked herself in the bathroom while she changed. Old people developed ridiculous whims. Harriet's words echoed in her ears. *Your job from now on is to keep the old bastard happy at all costs.* As Vivi said, he was well past it. She wasn't frightened. She could handle this. She had to handle it.

'That's better,' approved CC on her return. 'I want you to wear that dress every time I come, Gemma. Tell me, what colour are your panties?' He unzipped his fly. 'You know, this would be so much better if you did it for me.'

Gemma felt another wave of nausea.

'That's enough,' she said, trying to sound stern and authoritative. 'I won't put up with this a moment longer.'

She put down her brushes and made to walk past him. But he stuck out a leg, nearly tripping her up.

'Why are you running away from me, Gemma?'

'I find your behaviour offensive.' He was bluffing with his threats to sack Gerald. He couldn't run the risk of her exposing him. 'If you carry on like this, I shall have to speak to Gerald.'

'Perhaps I'll speak to Gerald as well. Tell him how you pleaded with me to give him a chance. How you offered yourself to me in exchange for his promotion, and suggested painting my portrait, so that we could be alone together.'

'He won't believe that!'

'I have the panties you were wearing, the first day I came. They still smell of you. You gave them to me, remember, as a souvenir?'

He put his hand in his pocket and waved them in front of her. He must have taken them from the dirty linen bin in the bathroom. The man was insane . . .

'Even if Gerald doesn't want to believe it, other people will. And they won't think you did it for his sake, believe me, they'll think you did it for your own. It won't take much to convince Harriet that you're another little tart, like your mother. Or Vivi. It won't take much to convince anyone of what your real motives in marrying him are.'

No, he wasn't insane. He must have worked all this out in cold blood. The threat of Harriet and Vivi turning against her was even stronger than the one to disinherit Gerald. She imagined herself misjudged, cast off, reviled, with a disillusioned, heartbroken Gerald breaking off their engagement. She would be back at square one again, a nobody going nowhere . . .

'Now get back to work,' he said. 'There's nothing to be afraid of. Play fair with me and I'll play fair with you.'

Frozen-footed, Gemma retraced her steps. She mustn't let this evil, power-crazed old man destroy her life, or Gerald's. She mustn't panic. He was just a pathetic old man who wanted something new to wank to. Gemma picked up her brush and got down to work on the eyes, ignoring his obscene gruntings, and did what Daniel had exhorted her to do. For once she painted what she really saw and didn't hide what she felt about her subject. For once she uncorked the bottle and let the genie out, and wondered, shuddering, if it could do that on canvas, what the hell it was capable of in real life.

## 9

'PRETTY AS A picture,' said Vivi dryly, standing back to survey the final effect of Gemma in her wedding dress. With Barbara and Fred driving straight to Little Moldingham from Alchester, and Harriet fussing over the groom and best man, it had fallen to Vivi, as reluctant bridesmaid, to put Gemma up for the night, help her dress, and travel with her in the bridal car to the church. 'Cheer up, for God's sake. You look as if you're going to the block.'

You're not the only one who's nervous, she was thinking, steeling herself for another encounter with Max. He had earned himself a wedding invitation by sending the bridal couple a canteen of Georgian silver cutlery and offering them the use of either of his two holiday homes for their honeymoon – one on a remote Bahamian island, and one in Monterey. By this time they had already arranged to go to CC's villa in Cannes but Harriet, never one to pass up the chance of a freebie, would be visiting California in their place.

'Max keeps asking after you,' Harriet had told Vivi hopefully, thinking, no doubt, that a millionaire son-in-law would provide an additional bulwark against an impoverished old age. 'You obviously made a big impression on him.'

'I can't bear it when you go into Mrs Bennet mode,' grumbled Vivi. 'Why don't you just make a play for him yourself?'

'Because it's you he's interested in, not me,' sniffed Harriet, not without chagrin. 'He's made that crystal clear.'

Max had made no attempt to see Vivi, or even phone her. On the other hand, huge bouquets would arrive for her at *The Courier*, with a card signed simply 'Happy sneezing. M.', which she would claim had come from a nutter – every female hack who had ever had a picture by-line attracted the attentions of nutters – and send round to Bart's by messenger. And on her birthday, in April, he had sent her a cheque for a thousand pounds, with the payee's name left blank, 'to be credited to the charity of your choice', making it impossible for her to return it. She felt as if she were being stalked by a killer beast masquerading as a cuddly toy.

'I can't,' announced Gemma suddenly.

'What's that?' said Vivi, still miles away.

'I can't go through with it.'

'You'd better,' said Vivi, not taking her seriously. 'Or I'll get the blame.'

'I mean it. I thought I could cope, but now . . .' Her voice broke and she covered her face with her hands.

'Don't start snivelling, you're going to ruin your make-up.' Her voice softened. 'I know it must be scary, getting married. But it's too late to chicken out now.'

Much too late, thought Gemma, hiding behind a tissue. She should have cut and run long ago. And now here she was, at the eleventh hour, blurting out half-truths to Vivi, groping desperately for an excuse, any excuse, to extricate herself from this nightmare without hurting Gerald's pride.

Vivi wasn't going to make things easy for her. She might not really want her in the family, but she cared about Gerald too much to connive at his public humiliation. The only person who would have listened, all ears, was Mum, Mum who had never listened to her in the past.

'Not like that, you'll smudge your eye shadow,' remonstrated Vivi. She took the tissue and dabbed carefully until the leak was stanched.

'I'm sorry,' said Gemma, rallying. What a wimp Vivi must think her. 'I'm just afraid of . . . making a mess of things.'

Aren't we all? thought Vivi. At the beginning she had credited Gemma with a certain smugness at having got her man, but the last few weeks had evidently taken their toll, what with Gerald working all hours, and Harriet putting her through her paces like a circus pony, and CC insisting she paint his rotten portrait.

'You'll handle everything brilliantly,' she said sturdily. 'All right, so I had my doubts about you. I wondered if you were tough enough to cope with my mother and the old man. But you've always been tough inside.' Which was a lot more use than being tough on the outside. 'You've given Gerald a lot of confidence, especially as far as the old bastard's concerned. Because whatever happens at the paper, he'll still have you. You're the one thing CC can't take away from him.'

Gemma looked for a long moment at her sister's reflection, absorbing the bitter irony of her words. And let her last chance slip by.


The clever part of it was that she hadn't been expecting it. Weeks of putting up with CC's vile behaviour had lulled her into a state of false security. He had never laid a finger on her, after all, despite his relentless assault on her eyes and ears. So conscious was Gemma of the constant, hovering threat to Gerald, that she had chosen to ignore the danger to herself.

The world was full of dirty old men who exposed themselves in public places, and sexual inadequates who terrorised women with obscene telephone calls. But both breeds, she had read, were relatively harmless. What CC was doing, she reasoned, was just a variation on these activities. He made his obscene suggestions face to face, he did his indecent exposure in private. As Nick had said that night in the restaurant, all kinds of respectable public figures were raging deviants on the quiet, *The Torch*'s safe was full of undisclosed revelations about so-called pillars of society. Someone more worldly than herself would probably have found the whole pathetic business funny, albeit in a sick kind of way.

When the longed-for final session came, the day before the wedding, Gemma was suffering from something akin to gate fever. Once the portrait was finished, once she was married, CC would leave her alone . . . wouldn't he? She had to believe, as an article of faith, that this would soon be over. It was all that had got her through it.

'Finished,' Gemma said, putting down her brushes in relief. She could have completed the picture sooner, and cut down on the number of sittings by using photographs, but naturally CC had wanted his pound of flesh. For once he hadn't indulged in his favourite activity; retrospectively that should have been a warning sign, but it didn't occur to her at the time. Especially as he had been at his most avuncular and benevolent today, commenting on the rise in *The Courier*'s circulation and what a good job Gerald was doing, as if to reassure her that her ordeal hadn't been in vain.

'Do I get to see it at last?' he said, crossing over to the easel. Gemma steeled herself for his reaction. But luckily he was too vain and too visually ignorant to see what she had done.

'Splendid, splendid. We can hang it in the hallway in time for the wedding, so that all the guests can admire it.'

'Oh, it can't be framed for a long time yet, not until it's properly dry.'

'To hell with the frame, then. It can get properly dry standing on the easel, by the front door. I'll send a van round to collect it. Meanwhile this calls for a celebration.'

He helped himself to a glass of Gerald's Glenfiddich, pouring an equal measure for her. Gemma wiped her hands and took the drink from him. Ten more minutes, she thought twitchily, fifteen at the outside, and he'll be gone.

'What music shall we listen to?' he mocked, looking through the cassettes. 'Wagner, for a change?'

Despite resolute efforts, Gemma couldn't warm to the *Ring* cycle, particularly the screechings of Brünnhilde, though no doubt she had been unwise to taint the music with CC's presence.

'Don't know how you can stand that din myself,' he grunted. Nonetheless he inserted *Götterdämmerung*, turned the volume up loud and chinked his glass against hers.

'To your first child,' he bellowed. 'Let's hope it's a honeymoon baby. And a boy.'

Embarrassed to endorse this wish, Gemma simply smiled and swallowed. She waited for him to sit down first, on one of the two settees, and then chose the one opposite, even though it was further from the door, with the coffee table between them.

'I thought of remarrying, you know,' he went on, 'after my wife died. To get myself a son at last. But as Vivi was quick to remind me, there's nothing more ridiculous than an old man in thrall to some young floozie waiting to become a rich widow. I don't like to be made a fool of, Gemma. In public or in private.'

'Well, I hope Gerald's proving to be the son you never had.' God, what a phoney she was. But such trite remarks had become automatic.

'It's my brother John he takes after, not me. You know he ended up shooting himself, do you?'

Gemma nodded. Both Gerald and Harriet had told her the story.

'It was all hushed up, at the time, of course. God knows how long he'd been poking the students and getting away with it. I still wonder if he'd been interfering with Gerald on the quiet. That would explain a lot. If there's one thing I can't abide, Gemma, it's queers. No wonder the country's going to the dogs, with all these legalised perverts running about.'

CC wasn't a pervert, of course. He was a normal red-blooded male. Gemma sat silently while he turned his attention to ugly lesbian bitches, and small wonder there were so many of them about these days, what with shirt-lifters chasing each other instead of women . . .

'If you'll excuse me, CC,' said Gemma finally, unable to bear it any longer, 'I have a lot to do before tomorrow . . .'

'Dying to get rid of me, aren't you?'

'Not at all. But I have a few things I still need to buy and I want to get out to the shops before they close.' If only Harriet would ring, or call round. But CC had decreed that no one was to disturb Gemma while she was working, and there was technically still a half hour of their session to go.

'Let's wait for the music to finish at least. You've been so nice to me, Gemma, you're not going to spoil things now, are you?'

Gemma began counting slowly up to a hundred in her head. The music was much too loud, but at least that helped drown out her thoughts. Twenty-two, twenty-three, twenty-four . . .

'I shall miss these little get-togethers, Gemma. But once you're married, I hope I can come round and visit you sometimes. With Gerald working so hard, I can't have you getting lonely.'

He stood up, perched on the arm of her settee and put his hand on her bare thigh – she was wearing the short blue dress he insisted on. Gemma removed it primly, struggling not to lose her cool, not to offend him.

'CC, I do wish you'd stop . . . flirting with me. I've tried to be tolerant, but –'

'Tolerant? Is that what you call it? I call it leading me on. I call it teasing, Gemma.'

She stood up. So did he.

'Please, Gemma.' He was plaintive now, pathetic. 'No one will know, except you and me. How about a little kiss?' He tried to plant his mouth against hers, his lips wet and blubbery. Gemma recoiled.

'I'd like you to leave now,' she said quietly. 'Please.'

But he caught hold of her upper arm, his horny fingers digging into it like claws, holding on even tighter as she tried to break away. Something snapped, like a branch finally giving way under a weight too great for it to bear.

'Let go of me, you revolting old man!' Gemma heard herself hissing, frightened now. 'You disgust me!'

She regretted the words as soon as they were uttered. All her good work – if you could call it good work – was undone in an instant. His eyes flickered furiously. No one insulted CC with impunity. Gemma faltered, fighting the absurd urge to apologise.

'I disgust you? But my money doesn't disgust you, does it, Gemma? My paper doesn't disgust you. It doesn't disgust you when I give you what you want. You wanted a rich husband, so you promised to make me happy, and now you're trying to get out of your side of the bargain. Which would mean that I'd have to renege on mine.'

His face was so near it seemed out of proportion, like a caricature, the eyes more protruding, the nose sharper, the mouth greedier.

'I didn't promise you anything. I –'

'All he's wanted all these years is for me to die and leave him everything. Well, now I intend to leave him something he didn't bargain for. You know how important it is for you to have a son, don't you, Gemma? One that doesn't have bad blood? One I can look upon as my very own?'

'Let go of me! Let me go or I'll tell him! I'll tell everyone!'

'So it's threats now, instead of promises.' He gestured at her with his stick, the fingers of his other hand still burrowing into her flesh. 'All that smiling and simpering and flattery. All that nice-girl coyness. I'd hate to have to tell the rest of the family what you're really like.' In desperation Gemma tried to kick him, in an attempt to loosen his grip on her arm, but he struck out with his stick, making her lose her balance, forcing her backwards on to the settee.

'You've got Gerald well fooled, haven't you? And you thought you had me fooled as well. You thought I wasn't capable. You thought that because I'm old, I'm not a man. You were laughing at me . . .'

Gemma tried to beat him off but he was too strong for her, pinning her down with his full weight, pressing his stick across her chest.

'No!' she screamed. 'Please don't!' But no one could hear. Her cries were swallowed up by the music as it thundered its way towards a roaring crescendo. The more she struggled, the more it excited him. And then . . .

And then she couldn't, or rather wouldn't, remember any more. Whatever had happened hadn't happened to her. She had been somewhere else at the time. She had run away and left Gemma to bear it all alone. And when she returned, after the old man was safely gone, to find her shaking and sobbing, she felt remote, detached. The silly girl had only herself to blame, she should have seen it coming. There was no question of taking her to the doctor's, if only because she was registered with Gerald's and Harriet's doctor. So she had better look after her herself.

Gradually she calmed her down. When the bleeding wouldn't stop, she told her not to be frightened, the shock had brought her on early, that was all. Which was good news, at least she wasn't pregnant. She helped her into the bath, added half a bottle of disinfectant to the scalding hot water, washed her hair, scrubbed her all over with a nailbrush and threw away her contaminated clothes. She dressed her in clean ones and put on fresh make-up. She took a phone call from Gerald, who was off on his stag night, and from Harriet, fussing about some last-minute wedding crisis, and neither of them guessed that anything was wrong. Nor must they. They would be bound to blame Gemma, rightly so, because it was Gemma's fault.

Then she rang for a taxi, and went round to Bamber Court, where she was due to spend her last night as a single woman. And neither Nick nor Vivi noticed anything amiss, other than to comment that she was rather quiet, but then she was always rather quiet. Gemma stood back and watched Gemma's performance, willing her not to break down, surprised at how well she was doing.

But in bed that night, Gemma gave Gemma no peace. When she wasn't weeping into the mattress with the covers over her head, she was threatening to go next door and tell Vivi everything. To ruin Gerald's career, to expose herself to CC's lies, to brand herself at best as an idiot and at worst as a manipulative little tease.

In the end she managed to terrorise her into silence. But there was one point they both agreed on. It would never happen again. Next time, if there was a next time, he would have to kill her first.

There was a cheerful knock on the bedroom door and Nick, unrecognisable in morning dress, put his head around it.

'The car's arrived.' He gave a building-site-sized wolf whistle. 'Too bad Gerald beat me to it, lucky bastard. What's up, Gem? You been crying?'

'Wedding nerves,' said Vivi, producing some drops from her bag and whitening up Gemma's eyes. She brushed a dusting of extra powder over her pink cheeks.

'No wonder, with you as tart-of-honour. Has she been trying to talk you out of it, love? Has she been telling you that marriage is a wicked instrument of male oppression?' Gemma smiled thinly. 'I get down on my bended ones at least once a week, begging her to make an honest man of me. But to her I'm nothing but a sex object . . .'

When Nick wanted to make a serious point, he invariably dressed it up as a joke. But the message wasn't lost on Vivi. He had never, in fact, asked her to marry him, knowing what her answer would be. He had never even suggested that she move in with him, even though she was regularly seduced into staying overnight, because the best part of sleeping with Nick was sleeping with Nick.

That they were still together was no thanks to her. Lately she had begun to resent him for loving her so much, for making her feel so inadequate and unworthy. She had punished him, and herself, by picking pointless quarrels, been cruel and hurtful and vicious, tried, like a wilful child, to find his limits. But even when he lost his temper he could never bring himself to hurt her back. Anger was just a prelude to making things up, a turn-on for both of them. Why oh why did the nicest men always fall for selfish bitches? Thank God it hadn't happened to Gerald too.

Nick sat between them in the back of the car, distracting Gemma with a steady stream of nonsensical patter. By the time they reached the village church in Little Moldingham she was all smiles again. A crowd of local people had gathered outside to watch. They raised a cheer as Gemma emerged from the car, clutching her bouquet.

'She looks like Princess Di!' Vivi heard one woman say. Which she did rather. Tall, blonde, with the same shy smile, the same habit of lowering her head and looking upwards. She even managed a little royal wave.

Vivi followed, one step behind, arms full of satin, feeling like the ugly sister. Nick took his place inside the church, leaving them with the old man, who had driven down the previous evening, following his usual Friday night practice. Gemma had been only too ready, at first, to agree to Harriet's suggestion that they flatter him by asking him to give her away, seeing it as a licence to snub her seedy stepfather. The honeymoon in Cannes, likewise, had been arranged in the flurry of initial goodwill. Too late, she regretted her compliance, the compliance which had led her to agree to marry Gerald in the first place.

'You're looking very beautiful, my dear,' said CC.

Gemma didn't answer, staring fixedly at her feet while Vivi spread out her train carefully so that it would drag evenly behind her.

'And so virginal,' he whispered in her ear. 'White suits you, Gemma. You should wear it more often.'

Gemma clenched her fists. The hatred was so intense it made her feel dizzy and short of breath. She was weightless with loathing as she allowed him to take her arm and lead her down the aisle, her mind inhabiting a different space from her body, looking down on her from some safe place where he couldn't touch her.

The church was packed with people she didn't know. Barbara had brought along a clutch of her relatives to swell the numbers on Gemma's side, but they were lost in a sea of strangers, people who wouldn't give her the time of day if she wasn't marrying Viscount Collington's grandson. She could see Gerald, waiting for her, with Daniel by his side. She couldn't believe that she had ever had a crush on Daniel, that she had ever been that innocent. Something inside her had died, or rather been brutally murdered.

Harriet turned and waved an invisible baton at the bride, reminding her to hold her head up and keep her shoulders back and take small steps. She was subtly elegant in pale blue, in contrast to Mum, sitting on the opposite side of the aisle, handkerchief at the ready, resplendent in shocking pink with matching hat, still sulking that Fred wasn't doing the honours in Dad's place; he had seemed so repulsive once, before Gemma understood the meaning of the word. Mum wouldn't be sympathetic if she knew. She would say it served her right and so it did.

Vivi took Gemma's bouquet and stepped to one side, uncomfortably aware of Max watching her, of Nick watching her. She had always hated weddings and certainly wouldn't have agreed to be 'tart-of-honour' for anyone else. She felt out of place listening to the vows, envying Gemma her ability to mean them and keep them. If she ever got married it would have to be a register office job, short and sharp and functional, with no promises made on either side. In which case, why bother to get married at all?

And yet she wished it was otherwise. Wished she had it in her to be a good wife and mother, as Gemma was destined to be. If she thought herself capable of that, she would opt out tomorrow, breathe a huge sigh of relief that she didn't have to compete any more. But then, Harriet had invested all her hopes in marriage and motherhood, and look at her now. A bored, neurotic, lonely, meddlesome woman presiding over an empty nest. Vivi recognised too many of her own faults in Harriet to blame everything on her disastrous choice of husbands. She would have been much less hard on her mother if she wasn't so hard on herself.

The vows made, the bridal party trooped off to sign the register. Gemma had recovered her usual composure, Gerald was being hearty, which didn't suit him, Harriet regal, which did, the old man nauseatingly sentimental, reminiscing about his own wedding, here in this church, and Daniel remote and detached as always, while Barbara twittered on about it being a lovely service, and the vicar grovelled to CC with a mind to the roof renewal fund.

'Doesn't she look perfectly vile in that colour?' hissed Harriet in Vivi's ear. 'The woman has no dress sense at all. Poor Gemma. She must be mortified.'

'Then do your best not to make things worse. Lay off the champagne, okay?'

Once the wedding and the trip to Monterey were over, Harriet would be back at a loose end again, behaving like some manic escapee from a sex-and-shopping novel. Vivi could only hope that she found herself a rich Yank who would keep her out of Gerald's and Gemma's hair, or more specifically out of their house. Vivi couldn't see her keeping to a granny flat, especially once there was a grandchild for her to fuss over. Harriet had always been a baby-freak, peering into passing prams, godmother to a dozen assorted bratlets whom she spent a fortune on. Poor old Gemma. Greater love hath no woman than she who agrees to live with an interfering old bag of a mother-in-law.

Vivi smiled her way dutifully through the photographs and the speeches – long-winded from the old man, well rehearsed from Gerald, and witty from Daniel, who, when it suited him – which wasn't very often – could out-suave the likes of Max Kellerman any day. It wasn't long before that slag Myra Shaw was busily chatting him up, and being Daniel he encouraged her, too lazy to pass up the chance of an easy lay, while Nick made it his business to take care of Barbara, Fred and Co., isolated as they were from the rest of the throng by a kind of social apartheid.

'Vivi, come and say hello to Max,' commanded Harriet, who had already broken her ban on the champagne.

'Do you have to be so obvious?'

'It's not obvious at all, he's talking to Gerald and Gemma and the old man.' She steered Vivi purposefully over to the group. 'Max is a great admirer of your column,' she carolled, making Vivi cringe. 'Aren't you, Max?'

'As long as I never find myself as one of your victims,' said Max in that soft, steady drawl.

'Now there's an idea,' said Vivi, who had already scoured the cuttings library for information about him. He had attracted a good deal of press coverage in recent years, projecting a hypable image of himself as a bad boy made good. Born 1949 in Bakersfield, California. Father James Kellerman, a war hero injured in the D-Day landings; married mother Margaret, a Scot, in 1945. Died when Max was seven years old. Max clashed with his stepfather, ran away from home, became a self-confessed juvenile delinquent. In and out of reform schools until drafted and sent to Vietnam in 1966. Trained as a radio operator and developed an interest in electronics. Subsequently put through college by the army under the GI Bill, took a masters degree in computer studies at MIT. Went on to devise and patent the K-script software system that had made him his first million. Now a majority shareholder in Kellerman International, based in Silicon Valley and quoted on Wall Street, with subsidiary companies registered in London, Frankfurt and Rome. Stated ambition to become the biggest, most successful hard/soft computer operation in the world. Famous for taking chances and pulling them off. A workaholic and proud of it; only listed recreations – all variations on a macho theme – 'flying, sky-diving and beautiful women', mostly airhead models and actresses, judging by a soppy feature on 'the world's most eligible men' listing his ex-girlfriends. Vivi's first instincts about him had been spot on. The man was a prize egomaniac bastard.

'Paper's put on forty thousand since she joined,' boomed Gramps.

'You mean since Gerald took over,' Vivi corrected him.

'Well, carry on the good work and *The Courier* will be worth a lot more when and if I decide to sell.'

Gerald laughed stolidly. Following his lead Gemma managed a tight smile.

'I hear you have a strike brewing, Gerald,' put in Max.

'Oh, I'm sure it can be averted,' said Gerald, with false but convincing sang-froid. A ballot had already been taken, authorising the union executive to call its members out immediately if pay talks broke down. Prolonged industrial action, or too large a settlement, and the old man was threatening to close the paper down altogether.

'The journalists deserve a lot of the credit for the rise in circulation,' Vivi reminded CC. 'If we want to hang on to good people, we have to pay everyone what they're worth, not just a few star names.'

'And where's the extra money going to come from?' growled Gramps.

'Long term, from extra profits,' said Gerald. 'In the short term, as I keep being reminded, the money's always been there for the print when they want it.'

'Dammit, man, you're supposed to be management now. You're talking like one of them.'

'It's time we got rid of them and us,' said Gerald.

'Don't talk shop at a wedding,' interjected Harriet hurriedly.

'I couldn't agree more,' grunted the old man. 'Mustn't have Gerald thinking about the paper on his honeymoon, eh Gemma?' Gemma blushed scarlet.

'Excuse us,' said Gerald stonily, 'we ought to circulate.' At which point Gramps was waylaid by another party of guests and Harriet, damn her, made herself scarce.

'How are you?' said Max, looking at Vivi as if she were naked.

'Never better.' And then, lowering her voice, 'I wish you'd stop sending me flowers. I give them all away in any case. And stop asking Harriet about me, will you?'

'At least it stops her getting the wrong idea. As for the flowers, you enjoy giving them away. Every time you do it you use up a little bit more of your anger.'

'I'm not angry. But I will be, if you carry on pestering me.'

'Smile,' said Max. 'Your boyfriend's watching.'

'If you dare say anything to him . . .' warned Vivi, fearing mischief.

'I wouldn't dream of it. He might hit me. And then I'd have to hit him back.' He caught Nick's eye, raised his hand in a hello-goodbye wave, and moved on.

'So what was all that about?' said Nick, approaching.

'What?'

'The cosy chat you and Kellerman were having.'

'What do you mean, cosy?'

'He fancies you. It's written all over his face.'

'Why shouldn't he fancy me?' scowled Vivi. 'You do.'

She ought to understand jealousy, being jealous herself. But as always Vivi was intolerant of her own failings in other people.

'It was the same at the old geezer's party. Every time I looked at him, he was looking at you.'

'Don't be ridiculous.'

'What's ridiculous about it? A big wheel like him is used to snapping his fingers and having any woman he wants.'

It didn't help to have him remind her of that.

'Nice to know you think I'm any woman.'

'I just don't trust him, that's all.'

'Don't worry,' said Vivi. 'I don't trust him either.' More to the point, she knew better than to trust herself.

'Gemma.'

'Daniel. Thank you for a lovely speech. I'm sorry I haven't had a minute to say hello, I –'

'I've just seen the picture.'

'Oh. I did tell the old man to wait till it was framed, but he insisted on putting it on display.'

'Shows how blind he is. Otherwise he'd hide it away.'

'Is it that bad?'

'It's that good. Has Gerald seen it?'

'I don't know.'

'Well, if Gerald could paint, that's how he would portray him. I take back everything I said about you prettifying things. Congratulations.' And then, almost shyly, for him, 'Am I forgiven for that row we had last time we met?'

'We have a row every time we meet,' said Gemma. 'I've forgotten what it was about.'

'Liar. I was putting the mockers on Gerald taking over the paper. And you got angry with me, and so you should. I want to be proved wrong, believe me.'

'You will be.' He must be. If he was proved right, all her agony would have been in vain.

'Then don't look so worried. Even if things don't work out, it won't be your fault.'

Oh but it will, thought Gemma. Once again she felt the crazy urge to unburden herself. Daniel had seen what no one else had seen in the picture, Daniel would understand . . . No, of course he wouldn't. The picture was evidence against her, proof that she had been forewarned.

'You must come to dinner, next time you're in London,' she said, taking refuge in a social smile.

'I'll ring you. Talking of which . . . I know Gerald and Vivi are all bound up with the paper at the moment. And Harriet's going to be playing hookey in California for as long as she can swing it. If you're feeling lonely and neglected and stuck for someone to talk to' – he fished a card out of his wallet – 'that's the number of my flat in Paris, and a twenty-four-hour freephone for the agency. If I'm away, they'll know where to reach me. Leave a message and I'll ring you back on expenses.'

Now that she was safely married, thought Gemma bitterly, he could afford to risk being nice to her.

'Thanks.'

'Now cheer up. Think of it. Two weeks in the South of France, away from Harriet and the old man . . .'

'Daniel,' purred Myra Shaw, approaching. She flashed Gemma a quick, false smile. 'You were going to give me a tour of the house, remember? I just love these old neo-Gothic buildings, full of nooks and crannies . . .'

'. . . and empty bedrooms,' hissed Vivi, overhearing, as Myra bore him off. 'Talk about a bitch in heat. Come on. Harriet says it's time to cut the cake. And then you can escape.'

If only I could, thought Gemma.

## 10

'POOR DARLING,' SAID Gerald on the drive back to London. 'You look exhausted.'

'I am a bit tired, yes.'

'Just as well we decided to stay in an hotel and put off the flight till the morning. It's been a long enough day already.'

Gemma agreed that they had been wonderfully lucky with the weather and that Harriet had done a marvellous job of organising the catering. No one would have thought, listening to their restrained, polite conversation, that they were a pair of newly-weds setting off on honeymoon. In the last few weeks they had spent hardly any time alone together, thanks to Gerald's hectic schedule – something Gemma had been almost glad of, ever fearful that he would notice something wrong. And now there was nowhere left for her to hide . . .

'The old man told me to put the hotel bill on my exes,' said Gerald jauntily, as they arrived at the Dorchester, 'so I thought we might as well push the boat out.'

The bellboy showed them up to a palatial suite, all antique furniture, thick wool carpet, gold taps and hothouse flowers, complete with four-poster bed. There was a card by the silver bucket of champagne on the bedside table, inscribed 'Best wishes for your honeymoon, CC'.

'Your influence,' said Gerald, showing it to Gemma. 'He'll never stop sniping at me, but he's got a serious soft spot for you. You've handled him superbly, I must say. Painting his portrait was a masterstroke, he's pleased as punch with the results. Even Daniel said it was a brilliant piece of work, and you know he doesn't give praise lightly.'

He smiled as the cork popped. It should have been a happy

sound. He poured two glasses, handed one to Gemma, and said, 'To my wife.'

'To my husband,' responded Gemma in a choked voice.

'I know I've been neglecting you dreadfully lately. I do appreciate how understanding you've been. Most women would have complained loudly, or at least sulked. But you've been a tower of strength.'

'I believe in you, that's all.' She mustn't cry. If she started crying she might lose control and confess that she wasn't fit to be his wife. The compulsion was always there, twinned with a determination not to give in to it, creating a constant tension.

'And I'm not going to let you down. That's a promise.'

The same promise she had made herself. Better white lies than black truths.

Dinner in the hotel restaurant seemed endless. Gemma found it impossible to concentrate on what Gerald was saying, still wondering if she ought to ring that new rape helpline Vivi had given a plug to in her column.

'For victims of rape,' she had written, 'the worst part, worse even than the attack itself, is the guilt they suffer afterwards, the mistaken belief that they must have "asked for it" in some way. Even women who have been threatened at knife point, or beaten within an inch of their lives, blame themselves for "letting it happen". Unfortunately husbands and boyfriends, however nominally supportive, tend to take the same view. The rate of relationship breakdown among victims is depressingly high . . .'

But what was the point in talking to some kindly fellow-rapee who would tell her that it wasn't her fault when she knew it was? She didn't want, couldn't cope with sympathy. Sympathy would reduce her to a gibbering wreck . . .

Half way through the *sole véronique* she had to make a sudden dash for the powder room, where she was violently sick, her discomfort made worse by crippling period pains.

'You've been gone ages,' said Gerald anxiously when Gemma rejoined him, white-faced. 'Have you been ill? You don't look at all well.'

'Actually . . . I know this is awful of me, but it's the wrong time of the month. I came on early, you see, and . . .'

And at least it would give her a few days' grace, a few more days for the horror to fade sufficiently for her to tolerate his touch.

'Don't apologise,' said Gerald. 'I expect it was just nerves. Let's get you tucked up in bed, you'll feel better once you've had some sleep.'

'I'm sorry, Gerald. I'm so embarrassed.'

'How can you say that? I'm your husband now, after all.'

Her husband. One whom she had already betrayed. She shut herself in the bathroom and showered interminably in a vain attempt to feel clean again. When she came out, wearing a new, demure, long-sleeved Laura Ashley nightie, Gerald, waiting in his dressing gown, went in to complete his own ablutions. He emerged in blue pyjamas, asked her which side of the bed she would like, drew back the covers and tucked her up before taking off his glasses and getting in beside her. He looked so defenceless without them, thought Gemma. So trusting . . .

'Sweet dreams,' he said, confining himself to a chaste kiss on the cheek. 'Do give me a poke in the ribs if I snore, won't you?'

She must have drifted off from sheer exhaustion, only to wake up with a start, arms and legs flailing in distress.

'Gemma? Gemma darling, what's the matter? You were crying out in your sleep . . .'

'What did I say?' demanded Gemma, panic-stricken.

'Just no, no, don't. You must have been having a nightmare. Do you want to tell me about it?'

'I can't remember. Probably someone chasing me. I've always had that dream, ever since I was a child.'

'With me it's all my teeth falling out,' said Gerald kindly, putting an arm around her. 'Shall I phone down for a hot drink? Or a brandy?'

'No, I'm all right now. I'm sorry I woke you.'

'I was awake anyway. I'm a terrible insomniac, as you'll discover. Always find it hard to switch off. Get my best ideas in the middle of the night. Go back to sleep now.'

But she didn't dare, afraid that she would have another dream and cry out something incriminating. And besides, sleep was no relief, swarming as it was with hideous images.

They flew to Nice next morning in CC's private jet, which was fitted with a luxurious cabin. They sat back in armchairs while a steward attended to their every whim, treating them like royalty. But his smile seemed full of mockery, the champagne and caviar tasted sour and stale, and even the brilliant weather which greeted their arrival struck Gemma as ominous, a calm before a storm.

The Collington villa in Cannes was in theory an idyllic setting for a honeymoon, with its stunning sea views, large blue pool, lush gardens, tinkling fountain, and cool marble-floored interior. A maid unpacked for them while they ate a seafood lunch on the terrace, served with more champagne.

'Harriet used to bring us here for holidays when we were kids,' said Gerald, while Gemma kept rearranging the food on her plate to make it look as if she was eating. 'She's a raving Francophile, of course, speaks the language like a native. Spends most of the summer out here, you'll be relieved to know, while CC's in London.'

'Why should I be relieved?' said Gemma. 'She's gone out of her way to be kind to me.' More importantly, Harriet living in the house was some protection against CC. Gemma hadn't bargained on her being away for so long, at the very time when CC would be back in town.

'She has very strong maternal instincts. You appeal to that side of her. Vivi's always rebelled against it, of course.'

Vivi had put it rather differently. 'She's always wanted a pretty little daughter she could dress up. Never much chance of that with me.'

'I suppose she told you about the baby girl who died?' added Gerald.

'She told me about your grandfather having her smothered, yes.' Gemma no longer had any doubts that Harriet's suspicions were true, despite Vivi's scepticism on the subject; she knew now that CC was capable of anything.

'I'm afraid that was some kind of warped wishful thinking, her way of coping with her loss. The old man wasn't even in the country at the time.'

'But he could have got someone else to do it, surely?'

'Not without his sister Emily knowing about it,' said Gerald with his customary objectivity. 'She was the one who ran the household, CC was hardly ever there. I never really knew her, she joined a convent when we were quite young, but by all accounts she was religious, even in those days. Hardly the type of person to condone foul play.'

'But she helped cover up the birth of the baby,' Gemma reminded him. Harriet was convinced that it was Emily's guilty conscience that had driven her into the nunnery. 'Harriet said it was never even registered, to avoid a leak. And that's a crime in itself, isn't it?'

'But hardly a hanging offence. You have to remember that Harriet wasn't totally compos mentis at the time. She nearly died giving birth, ended up having an ad hoc Caesarean in the middle of a snowstorm, and afterwards she became quite deranged, spent the next couple of weeks under sedation.'

'She said she was drugged to keep her quiet,' put in Gemma, almost argumentatively. Why was Gerald standing up for the old man? Would he think that she too was being hysterical if she were ever unwise enough to tell him the truth?

'She's really upset you with this story, hasn't she?' sighed Gerald. 'I'm afraid I must seem terribly callous, but we've all become hardened to her histrionics. Harriet's a survivor. When it came to it she was happy to trade her silence in return for a cookery course in Paris. Or rather to exploit the old man's obsession with respectability.'

Respectability, thought Gemma. It was as if he were sitting there, invisibly, beside them, enjoying a huge, obscene joke at Gerald's expense. And when Gemma went upstairs to change, he was waiting for her there as well. The wardrobe reeked of his cigars, contaminating her clothes and Gerald's, identifying this as his room; he must have instructed the maid to put them here specially. The thought of lying in that bed appalled her. But this room had the best view, and she couldn't think of a good excuse to change it without arousing Gerald's suspicions. She returned downstairs to find him on the telephone to his editor.

'I'm sorry,' he said sheepishly. 'You know how it is. Something you've forgotten about occurs to you out of the blue. It was a one-off, I promise.'

'You've been working far too hard.'

'It's not easy to take a back seat when there's so much at stake. Six months just isn't long enough to work a miracle. Every single budget will end up in the red, there's no way of avoiding it.

Traditionally it's editors who overspend and management which curbs their excesses, and the old man's always accused me of taking an editorial point of view, but as I told him, no successful newspaper was ever run by a bookkeeper . . .'

How she had grown to hate this constant talk of *The Courier*! Why couldn't Gerald turn his back on it, like Daniel? For as long as he remained obsessed with his wretched heritage, she would be condemned to live in fear . . .

Was it love that had got her into this mess, or guilt? Guilt that she had jumped at the chance to make a good marriage to a man with prospects, one who would hoist her into a higher social class, who owned the house she had always coveted, who would give her the sense of identity she lacked? Was that the real reason why she had put up with these last few weeks of torture? As penance for not loving Gerald enough?

When they went up to bed that night Gemma discovered, to her relief, that Gerald had asked the maid to move their things to another room, on the grounds that the other side of the house was cooler at night. She dozed fitfully, ever wary of the dark shapes lurking in the shadows, catching up on her sleep next day, on a deck chair by the pool, trusting the bright Mediterranean sun to keep the monsters at bay. The weather was glorious and Gerald, at least, seemed to unwind, having kept his promise not to ring the office again. They swam and sunbathed, went for walks along the beach and the promenade, admired the yachts in the harbour, sat by the hour in pavement cafés, ordered elaborate *menus gastronomiques*, and watched the gamblers in the casino, without participating themselves, because, as Gerald said, real life was enough of a gamble as it was. It should have been their opportunity to get to know each other better, but Gemma didn't want Gerald to know her better. She was glad to let him do all the talking, while she smiled and listened and pretended to be the girl he thought he had married.

She must have done a good job because he didn't appear to suspect anything. He began kissing her more confidently, more demandingly, his lips moving on to her breasts, his hands exploring her with a new candour, his body leaving her in no doubt that he wanted her. Which he wouldn't have done, of course, if he'd known. Gemma managed to disguise her frigidity as maidenly shyness; she could almost hear him counting off the days, one, two, three, four, five, reminding her that she couldn't put him off much longer. It wasn't just the physical terror of having her body invaded again but the fear that she wouldn't be able to go through with it, that she would end up telling him everything, forcing him to share her suffering, giving him no choice but to resign from *The Courier*, and wrecking their marriage before it had even begun. She couldn't do that to him. However much she hated it, she mustn't let it show, mustn't panic into making a disastrous confession . . .

On Wednesday night Gemma had a large Martini before dinner, more than half a bottle of Chablis with the *assiette de pêcheur* – an attentive waiter kept refilling her glass – and a *crème de menthe* with her coffee, in a desperate attempt at Dutch courage. Drink revealed your true character, so people said. If so, she didn't recognise herself, which was all to the good. Giggling, she retold one of Nick's interminable jokes. She penned a caricature of the waiter on the paper tablecloth. She was vivacious, extrovert and frivolous. Or loud, exhibitionist and silly, as it seemed afterwards.

'Please can I have another *crème de menthe*?'

'The one you just had was a quadruple, by English standards. I think enough's enough, don't you?'

'Spoilsport,' teased Gemma. 'Stick-in-the-mud.'

Gerald signalled for the bill.

'It's most unlike you to drink too much.'

'You've no idea what I'm really like. Nobody has. Everyone thinks I'm such a good little girl.'

'Well, be a good girl now and let's go home.' He bid a bland goodnight to the ogling waiters and helped her out into the street, where he hailed a taxi and bundled her inside.

'Kiss me,' demanded Gemma.

'Not here. When we get home.'

'The silly old taxi driver doesn't care.'

'Well, I do.'

Undeterred, Gemma kissed him instead, while the going was good, while her inhibitions were still submerged in a sea of alcohol. He smelt nice, Gerald always did. His face was smooth, thanks to his fastidious habit of shaving twice a day, but those glasses of his did tend to get in the way . . . She took them off and tossed them over her shoulder in a devil-may-care gesture.

'What's come over you?' said Gerald, groping on the seat. He was virtually blind without them.

'This is our wedding night,' Gemma told him boldly. 'Better late than never.'

'You mean . . .'

Gemma began fiddling with his bow tie, his one sartorial idiosyncrasy, and fumbling with the buttons on his shirt.

'I'm sorry I made you wait,' she hiccupped. 'But I'll make it up to you tonight. Give ya a good time, darlin'.' She gave him a grotesque streetwalker's wink.

'Ssh. The driver will hear you.'

'He doesn't understand English, do you, taxi driver?'

Gerald imprisoned her wandering hands in his.

'Gemma, you're embarrassing me.'

'And you're being a stuffed shirt, as usual.' She assaulted him with another brazen kiss, and this time he returned it, as if to shut her up. Hurry up and get us home, thought Gemma, before this wears off . . .

As soon as they got inside she dragged Gerald up the stairs, pulled him down on the bed and began tugging at his clothes. She hadn't thought she had it in her to take the initiative, the way magazines were forever urging you to do. But in a way it was easier than being passive, it gave the illusion, at least, of being in control.

'Gemma, you're drunk.'

'So what? Don't you want to make mad passionate love?'

'Of course I do. But –'

She silenced the but, took charge, astonished herself with her shameless behaviour. It was as if another Gemma had taken her over, the Gemma she had always longed to be . . .

'Stop it,' said Gerald, pushing her away in disgust. 'Stop behaving like a whore.'

Gemma stopped it, suddenly horribly sober.

'I married you because you were different,' he accused her. 'I married you because you weren't like my mother, like my sister, like Myra bloody Shaw, like the slags my brother goes to bed with. I respected you, dammit!'

'I'm sorry,' faltered Gemma, the balloon of her bravado losing all its air. It was the first time Gerald had ever been angry with her, a small, terrifying taste of how he would react if he ever discovered her deceit.

'I might have known Harriet would get her claws into you, plastering you with make-up and messing about with your hair and dressing you up like a Barbie doll. But you told me you were still the same inside, and I believed you.'

'I'm sorry. I was just trying to . . . to encourage you.'

'I don't need to be "encouraged"! Just because I haven't leapt on you before now doesn't mean I'm not capable, you know!'

'I never meant to imply . . .'

'I am capable, in case you've been wondering. In case CC has been putting any doubts in your mind. He'll tell anyone who'll listen that I'm gay, like my uncle!'

'Gerald, please. How can you think . . .'

'Well, I'm not. I'm perfectly normal and I can perform without you turning any tricks.'

Oh God, thought Gemma, seeing the suspicion in his eyes, he thinks I've behaved this way before, with other men.

'I . . . I was just terribly nervous, that's all. That's why I had too much to drink. It was stupid of me. I'm sorry, Gerald. It won't happen again. I'm so ashamed.'

'I think you'd better sleep it off. Now let's just forget this little fiasco, shall we?'

They spent the night without touching, with a wide space of no-man's-land between them. Gemma woke up very early with a filthy hangover to find Gerald already breakfasting on the terrace.

'Good morning,' he said, with a stiffer version of his usual courtesy. 'Looks like another lovely day.'

'Yes, doesn't it?' Gingerly she took a sip of orange juice, wishing she were dead. It wouldn't take much, Mum had warned her, for her new family to turn against her. It wouldn't take much, CC had taunted her, for people to believe she was just another little tart, like her mother. And now she had managed to behave like one. If it ever came to her word against CC's, Gerald would believe him, not her . . .

The telephone rang inside the house, and a moment later the maid appeared, saying that there was a call for monsieur from

London. Looking anxious, Gerald went indoors to take it. He was gone a long time.

'Is something wrong?' asked Gemma as he returned to the table with a face like thunder.

'Negotiations with the NUJ broke down late last night.'

'What negotiations? I thought everything was on ice till you got back?'

'Evidently CC decided otherwise. For reasons best known to himself he announced, quite gratuitously, that he will personally veto any pay increase in this financial year. With the result that the strike is on as from today. And it's looking like the print might well come out in sympathy.'

They couldn't very well refuse, thought Gemma, given that the NUJ had instructed its members not to cross print picket lines last year. And without the print, management wouldn't even be able to produce a skeleton paper to maintain a vital presence on the newsstands.

'I had the whole situation under control,' muttered Gerald. 'It could all have been settled without bloodshed. And then the minute my back's turned he starts sticking his oar in . . .'

This was CC's revenge for the insults she had hurled at him, thought Gemma, hoping disloyally that this would be the final nail in *The Courier*'s coffin. The sooner he closed the wretched paper down the happier she would be, however selfish that wish might be. Then perhaps Gerald would take Daniel's advice, take up an academic career, and then they would both be free.

'It's no use,' said Gerald. 'I'm sorry, Gemma, but I'll have to fly home straight away, see if I can save the situation. I daren't leave the old man to wreak any more havoc. If you want to stay here for a bit . . .'

'No, of course not. Don't apologise. I understand.'

'We'll go away again, once all this is sorted out.'

'It doesn't matter. I just wish there was something I could do to help.'

'You do help. I'm sorry I was so vile to you last night. I over-reacted. I should have realised it was just nerves. I know perfectly well how inexperienced and innocent you are, it's one of the reasons I fell in love with you.'

Gemma bowed her head, hating herself.

'I suppose I'm terribly old-fashioned,' went on Gerald. 'And a bit of a misogynist, except when it comes to you. I shouldn't have said what I did about Harriet and Vivi. But you know the way they carry on. Please forgive me.'

Please forgive me. If only she had the courage to say that to him. But how could she expect him to forgive her when she couldn't forgive herself?

'I might have known whose side you'd be on,' Vivi accused Nick. The print unions had voted to carry on working, which would enable management to produce a paper, of sorts, using agency bulletins and pre-written features. And Nick insisted on condoning their treachery.

'All the while the paper's being printed,' he said patiently, 'at least *The Courier* will be getting some revenue in, and there's less chance of it closing down.'

'That's got nothing to do with the way they voted. They've gone and sold the hacks down the river . . .'

'No more than your own brother'll be doing, by undermining NUJ action.'

'He's acting proprietor, dammit!' Gerald had phoned Vivi first thing that morning, from France, asking how strong the support was for the strike, and saying that he would be home later that day. 'You're contradicting what you just said, about keeping the paper on the streets!'

'I'm just putting it another way. Gerald's making the best of a bad job, same as my dad's having to do. He was all for coming out, but the vote went the other way. So he's going along with the majority, just like you are, by not turning in your column, even though you feel you're letting Gerald down. So let's beg to differ and leave our families out of it, shall we?'

Their dispute was curtailed at that point, not by another bout of conciliatory lovemaking, but by the sound of the key in the front door, succeeded by Jackie's voice calling 'Anybody 'ome?' Vivi's scowl deepened.

'Did you tell her you had the day off?'

'I might have done.' He got out of bed and shouted down the stairs, 'Be with you in a minute, love. We're not decent.'

So she was going to dump the kid on them again, thought Vivi sourly, while she and Spike took off somewhere on his motor bike. It wasn't the first time they had been landed with childminding duties; Jackie had adopted a policy of being nice as pie to Vivi's face, the better to exploit her ill-concealed soft spot for Cass (Vivi could never bring herself to use her real name).

'You'll have to change the nappies on your own this time,' Vivi informed Nick. 'I'm on picket duty. And besides, I've had just about enough of baby-sitting.'

'Be fair, doll, it's not all that often. Mostly they come here while we're out, we don't even know they've been.'

'Well I know when they've been because the fridge is always empty. And so is the jar of parking-meter money.'

'So what? I don't begrudge my own sister a bit of food and a few extra bob . . .'

It was an argument Vivi knew she couldn't win, which was why she chose not to mention the various bits of jewellery which had disappeared from the dressing table. Nick would only accuse her of mislaying the items and then jumping to malicious conclusions. Thwarted, she stomped off downstairs ahead of him to be accosted by a beaming Cass, who toddled out into the hall to greet her, arms outstretched, with a gleeful shout of 'Bibi! Bibi!'

Vivi bent to pick her up and gave her a quick, furtive hug. Try as she might not to get fond of the kid, it was impossible not to respond to her artless advances. And seeing her court Spike's attention in vain – he seemed totally indifferent to her – made Vivi want to make up for it, to tell her that fathers didn't matter, she had managed perfectly well without one and so would Cass, given time. The sooner Spike deserted the family the better.

It was then that she heard the sound of stifled sobs from the living room. Jackie was sitting there, eyes red and puffy, snivelling into a tissue.

'Are you okay?'

'Spike got picked up by the filth last night,' announced Jackie, blowing her nose. Aren't our policemen wonderful? thought Vivi. 'One of his mates fitted him up. Said he was in on this burglary. And he wasn't! They've set bail at five hundred quid. I asked Dad, but all he gave me was another sodding mouthful. I hate him.'

So now she was going to ask Nick instead, thought Vivi, as

Jackie poured out the story a second time to her brother. It must have been Spike who nicked her bracelet and earrings; she wished now that she had mentioned them. Cass, troubled by her mother's tears, began crying along.

'Vivi, do me a favour, love, and take Cass out for a walk, will you? Jackie and I have to talk.'

Weakening, Vivi strapped her into the pushchair and took her out to the shops for an ice cream on the way to the park. Cass grinned indiscriminately at passers-by, inducing a couple of old biddies to gurgle back at her and compliment Vivi on her pretty little girl. Cass wasn't particularly pretty in fact, but she had Nick's cheeky grin and sunny temperament. Vivi found herself wondering gloomily if Gemma was pregnant yet. She would no doubt do a Di and produce within a year of the wedding.

Once inside the park she let the child toddle alongside her for a bit, keeping a tight hold on her hand, talking to her constantly, whether she understood her properly or not, and listening intently to her burbled responses. Poor little brat. She might be well looked after physically, but what about mental stimulation? Another few years and that precious spark would have gone for ever . . .

After an hour or so, Vivi set off for home. She had just turned the corner of Nick's street when Jackie came running out of the house towards her, grabbed hold of the pushchair, turned it around, and took off without a word of explanation, leaving Vivi feeling as if she had just been mugged.

'So what was all that about?' she asked Nick.

'In a nutshell, I'm an even meaner bugger than Dad and she won't be coming round here no more ever again.'

'You didn't give her the money?'

'You think I'm soft in the head, don't you?' Vivi didn't answer. 'Look, I don't like Spike any more than you do. I just thought if he got to know the family, he'd act more responsibly. But if he's started thieving, I'm not going to be the one to bail him out. Satisfied?'

'Nothing to do with me,' shrugged Vivi. 'Can I go to the picket now, please?'

'I'll come with you,' said Nick, signifying a truce. 'But we'll have to get that wallpaper on the way. I've got a mate coming to hang it tomorrow, can't leave it any longer.'

They drove up to town via the local DIY emporium, where cosy nest-building couples were loading their trolleys with home improvements. Vivi felt almost as out of place as she had done in church the other day.

'What do you think of this one?' said Nick.

'If you like. Hurry up, this is taking for ever.'

Once she started picking out papers and curtains, she would be half way to treating Nick's place as home, the way she had never treated her own flat as home. Or even the house she had grown up in, somewhere she had longed to escape from at the earliest opportunity. They queued up at the check-out behind a snogging couple, their wedding rings still bright and shiny. If there was a one in three chance their marriage wouldn't survive, thought Vivi, what hope was there for someone like her?

'Shit,' said Nick, patting his pockets. 'I've come out without my wallet and cheque book.'

'I'll pay,' said Vivi, rummaging in her bag. He was very quiet on the way to the picket. It took Vivi all of five minutes to work out why.

'I'm awfully sorry, Gemma, but I'm not going to be home till very late. There's another bargaining session with ACAS set up for nine p.m. Which is good news, I hope. At least CC has agreed to stay out of it.'

'So what time should I expect you?'

'Early hours. Or not at all, if it goes on all night, which it may well do. Don't wait up for me and don't worry. Must go now. 'Bye.' He rang off.

Gemma turned the oven off and the television on. She had so looked forward to living in this beautiful house, to being the perfect wife. And now it seemed like a prison, and a lonely one at that. If only Harriet were here . . .

She jumped as she heard the doorbell, the third time it had rung since her return that morning. Yet again she crept out into the hall and peered through the spy-hole, consumed with a paranoid certainty that this time it would be CC, come to gloat, to let her know that he had instigated the strike deliberately, just in case she hadn't worked it out for herself. She had briefly contemplated staying with Mum for a while, to avoid him – she had nowhere else to go, after all. But her pride had got the better of her. And besides, she had to confront him sooner or later . . .

This time it was him at last, his face horribly distorted by the fisheye lens. There was a kind of warped relief in it, the reality was almost better than the suspense. Trembling, Gemma tiptoed downstairs to the basement kitchen at the back of the house. If she didn't answer the bell, she told herself feverishly, he would think she wasn't in and go away.

Was this to be her life from now on? Hiding like a fugitive behind locked doors? Please God let him close the paper down. I did my best for Gerald but I failed and I can't do any more . . .

She froze in horror as the front door opened and slammed shut again. 'Gemma!' boomed his voice from above. 'Gemma, I know you're in there! Ready or not, here I come!'

In her panic to escape via the back door, Gemma knocked over a kitchen chair, advertising her presence. Hearing his footsteps on the stairs, punctuated by the thump of his stick, she slid the bolts top and bottom, lacerating her fingers, only to find that the door was still double-locked, from the holiday, and the keys were upstairs, in her bag . . .

'Trying to run away from me, are you?' He stood in the doorway like Satan welcoming her to hell. 'That's not very hospitable, now is it?'

'Get out of here,' hissed Gemma, as he limped towards her. 'Get out before I call the police.' A futile threat; he was barring her way to the phone.

'The police? Come now. I'm hardly a trespasser. See the key you gave me?' He held it aloft.

'Where did you get that?' Stupid question. He must have got hold of Harriet's, or Gerald's, or even Vivi's, and had it copied.

'From you. You gave it to me so that I could come here whenever your husband was working late. Which he'll be doing a lot of from now on. Don't worry, there's no chance of us being disturbed. He'll be busy for most of the night.'

He advanced towards her, his mouth stretched in a rictus of anticipation.

'Don't touch me. If you touch me, I'll . . .'

'Come now. You're not going to make this difficult for both of us, are you? You're not going to force me to tell Gerald what's been going on between us, these past few weeks? Of course, he'll be furious with me, as well as with you. Most likely he'll refuse to work for me any more . . .'

'I don't care if he does. I don't care if you close the paper down, or sell it, I hope you do. I'm going to tell Gerald the truth. I'm going to tell him you raped me.' Which was what she should have done in the first place, if she hadn't been such a coward.

'Rape? Come now. You enjoyed it, you know you did. You were begging for it. I've thought about nothing else ever since. That's why I had to cut your honeymoon short, I couldn't bear to think of you with him. You're wasted on Gerald, you know that, don't you? You need a real man to satisfy you . . .'

He's going to do it to me again, thought Gemma, back to the wall. Seventy-four or not, he was bigger and stronger than she was, she wouldn't be able to stop him. She couldn't bear it. She couldn't bear to live this way any longer . . .

She would rather die.

## 11

'SHE STOLE YOUR wallet and cheque book, didn't she?' goaded Vivi, unable to button her mouth any longer. 'So she could help herself from your bank account and fence your credit cards to raise Spike's bail.'

'Most likely I left them at home,' said Nick, as Vivi made her usual fist out of parking the car. 'Or at work.'

'No you didn't,' said Vivi, with ruthless logic. 'It was your turn to pay for the meal last night, remember? You wrote a cheque and showed them your Barclaycard. I saw you put them back in your jacket pocket, the jacket you're wearing now, and you had no reason to take them out again between last night and leaving the house today.'

'Who are you, Miss Marple?'

'You weren't wearing your jacket when you came downstairs. All she had to do was go up to the loo, nip into the bedroom, and –'

'For God's sake belt up, will you? If she did, then I drove her to it by refusing to give her the money.'

How could a man who was hard as nails in his professional life be so pathetically soft when it came to his spoilt brat of a lying, thieving sister? He made the same kind of allowances for Jackie's putrid character, thought Vivi, as he did for hers.

'Your father's got absolutely no control over her,' she went on. 'She'll end up on the streets, and what's going to happen to the baby then?'

'That's rich coming from you. You were the one who did your pieces when she asked if she could come and live with us.'

'Us? I don't live with you, remember? As for "doing my pieces", I never said a word. You were the one who refused to take her in, not me.'

'You didn't need to say a word. You've always made it clear that you don't like her, that you don't want a kid around the place, that you want me all to yourself.'

'All to myself? I've told you a million times I want us both to keep our own space, I don't want to be a cosy twosome with you, with anyone . . .'

'Your trouble is you hate sharing people. You're even jealous of Gemma managing to hit it off with your mother.'

'Gemma's more than welcome to my mother!' lied Vivi, reeling under the onslaught of home truths. 'And you're one to talk about jealousy. Max Kellerman's only got to look at me and you start acting like a caveman.'

The mere mention of Max's name provoked a visible frisson, like swearing in front of a maiden aunt.

'At least I'm honest about it.'

'So why can't you be honest about Jackie? If you don't report those cards stolen right away, you'll be liable.'

'I'll report them missing, okay? Not stolen. I'll say I left my jacket on the tube. Now give that tongue of yours a rest, will you?'

But Vivi's tongue was still raring to go. They arrived outside the *Courier* building as Ferris senior's shift were lining on.

'Scab!' she yelled, pouncing on him and shoving a leaflet in his face. 'Blackleg! Management flunkey!'

Never mind that she was the proprietor's granddaughter, with a column of her own, to a union heavy like Bert Ferris she was a mere hackette, one who owed him some respect. Unable to let the insult pass, he wagged a callused finger in her face.

'Listen to me, love,' he began.

'Don't call me love, you patronising sexist pig. I'm not your love . . .'

'Listen to me, darling. I've been on more pickets in my time than you've had hot dinners.' God, what a cliché. 'A scab's someone who disobeys a union instruction to strike. And there isn't one.'

'Thanks to the likes of you! Thanks to the bunch of hypocrites who run the Chapel!'

Nick stood by silently, hands in pockets, making a show of not taking sides. Vivi was aware that everyone was watching and listening, too intent on the cabaret to bother to harangue the other workers who were crossing the picket. A few of them turned back voluntarily, but not many.

'The *Courier* NUJ's always supported you,' went on Vivi, playing to the gallery. 'And now you're spitting in our face. Talk about I'm all right, hack.'

There was a chorus of titters at this feeble witticism. Ferris senior didn't get the joke.

'We are supporting you. All the lads are contributing to your strike fund. Some of them, me included, are donating their wages in full . . .'

'Well, God knows you can afford it. You've been bleeding the paper white long enough!' Hardly the sort of sentiment a wise journalist voiced out loud.

'Get this hysterical bird out of my hair, will you son?' said Ferris, pushing Vivi to one side. 'What she needs is a bloody good shafting.' There was a supportive cheer from his mates.

'Come on,' sighed Nick, taking Vivi's arm. 'Let's go.'

'I'm not going anywhere with you!' spat Vivi, her dander well and truly up. She wrenched her arm free. 'You're as much of a traitor as he is!'

She knew she was going completely over the top, and she knew why, and so did he, but it was too late to back down now.

'I'll see you later then,' shrugged Nick, leaving her to it. 'It' being a deathly silence, with everyone acting as if she wasn't there. If a man had had a set-to with Ferris, he might have earned a round of slaps on the back for his pains. But such behaviour in a woman emasculated the males and alienated her fellow-females. Harriet wasn't the only one, thought Vivi, who wished she had been born a boy.

After the rest of the shift had arrived – or rather, once Nick had gone – there didn't seem much point in hanging around any longer. She had done what she had set out to do – picked another quarrel. 'See you later,' he had said, when he would reap the benefit of her rage and remorse, and afterwards she would look at him sleeping and hate herself for being the biggest bitch that ever walked the earth.

He had a genius for making her connive at her own humiliation. If she refused to pick up the phone tonight, he would simply turn up, con someone else into buzzing open the front door, and have a one-sided conversation with her on the landing, loud enough for Pulowska to hear, until Vivi gave in and admitted him. Alternatively, he might not phone, might not turn up, just to teach her a lesson, an even worse prospect. The only solution was not to go home at all . . .

So why not spend the night at Lansdowne Gardens? Nick would never think of looking for her there, knowing that Gemma was the last person she would confide in after a row. Nor would she now. She would claim she had come to keep her company; the latest bargaining session was expected to last all night, and ten to one Gerald would end up snatching a couple of hours' sleep on the couch in the management suite before starting work on the next day's paper. Yes, she would be nice to Gemma for a change, and earn herself some brownie points with Gerald into the bargain.

In fact Vivi couldn't help feeling sorry for her, losing out on her honeymoon. Still, that was the kind of business she had married in to. Fleet Street was no place for clock-watching home-lovers. Small wonder that so many deserted it for PR, periodicals and the provinces, bowing to the pressures that had finally broken a so-called hard man like Dad. In his case, of course, working late every night had been good cover for running a mistress. At least Gemma wouldn't have to worry about that kind of thing with Gerald. Nor would Gerald have to worry about a neglected wife seeking solace elsewhere. That pair were made for each other, right enough.

It was pouring when she got to the house. The old-fashioned roses in the front garden were out early this year, heads bowed under the weight of the rain, dripping perfumed tears into the sodden earth. There was no answer to Vivi's impatient ring on the bell. Perhaps Gemma was in the kitchen, you couldn't always hear it down there, specially if the radio was on. Getting wet now, Vivi fished for her keys – she supposed, vaguely, that she ought to return them now – and let herself in. Seeing the light on in the basement, she shed her damp jacket and went downstairs, calling 'Gemma! It's only me, Viv –'

The last syllable of her name died in her throat. Gramps was lying, face up, on the kitchen floor, covered in blood, with one of Harriet's Sabatier knives lying by his side. Vivi recoiled, horrified, as the faecal stench hit her, felt gingerly for a pulse and found none. He was dead. Not just dead. Someone had killed him. Someone must have broken in . . .

'Gemma!' she screamed. CC must have collected her from the airport, she thought numbly, fumbling for the illegal can of Mace she carried in her bag. He must have brought her home while Gerald went straight into the office, only to interrupt a burglary ... Holding the can at the ready to ward off attack, she began a feverish search of the house. 'Gemma!'

She wasn't in the dining room or the basement loo. She wasn't in any of the rooms on the ground floor. There were no open drawers, no overturned furniture, no sign of forced entry. Everything looked perfectly normal. 'Gemma!' Vivi forced herself to go upstairs, barely able to breathe for fear of what she might find there. Please God, don't let them have hurt Gemma. Don't let them have killed her too ...

'Gemma!' She was lying on top of the bed, fully clothed, facing away from the door. 'Gemma?' Vivi turned her on to her back. There was blood on her blouse and on her hands. Vivi put her ear to her chest. Her heart was still beating, but her breathing was shallow, her skin felt cool and damp, and she didn't respond to Vivi's frantic attempts to rouse her. What had happened to her? Had she fled upstairs to avoid the intruder and been hit over the head? Vivi struggled to remember the first aid she had learned at school. She mustn't move her, in case she had internal injuries. She must keep her warm, because of the shock. Stay alive, Gemma. If you die on me, I'll never forgive you ...

Trembling, she dialled 999, telling them to send an ambulance quickly, her sister had been seriously injured, and asking for the police as well, there had been a murder. She wrapped the duvet around Gemma and sat helplessly holding her hand, checking her breathing every few seconds, weeping with the sheer horror of it all. The wait seemed endless. If she'd been physically capable of it, and less fearful of doing her further damage, she would have carried her downstairs and driven her to St Mary's herself, speeding all the way ...

So intent was she on willing Gemma not to die that it was only when she heard the siren in the street outside that she noticed the bottles of pills on the bedside table. Half a dozen of them. Harriet's name was on the labels; the bathroom cabinet was always full of dog-ends of sleepers and tranks ...

All the caps were off. And every one of them was empty.

The Echo, *12 May 1984*

*VISCOUNT COLLINGTON SLAIN IN MYSTERY STABBING*
*GRANDSON'S WIFE RUSHED TO HOSPITAL*

Courier *proprietor Lord Collington, 74, was found dead of stab*
*wounds last night at the luxury Holland Park home of his*
*grandson, Gerald Lawrence, 33. Newlywed Mrs Gemma*
*Lawrence, 21, was rushed to St Mary's Hospital Paddington,*
*where her condition was described as critical following an*
*overdose of prescribed drugs. Police are waiting to question*
*Mrs Lawrence in connection with the incident. A post-mortem*
*on Lord Collington will be carried out later today . . .*

'In other words, she done it,' muttered Vivi, tossing the paper to
one side. She had despatched Nick to pick up the first editions,
which came out between ten and midnight. Coverage ranged from
a bare paragraph in a thinner-than-usual *Courier* to front-page
splashes in all the tabs. The old man's death should have been a
relief, a cause for jubilation, even. Mealy-mouthed hypocrisy to
pretend otherwise. But he had contrived to die as he had lived,
leaving fear and confusion behind him.

At first Vivi had clung to the belief that a third party must be
involved, but as the CID man had pointed out when he took her
statement, a third party would surely have stabbed her sister as
well, not forced her to take pills. Pills would have left her
conscious long enough to get help, and survive to give evidence.
No murderer would sit there, patiently waiting, until she passed
out.

'It's obvious what happened,' said Nick. 'The old bugger must
have tried it on. Gemma picks up a knife, tells him to back off,
there's a struggle, and he gets stabbed by accident. She thinks
Christ, I've killed him, panics, and ODs. Poor kid. She must have
been scared witless.'

'No,' Vivi insisted, still groping for another explanation. 'I can't
imagine Gemma knifing anyone to save her life. As for CC trying it
on, he was a bloody geriatric, for heaven's sake.'

'Don't kid yourself. I can tell a dirty old man when I see one,
even if you can't.'

'Are you saying I should have known? That I should have warned her against him? A man his age?'

'I'm saying you were too close to see it. Things look different to an outsider. Specially a professional dirt-dredger like me. I'm the one who should have warned her. I tried, once, but your brother jumped down my throat for casting aspersions, and you laughed and said he was past it.'

So she had. The thought of wrinklies having sex had always filled Vivi with incredulous ageist disgust. It was hard enough to accept that Harriet still indulged at the grand old age of fifty-one. Had the old man 'tried it on' before? If so, why hadn't Gemma told her? What the hell had been going on beneath the still, deep waters of Gemma's surface calm?

'How is she?' she demanded, jumping up as a haggard Gerald joined them in the hospital waiting room.

'She's regained consciousness, thank God. As far as they can tell there's no brain damage, they're going to run all kinds of tests on her tomorrow. She's still very groggy, I couldn't get much sense out of her. But at least she's out of danger now.' Out of danger, thought Vivi. That was a joke. She sat down again, weak at the knees with relief, and lit a fresh cigarette, or rather let Nick light it; her hands were shaking too much.

'I got Nick to ask *The Torch*'s crime people about solicitors,' she said, hiding behind a show of brisk practicality. 'They recommended Simon Bartlett, if we could afford him. Nick got hold of his home number, and I gave him the gist on the phone. He's on his way.'

'Thanks. Did you get through to Harriet?'

He seemed unnaturally calm. Gerald had always been the best of them at keeping his emotions in check. But Vivi sensed that it was the thinnest of veneers that could split wide open at any moment.

'She wanted to come home straight away but I persuaded her to stay put for the moment. The last thing we need is her faffing around, playing the drama queen and getting under everybody's feet.'

'What about Gemma's mother?'

'She should be here any time.' For all the good it would do. Barbara had had hysterics on the spot and passed the phone over to Fred, who had made Vivi repeat everything twice while he wrote it all down.

A moment later Simon Bartlett arrived, a chubby, rosy-cheeked individual who exuded an air of mildly dishevelled efficiency. No wonder he had come running, thought Vivi cynically, as he shook Gerald's hand. Talk about a juicy high-profile case to add to his portfolio. Bartlett specialised in high-class crime; thanks to his impressive track record, he was the first choice of insider dealers, embezzlers, and the parents of rich-kid drug-pushers, and charged accordingly. Recently he had handled the headline-making case of a well-known actress who had shot her lover, and another of a Harley Street dentist who had mercy-killed his ailing wife; both had got off with a suspended sentence. In principle, Vivi disapproved of the two-tier justice system, one for the rich and one for the rest, except when it came to getting Gemma off the hook.

'Thank you for coming out at this time of night,' said Gerald. 'But I'm afraid my wife's still in shock, she's in no fit state to answer any questions.'

'That's all to the good. The police can't actually ask her any till she's well enough to go down to the station. Which should give us plenty of time to talk to her first. Is there somewhere we can speak in private?'

'The house is still swarming with scene-of-crime people, we'd better go back to my office. Are you coming, Vivi?'

'You go on ahead, I'll join you there.'

She had to see Gemma before she left, riddled as she was with guilt at having shopped her, however unwittingly. If only she'd put two and two together before dialling 999 she could have disposed of Gemma's bloodstained clothes, left the old man's body in the kitchen till after the ambulance men had left, and then found some way of dumping it in the river, or in a back alley somewhere. A fanciful scenario, perhaps, not to mention an illegal one, but better than setting her own sister up for a murder charge.

'She'll be all right,' murmured Nick into her hair as she gave in, finally, to tears. 'The lawyers will sort it all out. It was obviously self-defence, the DPP won't even bring the case to court, you'll see.'

'Self-defence involves using what they call "reasonable force",' pointed out Vivi, sniffing. 'It doesn't give you a licence to kill. CC was an OAP with a gammy leg, remember. And a peer of the realm. And unarmed. It's not as if some low-life broke into the house and jumped her.'

If using Mace against a poor defenceless mugger was enough to land you in court – one of Vivi's pet hobby horses – what hope was there for Gemma? Only the other week she had sounded off in her column about a case of a woman convicted of the manslaughter of her husband, a brute who had beaten and sexually assaulted her all the years of their marriage. He had burned her genitalia with lighted cigarettes, raped and buggered her with bottles and broom handles, broken, at various times, her jaw, ribs, arm and collar bone, kicked her while she was pregnant, inducing a miscarriage, caused permanent damage to her kidneys, and threatened to kill her and their children if she ever tried to leave him or reported him to the police. Being neither big nor foolish enough to fight him on equal terms, she had finally resorted, in despair, to poisoning his food. Self-defence in Vivi's eyes, but not in those of the law. The raving misogynist of a judge, anxious to discourage similar outrages against his sex, had seen fit to send the poor bitch down for seven years, never mind that she had young children. Of course that woman had been poor, without connections, reliant on legal aid. On the other hand, her victim hadn't been Viscount Collington, CBE . . .

Gemma was still in intensive care; Vivi was granted five minutes with her and told not to tire her. She was as white as the sheet, attached to a drip, with a tube coming out of her nose. Vivi sat awkwardly by the bed, trying to be calm and positive and reassuring and above all not to cry.

Gemma opened her eyes. They were hideously bloodshot.

'How do you feel now?' said Vivi, feeling fatuous. Gemma didn't respond. 'Gemma, what happened?' Perhaps it was too soon to ask but she had to know.

'I killed him,' said Gemma thickly.

'Yes, but why?' No answer. 'Come on, Gem. You can tell me. I'm on your side.' Though why should she believe that? There had never been much evidence of it in the past.

More silence.

'Gerald's talking to a lawyer at the moment. You have to tell him exactly what happened, so that he can help you . . .'

'I don't want any help. I don't need a lawyer. I'm guilty. I did it. I'm a murderer.' Her voice was toneless, robotic. 'When the police come, I'm going to tell them that. I don't want anyone making excuses for me. I want to go to jail. I want Gerald to divorce me.'

She's still in shock, Vivi reminded herself, she doesn't know what she's saying.

'Of course he's not going to divorce you. Did the old man make a grab for you, or what?'

'I don't want to talk about it.'

Not to me, anyway, thought Vivi with a pang.

'Wait till you're feeling better. Then you can talk to Gerald. Whatever happened, I promise you he'll understand –'

'I wish you hadn't found me. I wish you'd left me to die. Go away. Go away and leave me alone.'

She shut her eyes, dismissing her. Vivi fell silent, afraid to harangue her further in her present feeble state. She sat by the bed until Gemma, exhausted from the effort of speaking, lapsed back into unconsciousness, and waited until she was sure, from the sound of her breathing, that she was really asleep. Then she bent over her and kissed her very lightly on the forehead before tiptoeing out of the room.


Gemma wished her mother would go away. Or at least stop nagging. This was the third, no fourth time she had told her that she didn't know what she was going to say to the neighbours, she and Fred would have to move away somewhere where nobody knew them.

'I just thank God your father isn't alive,' she lamented, wiping her eyes. 'This business would have killed him, that's for sure. And to think you won't confide in your own mother. Or even talk to that nice solicitor Gerald found for you. Do you want to be put away for murder?'

She would rather be put away for murder than admit to the far worse crime of being raped. She wished that the police would hurry up and arrest her, but they weren't even allowed to talk to her yet. And in the meantime everyone else insisted on treating her as if she were mad.

Why else would the sane, wholesome, unassertive Gemma have metamorphosed into a killer? They couldn't believe that the person who had wielded the knife had been the real her, that the other Gemma had been an imposter. Gerald's patient, anxious coaxing, like Vivi's insistent cross-examination and Mum's endless hand-wringing, made her want to scream. And the solicitor had already given up on her, passed her over to a psychiatrist who was doing his level best to prove that she was 'incompetent'.

'What people will think of me I just don't know,' Mum was bleating. 'They'll blame me, they always blame the parents when children go wrong. I knew you'd get yourself into trouble once you left home. You were always so secretive, I never knew what you were thinking . . .'

Gemma shut her eyes again, wishing she could shut her ears as easily. She hurt all over, especially her brain, which seemed to have escaped from the safety of her skull, leaving it as vulnerable as a mollusc without a shell, shrivelling under the pitiless onslaught of words. It shrivelled some more as she heard a knock at the door. Whichever one of her tormentors it was this time, she didn't want to see or speak to him, her, anyone, unless it was the police, at last, come to take her away, away from Mum's eternal yakking . . .

'Gemma. I came as soon as I heard.'

Striding past her mother, Daniel sat on the bed, stretched out his arms, and lifted her into the kind of hug you gave to a frightened child. Nobody else had done that, not Gerald, not Vivi, not her mother. It was as if they were all afraid to touch her.

'I don't know what to do with her, I really don't,' Mum resumed eagerly, seeking an ally in Daniel. 'The solicitor said to me, he said, they can only help her if she agrees to help herself. I told her time and again, she's my own flesh and blood, no matter what she's done I'll stand by her. I told her . . .'

'I'll bet you did,' muttered Daniel.

'I beg your pardon?'

'Mrs Palmer, would you mind excusing us for a moment? I'd like to talk to Gemma in private.'

Affronted at this polite but curt dismissal, Barbara marched, with much huffing and puffing, out of the room.

'Thank you,' Gemma managed to say. 'She's been driving me up the wall.' He adjusted the bed so that she could sit up and rearranged her pillows, giving her a second tantalising glimpse of a Daniel she had never seen before, warm and gentle and caring. 'She can't understand why . . .' She didn't finish the sentence.

'Why you're being so bolshie?' His voice was clipped, hard, the spell broken. He pulled up a chair and looked at her grimly, arms folded across his chest.

'I'm not being bolshie,' muttered Gemma, sheepish now. 'I just want to get it over with, that's all.'

'You mean, the pills didn't work so you'll settle for the next best thing. You don't just want to punish yourself, do you, you want to punish everyone else as well. Gerald, and Vivi, and Harriet and your mother, all the people you were scared to turn to for help. And I include myself in that. I should have known when I saw that picture that you were in trouble. No more stonewalling, Gemma. I'm not leaving this room till you tell me everything.'

He was right, she had wanted to make them all sorry. Gerald for being so obsessed with the paper, Harriet for the relentless pressure she had put her under, Vivi for saving her wretched life, Mum for having been proved right, in her ignorance, Daniel, for reasons she preferred not to analyse, and most of all, herself.

Anger had kept her silent; anger gave her her voice. She thought she had blotted the rape out of her mind, but now she forced herself to recall every appalling detail, seeking to nip Daniel's sympathy in the bud, to shock and repel him, to invite censure, most of all to test him. She lanced the wound and let the poison flood out, dizzy with the pain and relief of it. When the worst of it was over she searched his eyes for scorn, or at best pity. But all she could see was a reflection of her anger and something else, something even more threatening.

'He must have known I wouldn't say anything to Gerald,' she resumed, 'not on the day before the wedding. The only alternative was jilting him, and I couldn't bring myself to do that either.' That sounded like an excuse, and she hadn't meant to make excuses. 'I was stupid. I played into his hands.'

'What about the other day? Did it happen again?'

'No.' That was the only solace. 'But it would have done. I'd given in once before after all. I didn't even fight back, not hard enough, anyway. I remember thinking, if I get any bruises, Gerald will see them and ask how I got them. That was the worst part of it. Knowing I might have been able to stop it if I hadn't been such a coward . . .'

Another hideous flashback robbed her of speech for a moment. Daniel waited, not prompting her, not helping her, letting her take her time, while she explained how CC had got into the house, blamed herself for not anticipating it, and described how she had been trapped in the kitchen.

'He was so smug. He thought I would do anything to stop him closing down the paper. He'd even convinced himself that I'd enjoyed it the last time, that I'd just been playing hard to get. He kept saying he wanted me to give him a son, and what a fool we would make of Gerald together . . .'

She hesitated again, taking a long run at another hurdle of memory. This time Daniel reached for her hand and held it while the words tumbled out in a rush.

'That's when I grabbed the knife, from the rack on the wall behind me. But he just kept coming nearer and nearer, with that horrible leer on his face, he didn't think I'd dare to use it. I was afraid he'd get it away from me and use it to threaten me instead, so I raised my hand, like this, and brought the knife down as hard as I could. But he moved at the last minute, I just got him in the arm, and I knew it wouldn't stop him, so I did it again. And again. I can't remember how many times. And then he sort of tottered to one side, and I managed to get past him. But he wasn't dead, not then. I mean in films, people just keel over instantly, but he didn't, he was still on his feet, so I locked myself in the downstairs loo, next door, before he could come after me. I know it sounds ridiculous, that I should have got out of the house, but I wasn't thinking straight, I thought he was right behind me. I don't know how long I stayed in there, I was too scared to come out in case he was lying in wait, and the window was too small to climb through. But after an hour or so, when I didn't hear anything, I began to think, God, what if he's bleeding to death in there? I waited, and waited, and then I finally forced myself to take a look, and that's when I realised I'd killed him. And that I'd have to explain why.'

And then Gerald would know that she wasn't the pure, unsullied virgin she had pretended to be. That she had been defiled by the man she hated most in all the world, the man who had ruined the few, false days of their marriage.

'So I decided to kill myself,' she finished lamely. 'The easy way out.' Even though it hadn't seemed the least bit easy at the time. If she hadn't spent so long trying to pluck up courage, Vivi would have found two corpses, not just one.

'Well, now you're going to do something difficult.' His grip on her hand tightened, as if to imbue her with strength, making her feel weaker and more helpless than ever. 'You're going to survive.'

Yes, thought Gemma, bleakly. She should have thought of that. Living was a much better punishment than dying.


12 May 1984
Dear Vivi
I don't want to intrude at a time like this. But if there's anything I can do to help, just say the word.
Max


'You're both handling her all wrong,' Nick had said. 'Let me speak to her.' Only for Vivi to tell him to mind his own business, he ought to be worrying about his own delinquent of a sister, not hers. And then, when the full, horrifying truth came out, it was Nick who had held her in his arms while she wept and raged.

Trust Daniel, cool and detached as always, to arrive like the cavalry and show the rest of them up. The whole family, bar him, had contributed to Gemma's downfall, however unintentionally. Gerald by being so wrapped up in his work that he hadn't noticed anything wrong. Vivi by dismissing the frantic signals Gemma had sent out, on the morning of the wedding, as pre-nuptial nerves. Harriet by transforming the pretty little country mouse into a raving beauty, thereby inflaming the old man's lust. And all three of them by impressing on her, in their different ways, that Gerald's future was in the balance, thus preparing a perfect seed bed for CC's threats to take root and grow to beanstalk proportions.

It was so bloody typical of her to have suffered in silence. She had always been a pleaser and appeaser. Vivi had learned aggression at her mother's knee, grown up in an atmosphere of marital strife, learned to play her parents off against one another. Whereas Gemma had come from a peaceful home where Dad's word was unquestionably law and Mum the quintessential little woman. Vivi could argue with Dad, and play up, and swear at him with impunity, knowing that Harriet would get the blame for turning her against him. Gemma had no such fall-back position.

She had had to live with the moody, sexist bastard, she had been trained from birth to be the kind of daughter he had always wanted.

Dad was every bit as guilty as the rest of them. Thanks to him Gemma had grown up expecting to be bullied. By him, by her nagging cow of a mother, by the gang of Alchester mini-thugs who had divested her of her pocket money – when Vivi wasn't around to fight them off – and most of all by Vivi herself. Not once had Gemma ever told tales on her, however great the provocation, for fear of reprisals. She had learned to bottle up her anger, accepted the futility of fighting back, mastered the art of stubborn, passive resistance. They had all done a wonderful job of teaching her to be a victim, a sitting target for CC, the biggest bully of them all. Even now, despite Daniel's pep talk, she was giving in to force majeure rather than making a stand.

After a carefully managed interview, conducted in the presence of her solicitor, Gemma was charged with murder, hauled before a magistrate and mercifully bailed, albeit to the tune of fifty thousand pounds. Whereupon she was transferred to a high-class private shrinkerie, with a view to securing sufficient gold-plated psychiatric evidence to mitigate her alleged crime.

The presence of 'provocation', Simon Bartlett explained, was sufficient in itself to reduce murder to manslaughter, with the onus on the Crown to disprove that provocation had taken place. Which sounded like good news, on the surface. It wasn't up to Gemma to provide any evidence that she had been in fear of rape, which was just as well because there was none; a medical examination had revealed no physical trauma to corroborate her story, or to counter the credibility problem, given the age and social standing of her attacker.

On the other hand, they were on shaky ground with self-defence. Again the burden rested with the prosecution to prove that the claim of self-defence was untenable, but they would make hay out of the post-mortem, which had revealed not one but four stab wounds, which was three too many to make a convincing case for 'reasonable force'. None, as it turned out, had pierced any arteries or vital organs; the old man was deemed to have taken over an hour to die, as a result of heart failure brought on by shock. But that didn't alter the fact that he had died as a result of his wounds, and Gemma's neglect to summon the ambulance which might have saved his life did her case no good at all.

It would be up to a jury to decide on the issues both of provocation and self-defence, which was why the initial charge remained one of murder. If the jury accepted provocation, which seemed likely, they would find Gemma guilty of manslaughter. If they accepted self-defence, which was much less certain, they would acquit her. The claim of diminished responsibility was another way of reducing murder to manslaughter, and if accepted would help secure a lighter penalty, but this time the burden of proof rested with the defence.

Counsel's opinion was that Gemma's best bet was to avoid a trial altogether. There was a good chance that the Director of Public Prosecutions would accept a plea of 'guilty to manslaughter with diminished responsibility', backed by the necessary psychiatric reports – the best verdict the defence could reasonably hope for if the case went to court. This way there would be a good chance of a suspended sentence, or even probation, depending on the judge. Judges were unpredictable, of course, Bartlett added, to cover himself, but less so than juries, who were notoriously subjective. If Gemma went for broke by relying on a jury to acquit her on the grounds of self-defence, she ran the risk, however slight, that they would swing the opposite way and convict her of murder instead, a verdict which carried a mandatory life sentence.

On the one hand, Vivi accepted the logic of this argument. She shuddered at the thought of Gemma's fate being decided by twelve random members of the public. Talk about a lottery. On the other hand, it seemed outrageous that she should have to resort to pleading guilty to anything at all. Gemma went along with the advice in typically passive fashion; as the self-perceived architect of her own misfortune, she displayed a masochistic need to suffer for her so-called crime, as if she hadn't suffered enough already. Gerald, meanwhile, was anxious to spare her the trauma of a trial, and Daniel, laconic as always, said merely that he hoped bloody Bartlett knew what he was doing.

He ought to, at the rates he was charging. Not that Gerald needed to worry about money any more. The only good thing to come out of the whole ghastly mess was a will which had not, despite years of threats, disinherited him in favour of Battersea

Dogs' Home. On the contrary, CC had left him everything, including all his *Courier* shares, 'and I wish him all the joy of them, he's wished me dead long enough'. He had chosen not to increase Vivi's holding – her punishment, no doubt, for spurning his attempts to turn her against her brother – or even to leave her a token bequest, but Vivi was too relieved for Gerald's sake to care.

The full worth of the estate would not be known until the accountants had finished valuing CC's assets and calculating the inheritance tax, which would be substantial; he had never taken any steps to minimise it by setting up trusts or disposing of property while he was still alive, having more affection for the Inland Revenue than for his family. Even so, there should still be a good few million to play with once the Exchequer had taken its cut, with most of it earmarked for the revamping of *The Courier*. Gerald's commitment to the paper seemed as strong as ever, despite all that had happened, work being his only refuge from worrying himself sick about Gemma. Vivi preferred not to speculate as to how they had fared on their honeymoon, or what long-term effects all this would have on their marriage. Other men might turn against wives who had been raped, but not Gerald, not her brother; he would stick by Gemma through thick and thin. There were some questions she would never ask them, some topics she would never discuss with anyone else, even Nick. Not only out of profound embarrassment but because their privacy had been invaded quite enough already.

The other positive outcome of the old man's death was the calling off of the journalists' strike, pending fresh negotiations with Gerald as the new proprietor. The atmosphere on the paper was tense but hopeful, with the old guard busy calculating their severance payments, and the new, like serfs released from bondage, looking forward to a better world.

Meanwhile there was no keeping Harriet at arm's length any longer. Having phoned long-distance a dozen times a day, often the worse for drink, she turned up, unannounced, at Lansdowne Gardens one morning, with an unpaid taxi bill and a Californian beach bum called Seth. Daniel broke the news to Vivi on the phone while she was struggling to complete her column against a fast-approaching deadline.

'She refuses point blank to stay here with Gerald and me,' he told her. 'The minute she walked in she got the screaming ab-dabs, reckoned the place was haunted. And suggesting Little Moldingham or the old man's flat in Albany was a waste of time, for the same reason. So I'm afraid it looks like you're lumbered.'

Vivi groaned. Harriet would take complete possession of the flat, run up enormous phone bills, and harp on endlessly about how nice the place could be if only Vivi would let her do it up. But she didn't have the heart to tell her to piss off to an hotel. She was her mother, after all, worse luck.

'I'm so sorry to be a nuisance, darling,' said Harriet, taking over the phone, 'but I'll start house-hunting right away. I just had to be near you all, to do my bit to help, I felt so cut off, not knowing what was going on, and fretting about poor Gemma . . .'

Her speech had that familiar hectic edge.

'Have you been drinking?' Harriet could never resist the free booze on planes.

'Oh darling, don't nag. After all I've been through can you blame me? It won't be for long, just till we find somewhere else . . .'

'We?' echoed Vivi, playing the prude.

'It's not as if CC's around to disapprove any more,' Harriet pointed out petulantly. 'Old hypocrite that he was. So don't you start.'

Seth turned out to be a muscle-bound blond with a Sundance Kid moustache, sweating fragrantly under the weight of Harriet's luggage, which Daniel had left him to carry unaided. Vivi refused to discuss family business in his presence, so he was banished to the kitchen, with a hospitable Harriet inviting him to help himself from Vivi's fridge.

'This dreadful business won't hold up probate, will it?' she said, offering round duty-free cigarettes.

'Gemma's not a direct beneficiary of the will,' said Vivi, 'and no one's suggesting that Gerald was an accessory to the crime, for want of a better word. So there's no bar to him inheriting. Which is just as well. He had to take out a whopping bank loan to raise bail, and he's been running up a small fortune in legal fees and hospital bills. You know what rip-off artists shrinks are. Now they've got her in their clutches they won't want to let go of her in a hurry. Not at two hundred and fifty quid a day.'

'I don't suppose it's occurred to you,' put in Daniel, 'that Gemma might actually need treatment? Just because she puts on a brave face for visitors doesn't mean this is all a put-up job.'

'I never said it was,' retorted Vivi. 'I just think it's wrong that she has to jump through all these bloody hoops when —'

'Two hundred and fifty a day?' echoed Harriet, horrified. 'But that's absurd . . .'

'Not you too,' exploded Daniel. 'You're all more concerned with money, and the will and the bloody paper than you are with her! Which considering you're all to blame for what happened is adding insult to injury!'

'Well, I'm not to blame, I'm sure,' protested Harriet.

'Not half you're not,' accused Vivi. 'Talk about leading a lamb to the slaughter.'

'That's not fair. If I'd just left her to her own devices, you would all have accused me of cold-shouldering her. You and Gerald were both too busy to spend any time with her, the poor child relied on me for advice and guidance. At least, I thought she did. Why she didn't confide in me, I'll never know . . .'

'I've got to go,' interrupted Daniel impatiently. 'I'm meeting someone for lunch.'

Vivi saw him down to his hire car, resenting him for dumping Harriet on to her, for walking away, for taking the moral high ground over Gemma.

'It's all very well for you,' she accused him, 'turning up out of the blue and lecturing the rest of us about what we should and shouldn't have done. You weren't around at the time, you never are. And soon you'll be gone again. You always manage to duck responsibility for everything.'

'And you've never ducked responsibility, I suppose?'

'I'm not saying we're different. I'm saying we're alike.' Hadn't she modelled herself on Daniel for as long as she could remember? 'Except that it's easier for men, the way everything always is.'

'That just shows how little you know about men,' said Daniel, leaving her wondering.

## 12

*Summer 1984*

VIVI HAD HAD enough. Enough of having her sleep disturbed by the grunts and thumps and squeals from the bedroom next door. Enough of Seth's moustache-clippings infesting the wash-basin like so many dead insects. Enough of Harriet helping herself to her hats and shoes and earrings – the only items of her wardrobe that fitted her, thank God – and overwatering her precious pot plants. And when Harriet heard that Max was in London and took it upon herself to invite him to supper, to make up a cosy little foursome with Seth and Vivi, that was the last straw.

'Stop trying to play Cupid, will you?' Vivi flew at her. Seth, who was into meditation, was sitting cross-legged on the floor, chanting mantras, with a beatific smile all over his stupid face. It was impossible to have a satisfactory row with him around. 'I've told you before, I don't even like the man.' That much was true enough.

'I really don't know what you've got against him when he's always been perfectly charming to you. Most girls would jump at the chance to get to know him better.'

'Well, find one of them and invite her instead because I won't be here. I'm seeing Nick tomorrow night.' Which she wasn't; Nick would be away on a running job till the end of the week.

'What you see in that boy I can't imagine.' Here we go again, thought Vivi, feeling her temper come to a rapid boil. 'He's not even good-looking. It was bad enough when you kept bringing home all those horrible punks and Hell's Angels and whatever, just to annoy me, but I thought you'd grown out of all that. And now you come up with this gor-blimey type with a shop steward for a father . . .'

'God, you make me sick with your snobbery and your ignorance. You're one to talk, with that pea-brained human vibrator of yours. Nick's kind, and funny, and intelligent and a bloody good reporter and I love him!'

There. She had said it. Thank God he hadn't been here to hear it. Having shocked Harriet into gratifying silence – love was not a word her cynical daughter used lightly – Vivi couldn't very well retract her ill-considered declaration. But neither could she live with the embarrassment of having made it. Carried away with her own momentum, she began packing a suitcase.

'Where are you going?' demanded Harriet.

'Nick's place. If I stay here another minute you'll end up with a knife in your guts like the old man.'

'You don't mean you're moving in with him?'

'You've always wanted me to settle down, haven't you? Well, perhaps you'll get your wish at last.'

That should give her a few sleepless nights, thought Vivi grimly. She knew that she would repent at leisure. But that had never stopped her doing anything in the past. And besides, it was just a temporary thing. Once the old man's funds were released Harriet would be buying a place of her own. As Vivi would be quick to point out to Nick, if he took too much for granted.

Nonetheless, she began to have second thoughts on the drive to Stockwell. This was another step down the slippery slope. This was what he had wanted all along. Just because he had never suggested moving in with him didn't mean he hadn't seduced her into it, tapped that deep, inadmissible need of him. It frightened her how emotionally dependent she had become on him, and how vulnerable that made her. A perverse, destructive part of her wanted to drive him away, to go back to being the brave, free, tough, self-sufficient Vivi he had weakened and corrupted. He had seemed so safe and unthreatening at the beginning. And now he made the likes of Max Kellerman seem positively harmless by comparison.

Just as well he wouldn't be home till Friday; it would give her time to think better of it. He was holed up in a *Torch* hide-out with a couple whose baby had been abducted and later recovered, a human-interest our-week-of-hell tear-jerker that they would be milking for all it was worth, running the story over three days.

Nick had pinched it from a rival paper with typical aplomb. It was common practice, following a buy-up, to transfer the interviewees to an hotel and guard them round the clock, to keep them away from the competition. The reporter assigned to the case, however, had recently moved in a new girlfriend, and never missed a chance to brag about their sexual exploits, leading Nick to suspect that he would book the couple in somewhere as near as possible to Basildon, where he lived, and then desert sentry duty in favour of a night of lust. Working on this hunch, he had identified the most likely hotel, recognised the luckless hack's car in the car park, waited for him to drive off into the night, and bowled into reception half an hour later, posing as a colleague of his and announcing that he had to move the couple urgently to a new, secret location because another paper had found out where they were. The bleary-eyed scribe had arrived next morning to find his property stolen and his job on the line.

Which just proved what a ruthless, thick-skinned bastard Nick could be. So why did he have to be so soft and sensitive with her? Why didn't he make her work for his love, instead of giving it away? What should have been a precious, well-earned reward felt like a charity hand-out, a measure of his generosity rather than her worth. And yet he wasn't so soft that he didn't manage to get his own way in practically everything, just as he was doing at this very moment.

Nick's house had been transformed in recent months, thanks to new plumbing and wiring and the installation of central heating. Never mind all his talk about it being a good investment, he was a domestic creature at heart, who wanted a wife waiting for him at home and kids to rush at him as he came through the door. So why hadn't he found himself a nice, cheerful, uncomplicated girl who would put him first and make him happy? Why did he have to make life so difficult for both of them?

As Vivi let herself in she heard Cass's plaintive wail from the living room; Jackie must have found out that Nick was away and moved in for the duration. Sure enough the living room was full of baby paraphernalia, including the cot and high chair, with Cass sitting woefully in her playpen, her normally sunny expression contorted by misery. There was no sign of her parents; they must have gone upstairs, damn them, leaving her to cry.

'It's okay,' soothed Vivi, lifting her out of her cage. She was wet, poor little brat . . . It was then that she spotted the note, labelled 'Nick', attached by safety pin to the front of Cass's little pink jumper.

*Dear Nick*
*I rang the paper but they wouldn't tell me where you were. Spike said we had to get away, the police are trying to stick him with another burglary. We've found this squat but it's damp and it's got cockroaches. If I take Casey she'll get sick and if I leave her with Dad he won't give her back, not unless I leave Spike and go home. I can't afford a minder but you can and I'll come and fetch her as soon as we get a place. Don't be mad at me.*
*Love Jackie*

So Spike had jumped bail, surprise surprise. God, what a fool Jackie was. Didn't it occur to her that Nick might not be back tonight? As for finding a minder, what would happen when he was away, like now?

'Are you hungry, Cass?' Vivi soothed, changing her nappy. 'How about some scrambled eggs?' Just as well she had got in some practice at this, willy nilly. Jackie had left a large holdall stuffed with clothes, toys and toiletries; supper over, Vivi took Cass upstairs, ran some baby bubble bath under the tap, and spent a gleeful half hour racing her two plastic ducks and making huge puddles on the floor. She had just dressed her in her night things and started telling her a bedtime story when the phone rang. There was the sound of pips at the other end.

'Nick?' Jackie's voice.

'Nick's not here. He won't be back till Friday. Cass – Casey's all right. I read your note.'

'You're not to dump her on to my dad. You're not to –'

'Your dad and I aren't on speaking terms, remember?' Vivi muzzled the accusations and reproaches. She didn't want Jackie turning up and dragging the kid off to some filthy vermin-infested squat. 'Don't worry, I'll stay here with her till Nick gets back, and then it's up to him.'

A strangled sob.

'I do l-love her,' croaked Jackie. 'That's why I couldn't take her with me. She catches cold ever so easy. But this is the only way Spike'n'me can be t-together . . .' The pips went again. 'I've no more change.' And then, in a last desperate plea, before the line went dead, 'Take care of her for me, Viv, won't you?'

I'll take care of her, thought Vivi grimly. And I'll do it a hell of a lot better than you.


6 April 1984
> Gerald's fiancée offered to paint my portrait. I was reluctant but she flattered me into it. A charming girl. Although Gerald and I have never seen eye to eye, I am glad to see him settling down at last.


9 April 1984
> My first sitting with Gemma. Afterwards she begged me to stay and talk for a while, saying she was lonely. A very beautiful young woman. And a very flirtatious one. I can see now how she brought Gerald out of his shell.


12 April 1984
> I arrived for my sitting today to find the flat ridiculously overheated, and Gemma wearing shorts and a skimpy top. When I complained of the heat, she suggested I take off my jacket and tie. Afterwards she sat down next to me on the settee and began to cry. When I asked what was the matter, she complained that Gerald neglected her. Then before I could stop her, she was kissing me and removing her clothes and begging me to make love to her. I told her no, she was engaged to my grandson, and if she compromised me like this I would have to cancel the commission . . .


Gemma read on, appalled, acutely aware of Gerald watching her. The certified transcript of CC's diary ran to fifteen typed pages and recounted how she had supposedly seduced him, claiming that Gerald couldn't satisfy her sexually and confessing to a fetish for older men. He listed several futile attempts to end the affair, with a hysterical Gemma threatening to create a scandal or even —

horrors – to kill herself if he refused to see her again. All such encounters culminated in another steamy, minutely detailed sex session. The final entry was dated the day of his death.

11 May 1984
*Gemma phoned me at the office on her return from honeymoon, begging to see me again. Gerald will be working late tonight, she said, and we can have several hours alone together. The usual dirty talk. How can any woman look so innocent and be so depraved? When I told her that this cannot go on now that she is married she threatened to come to the office and cause a scene. So like a fool, I have agreed to go to the house, in the hope that I can make her see sense . . .*

Gemma looked from Gerald to the solicitor and back again.

'You surely don't believe any of this, do you?'

'No one's suggesting that we believe it, Mrs Lawrence,' said Simon Bartlett. 'But now that this diary has come to light, neither the police nor the Director of Public Prosecutions will be inclined to ignore its existence. Our intended plea of diminished responsibility was based on the Crown accepting, in principle, your own account of events. At the time there was nothing to contradict your story. Now, unfortunately, there is.'

'You're saying that the diary is acceptable as evidence?'

'That is a matter for the judge to decide, at the hearing. But the prosecution will be pressing for him to allow it, and we have to be prepared for that eventuality. The handwriting has already been authenticated.'

'But why did he invent all this? He couldn't have known what was going to happen!'

'To cover his back, presumably, in case you exposed him,' said Bartlett. 'Or it may simply have been lurid fantasy.'

Gemma shuddered, assailed by an image of CC drooling over his home-made pornography.

'So how do we prove that it's a pack of lies?'

'The defence doesn't have to prove anything, Mrs Lawrence, apart from diminished responsibility. The burden of proof, as regards everything else, rests with the prosecution. But you can see that there's no way we can avoid a trial, in the circumstances . . .

unless, of course, you chose to amend the terms of your plea.'

It took Gemma a moment to catch his drift.

'You mean . . . admit that what he says about me is true? That I killed him in a fit of passion because he tried to break things off? You're not seriously suggesting that I make a false confession?'

'I'm not suggesting anything, Mrs Lawrence. I'm simply clarifying your position. We've already discussed the perils of pleading not guilty to a murder charge, rather than guilty to manslaughter. And that was before we knew about the diary.'

'In other words, if I stick to my original story, the Crown won't accept my guilty plea any more, and if I go to trial a jury might convict me of murder?'

'In a nutshell, yes.'

'So I have a choice between lying, in the hope of a lighter sentence, and telling the truth and perhaps going down for life?'

'I would never advise a client to lie,' said Bartlett impassively. 'That would be unethical.'

Still Gerald didn't speak. But Gemma could guess what he was thinking. To twelve randomly chosen members of the public, CC's side of the story would seem far more plausible than her own. Easy enough to believe that he might have been tempted into an affair. Life in the old dog yet. And that he had tried to end it. But rape? At his age? Never! The little hussy was obviously making it up . . . God. Surely Gerald didn't think that too?

'Then I'd better stick to the truth, hadn't I?' said Gemma. 'I'd better go in the box and tell the whole story. After all, I'm the only eyewitness we've got.' Still Gerald didn't comment.

'As long as you realise,' said Bartlett, 'that if you waive your right to silence you open yourself up to cross-examination.'

He doesn't think I'm up to it, thought Gemma. Evidently he had expected her to take the soft option; she had sold her soul to CC once already, after all. All the more reason not to do it again. For the first time since it had happened, she was glad to be still alive and able to defend herself. The diary was like an absolution, relieving her of guilt and remorse. She wouldn't let that evil old man continue to harass her from beyond the grave, wouldn't let people believe his filthy masturbatory lies about her . . .

Giving in to him had cost her her self-respect. And now she had a chance to get it back.

*

'You mean there's no money at all?' echoed Vivi incredulously, shushing a fractious Cass.

'No,' said Gerald heavily. 'There's less than no money at all. In accountancy parlance, the total value of the old man's assets is exceeded by the sums borrowed against them, resulting in a net deficit. In simple language he hocked just about everything, including the freehold of the *Courier* building, which he managed to do without the board knowing anything about it. The deeds to Collington Hall, the flat in Albany, the house in Cannes, they're all being held as security for loans. As for his portfolio of investments, he's been selling them off, year by year. Given that he didn't have an heir worthy of the name, as he never ceased to remind me, I suppose it made sense not to leave anything behind him. No wonder he didn't cut me out of his will. He didn't need to. He's even borrowed against the shares he so kindly left me.'

So far Gerald had maintained a frozen, white-knuckled calm, sustained by the prospect of being his own master at last. But now that CC had delivered the final blow, he seemed near to breaking point, visibly struggling to maintain his customary rigid self-control.

'But why did the banks keep on lending him money?' said Vivi, still too stunned to take in the full significance of the news. 'Didn't they check up on what other debts he had? Didn't they ask to see any paperwork?'

'CC was a distinguished and ostensibly wealthy public figure. He seems to have spread the loans here there and everywhere, used one to pay the interest on another, conned people right and left. Nobody seems to have questioned his good faith, on the contrary they were falling over themselves to oblige him. At that level business is done on a handshake over a boozy lunch at somebody's club. If he'd lived he would have carried on getting away with it, perhaps indefinitely.'

And his family had been taken in by the charade, thought Vivi, along with everybody else. All the things they had seen as indicators of his wealth had in fact been consuming it. CC had always maintained a hugely extravagant life style – three luxurious homes, all with live-in staff, a private jet on permanent standby to commute between them, racehorses stabled with one of the top trainers in the country, and a reputation as a lavish host.

And of course the biggest status symbol and money-gobbler of them all, *The Courier*, the emblem of his power. He must have spent the last thirty years frittering away his father's fortune, intent on spending every penny of it before he died. What a waste of a life. What an exercise in greed and spite. And all because he didn't have a son.

'We don't know the half of it yet, of course,' Gerald went on, 'but what we do know is that a dozen different banks are holding *Courier* share certificates against outstanding loans. I can't see them forming any kind of useful controlling consortium, so unless one of them's prepared to buy the others out, or an outside investor is prepared to pay them all off, they'll probably end up closing the paper down.'

Vivi exchanged glances with Daniel, who was standing there, arms folded, saying nothing. Harriet hadn't been included in the family conference. Gerald, anticipating hysterics, no doubt, had put off the evil moment till she returned from a weekend visit to friends in the country. In high dudgeon at Vivi's decampment, she had spent the last week house-hunting and had set her heart on a dear little mews in Chelsea, a snip at a hundred and eighty grand.

'What's going to happen about Gemma?' said Vivi. 'How are you going to manage to pay the legal fees, or keep her in that nursing home?' Gerald had been counting on his inheritance to pay the astronomical cost of hiring a top QC to represent her in court. Theoretically, a top QC had to take legally aided cases, if it came to that, but in practice he might well prove 'too busy' to do so. 'I mean, you can have all my savings, right this minute, but they're not going to be nearly enough to –'

'Thank you,' said Gerald, interrupting her, 'but I'll manage. The house is already up for sale, neither of us wants to live here any more.'

'Could be hard to find a buyer, in the circumstances,' pointed out Daniel, speaking for the first time. 'I can always raise a loan against salary to help you out . . .'

'Whereas I soon won't have a salary,' said Gerald touchily. 'Be that as it may, Gemma's my wife, my responsibility, and I'd prefer to take care of her myself, thank you all the same. I'm late for another meeting with the bloody accountants. I'll keep you both posted.'

He left, slamming the front door behind him. There was a vein throbbing in Daniel's temple, belying his apparent sang-froid.

'I hate to be the one to say it,' he shrugged, with forced flippancy, tapping the ash off his cigarette, 'but what Gerald needs is someone filthy rich enough to redeem the old man's shares, pump the paper full of cash, and keep him on the staff at a big fat salary. Any ideas?'

Vivi's heart stalled briefly and then revved back into juddering life.

'I wish I had,' she said.


For once Vivi was glad that Nick was soft on his sister. Though in fact on this occasion he had taken his cue from her. Without Vivi playing peacemaker for a change, there would have been a deadlock, with Nick unwilling to take charge of such a young child, and Jackie stubbornly refusing his alternative offer to set her up in a flat, well aware that if he knew where she was living he would shop Spike to the police. As things were, Cass was safe, thank God, for the moment at least.

'I'm still not happy about this,' said Nick when Jackie had gone, having put her daughter to bed. 'If you weren't going to this press junket tonight, I'd tail her back to this squat and then have a quiet word with one of my tame coppers. I'll find a minder tomorrow.'

'It's not worth it,' said Vivi nobly, still striking a careful pose between nonchalance and martyrdom. 'Another week of roughing it and Jackie will have had enough, you'll see. I can manage a bit longer.'

'Are you sure you don't mind?'

'Of course I mind. But you've had to put up with a lot from me lately. My turn. And it's not fair on the kid to dump her on some stranger. None of this is her fault, after all.'

'Well, if it means you moving in for a bit, I'd be a fool to knock it, wouldn't I?'

No longer sure who was manipulating whom, Vivi returned his kiss, if not his 'I love you'. It never ceased to amaze her how unembarrassed he was about saying it, how he made it sound the most natural thing in the world.

'Do you really have to go to this do?' he coaxed. 'I was looking forward to a night at home, after being stuck in that hotel all week.'

'The sooner I leave, the sooner I'll be back.' Vivi, who had lied all her life with the greatest panache, hated lying to Nick. But she was nervous enough already about meeting Max without inviting Nick to put the mockers on it.

He was waiting for her at the restaurant, an unfashionable one, chosen by Vivi, as being somewhere no one was likely to spot them; if this encounter was fruitful, she didn't want any of the credit for it. And if it wasn't, all the more reason to keep it secret. He stood up to greet her and held out his hand. Vivi shook it, feeling like a dried-out alcoholic faced with an open bottle of Scotch.

'I don't flatter myself this is a social call,' he said, going straight to the point. 'As a matter of fact, I know why you're here.'

'So tell me why I'm here,' said Vivi, trying to sound off-hand.

'Because your grandfather left nothing but debts. Because you're looking for a buyer for *The Courier* and you think I might be interested.'

Damn him to hell for robbing her of the advantage of surprise, for making her look flat-footedly obvious.

'Who told you?' The news hadn't been made public yet.

'I was trying to do business with the old man at one time, remember? And despite my reputation as a chancer, I avoid bad debts like the plague. Unlike the financial institutions he had dealings with, I made a point of checking him out. And put him on my black list.'

'How the hell did you manage to rumble him when nobody else did?' She realised, too late, that the question must sound naïve.

'Come now. There's no such thing as information that can't be bought, as a journalist you ought to know that.' He broke off to discuss the menu, chatted interminably to the waitress about the dishes of the day, consulted Vivi politely about her tastes in wine and did she prefer still or fizzy water? Even in a second-rate place like this, he managed to get treated like royalty.

'How's your sister bearing up?' he asked, changing the subject.

Now that it looked as if Gemma would have to go to trial, Vivi had been spreading the real story at every opportunity, and she did so now, anxious to counteract the inevitable rumours about

Gemma being some kind of scarlet woman. Even if CC hadn't written that diary, people would have dreamed up a similar theory for themselves. Anyone as good-looking as Gemma had to be a scheming little slag, now didn't she? The digression gave her time to gather her wits and review her intended approach.

'Obviously the old man was thinking like a journalist,' she said. 'If you know bloody well you're misquoting someone, and you think they might make trouble, you keep a false record of the interview, don't you? If you've got any sense. I know people who've rewritten entire shorthand notebooks for the benefit of the Press Council, beats me why they bother to ask for them at all. Or how that diary can be taken as proof of anything except a warped imagination.'

'If there's anything I can do to help . . .'

'That's why I'm here, remember?' And then, reluctant to sound like a supplicant, 'But that doesn't mean I'm asking for any favours. You need a Fleet Street showcase for Kellerman technology. Owning your own paper would give you a chance to prove it can work. And this way you can buy one cheap, before somebody else beats you to it . . .'

Her pre-rehearsed sales pitch tumbled out too fast in her eagerness to convince him. He listened without interrupting her, subjecting her to the unwavering attention of those dark, dissecting eyes. They were like smoked glass, thought Vivi. He could see out, but she couldn't see in.

'Gerald's worked wonders already,' she said finally. 'He'd have done a lot more if both his hands hadn't been tied behind his back. The important thing is continuity, to preserve what he's achieved so far, combined with the changes he's been dying to make all along . . .'

How Gerald would react to an all-out battle with the print was another matter. But one hurdle at a time.

'Does he know you're here?'

'No. And I wouldn't want him to.' Canute-like, she ordered back the hot tide of colour that rose to her cheeks.

'Working for me wouldn't be the same as owning the paper,' commented Max, dipping asparagus into hollandaise. 'His pride's involved. If I asked him to stay on as vice-chairman, he'd most probably turn me down.'

'He won't. Not with Gemma in the trouble she's in. He can't afford to.' Tarnished as Gerald was by CC's mismanagement, however unjustly, he was unlikely to get a better offer.

Max considered for a moment, like an angler inspecting a dubious catch, debating whether to keep it or throw it back in.

'If I just wanted a shop window for new technology it would be easier, and probably cheaper in the end, to start a paper from scratch. If I bought *The Courier*, and all the problems that go with it . . . I'd be doing it for you.'

God, thought Vivi, what I couldn't get out of this man if I played my cards right. But her integrity got the better of her cynicism.

'It's the paper that's for sale, not me,' she countered, at the risk of blowing the deal. 'So don't think you can blackmail me the way the old man blackmailed Gemma. I love my brother, but not that much.'

'You're jumping to conclusions, Vivi,' drawled Max, mocking her over-reaction. 'That's the trouble with journalists, I find. They're inclined to make snap judgements, to simplify, to stick a label on everything. Because there's always a deadline hanging over their heads and an editor breathing down their necks and never enough time to do all the research. Well, the deadline on this story's still a long way off. So don't be in such a hurry to file it.' He selected another green spear and bit its head off. 'And don't kid me you're doing this just for Gerald. I'm willing to bet a lot of his bright ideas have been yours. And you want things to stay that way.'

Vivi glared by way of an admission rather than stoop to denying her own self-interest.

'Any offer would be conditional on you keeping up your column and writing exclusively for *The Courier*. Your fee would reflect that, of course. A year's contract initially. Agreed?'

Silly question, thought Vivi, heart racing. The thought of losing her precious column, just as it was taking off, had been one of her less admissible worries. Like Gerald she was technically the product of nepotism, the first likely victim of new management. An even worse prospect, ego-wise, than the paper closing down altogether.

'Agreed.'

'Good. I'll make Gerald staying on a pre-condition as well, so he doesn't feel patronised. I'll talk to him first thing tomorrow, suggest we set up an early meeting with the banks and the board before anyone else tries to get in on the act. Don't worry, I won't mention you. Easy enough to invent a leak.'

It was almost an anti-climax. Vivi hadn't expected to get to this stage till the coffee, let alone half way through the starter. It was her first experience of his do-it-now style of management, a taste of things to come.

'From my point of view this is good timing,' he went on. 'Once the unions find out that there's nothing in the kitty, they'll be forced to accept any proprietor prepared to pay their wages. Even an arch-enemy like me. That should give me some breathing space.'

*The Courier* would clearly be just one small cog in the expanding Kellerman empire. He spoke confidently of the imminent second wave of the computer revolution and his intention to oust the current giants from the top of the tree. The offices and warehouse he was building on a derelict site in Bermondsey were the first stage in a big expansion of his British operation. The competition wouldn't know what had hit them, he said, once his new products hit the market, his research team was on the brink of a technological breakthrough.

Vivi respected naked, unapologetic ambition. She mistrusted people who were coy about success, who tried to pretend it was accidental and affected to despise money. A self-made man would always be brasher than the CCs of this world, and what was the shame in that? Here was someone who had what it took to make things happen. If anyone could get *The Courier* out of its present hole, it was Max can-do Kellerman. He might seem like a gambler but his risks were all carefully calculated. Vivi wished she could say the same for herself.

'I didn't want you to know just yet,' said Gerald. 'But you would only have read about it in the papers. Or Harriet would have blurted it out, you can imagine the state she's in. There's no need to worry, everything's under control. I've still got a job. At a much higher salary, I might add.' He tried to smile, but it didn't work.

First the diary, thought Gemma, now this.

'A high enough salary to pay what I'm costing you? I've been here for over a month, clocking up a fortune in medical bills, and now . . .'

'I sold my original fifteen per cent holding to Kellerman as part of the deal. So the money side is taken care of.'

'You mean you've got no stake in the paper any more?'

'I don't want a stake in the paper any more. At least I know where I am now. I'm just an employee. Which is all I ever was. He insisted I commit myself for a minimum of a year, to ensure a smooth transition, he says. God knows, the fellow doesn't know the first thing about running a newspaper. But once all this is over, I intend to move on.'

'You should have held on to your shares,' protested Gemma. 'At least until they increased in value. I can't bear to think you've given them up for me . . .'

'Don't. Please. I've had enough of that from Vivi and Harriet. Quite frankly it was a relief to get rid of them. I only wish I'd done it years ago.'

Gemma fell silent. Useless to tell herself that he would have lost the paper anyway, even if he'd never met her, she still felt responsible. All her sufferings had been for nothing. The only solace open to her now was revenge.

'I've got to go,' said Gerald. 'Big meeting this evening, to break the news to the staff, and I've still got the press release to write.'

He gave her a brief peck on the cheek. Gemma would have liked to say, it's all right to hug me, I'm not infectious, but of course to him she was. That was why he wanted to keep her here. He didn't want her at home, didn't want to have to live with her or share a bed with her. And she had gone along with it, because the mere thought of walking into that house again brought her out in a cold sweat . . .

No. The longer she put it off, the harder it would be, for both of them. She had played the invalid long enough, hiding away in this pretty pale green cocoon with its view over the gardens. It was time to pick up the threads of real life again, salvage what was left of her marriage. If she didn't the old man would have scored yet another victory.

She picked up the phone and dialled. Daniel answered.

'Can you come and fetch me?' said Gemma. 'I want to come home.'

The Echo, *15 June 1984*
## KELLERMAN BUYS COURIER
*Max Kellerman, the American computer tycoon, has bought a controlling interest in* The Courier *in the wake of the financial crisis following the violent death of former proprietor, Viscount Collington. At an informal meeting with* Courier *employees yesterday, Kellerman pledged a large injection of funds to modernise and improve the paper and answered heated questions from the floor. There would be 'rationalisation' procedures, he announced, involving staff cuts, but it was hoped that a voluntary severance scheme would avoid the need for compulsory redundancies. Negotiations will begin immediately to settle the journalists' outstanding pay claim. Meetings are also scheduled with print unions to discuss the introduction of new technology . . .*

'So he pulled it off,' said Nick.

'He saved the paper, if that's what you mean.'

'As long as you were part of the deal.'

'Me and Gerald. What's wrong with that?'

'Come off it. You're not telling me everything.'

'What is there to tell? My column's just about the best thing in the paper. Max wanted to make sure he kept it, and the readers that go with it. And Gerald knows *The Courier* inside out, it made sense to keep him on board. It's only for a year, to start with.' There was no need for her to feel guilty, dammit. She hadn't done anything . . . yet. 'People weren't exactly queuing up to buy, you know. Would you rather your dad and all his mates were out of a job?'

'They will be soon enough if Kellerman gets his way.'

Damn him for being such a wet blanket. And damn Gerald for being so bloody-minded and ungracious. He could have borrowed against his shares, if need be, rather than sell them all to Max, a gesture which smacked of sour grapes.

'Well, I'm sorry, it's the best we could do. At least this way I can carry on working from home. Which is just as well, in the circumstances, isn't it?'

'Don't pretend that Casey had anything to do with this. What's he promised you, Vivi? A whole page? Your own office? Unlimited exes?'

'Think how pissed off you would be if I got all that.'

'What's that supposed to mean?'

'Just because you're not ambitious doesn't mean I have to be the same. You're happy to stay in your well-paid little rut, you'll end up as one of those old Fleet Street stagers who's seen it all, done it all, and never realised his full potential.'

'Meaning, I don't creep to the bosses and I loathe office politics?'

'Don't try to paint me as some kind of arse-licker. If I was any good at office politics I'd still be working for the Hun.'

'Then don't try to paint me as some kind of also-ran. I happen to be good at what I do.'

'Good at sniffing out scandal? Good at conning people? Good at writing all your copy in words of one syllable?' She didn't mean it, of course she didn't, but as usual her tongue had a life of its own.

'And what do you do, apart from parading all your feminist hang-ups and right-wing prejudices?'

'Here we go again. Me working-class hero, you stuck-up bitch . . .'

'Is there something going on between you and him?'

'No!'

'Don't lie to me. I can smell it. I was right about the old man and Gemma, and I'm right about him and you.'

'I'm not lying. All right, he's come on to me a few times, but men come on to me all the time. What do you want me to do, have my tits removed?'

'Have you ever been to bed with him?'

'Once,' admitted Vivi desperately, knowing that he would see through a denial. 'But it was last year. Long before I got involved with you.'

'Was he the one who had you so screwed up? The one who put you off sex?' Trust him to remember that self-pitying little speech.

'Oh for heaven's sake.'

'I knew it. The first time I saw him looking at you I knew he'd had you.'

'He didn't "have me",' snapped Vivi. 'I had him. And who's being jealous and possessive now?'

'I'm afraid for you. Types like him don't care who they hurt, as long as they get what they want. So are you finally going to tell me what he did to you?'

'What is this, the Spanish Inquisition? If you must know he screwed me senseless all one night and then never bothered to ring me. Big deal.'

'No. No, it was more than that.'

'All right, damn you!' He would never let up now until she told him. 'I got pregnant. I had an abortion. Which was entirely my own fault. Happy now?'

'Bastard.' When his eyes went hard like that she didn't know him any more. 'I ought to lay him out.'

'Don't be ridiculous. What did you expect him to do? Marry me? It was just sex.'

'Was he better than me?'

'Here we go. Now we're getting down to what this is really all about. Your precious ego. God, men are all the same. Full of macho shit.'

She flounced out of the room, furious with herself. The one thing she had sworn not to tell him and he had got it out of her, the way he always did. Just sex, she had said. God, how brilliantly uncomplicated 'just sex' was. It took a man like Max to blind you to that. And one like Nick to open your eyes.


'Would you like to sleep on your own for a while?' said Gerald. His way of saying that he wanted to use the spare room.

'No. No, I want things to get back to normal.' As if they had ever been normal.

It had been a mentally exhausting day. First the doctors trying to talk her out of discharging herself and then Gerald shouting at Daniel for having brought her home without his permission, as if Daniel had any choice in the matter. If he hadn't agreed she would simply have rung for a cab, as she had pointed out to Gerald, trying to sound calm, while she battled against another paralysing flashback of CC lying dead on the floor.

'I never bargained for you coming back here,' he muttered. And then, realising his gaffe, 'That is, I'd planned to find a place for us to rent, pro tem.'

'It's all right. The house doesn't bother me.' She had forced herself to go down to the kitchen on arrival. Daniel had been with her then, of course. Tomorrow she would have to do it alone. He had already moved out to stay with a 'friend' – female no doubt – rather than intrude on their privacy. He was due to go back to Paris next week in any case, after taking over a month's leave, ostensibly to give Gerald moral support.

Gemma knew he had done it for her sake. But she had also felt him withdrawing from her with every day that passed, not wanting her to become too dependent on him, or to risk getting too close to her. It would be almost a relief when he had gone, despite the wrench. She felt quite guilty enough about Gerald already.

She undressed and got into bed. Gerald followed suit. He switched off the light, kissed her on the cheek, and said, 'Sleep tight.'

'Gerald . . . will you hold me?'

'I thought you'd prefer me to leave you alone, for the moment.'

'Thank you. I appreciate that. But putting your arm around me is okay.'

The shrink had warned her that she and Gerald might have 'difficulties' and recommended an out-patient clinic where they could be seen as a couple, but Gerald had ruled it out of hand, claiming that he was perfectly all right, it was Gemma who needed therapy, not him. Responding to her request, he stretched an awkward arm across her.

'Did they give you anything to help you sleep?'

'I'm trying to manage without.'

'I remember that night on our honeymoon, when you woke up shouting "no, no".'

'I still do.'

'If I'd known . . .' For a moment she thought he was actually going to talk about it, for the first time since it happened, but he checked himself, saying, 'Never mind. No point in rehashing it all. Goodnight.'

His arm felt stiff. After a while he removed it, saying, 'Sorry. Have to lie on my other side,' and rolled over. Gemma lay wakeful, telling herself that it was early days, this was bound to be a long, slow haul . . .

She woke up at dawn, as always, in the throes of a panic attack. Seeing that Gerald's side of the bed was empty, she was gripped by the absurd fear that he had left her and felt compelled to pad downstairs in her bare feet in search of reassurance. The light was on in the living room. Tentatively, she opened the door. Gerald was sitting slumped on the settee, with a glass of whisky in his hand. He looked round, startled, and she saw that his face was wet with tears.

'I warned you, I'm an insomniac,' he said thickly, turning away. 'Always have been. Go back to bed.'

'But –'

'Go back to bed, Gemma. Please.'

She wanted to do to him what Daniel had done to her, put her arms around him and comfort him. But the warning note in his voice was unmistakable; she didn't dare risk a rebuff. It took her a long time to go back to sleep, and when she woke again, unrefreshed, at seven, he had already gone. There was a note by her pillow, saying 'Didn't like to wake you. Early start. Back about eight. G.'

The day stretched out ahead of her like a desert. She set about cleaning the house from top to bottom, or rather from bottom to top, starting with the kitchen floor. Harriet rang while she was scrubbing away at an imaginary bloodstain and talked for half an hour. She thought it was terribly brave of you, darling, going back to the house, personally she couldn't face it just yet, but you must come over to Bamber Court for lunch. Knowing that Seth would be there Gemma pleaded fatigue, unwilling to play gooseberry, and went back to her chores.

There was another call, much briefer this time, from Mum, doing her duty. If they needed a loan, she repeated, now that Gerald wasn't due to inherit anything, Fred had offered to help them out. Which may not have been intended as rubbing it in, but it certainly sounded that way. For richer for poorer, thought Gemma, politely declining her offer. At least now she had a chance to prove, if only to herself, that she hadn't married Gerald for his money.

Another bout of housework took her up to lunchtime. Allow an hour for shopping, an hour for cooking, and that still left her with time to kill before Gerald came home for dinner. There were a few more wedding presents to take out of their boxes and put away, a few outstanding thank-you letters to be written. But how could she possibly write thank-you letters to all those friends of CC, people who regarded her as a monster?

Suddenly all her energy deserted her, leaving her as limp as a puppet without strings. In hospital she had felt obliged to put on a coping front to convince them she was making progress, but here, alone, there seemed no point in pretending she wasn't in pain. Giving way to a wave of despair, Gemma sat down on the stairs and wept.

But there was no relief in it. Cursing her own weakness, she blew her nose and went out to the shops to buy food for supper. The woman in the greengrocer gave her an odd look, she thought. And the butcher, hacking out lamb cutlets, seemed to wield his cleaver with a certain malice. There's that loony, they were thinking, that done Lord Collington in, they reckon she was his bit on the side. As she waited to be served in the delicatessen, the customer ahead of her set up a conversation in Italian with the man behind the counter, both of them bursting into sudden gales of incomprehensible laughter, and she found herself thinking, they're talking about me, they're laughing at me . . .

Paranoia, of course. But as soon as she got home, she roughed out some caricatures, to cut her tormentors down to size, to take away their power and make it her own. The butcher became a pig, the delicatessen's limbs were made of salami, and the greengrocer woman was a large pear. They were cruel sketches, but they would give her the courage to go shopping again tomorrow. She wasn't going to hide away, she was going to enjoy her freedom while she could. Plenty of time to stay indoors if and when they locked her up . . .

She jumped in alarm as she heard the doorbell, half expecting CC to be there; it was all she could do not to run and hide. She had to force herself to go out into the hall and look through the spyhole, mouth dry with apprehension, swallowing with relief as she saw that it was only Vivi. She had the child with her, a little girl of about eighteen months in a buggy.

'Daniel rang to say you'd gone AWOL from the bin,' she said, by way of greeting. 'I just wanted to check if you were all right for Lucozade and grapes.'

'I've just been shopping, thanks. Come in, I was about to make coffee.'

She spooned the grounds into the little stove-top percolator she had bought for her Balham bedsitter, a lifetime ago. The electric espresso machine she had selected for her enormous wedding list was still in its box. There were no ginger nuts – Gerald preferred Bath Olivers; she put half a dozen on a plate.

'What would Casey like to drink?'

'I've got hers with me, thanks.' Gemma fetched an ashtray. 'No need. I don't smoke in the house. Bad for her lungs. That's Chapman, the butcher, isn't it?' She picked up the sketch pad lying open on the settee and began showing the pictures to Casey. 'See her, Cass? That's the old bag in the greengrocer that always gives short weight. And that one's Mario, Marco, whatever. Harriet had a fling with him once, would you believe. I never realised you did stuff like this.'

'Neither did I. I was feeling a bit vicious. The pencil is mightier than the carving knife. I hope.'

'That's not like you either. To crack a joke, I mean.'

'I think it's what's known as gallows humour.'

'You're definitely going to go into the box?'

'Yes.'

'God. I wish it was me. That is, I wish I could do it for you.'

Meaning, she could do it better, thought Gemma, the way she did everything better.

'This isn't a plate of fish pie. I've got to do it for myself.'

'What's the latest from the solicitor?'

'I have to meet with counsel next week. Geoffrey Spinet.'

'He's the best.'

'Best being the most expensive.'

'It costs money to play golf with the right judges, I suppose,' observed Vivi, pulling a face. 'God, I tell you, when this is over, I'm going to take the legal profession apart. Talk about restrictive practices. That mob could teach the print a thing or two . . . Sorry. Am I winding you up?'

'Actually, I prefer to talk about it.'

'And knowing Gerald, he isn't talking about it, right?'

'He's got a lot else on his mind. Specially now.'

'Losing the paper was tough, I know. But at least this way he has a say in what happens. And I get a chance to whip up public opinion in your favour in the run-up to the trial. Just because it's all sub judice doesn't mean I can't discuss general issues, does it? Like how the law discriminates against women.'

'Thank you.'

'I've been busy making contacts in all these feminist groups. I plan to gee them up like crazy, get them all set to campaign for your release if the bastards send you down. Whoops. Cass has gone and spat Ribena all over Mr Butcher.' She mopped it up with a tissue. 'Harriet's just about disowned me, you know. I mean, moving in with Son of Ferris was enough to freak her out without getting lumbered with the bratlet. I expect she's already given you an earful.'

'She mentioned it, yes.'

'She'll get ridiculously attached to this child,' Harriet had predicted, 'and then break her heart over having to give her back. When she was little she was forever bringing home flea-ridden strays, birds with broken wings, and then they would die, or go missing, and she'd take it all so personally. She made such a fuss to have a dog, when she was small, I hate the way they bark and fart all over the place, but Trevor insisted we get her this Jack Russell she'd set her heart on. She used to sleep with it and pinch fillet steak out of the fridge for it and generally spoil it to death, and then of course it got run over one day, just after her father left home, and she became quite uncontrollable, started smashing her bedroom up, I had to give her one of my Valium to calm her down . . .'

'Kids are easy to please,' shrugged Vivi. 'Same as pets. You can be the worst person in the world and a kid'll still love you, same as a dog. For a few years, at least. That's where dogs have the edge, of course. They don't grow up. They love you for ever.' And then, squinting at Gemma's sketch pad again, 'Could you draw a picture like one of these to illustrate my column? A nice unflattering sketch of my victim of the moment in a suitable setting? You know, like a cartoon but without a caption. To draw the eye to the copy.'

'I suppose so,' said Gemma, taken aback.

'Might be worth showing a few samples to the editor, see what he thinks. It might cost me some space at first. But it could end up getting me more. Can you knock out some stuff by the end of the week if I chuck some ideas at you?'

'Would I get paid?' said Gemma, thinking of Spinet's fees.

'If I can get it accepted, yes. Anything's worth a whirl at the moment, it's new-broom time . . .'

She began reeling off possible subjects. Already Gemma could feel the images taking shape in her mind; for a moment she almost forgot the shadow hanging over her. As soon as Vivi had gone, she got down to work, and for the next couple of hours, incredibly, she managed to forget it altogether.

# PART TWO

*Journalists say a thing they know isn't true, in the
hope that if they keep on saying it long enough it will be true.*

Arnold Bennett

# PART TWO

# 13

GEMMA NOTICED A change in Vivi once Spike and Jackie were safely on the other side of the Channel. After months of flitting from squat to squat one jump ahead of the law, they had decided to try their luck at finding work and accommodation abroad. An eventuality which Vivi regarded as highly unlikely, which was why she had encouraged the feckless pair to back-pack their way around Europe and offered to look after Cass for them 'just until you find a place'. By this time an unsuspecting Jackie had come to regard Vivi as a friend and ally.

Jackie had kept in touch by phone, reversing the charges, and claiming to miss the child, but she was evidently enjoying her first taste of freedom, just as Vivi had intended her to do. In the six months since she had left the country, Vivi had relaxed into her role of surrogate mother, going so far as to appoint Gemma as part-time minder. Gemma was surprised and gratified that Vivi thought her capable of coping with the demands of a boisterous, not to say wilful, toddler, one whom Vivi herself seemed reluctant to discipline in any way.

'I know I spoil her,' she admitted unrepentantly. 'But then I was spoilt myself. You're the well-brought-up one. So I'm counting on you to teach the little cow some manners.'

This was Vivi's way of warning her not to compete in the popularity stakes. But it was also her way of sharing, and showing confidence in her, and relieving her of the scourge of introspection. Little cow or not, the time passed more quickly when Cass was there.

Certainly Vivi couldn't have managed without help, given her increasingly busy schedule. She was now a frequent contributor to radio discussion programmes, breakfast television chat sessions, and late-night TV debates, with the full approval of her editor, given that her increasingly high profile was deemed to be good publicity for *The Courier*. She could always be relied upon to be as outrageous on the air as she was in print and to ruffle the feathers of her fellow-panellists. People either thought her refreshingly outspoken or self-opinionated and strident; like her or loathe her, no one was indifferent to her. Vivienne Chambers was fast becoming a media personality.

Gemma, meanwhile, took refuge in anonymity. Although her occasional sketches for Vivi's column had become a regular fixture no one knew her real identity, at her insistence – her pictures were signed merely 'G'. It wouldn't do, in her present position, to acquire a reputation for a warped, savage, often sick sense of humour. But without that release she would have found the strain unbearable, as the trial loomed ever nearer and she and Gerald grew further and further apart.

She had hoped that the move to a rented flat in Westbourne Park would help lay CC's ghost (thanks to which there were still no takers for the house, despite a constant stream of ghoulish sightseers) and encourage Gerald to spend more time at home, with her. But he continued to put in long hours at the paper, often not returning till late at night, when Gemma was in bed.

Bed. It wasn't so much a battleground as a no-combat zone. It had been months now since Gerald had last attempted, or rather failed, to make love to her. Gemma knew, though he never said so, that he blamed her for the rape, or at least for not fighting back, even though her current predicament was surely an advertisement for not fighting back. His habitual black moods alternated with guilt-ridden, short-lived bouts of being extra nice to her, but such respites were like candyfloss – sweetness without sustenance. It was as if she were living with two different people, both at constant war with each other, and one of them, at least, at war with her.

One evening, when the hostile half of Gerald had bitten her head off once too often, Gemma heard herself saying, 'Look on the bright side. Not long till I go to court now. And then, with a bit of luck, you'll be free of me at last.'

'How can you say that?' said Gerald, aggrieved. 'If I felt that way, why would I have hired a big gun like Spinet?'

Precisely because you feel that way, thought Gemma.

'We have to be realistic,' she went on, sidestepping the question. 'If the worst comes to the worst, I won't expect you to wait for me. Even if I get off, I don't want you staying with me out of duty.'

'If you mean that *you* don't want to stay with *me*, why don't you just say so?'

'Because I do want to stay with you!' To admit otherwise would be to admit defeat. 'But not if we're going to carry on like this . . .'

'In other words, not if I can't get it up.' It was unlike Gerald to express himself so crudely.

'It's nothing to do with that!' Anyone would think that she wanted sex for her own benefit, rather than his.

'I would have thought, after what happened, that you'd be only too glad to be left alone, instead of putting all this pressure on me to perform. God, when we were on honeymoon, you had to get yourself drunk before you could bear me to touch you –'

'But that was only because –'

'Well, it's only because for me as well. Only because I can't forget as easily as you've obviously managed to do, only because every time I think of it, I feel physically sick. Not because there's anything wrong with me!'

'Do you think I don't realise that I'm the problem, not you? I'm just saying if you want a divorce, I'd understand.'

'A divorce? What do we want with a divorce, when you can get an annulment for non-consummation?'

His tone was angry, accusatory, but his eyes were full of pain and humiliation and . . . fear.

'I would never do that,' said Gemma, chastened. 'I'm sorry I brought the subject up. But I can't bear to see you so unhappy. And I suppose I'm a bit tense at the moment' – she was developing his gift for understatement – 'because of the trial coming up.' If in doubt, apologise.

'I shouldn't have snapped at you,' said Gerald. It wasn't a question of making up, just a mutual retreat from conflict. 'But if you're tense about the trial, then so am I. And in my case it doesn't help being shackled to bloody Kellerman.'

It was a familiar excuse, his way of deflecting their problems on to someone else. It wasn't as if Max gave Gerald a hard time; on the contrary he treated him with unwavering respect. And Gerald couldn't cope with that. After years of walking a tightrope between CC and his ever-changing editors, surviving by stealth and stubbornness, he simply didn't have enough self-esteem to believe that Max was sincere in wanting him to stay on.

At first he had suspected him of doing it as a favour to Harriet, convinced that the two of them were having an affair. An impression which was reinforced when Max had set Harriet up in a flat off Sloane Square at an absurdly low rent; officially it belonged to a friend of his who was working abroad, and who wanted someone 'reliable' (not a word which best described Harriet) to live in it in his absence. Not content with that, Max had asked her to handle the interior decoration of his new penthouse in the Barbican, a commission which had led, by word of mouth, to others, thus providing her with an income. When Gerald had finally challenged Harriet she had insisted that of course there was no romance between them, it was Vivi Max was interested in, not her – an assertion which did nothing to improve his state of mind.

'What would you do,' ventured Gemma, 'if you were free to leave *The Courier*?'

'Write, ideally. History, biography, lit. crit., that sort of thing. Of course, there's not much money in it, that's the trouble.'

'I'm earning as well now, remember,' began Gemma, forgetting for a moment that she might soon be sewing mailbags for a couple of pounds a week. As for the other possible source of income, she didn't dare mention that to Gerald in his present mood.

'I wouldn't dream of letting my wife support me. And anyway, I'm in no position to turn up my nose at a well-paid sinecure.'

'Some sinecure, given the hours you work. You didn't get back till ten last night . . .'

She shut up, reluctant to seem like a carping wife, aware that she was 'appeasing' all over again. And yet, what choice did she have when she felt so thoroughly in the wrong?


There was no harm, Vivi told herself, in meeting Max occasionally. Or even in leading him on a bit. If the editor vetoed your bright ideas, and you had a chance to go above his head, then why not take it? Especially if the editor was obviously on his way out. A source of great angst to Gerald, who had originally appointed him, and one of no surprise to Vivi, who had known that he wouldn't fit in with the new, racier *Courier* Max had in mind.

Vivi's column had expanded, by popular demand, to a whole half broadsheet page. Bumbling bureaucrats, the Oxbridge mafia that ran Whitehall, posturing politicians, bleeding-heart busy-bodies who thought they knew what was best for the proles, menopausal men who traded in their ageing wives for newer models – all were dunked in the vitriol of her invective. Market research showed that Vivi's was one of the first pages people turned to and the biggest generator of readers' letters. Gerald, having launched the column in the first place, now muttered about it being in poor taste and over the top. Which Vivi didn't deny. But then, so were Gemma's cartoons. Give her a library photograph of the victim and a preview of the copy and she would come up with a grotesque, eye-catching image that doubled the impact of Vivi's words.

If only Gerald wasn't so prejudiced, he would admit that Max was only taking his own improvements to their logical conclusion. Gerald had always stressed the need to 'catch the demographic wave' – attract the baby-boomers – well aware of the old Fleet Street joke that whenever you saw a hearse, that was another *Courier* sale gone. He had wanted more features, more competitions, more special offers, above all more readers, because more readers meant more advertising, more revenue, more money to make the paper even better.

But Gerald, of course, had had to make numerous compromises, hampered not only by lack of resources but by the need to tread carefully vis-à-vis the old man. He certainly couldn't have afforded to poach the editor of *The Echo*, whom Max was head-hunting at the moment, and naturally he resented Max for having the power he had lacked.

And so did Vivi. Which was why she was keen to get some of it back, by working on him behind the scenes. Or rather in secret, to avoid gossip. There would be no satisfaction in resisting him if everyone else thought otherwise. Particularly that gossipmonger Myra Shaw, who had recently been paid off, one of the many disgruntled casualties of Max's new regime and Vivi's unseen influence. And even more particularly, Nick.

Despite all Vivi's protestations and precautions he remained perennially suspicious, forcing her to take the easy way out and lie rather than be disbelieved for telling the truth. Sexual jealousy was only part of the problem, and one which became submerged in a different, if related quarrel, that of hot metal versus new technology, a topic on which Nick remained inflexibly on his father's side.

In recent months there had been an unprecedented number of 'plate breaks' in the print shop – a normally rare occurrence, which not only incapacitated the machine in question but endangered nearby life and limb from flying fragments of metal. Mercifully, there had been no injuries, but that in itself was suspicious; Vivi, like Max, was convinced that the breaks were pre-planned, not only as a piece of power-play but to justify the introduction of 'double-roll locking', a laborious safety measure which not only delayed production but led to massive overtime claims. A theory which led Nick to accuse her of toeing the Kellerman party line, the prelude to yet another bitter dispute.

Vivi would surely have stomped off back to Bamber Court by now if it hadn't been for Cass. She knew if she tried to take her with her, even with Nick's consent, Ferris senior would undoubtedly step in; he was unhappy enough about her influence already. Meanwhile the fifty quid a week he insisted on giving Nick for Cass's keep served, by his lights, to reduce Vivi to the status of a hired help.

'I know all the arguments against investigative journalism,' Vivi told Max, over another clandestine lunch. 'It costs too much and we mustn't upset the advertisers. Which is precisely why a consumer page would build us a reputation as a real campaigning paper, one that hasn't sold out to its own vested interests . . .'

'Think how many staff you'd need to run it. People would write in in their thousands. There are organisations set up to deal with this sort of thing. The Office of Fair Trading, the Ombudsman –'

'We could restrict our interest to consumers who've already used the existing complaints machinery and failed. All right, so most of them won't have a case, but the ones that do will throw up really good stories.'

'Perhaps. But something like this will have to wait till we go tabloid. Which I don't intend to do by converting outdated machinery.'

'So, how long are you going to wait? The print think they're calling the tune, you know.' Another pay claim was brewing, even more exorbitant than the last, while negotiations on new plant had reached a stalemate.

'Then I've got them well fooled, haven't I?'

'Is that why you're using Gerald as a front man?'

'Oh, I wouldn't put it quite like that.'

'He's not happy, you know. And he'll be even less happy when things get confrontational. He may have worked for a right-wing paper all these years, but his own politics are well to the left of centre.'

'Actually, I'd like to see *The Courier* shape up as politically independent. I don't qualify for a knighthood, or a peerage, or any of the rest of that crap, so I've got no reason to brown-nose the establishment.'

'Except that Kellerman's is pitching for government contracts at the moment.'

'All the more reason to show myself to be impartial.'

'Impartiality's all very well. But readers like to buy a paper that matches their prejudices.'

'Well, you manage to match reader prejudices without coming down either side of the party fence. Though of course, as you've said, journalists don't always write as they feel.'

Dad had once said that there were a lot of emotional cripples in the business. That it attracted people who stood back from real life, observed it, reported it, but remained essentially aloof, detached, able to hold their own opinions in suspension, to serve masters they despised. True enough, journalism was full of cold fish like Daniel, malcontents like Gerald, and split personalities like Nick, who donned a suit of impenetrable armour before he went to work each morning.

'Well, I do write as I feel,' said Vivi. Though in fact to attack people effectively you had to reduce them to caricatures, much as Gemma did in her sketches. Once you started thinking of them as real live fellow human beings, you risked losing your edge.

'Only because it suits you. You're a grandstander, Vivi. You know what people think, what they want to read, and you pander to that quite shamelessly. You're a born manipulator.'

'No more than you are,' said Vivi, with the grudging admiration of one cold-blooded schemer for another.

'As long as we both understand that. I value your opinions. And I don't want to lose you. That's why I'm keeping these little meetings strictly business. For the time being, anyway.'

He was treating her like he was treating the print, she thought. They might underestimate him, but Vivi never had done. She knew that she was playing with fire. But then, that was the whole point.


On the Wednesday before the trial Gemma spent the day at Geoffrey Spinet's chambers, rehearsing a gruelling mock cross-examination, if not quite as gruelling as the practice runs Vivi had put her through. She arrived home, drained, to find Daniel sitting on the doorstep. The sight of him after such a long absence – he hadn't been home since her discharge from hospital – provoked a treacherous surge of powerful emotions, emotions she dared not examine or identify.

'You should have phoned first,' she said, flustered. 'We weren't expecting you till next week.'

'They were about to send me to Libya and I was afraid it might drag on, the way these Middle East jobs tend to do. So I decided to extend my leave. How are you?' His embrace was brisk, his manner guarded.

'Scared to death. Come in. I'm afraid it's a bit cramped, we had to leave most of the furniture behind. But there's always the divan in the living room, if you'd like to stay . . .'

'It's all right. Vivi's place is free at the moment.'

'It didn't seem worth getting anything bigger, what with Harriet in her own flat, and Gerald still having the mortgage to pay, and not knowing what's going to happen in court. I put a casserole in the oven, on the timer, it's not ready yet, but I can fix you something else in the meantime . . .' She tailed off, aware that she was babbling.

'I'm not hungry. Sit down, don't go all hostessy on me.'

How she had been looking forward to seeing him again! And how she had been dreading it! On the phone they would talk by the hour, always, by some unspoken agreement, when Gerald was at work. But face to face they were tongue-tied, or rather Gemma was tongue-tied and Daniel was back to his other, taciturn, inscrutable self. Their relationship might be totally innocent, but that didn't stop Gemma feeling guilty about it.

'It was nice of you to come,' she began, breaking the silence.

'I nearly didn't,' he said shortly, letting her know that he was dreading the trial as much as she was.

'If the worst comes to the worst, I stand a good chance, so they say, of getting a transfer to one of those cushy open prisons for middle-class offenders. I thought I might try to get on to a fine arts course, by correspondence.'

' "G" is much too subversive for a fine arts course. They'd probably have knocked that out of you at college, I'm glad now you didn't go.'

'Subversive?' She had never thought of herself that way, but she could hardly dispute it. She was a criminal, after all.

'Misfits tend to be. You've more in common with Vivi than you think.' He caught her eye for a brief, endless moment; they both looked away at once. 'How's Gerald?'

Daniel knew nothing of the problems in her marriage. Officially, Gerald was being a tower of strength; even to have hinted otherwise would have seemed like an infidelity.

'Worrying about money. If it wasn't for that he'd have resigned by now.' And then, seizing the chance to sound him out about a possible solution to the problem, 'Do you think . . . do you think, if I get off, and I know that's a big if . . . that it would be morally wrong to sell my story to the papers?' Daniel, unlike Nick or Vivi, would give her an objective answer.

'Have you had an offer?'

'Several, via the solicitors.' Much as the prospect of telling all appalled her it was the only way of recovering Gerald's losses. Spinet had warned them that there was little chance of the judge granting costs if she was acquitted; if you chose to hire a top name, you couldn't expect the public purse to underwrite your extravagance.

'Including one from *The Courier*?'

'No. Max vetoed it, Vivi said.'

'A case of dog not eating dead dog,' Daniel commented, lighting up one of his filthy untipped cigarettes. If a bomb or bullet didn't get him, thought Gemma anxiously, thinking of Dad, tobacco surely would. 'I wouldn't have credited him with so much tact. Could you bear to expose yourself in print like that?'

'I'd be exposing CC, not myself. I know it will be horribly

embarrassing, but the facts are all going to come out in court in any case. If we had a bit of money behind us, Gerald could afford to take a sabbatical, to write a book. And if I gave the story to Nick, at least I could be sure he wouldn't misrepresent me.'

'You have touching faith in friend Ferris,' smiled Daniel.

'I know what he's like, but he promised me, and Vivi would flay him alive if he broke his word. And besides,' she added, practically, 'The Torch offered more than anyone else. What do you think?'

'That you should leave it to Gerald to decide. Sorry to sound like a male chauvinist, but I know my brother.'

'Yes. I suppose you're right. But I didn't like to mention it yet. He's got so much else on his mind at the moment, he's up to his eyes in negotiations with the print and . . . there he is now,' she said, jumping up as she heard Gerald's key in the lock, half relieved and half disappointed that he was home early for once. 'Gerald! Daniel's here!'

She greeted him with a sunny welcome-home smile and received his customary peck on the cheek.

'Daniel.' He wrung his brother's hand. 'How about a very large Scotch?'

'Bad day?' said Daniel.

'Wasted day. I just had to escort a bunch of union heavies round the Kellerman warehouse, in Bermondsey, to show them the new machinery.'

'I thought that place was top secret?' said Gemma, pouring the drinks.

'So it is. I've only seen one tiny portion of the complex myself. It's guarded round the clock, with good reason. A spot of arson would solve the dispute nicely, from the print's point of view. The men must realise there's enough equipment in there to do the changeover tomorrow, if they would only agree terms.'

'Which they won't, of course,' said Daniel.

'To quote Bert Ferris, Kellerman can put his effing toys up his effing arse, no way are they selling the lads down the effing river.'

'He's got a point,' shrugged Daniel. 'From what I've heard, these machines put the hacks in the driving seat. Can't have that.'

'Quite. Even with big pay-offs, and enhanced hourly rates, they're never going to accept the reduced manning levels Max is after. And as for the no-strike deal, and the new rota, he's living in a dream world. At least getting a flea in my ear gave me an early night, for a change. He can wait for his report until tomorrow. Damn,' he added, as the telephone rang in the hall. 'I'll bet that's him.'

'I'll get it and say you're out,' said Gemma.

'No. No, best get it over with.'

He went to take the call, shutting the door behind him.

'Rather him than me,' said Daniel.

'Oh, if anyone can talk them round, Gerald can. He's a born diplomat. Max has said he wants to avoid confrontation, he's told Gerald to keep everything very low key.'

'Sounds like a PR job to me,' remarked Daniel, 'to show what a reasonable guy he is, before he brings on the artillery. Kellerman didn't get where he is without being totally ruthless. And he's not going to let expensive computerised presses sit idly in a warehouse gathering dust.'

Vivi had said much the same thing. 'Max is too clever to be the aggressor. He'll wait for them to declare war first. And then . . .'

And then what? A lock-out? Mass sackings? Gerald wouldn't want to be a party to that. Gemma couldn't bear for him to be any more miserable at work than he was already . . .

'How did it go?' said Gemma, as he rejoined them.

'He wasn't surprised. Said he was sure I'd done a good job of putting the case. Thanked me for my trouble. "Have a nice evening",' he mimicked, taking off Max's accent. 'How I hate that phoney charm. Come back CC, all is forgiven.' And then, realising what he had said, 'Sorry.'

He could forgive CC with her blessing, thought Gemma, if only he would forgive her as well.

The week of Gemma's trial at the Old Bailey was the worst of Vivi's life. There was nothing more unnerving than sitting outside the courtroom, waiting to be called as a witness, and wondering what the hell was going on inside. And once she got into the box, it was almost as bad, especially as it was the Crown who called her, making her feel like a traitor. She was obliged to confirm that yes, she had found the body, and yes, she had called the police, and yes,

237

the knife produced as exhibit A was the one she had seen lying next to the corpse. And all the while she was sneaking despairing glances at the jury, if only to stop herself looking at Gemma, pale and calm in the dock.

That blue-rinsed woman with the winged spectacles looked a real old ratbag, she would have a down on Gemma just because she was young and pretty, never mind the sober grey dress and minimal make-up she was wearing on Spinet's advice. And that yob with the earring in the second row bore a disheartening resemblance to Spike. As for that vacant-looking girl with the greasy hair, you could tell just by looking at her that she was completely brainless. You weren't allowed to drive a car without passing a test, but you could sit on a jury with an IQ in single figures and no one was any the wiser. The system was insane. As she would be quick to point out in her column . . . unless the system worked in Gemma's favour.

Much to Vivi's frustration, the defence chose not to cross-examine her, well aware that she was itching to deliver a harangue on what an evil old sod CC had been, which would end up doing more harm than good. As Spinet had pointed out when Vivi had rung his chambers to tell him how to do his job, if Lord Collington was such a depraved character, then why had neither she nor any other member of the family warned Gemma against him? Because he had seemed too old to be dangerous, Vivi had protested. Precisely. Which was exactly what the jury would be inclined to think, exactly the point the prosecution would be hammering home. So the less said on that particular subject the better. As for Vivi's brilliant idea of swearing under oath that CC had once raped her as well, Gemma had refused point blank to let her perjure herself.

Her evidence given, the defence was granted leave for the witness to be discharged, enabling Vivi to take a seat alongside her mother and brothers, from which she could see the scribbling hacks, reminding her of the cases she herself had covered with callous disinterest. Like Daniel, she had been philosophical about the pack of photographers waiting to snap her as she walked into the court; they were only doing their job, after all. But that didn't mean it was easy, being on the other side of the Fleet Street fence. Harriet, congenitally unable to shun the limelight, had gone so far as to stop and pose for the cameras. But Gerald had turned his head away, muttering about bloody vultures. No wonder he had vetoed any possibility of Gemma making a few bob – or rather a small fortune – out of her ordeal.

Nick had stayed at home, to mind Cass. Max was in Washington all week, pitching for a contract with the Pentagon, aware, no doubt, that Gerald didn't want him getting any more involved in family affairs than he was already. Barbara, meanwhile, was now installed in a flat in Marbella, Fred having taken early retirement from the *Post*. She was purportedly 'not very well' and unable to attend the trial, her excuse for not risking a mention in the English press which might blow her cover with her new fellow-expat neighbours.

The prosecution wheeled out various police witnesses, who testified to Gemma's fingerprints on the knife and the presence of CC's blood on her clothes. The pathologist who had performed the post-mortem on CC confirmed that he had been suffering from a degree of arteriosclerosis. But for this, he conceded under cross-examination, he would not necessarily have suffered heart failure and might well have been capable of summoning help himself, or even walking away from the scene unaided. This didn't alter the fact that he had died as a result of his injuries, but it did help excuse Gemma's failure to call an ambulance. A point which Spinet intended to return to later when he called CC's doctor, who would testify that his condition had remained undiagnosed and that Mrs Lawrence could not therefore have been aware of it.

Why couldn't he point that out to the jury now, thought Vivi, frustrated, to make sure the stupid buggers made the connection? Were they even listening? They looked half asleep. It was all she could do not to jump out of her seat and shout at them to bloody well pay attention, this bit was important. She veered jaggedly between Gerald's entrenched gloom and Harriet's stubborn head-in-the-sand optimism, envying Daniel his customary fatalism, or at least his show of fatalism. Sitting next to him, she noticed the body language that gave him away – arms folded tightly across his chest, an impatiently tapping foot, the tell-tale throbbing vein in his temple.

Like Vivi, he was a doer, he hated sitting there watching, dependent on the expertise of others and the dubious goodwill of twelve anonymous strangers. But if things went wrong, at least he wouldn't have to live with the collective responsibility that burdened the rest of them, even Harriet, especially Harriet, despite her hectic insistence that everything was going so well, she was sure that justice would prevail. Justice. Since when had the law been about justice?

Vivi began to feel marginally less desperate once the defence brought on their troops, in the shape of expert witnesses testifying to the post-traumatic effects of rape, which would have magnified the threat of a second attack, thereby diminishing Gemma's responsibility for her actions. The stabbing itself would have induced denial, numbness, and an inability to think clearly, hence her failure to leave the house, or to summon help. As for the suicide bid, that had undoubtedly been genuine, given the massive overdose she had taken; had she been found even half an hour later she would not have survived. So much for the prosecution's veiled implication that it was some kind of sympathy-seeking stunt.

And then, at last, it was Gemma's turn, with the defence pointing out that she was waiving her right to silence because she had nothing to hide. In her place Vivi would have lied through her teeth, exaggerated, wept, fainted, whatever it took to persuade that bunch of dimwits to vote not guilty. But Gemma played it absolutely straight, relating her story in a quiet, unemphatic way, relying on the facts to speak for themselves. She was in the witness box for almost five hours and not once did she falter or lose her temper or resort to tears, treating the prosecution counsel with a dignified courtesy that made him look like a hectoring bully. No matter what he flung at her, she didn't take the bait, never wavering from her original position – that she had struck out merely to ward off another attack, and then fled to evade pursuit, unaware that Lord Collington was on the verge of collapse and in need of urgent medical attention. Asked to comment on the diary, which the judge had allowed to be entered into evidence and read out loud in all its sickening detail, she said merely that it fitted in precisely with the threats CC had made to expose her if she reported him, and proved, moreover, that those threats had been real.

Would the jury regard her as cold and calculating or honest and sincere? If journalism had taught Vivi anything, it was that truth was what people wanted to believe. Her postbag was proof of that. Endorse people's prejudices and they treated you like a prophet;

question them and you were a heretic who ought to be burned at the stake. Forget about trying the case according to the evidence. Juries worked on gut reaction, however much they tried to rationalise it. What it all boiled down to was whether they chose to believe Gemma's story or not. And whether they did or they didn't was down to the mix of personalities, the phases of the moon, the luck of the draw. Rather than go through the rigmarole of a trial, the judge might as well toss a coin and be done with it.

There was nothing left now but the closing addresses and summing up. As after every day of the hearing, Gemma and Gerald spent the evening alone, while Daniel nobly went home with Harriet; she had sent Seth packing long ago as a gesture towards economy. Which left Vivi to relate the day's proceedings to Nick, punctuated by diatribes against both counsels, the thick-as-shit jury, and the bloody fool of a geriatric judge. This wasn't the first time Nick had been there for her in a crisis, and now, as always, she was torn between gratitude and not wanting to feel grateful, gladder than ever of the cover Cass gave her for still being under his roof and not her own.

'Jackie phoned today,' he said casually, after serving her a boil-in-the-bag supper. Perversely, she couldn't have borne for him to be one of those men who could actually cook.

'Where from?' The further away the better.

'Corfu. Spike's landed some kind of unofficial labouring job. And Jackie's found work in an English bar, with a room thrown in.' Work and accommodation, thought Vivi. They had actually found work and accommodation, damn them . . . 'She's talking about fetching Casey.'

Over my dead body, thought Vivi.

'And meanwhile you can bet your life neither she nor Spike has a work permit. They'll end up being deported. You can't let her take Cass back to a situation like that . . .'

'I can't stop her either. She's eighteen now, an adult, she can do what she likes.' He put a placatory arm around her. 'I'm sorry, doll, I've been dreading this. I knew how upset you'd be.'

'I'm not upset! It's just that Cass is settled now, she's got a routine, she's –'

'She's not yours, Vivi. I know you love her. But Jackie loves her too.'

That was the whole trouble. Jackie did love her. How Vivi had hated her visits, hated all the kissing and cuddling and the way Cass would cry when she left, aping her mother's tears. How she hated it when Jackie phoned, long distance, and made her parrot, 'I love you Mum' . . .

'I know Jackie's immature,' soothed Nick, 'but she's not a bad mother and . . .'

'Oh, she's a terrific mother. She just abandoned her child, that's all.'

'God, but you're a liar to yourself sometimes. You were the one who said it would be good for her to travel, remember? You said she'd missed out on her youth by having a baby so young and it would help her grow up. You were all for her making this trip . . .'

'I thought she was only going for a few weeks . . .'

'You were hoping that she'd never come back.'

'Oh, naturally. I just love having to juggle my life around a child who's not even mine. Have you any idea how complicated it all is? No. Because I'm the one who has to park her at Gemma's and collect her, who has to organise my entire life around her, who has to –'

'You're the one who's ambitious, who's taking on more and more commitments. You can only spread yourself so thin.'

'Don't you dare accuse me of neglecting her!'

'Spoiling her is a kind of neglect. You let her have her own way in everything, she's becoming a right little madam, and if I tell her off, you take her part against me. And all because you want to make sure she loves you best. You're treating her the same way your parents treated you.'

'Did you have to bring this up, today of all days?' accused Vivi, well aware that she was losing the argument and afraid of losing control.

'Would you rather I'd kept it from you?' He sighed. 'Look, I'll tell Jackie that she'll have to save the money for her own fare home and back, to prove she's serious. All right?'

It wasn't all right. But it would have to do, for the moment. With luck this arrangement in Greece would break down and they'd have to move on again. Or perhaps Jackie's plane would crash, leaving no survivors . . .

See what love did to you? And they called it a force for good. Love was like religion. It preached peace and caused wars. And she had gone into it with her eyes wide open, convinced herself that it was somehow safe to love a child that wasn't hers, because it was only temporary. She was like some pathetic junkie who claimed to be able to kick the habit any time she liked . . .

'Let's go to bed,' said Nick gently. Vivi knew what he was thinking. And the worst of it was, she was thinking it too.


Not guilty. Not guilty of murder. Not guilty of manslaughter. The defendant was free to go.

Never mind the diary, or the multiple blows, or her failure to call an ambulance, never mind that the jury had taken two nailbiting days to reach a verdict. All that mattered was that they had convinced themselves that she had acted in self-defence, agreed that they didn't want to see her punished, allowed their collective subjectivity to get the better of them, partly thanks to Geoffrey Spinet's truly spellbinding closing argument which had reduced two of the female jurors to tears.

There was more weeping now, with Harriet and Vivi kissing and hugging each other for the first time in years, in contrast to Gerald and Daniel who shook hands with their usual stiff-upper-lip restraint. Gemma, having spent the trial in a trance of self-imposed calm, was now shaking from head to foot, unable even to speak. She left the court with Vivi on one arm and Gerald on the other, Spinet riding triumphant shotgun in front and Harriet and Daniel bringing up the rear, forming a protective circle around her.

A huge crowd was waiting outside, mostly feminists who had assembled, with prepared placards, to protest at Gemma's conviction, now delightedly cheering her acquittal. Someone tried to thrust a microphone in her face, whereupon Gerald swore at him and hustled her away into a waiting car, leaving the rest of the family behind. The driver took a circuitous route to the hotel they had booked under a false name, to throw off any following pressmen. Neither of them spoke. It was over. The nightmare was finally over. She wasn't going to prison, she was free. Everything was going to be all right from now on . . . wasn't it?

As soon as she got inside the safety of their room, Gemma lay down, fully clothed, on the bed and slept soundly for the first time in a year. When she woke, Gerald was on the telephone, with his back to her.

'I still have to talk to my wife, of course,' he was saying. 'A lot depends on her. In the meantime, if you can push the money up, so much the better. I'll ring you tomorrow. Goodbye.'

'Gerald?'

He turned, startled.

'How are you feeling now?'

'Better. It just all caught up with me. Who were you talking to just now? Have you changed your mind, about selling my story?'

'No. I won't hear of it. These tabloids make you sign away all your rights and then write what the hell they like.'

'But Nick promised me . . .'

'Have you ever read any of his so-called interviews? The fellow ought to be writing pulp fiction.'

'But they're offering fifty thousand pounds!'

Gerald fetched himself a Scotch from the mini-bar.

'Suppose I told you I could get just as much, maybe more, for writing the old man's biography?'

'His biography?'

'If I don't write it, someone else will. I had a letter from an author some months ago, wanting access to CC's private papers. And then it occurred to me, why not do the job myself? Your name's been dragged through the mud, our privacy's been shot to pieces, now let's do the same to him.'

Gemma's heart sank. Spending a day or two talking to Nick was one thing. Spending a year or more writing a book was quite another.

'I've been in touch with a literary agent,' he went on, unable to keep the excitement out of his voice, 'and it seems that there are several publishers interested in commissioning a warts-and-all exposé of the man behind the public mask, to cash in on all the public interest caused by the trial and the financial mess he left behind him. With them bidding against each other, I could end up with a pretty substantial advance. Of course, I wouldn't do it without your permission, because there's no leaving out your part in the story. That's one of the reasons I couldn't trust anyone else to write it.' He sat down on the bed beside her. 'What I'm sure of, once I start digging around, is that we'll discover all kinds of skeletons in the old man's cupboard. The dead can't sue for libel, remember.'

This isn't about money, thought Gemma. This is about revenge. Thanks to the catharsis of the trial, she had got beyond that, but plainly Gerald hadn't . . .

She owed him this much. He had been so generous to her, insisting on the best QC in the business, selling his stake in the paper, slaving away in a job he had no heart for any more. Perhaps writing this book would help exorcise his demons, as well as launch him on a new career with a potential best-seller.

'If this is what you really want to do,' said Gemma, swallowing her misgivings, 'then I'm right behind you '

'You're sure?'

'Of course. Does this mean you'll be resigning from the paper?'

'It means I won't be renewing my contract. By the time it expires I should have received the first part of the advance. Meanwhile I can start sorting through the old man's papers and letters, some of them go back years and years.'

A labour of hatred, thought Gemma. But at least it gave them something new to talk about over their room service dinner, complete with bottle of champagne. The pop of the cork reminded her ominously of her wedding night.

'To the future,' said Gerald, raising his glass.

'To the future,' echoed Gemma. Gerald polished off the lion's share of the bottle, together with a brandy to follow, after which he declared that he was bushed and went to bed, falling asleep, or pretending to, the minute his head touched the pillow.

Gemma was almost relieved. She couldn't expect everything to change overnight, just because she had been acquitted. Whatever happened she mustn't let this book drive a further wedge between them. She would offer to type the manuscript and help with the research, use it as a common interest on which to rebuild their marriage. But no matter how big the advance, she had better hang on to her job at *The Courier*. If things went wrong, she would need it more than ever.

Being prepared for the worst had become second nature. But it wasn't about giving up hope. It was about not giving in to it, the way she had done before.


'We ought to treat ourselves to a long weekend,' said Nick. 'Now that Gemma's decided not to sell her story, I can put in for a few days' leave.'

With Gemma and Gerald still holed up in an hotel till the dust died down, and Daniel already back in Paris, there was no reason to stay in London. As for Harriet, she had more invitations than she could cope with at the moment and would be dining out on the trial for the foreseeable future.

The decision made, they were packed and bound for the Devon coast within an hour, arriving in time to buy Cass a bucket and spade and a swimsuit before dinner. Vivi, still euphoric with relief, would have been in excellent spirits if it hadn't been for the prospect of Jackie's return. It wasn't until next morning, after a celebratory night of love, that she discovered that she had left her Pill in her other handbag – an oversight, of course. She could have gone to a local doctor to ask for a new prescription. But it was only for a few days, after all . . .

She didn't say anything to Nick. If it happened it would happen by accident, against her better judgement. The same as falling in love.


'I could help,' volunteered Harriet eagerly, calling in on Gemma the day after their return from the hotel. 'The more dirt Gerald can dig up on the old man, the better his book will sell. Wouldn't it be wonderful, after all these years, to get to the bottom of what happened to my baby?'

As always when the subject came up, there was a tremor in her voice. It might have happened a long time ago, but it had been the first of many blows, a precursor of the losses to come.

'Is there anyone we can talk to who was there at the time?' Privately Gemma doubted that anyone would admit to having been a witness, let alone a party, to the killing of a child, but of all the skeletons in the Collington cupboard, this was surely the one with the biggest sensation value.

'Well, Emily's dead of course . . .' She faltered. 'Darling, do you think I could have a teeny-weeny drink? There's no need for Gerald to know.'

Unable to deny her an anaesthetic to dull the pain of remembering, Gemma poured her a small shot of whisky. Harriet knocked it back gratefully.

'Not that I'd trust anything she said in any case,' she resumed, reverting to her customary forced flippancy and lighting a cigarillo. 'She was always under CC's thumb.'

'Anyone else?'

'The doctor was in his sixties even then, he must have kicked the bucket long ago. Then there were the Bradys. Maureen, the housekeeper, and her husband, he was a sort of chauffeur-cum-handyman. I don't know where they live now, they must have retired a good ten years ago. She worked at Collington Hall all her life, started off as a scullery maid, knew CC from when he lived there as a boy. Bit of a tight-lipped old hag, mind you. In those days, servants had to be discreet or they'd be out of a job without a reference. But nothing much could have gone on in that house without her knowledge. I've always suspected her of doing CC's dirty work. She'd have strangled her own mother for a fiver . . .'

It occurred to Gemma, as she made shorthand notes, that this Maureen Brady might know if CC had forced himself on a servant, for example, and be willing to spill the beans now that he was dead – especially if Gerald made it worth her while. If only they could prove that Gemma wasn't his only victim, it might help convince those diehards who still doubted her story.

'Oh, I remember Brady,' said Gerald, when Gemma related this conversation over dinner that night. 'A kind of downmarket Mrs Danvers. Couldn't stand the woman myself.'

'I could start trying to trace her, if you like.'

'Waste of time. She's probably dead by now.'

'But it's worth finding out, surely?'

'She's well down my list of priorities.' Which seemed odd, given her long association with the family. 'I've got some papers to plough through after dinner,' he added. 'You ought to have an early night, you look exhausted.'

By the time Gemma brought the coffee in, he was hard at work at his desk, with *Götterdämmerung* blasting away on the hi-fi. Gemma had never got round to telling him how much she hated that piece of music and why, unable to bring herself to spoil his enjoyment of one of his favourite operas. She went to bed with earplugs in, knowing that he would put off joining her for as long as possible. A court might have acquitted her, but Gerald hadn't, not yet. Gemma wondered if he ever would.

# 14

*Summer 1985*

GERALD HAD BEEN surprised and touched at the send-off he had received. The entire staff had assembled in *The Courier*'s composing room to 'bang him out', a farewell ritual involving the collective clash of metal against metal, and one which was accorded only to the few. He had never, in his own mind, shaken off the nickname of 'the Herald', or given himself credit for the respect he had earned from the print unions over the last year of patient if unproductive negotiations. Lawrence was a bloke you could trust, according to Bert Ferris, which was more than you could say for his boss. Or his snooty bitch of a sister.

Gerald's final report to Max had reconfirmed – not without a certain satisfaction – that no agreement would be possible regarding new plant until the print's outstanding pay demand was settled in full. Even then, the proposed innovations would only be acceptable if present manning levels and practices were maintained, thus defeating the object of the exercise – to cut costs and improve efficiency.

'Things are bound to hot up now that Gerald's not there to keep the peace,' Vivi predicted, risking another spat with Nick. 'If necessary Max'll let them strike themselves out of a job.'

'You'd really like to see that happen, wouldn't you?'

'Well, it's better than overpaying seventeen men to operate a press that only needs four. You're the one who's always saying what a dangerous, dirty job they do. You ought to be all for new, safe electronic machinery.'

'God, the hypocrisy of the woman. This is about maximising profits, not improving working conditions, about putting hundreds of men out of work. Still, why should you care? They're just the nobodies who shovel the shit while you sound off in your column telling people what to think.'

'I do not tell people what to think! I *make* them think! I reflect what *they* think! When the print allow me to, that is.' Vivi's comments on the dispute had been blacked on more than one occasion, with a blank space appearing in the middle of her page. 'So much for the freedom of the press. Or are you suddenly in favour of censorship?'

'You're twisting things again . . .'

'Why don't you admit what we're really arguing about? The real issue is that you wanted me to leave *The Courier* when my contract ran out.'

'Oh, God forbid. Not with Kellerman upping your money when you got that offer from the *Standard*.'

'And you hated that. You never bargained for me being more successful than you.'

'I always knew you'd be more successful than me. You won't be happy till you're editing the paper. No matter what it costs you.'

'It's the cost to yourself you're worried about. You'd like to have me sitting at home, knocking out the odd article for pin money and polishing the light bulbs . . .'

'Fat chance of that. God knows what I pay that cleaning woman for, the place is always a tip.'

'You can't expect a two-year-old to be tidy. I'm the one who has to pick up after her and do two jobs, not you. If you tried to do what I do, you'd keel over with exhaustion, like the typical bloody man you are!'

'A typical man, am I? That just shows how much you take me for granted.' He threw on his jacket.

'Where are you going?' He had only just got in.

'To meet the old man at the Printer's Pie for a few jars before he lines on. That's what your typical man does. Goes down the boozer on a Friday night. Perhaps I'll come home drunk and knock you about a bit. Sometimes I think you'd respect me more if I did.'

He slammed the door on his way out. Vivi shrugged and got back to work. He would say he was sorry when he got back. If she didn't say it first.

*

'It looks terribly complicated,' said Gemma, inspecting her new Kellerman state-of-the-art word processor, a personal leaving present from Max to Gerald, who had shown no interest in it, other than to say that Gemma was welcome to use it, if she liked, as long as it didn't clutter up his study.

Thanks to a handsome advance for the book, the Lawrences were now installed in a new house in Pembridge Close, not far from Lansdowne Gardens, which Gerald had sold ridiculously cheap for the sake of a quick sale. They could have, should have saved money by moving to a cheaper area, or settling for a flat, or somewhere in need of renovation, especially as their mortgage had been secured on the basis of Gerald's *Courier* salary. But for Gerald it had become a point of honour to re-establish their former standard of living; to preach economy was to express doubt in his ability to succeed in his new career.

'It's a piece of cake,' said Vivi, who had been using a similar machine at home for months. 'I'll show you how to do the basics, and then Max'll send one of his people round to teach you the clever stuff. I know Gerald will bash away at that old manual of his till kingdom come, but a PC will save you hours on typing up the fair copy. And on the research side, you can forget about tatty index cards and build up a proper database, so you can cross-reference and call up any entry you want in a couple of seconds. You can even keep an appointments diary on it, all the right software's already been booted up.'

'Is this the kind of system Max wants to bring in at *The Courier*?'

'More or less. Once it's up and running, I'll be able to file my copy down the phone lines from home. And now that you're fixed up, I can send a draft of my column straight from my hard disk to yours, via the modem.' Cass began bashing keys at random and dripping a melting ice lolly on to the keyboard. Gemma moved her gently but firmly away.

'I just hope Gerald's doing the right thing, writing this bloody book,' went on Vivi. 'Trust you to agree to it without a murmur. But I suppose it's better than him working for Max, right?'

'That had something to do with it, yes.'

Vivi had done her best to dissuade Gerald from signing the contract, saying that Gemma had suffered enough, and so had he for that matter, without having the old man as a house guest. Why couldn't he go for easy *Torch*-style pickings, and then bury the old sod for good and all? It was the nearest Gemma had seen to the two of them having a stand-up fight. Having predicted darkly that either Gemma or he would crack up under the strain, just you wait and see, Vivi now seemed anxious to mend fences by offering practical support, without pretending to any enthusiasm for the project.

'Max did his best for Gerald, you know. He did offer him a whopping great rise to stay.'

'Gerald thinks that you were behind that. He reckons you two are having an affair. Or that you soon will be.'

A remark she would never have made while Gerald was still at the paper, and one which he had been too inhibited, even in the middle of a row, to make himself. But now Gemma's curiosity – or rather her misgivings – got the better of her.

'Does he now,' commented Vivi dryly. 'What did you say to that?'

'That I couldn't believe you'd be stupid enough to risk losing Nick.'

'Perhaps I'm not stupid enough to risk staying with Nick. Oh, he looks harmless enough, your ultimate nice guy, puts on his new man act by taking his turn to cook supper and putting down the loo seat and doing his share of the baby-sitting. But it's all camouflage, you realise. At heart he's your ultimate control freak. Won't you come into my parlour? said the spider to the fly. No wonder I've started to feel so bloody trapped.'

And yet it was Max who reminded Gemma of a spider. As for Nick being a 'control freak', he provided Vivi with just the kind of unconditional love she needed, refusing either to dominate or be dominated and striking a skilful balance between humouring her and keeping her in line. Vivi might deny her feelings for him – she had never repeated the outburst which had so shocked Harriet – but Gemma could see the love in her eyes every time she looked at him, whether she was aware of it or not.

'Still, it won't be for much longer,' Vivi went on. 'If his dad ends up out of a job, and I carry on working for Max, that'll be the end of it. I'm not giving up my column for him, for anyone.'

'And what's going to happen about Cass then?'

Vivi made a big production out of unwrapping a Glacier Mint, her alternative vice to cigarettes when the child was around.

'Whatsername's due in from Corfu at the end of August,' she announced finally, between sucks, 'on one of those cheap charters you have to book weeks in advance. Then she's taking the bratlet back with her.'

So that explained why she had been so nervy lately.

'It'll be a relief, really,' went on Vivi, keeping up the pose. 'You know what I'm like. I hate being tied down. If it wasn't for Cass I'd have left Nick long ago. We've been fighting like cat and dog.'

'In other words you've been testing him to destruction.'

'If I have, it's only for his own good. What he needs is a perfect-wife type like you. Not a selfish cow like me.'

A perfect-wife type whose husband now slept in a separate room, officially because of his insomnia and his wish not to disturb her, but in reality because he couldn't bear to touch her. Not that she could admit that to Vivi, to anyone. Outspoken and tactless though Vivi was, she had never asked any nosy questions about the state of their marriage.

'Then stop being a selfish cow,' said Gemma. 'Stop despising your good fortune, before it's too late. Don't you realise how lucky you are, to have someone who loves you, faults and all? It was the same when we were kids. You played up all the time, and Dad let you get away with it. And now you're treating Nick the same way.'

'Listen to her. Quite the little amateur psychiatrist. You've never been the same since they banged you up in that funny farm.' And then, grudgingly, 'I know I go out there looking for trouble. But I never had any practice at being good, like you did.'

'I wasn't being good. I was just pretending.' And I still am, she thought. 'Just like you pretend to be bad.'

'Give it a rest, will you?' snapped Vivi, withdrawing, as she always did, when a discussion threatened to become too personal. 'I came here to give you a lesson on how to use the machine, not to discuss the meaning of life. So let's get on with it, I haven't got all day.'

She's going to break his heart, thought Gemma sadly. And her own.

*

Nick was away on an overnight job the day Jackie was due to fly in. Teeth gritted, Vivi went to collect her from Gatwick as arranged, only to bump into Ferris senior at the barrier. Nick had mentioned that he and Jackie had patched things up, long distance, but there had been no mention of him meeting her at the airport.

'How's my little girl?' he cooed, scooping Cass up in his arms. 'Let's have a big kiss, then.' Cass obliged him, grinning; much to Vivi's frustration she adored her granddad. Nick had taken her regularly to the Barking house, while an unwelcome Vivi had stayed at home.

'Look what I've got,' he teased her, reaching into his pocket and holding a packet of E-numbers just beyond her reach.

'Please don't give her those,' said Vivi, intercepting the cellophane bag and eliciting a howl of protest. 'It's the artificial colours. They make her hyperactive.'

'Can't I give my own grandchild a few sweets without your permission?' He snatched them back and handed them to Cass who rewarded him with a treacherous grin. 'Jackie'll be coming home with me,' he added, 'if you want to get off.'

The curt dismissal was like a slap in the face.

'When I spoke to her on the phone, the other day, she said she would be staying with us.' Vivi tried to keep her voice steady, but it came out horribly shrill.

'Well, I've spoken to her since, see. And she's decided to stop at home for a week or two, before she goes back. I'll come over and fetch Casey's gear tonight.'

Vivi had prepared herself for this moment, so she thought, but she hadn't expected it to be so sudden, and brutal, and final. She knew she ought to go, now, before Jackie arrived, but she waited till the bitter end, squeezing every droplet out of the last few minutes, watching while Jackie, looking tanned and healthy, dropped the huge teddy bear she was carrying, bent down to pick her daughter up and cuddled her half to death, laughing and crying at once. Ferris senior enveloped them both in a big hug; Cass, still munching happily, laid delighted claim to the teddy. God, kids were so damned promiscuous, thought Vivi bitterly. Talk about cupboard love.

'Thanks for everything, Viv,' Jackie greeted her. 'Hope Case hasn't been too much trouble.'

'No. No, she's been very good.'

'We're stopping at Dad's, did he tell you?'

'Yes.' And then, to make matters worse, Jackie hugged her. Not just because she was so obviously, pathetically happy to see Cass again but because Viv was a good mate. Viv was the one who had softened up Nick, encouraged her to spread her wings, told her not to worry about Case. Viv was on her side. Little did she know.

Vivi tried hard to hate her; it would have made things so much easier. But she couldn't. The poor kid was too dim to realise she had been conned. Unlike Nick, who had realised it from the start. He had set Vivi up every bit as much as Vivi had set up Jackie, smelt her broodiness, the way he had smelt out everything else about her. He wanted to make a good little wife and mother out of her, he had wanted that from the start. Well, screw him. She was glad she hadn't fallen into the trap he had dug for her, glad that she was shot of Cass and free to concentrate on her career, glad that she had no reason – or rather no excuse – to stay with Nick any longer. And more miserable than she had ever been in her life.

'How did it go?' said Nick on the phone that night.

'It went. That is, she went. Or rather they went. Back to your dad's place. Hardly saw them for dust.'

'I'm sorry, doll.' She had given up objecting to the sexist endearment, learned to like it, even. But right now it was just another irritant. 'I wish I could have been there with you.'

'Why? To tell me never mind, doll, let's make a dear little baby of our own?'

He wasn't to know that she had been playing Russian roulette with her Pill, not that it had done her any good. Most likely that abortion had left her sterile. Just as well. Kids were the ultimate hostage to fortune. They might die on you, like Harriet's baby, or turn out too like you for comfort, or end up hating you. She never wanted to get this attached to another human being ever again. It was time to cut her losses.

'Would that be such a bad idea?' said Nick.

'As you pointed out yourself,' Vivi reminded him tartly, 'I'm ambitious, I've been taking on more and more commitments, and I mustn't spread myself too thin. I'd hate to neglect another child the way I've neglected *Case*. When I wasn't spoiling her, that is.'

'Sometimes I think you save up every word I've ever said to you, just to throw it back in my face . . .'

'You were right. I'm too selfish to love anybody more than I love myself.'

'I never said that. I said you don't love yourself enough. That's your whole trouble.'

'You never give up, do you? You're like some bloody missionary hellbent on saving my soul.'

'And you're your own worst enemy. Why are you so afraid of being happy?'

Because I don't deserve it, thought Vivi. Because I'm not in control of it. Because one way or another I'm bound to fuck things up.

'Happy? We never stop bickering.'

'You're the one who picks the fights, not me.'

'I don't pick fights. I have the nerve to state opinions you don't agree with, instead of knowing my place as a mere woman.'

'And I have the cheek not to sit there saying yes dear, no dear. What is it you want, Vivi? A henpecked wimp you can walk all over? Or an even bigger bully than yourself?'

'Neither. I'm moving back to my place tonight.'

A long, knowing, infuriating sigh.

'Do you have to be so predictable? Look, I know how upset you are. I –'

'You're revelling in it! You think you've got me where you want me now. You think now Cass is gone I'm going to need you more than ever . . .' Shit. What was she saying? 'Well, I never needed you. You're the one who needed me. I've had enough of people being dependent on me, making demands, draining me dry. It's over, Nick. I mean it.'

'Here we go. Back to the old routine. On, off, hot, cold –'

'It's not the old routine. It's a completely new routine. I've had virtually no freedom for the last year, and now I intend to make up for it.'

'We can't discuss this over the phone.' He was using that calm, patient, humour-her voice of his. 'We'll talk about it when I get back . . .'

'I don't want to "talk about it",' exploded Vivi, fighting back the tears. Thank God he wasn't here to squeeze them out of her. Nick was in his element when she was in crisis. 'Can't you take a hint? I don't want any more of your soft soap and your so-called understanding and your non-stop emotional blackmail! I feel suffocated by you! And if you've got any self-respect you'll accept that!'

'Have it your own way, then.' He sounded weary rather than hurt. When you lashed out at someone as often as she did, it was like crying wolf. There's Vivi blowing her top again, putting herself in the wrong, as usual. Give her time to cool off and she'll climb down, the way she always does. He thought he knew her inside out, damn him. He thought she couldn't live without him.

I'll show him predictable, thought Vivi, slamming the phone down. I'll show him.

'Vivi.' Max stood up to greet her and extended a hand. He had got rid of CC's mahogany desk and button-backed leather chair and brought in functional steel-and-laminate office furniture. There was a computer terminal where the drinks cabinet had been; Max was known for his abstemious habits and his disapproval of drinking in working hours. The contingent of confirmed old resident soaks had either sobered up or taken severance; if you wanted to get on at *The Courier* these days, you didn't brag about your hangovers. 'Good piece for tomorrow.'

'Thank you.'

'Something you wanted to discuss?' He glanced at his watch. She had deliberately hung around the office till late, knowing that Max always came in on Thursdays, arriving in the early afternoon and seldom leaving before nine or ten. She couldn't face going back to that empty flat for the fourth night running and waiting for Nick to phone her, or rather not phone her, while she struggled against the compulsion to phone him first. She didn't kid herself he had got the message. He was just making a point, and making it more forcefully with every lonely day that passed. She knew that she couldn't hold out much longer, that there was only one sure way to cut off all possible retreat.

'If you're in a hurry it can wait,' she said. Not true. When you had made up your mind to do something irrevocable, it was best done now, soon, quickly. If it wasn't Max, it would be someone else, she told herself. Max was just a catalyst, not a cause . . .

'I'm in a hurry to eat, that's all,' said Max, shooting her that film-star smile of his. 'Care to join me? Or do you have to get home?'

He must know that she was back at Bamber Court. Harriet would have told him; she had phoned Vivi at Nick's place the other night, only to learn that she had moved out. Perversely enough, she had expressed regret; she had been gradually seduced, over the last year, by Nick's ability to make her laugh. Or perhaps Gemma had been doing a PR job behind the scenes. Nick was good for Vivi, he could handle Vivi, given time he could turn her into a nice person . . .

'No. I don't have to get home.'

'Right then. You suggest one of your obscure eateries, and we'll leave separately as usual.'

'Why don't we just go to the Savoy Grill, together?' They were bound to be spotted there.

'This wouldn't be because you've had a row with your boyfriend, by any chance?' How she had always hated that word. It reeked of pimply youth and sex in the back of cars.

'I'm just fed up with all the subterfuge. Why shouldn't we meet for dinner? I'm a shareholder, after all. And I wish Harriet wouldn't tell you my business.'

'Even if she hadn't, my secretary keeps me abreast of all the gossip. And you two are the latest hot news.' Damn the incestuous goldfish bowl she lived in.

'Care to make it we three? Or aren't I brainless enough to be seen in public with you?' she added slyly, referring to the interchangeable, if ever-changing, Kellerman escorts.

'I see Harriet's been telling you my business as well,' he said equably. 'Come on, then. Let's go.'

They left the building together, got into Max's chauffeur-driven Merc together, walked into the restaurant together, and who should be sitting at the very next table but bloody Myra Shaw, now women's editor of *The Torch*. Perfect, thought Vivi, smiling brightly at her, watching her eyes narrow. Nonetheless she chose the seat with its back to her so that she couldn't see her face.

'Harriet also mentioned that the child's mother arrived to collect her the other day,' said Max, once they had gone through the rigmarole of discussing the menu and ordering. 'I guess that must have been hard for you, after all this time.'

'Not really. She's not a bad kid, but I'd had just about enough, I'm not the maternal type. And if this new consumer page gets off the ground, I'll have to come into the office a lot more.'

'I told you, it'll have to wait until we go tabloid.'

'Which we can't until you reach a deal with the print. Are you going to let this strike go ahead? How much longer can you stall them?'

'Don't fish, Vivi.'

'Don't you trust me?'

'Frankly no. You were living with Bert Ferris's son until last week, and the general consensus is that you'll be going back to him, once this latest little tiff is over.'

'The last time someone accused me of giving Nick confidential information, I resigned,' said Vivi tightly.

'I'm not accusing you. But you have to admit, your boyfriend' – Vivi winced again – 'has quite a reputation for finding things out. He's bound to find out about this evening, for example. I assume you're trying to make him jealous?'

'What exactly would he have to be jealous about?'

'Don't play games with me, Vivi. What is all this in aid of?'

'Talk about looking a gift horse in the mouth. You didn't use to be so slow.' She gave him an explicit come-to-bed look, putting just enough satire into it to pass it off as a joke if it didn't work.

'Last time we discussed this, you said Nick was a good, kind, decent man who loved you and you weren't about to hurt him.'

'Then perhaps I don't want a good, kind, decent man. Perhaps I don't want love. Perhaps I'm looking for someone I don't mind hurting.' Or better still, someone she couldn't hurt. Even if she got hurt herself, there would be a certain masochistic satisfaction in that. At least she was in no danger of falling in love with Max. Quite the reverse.

'And I fit the bill?'

'Take it as a compliment.'

'Are you saying this split is permanent?'

'What difference does it make?'

'The difference between making a fool out of him and making a fool out of me.'

She should have known he wouldn't make this easy for her.

'Are you giving me the brush-off again?'

'On the contrary. I'm asking you to marry me.'

He said it quite matter of factly, while buttering a bread roll.

'You've got to be joking.' But she knew he wasn't. Max rarely joked about anything.

'You'll excuse me for not being more romantic. But you've just made it clear that you don't want love. What you do want, and don't deny it, is *The Courier*. Which is why I bought it, remember? Because what I want, what I've always wanted, is you.'

He gave her a look which melted her bones, reminding her of that early, instant mutual attraction, the mind-blowing sex, the false hopes he had raised in her, the crushing sense of rejection, the determination never to give in to him again, even after his subsequent apology: *I didn't want to get involved and so I tried to end it quickly. But it didn't end. So here I am.*

And here he still was. Far from slaking his desire that night, she must have inflamed it, which was why he had tried to dump her. He didn't like needing or wanting anyone, any more than she did, hence the appeal of marriage. Marriage was a clearly defined contract which would bring the wanting and needing under control . . .

'Well? Do we have a deal?'

The worm of ambition burrowed a little deeper into Vivi's soul. It hurt.

'I told you before, I'm not for sale,' she said, in a knee-jerk response to the pain.

'And I don't give anything away. So don't ever come on to me again unless you intend to do business.'

And with that he changed the subject to the multi-million-dollar contract he had just landed with the Pentagon, well aware that she wasn't listening. The rest of the meal passed in a blur, with Max at his most relaxed and urbane, and Vivi too preoccupied to offer more than token responses. *The Courier* was just a sideline to him. A rich man's hobby. And now she had a chance to get it back, unhampered by loyalty to Gerald. It wasn't as if she didn't fancy him something rotten, she always had done. It wouldn't be like marrying some disgusting old man for his money. The money didn't interest her in the least . . .

Vivi had come to the office by tube; Max insisted on taking her home. She steeled herself to finish what she had started before she shamed herself out of it.

'Would you like to come in?' she said, as the chauffeur stopped outside Bamber Court.

'Not until you've given me an answer, no. Take time to think it over, Vivi. Because I won't be asking you twice.'

He leaned across and kissed her with sudden passion, hurtling her back to the first time he had done so, getting on for three years ago now, and in all that time, incredibly, there had never been anyone else but Nick. His mouth felt uncomfortable, like new shoes. Or perhaps hers had changed to fit Nick's and nobody else's. She forced a response, to keep him warm, feeling guilty. Another weakness Nick had nurtured and exploited without mercy.

'Looks like your boyfriend's waiting for you,' said Max, nodding over her shoulder to where Nick stood by the outer door, watching them. Just as Max must have been watching him, all the while he was kissing her . . .

That was why he had done it, of course, the machiavellian bastard. He knew that she wasn't strong enough to do this without help, or rather duress.

'It's make-up-your-mind time, Vivi. Goodnight.'

The chauffeur got out and opened the door for her. Marching past a grim-faced Nick with what dignity she could muster, Vivi let herself in, trying unsuccessfully to shut the door in his face.

'How dare you come here spying on me,' she hissed, pre-empting an accusation.

'I was worried about you. But not as worried as I should have been, obviously. What am I supposed to do now, Vivi? Go round to his flash penthouse and belt him one?'

'Stay out of this. I told you, I'm a free agent now.'

She got into the lift. By the time it creaked its way to the fourth floor, he was waiting for her on the landing.

'What's the matter with you?' she demanded, willing herself not to weaken. 'Haven't you got any pride?'

'Did you have it off with him?'

God, Pulowska must be having a field day. But once she let him into the flat, she would be done for.

'What do you think?'

He gripped her by the shoulders, his fingers biting into her flesh, hurting her. There was some relief in that. Vivi couldn't look at him.

'You did, didn't you?'

'What do you think?' she repeated. Still she couldn't meet his eyes, for fear he would see through her.

'Who's the one without any pride now? Everyone knows he gets through women like socks. Don't you realise he's just using you?'

'I'm the one who's using him!' countered Vivi, stung. 'Because I'm ambitious, remember. Because I'm after the main chance. Because I want *The Courier* back. And this way I'll get it. Just you wait and see.'

That did the trick nicely. She would never forget the look on his face.

'You just had to revert to type, didn't you?' he jeered, letting go of her abruptly. 'Some bloody feminist you are. You're just another killer bimbo hitching her wagon to a hotshot. I've had just about enough of being good old Nick, poor old Nick, who's always there, who puts up with any amount of crap, who thinks he's lucky to have you. Go and sell yourself to the highest bidder with my blessing. Good riddance.'

She had never seen him so angry. For a moment she thought, hoped that he was going to hit her. But he didn't give her that satisfaction. It was as if she had flicked a switch somewhere inside him, blocking off the light and warmth that had blinded and burned her, condemning herself to shiver in the dark.

She stood watching as he disappeared down the stairs, limp with a sense of anti-climax. It had been bound to end like this. She had always been a great one for breaking things, losing things, giving things away. She would always prefer running in the rain to snoozing in the sun. Or having sex to making love. Never again would she let a man have that kind of power over her. Specially not Max Kellerman.

Vivi woke up next morning – not that she had slept – with a filthy migraine, Nick's words still hammering nails into her skull. A killer bimbo hitching her wagon to a hotshot, selling herself to the highest bidder. He wouldn't be the only one to think that, never mind that she had brains, and talent, and was successful in her own right . . .

So what? She didn't care what people thought of her. And besides, everyone got married because they wanted something. For most women it was a home, children, security. For men it was sex on tap and domestic comforts. So why shouldn't she marry for the paper? It was a hell of a lot safer than marrying for love.

Unable to summon the energy to get out of bed, even to answer the phone, Vivi let the machine take her calls.

'Hi Viv, it's me,' sang out Jackie's voice over the loudspeaker. 'I just rang Nick and he said you'd moved back to your own place. I'm here till Friday week, so if you give us a ring I'll bring Case over one night. Hope you and Nick kiss and make up, he sounded ever so depressed. Say goodbye to Viv, Case.' Vivi covered her head with the pillow as she heard Cass warble, "Bye 'bye Bibi.'

Then there was Harriet, obviously at a loose end and in need of a chat, happy to talk into thin air, followed by Gemma asking her to dinner next Friday, Gerald was off to Cannes to do some research and she would be on her own – her excuse for trying to play peacemaker, no doubt. The next call was from the managing editor's secretary, saying that there would be an emergency meeting of all staff that evening at six p.m.; the pay talks with the print had finally broken down.

Bleary-eyed Vivi squinted at her alarm clock. Four o'bloody clock already. She ran a cold shower and forced herself to get under it, to wake up her system. No time for a run this morning, or rather this afternoon. Without her daily fix of endorphins she would feel sluggish and grumpy all day, or what was left of it. She chose a flamboyant yellow suit to negate her black mood and tied her hair back with a matching scarf; there wasn't time to untangle the dark, heavy mass of curls. No amount of make-up would hide the puffiness around her eyes, but with luck people would be too intent on the meeting to notice.

By the time she arrived at the office a posse of militant inkies were picketing the building. One of them shoved a leaflet at her.

'Do me a favour,' snarled Vivi. 'You're the scabs who crossed our picket line last year.'

'NUJ have already instructed you lot to support us, love. Not that it makes much difference if you show up for work or not. Not as if you can produce the paper without us.'

'No. You're the ones who produced it without us. Whose side is the NUJ supposed to be on? Ours or yours?'

'Same thing. We're all in this together, see . . .'

'Don't waste your breath, mate,' boomed a voice in her ear. 'She's sleeping with the Yank, didn't you know?'

Vivi turned and glared at Ferris senior, momentarily lost for words. He caught hold of her arm and pulled her to one side.

'You pleased with yourself now?' he growled.

'Aren't you?'

'Don't act like it was my doing. I've kept my trap shut all this time, for Nick's sake, but now I'm going to say my piece. He was happy before he met you. Nothing ever got him down. I've seen a big change in that boy and you're the cause of it, stringing him along and screwing other men behind his back.' Vivi drew breath to deny the accusation and thought better of it. 'You think you're so bloody important, what with your shares in the paper and your own page and being on telly and lord knows what else, you think we ought to be grateful to you for teaching young Casey to talk posh and letting her run wild. I told him, son, there's a woman who's always going to want to wear the trousers. And it's time you stopped kidding her you like it. Christ alone knows what he ever saw in a little whore like you.'

Vivi slapped him hard across the face. It hurt her hand more than it hurt his jaw.

'You know what you need, love?' he sneered, unimpressed by this puny attempt at violence. 'A bloody good hiding. Now piss off to your meeting. Your new boyfriend's waiting.'

Vivi further distinguished herself by spitting at him before storming into the building. Good riddance, Nick had said. Well, good riddance to him as well, and to his stinking lousy family. She had quite enough problems with her own . . .

She was trembling as she joined the throng in the news room, barely aware of the hubbub going on all around her.

'Those boneheads are going to cost us all our jobs . . .'

'What about their jobs? You can't blame them for not wanting to commit hari-kari.'

'You're breaking my heart. I wish Kellerman'd sack the bloody lot of them.'

'What kind of fascist are you?'

Ferris was right, she thought as outrage gave way to depression. Nick would be better off without her. At least there was no room now for a climb-down, however much she lived to regret her decision. How ironic, to be judged for an infidelity she hadn't actually committed, yet. All the more reason to redeem the lie, as soon as possible . . .

There was silence as Max walked in; his presence seemed to fill the room. He appeared confident and untroubled as always, unlike his new editor, who looked harassed, as well he might. He must have known he was taking a gamble, leaving the relative security of *The Echo* for a hotbed of industrial unrest, and soon he would know if the risk had paid off.

'You all know why we're here,' began Max. 'The last time we met like this was when I took over. I made it clear that I wasn't going to carry on mopping up the paper's losses and that I intended to bring in new technology. Since then I've been negotiating non-stop with the unions to achieve that, without success. And now the print workers have elected to strike in support of a pay demand which ignores the proposed settlement altogether.'

So he's going to call their bluff, thought Vivi, forgetting her own troubles for a moment. He's going to starve them out . . .

'The situation was, however, predictable. Which is why contingency plans were made. As you know, Kellerman International has built a warehouse and offices in Bermondsey, supposedly housing new equipment which isn't yet available on the open market.' The word 'supposedly' sent a murmur round the room.

'If I'd made it public, at the time, that this was in the process of being converted to an alternative site for *The Courier*, fully equipped to produce the paper with non-union labour if necessary, we'd have faced an immediate walk-out long ago, before the installation was complete. But now it is. Now we're ready to roll with or without SOGAT and the NGA, though they're more than welcome to join us, if they're willing to settle, even at this late stage. I'm telling you first, not them, because it's thanks to you that we've put on two hundred thousand copies in the last year, and the journalists are going to come first from now on.'

Brilliant psychology, thought Vivi. After years of having to pussy-foot around the masters who operated the presses, the worms were getting a chance to turn at last.

'Starting tomorrow, *The Courier* will be created and printed in its new home. And I hope you're all going to be in at the birth. A whole technical team is ready to act as midwives, steer you through the technology, and iron out any bugs in the system. The alternative is to follow your union instruction to down tools, and that decision must rest with you, individually and collectively. Meanwhile I'll leave you to talk this over and take a vote. Your editor can answer any questions. I'll look forward to hearing your verdict.'

There was silence for a moment after he left the room, followed by a buzz of chatter, a call to order and two hours of heated debate, with some people afraid to disobey the NUJ instruction, in case they lost their union cards, and others saying, what the hell, what had the bloody union ever done for them, and if Kellerman was getting rid of the closed shop, who needed it anyway?

Vivi kept her mouth shut, for once in her life. She had only recently joined the permanent payroll and still felt like a newcomer, one who attracted envy and resentment, who was more likely to antagonise people than secure their support. Especially now that she was known to be Kellerman's bit of stuff. No, not his bit of stuff. His future wife. Who would one day take over as proprietor of *The Courier*. Then she'd show them all what she was really made of, prove that she could run a paper better than any man . . .

What swayed the argument, in the end, was the print's treachery of the previous year, and the knowledge that what was happening here was the beginning of something bigger, inevitable, the first stage in a revolution that would change the face of Fleet Street for ever. Out of two hundred and forty journalists, all but thirty-two voted in favour of the move.

Max reappeared to thank them for their support, without any show of triumph, warning them that things would be difficult for a while, and adding that special buses would be laid on, to pick up those who didn't drive to work, or who preferred not to put their cars at risk. The new site would obviously be picketed, and he didn't advise anyone to try to cross the lines on foot, in case things got ugly.

He caught Vivi's eye across the room and smiled in a way that no one else could see. Then he went to talk, one last time, to the print, already knowing what their answer would be.

<br>

## 15

A S DANIEL HAD always said, Gerald was a born academic, never happier than when ploughing through a heap of yellowing papers. Unfortunately these had not, as yet, yielded up any secrets. There were no letters from former mistresses, no evidence of any illegitimate children, no blackmail demands. And no other diaries, which to Gemma's mind spoke for itself. No one suddenly started keeping a diary at the age of seventy-four. Gerald was despondent at his lack of progress so far, but as Gemma pointed out, CC had obviously had the sense to destroy anything incriminating.

'What about Maureen Brady?' she reminded him. She had entered her in her computerised index under 'B' with a subheading describing her connection and the annotation 'Possibly deceased. Current address unknown.'

But Gerald remained perversely unwilling to seek Brady out, despite her intimate knowledge of the Collington household. He was still working through a long list of the prominent public figures who had known CC personally, reasoning that the old man would have made many enemies among them; now that he was dead they might be glad of the chance to settle old scores. So far, however, such people had proved unwilling to find themselves quoted in a potentially sensational book, or to damage their own reputations by association. So most responded with a simple 'Sorry, but I've nothing useful to contribute', rebuffs which Gerald took personally, lacking both the thick skin and the persistence of a seasoned hard news journalist.

Which was hardly surprising. His early career had been spent in backroom jobs and subbing, and during his years as a lobby correspondent he had relied on official briefings, unofficial ones in Annie's Bar in the Commons, and a tight circle of regular contacts for information. Leader writing, a post traditionally filled by intellectuals, had suited his bookish, analytical talents but done nothing to teach him the investigative skills so vital to a biographer.

Vivi would no doubt have made a much better job of sniffing out any scandal, or making things up, if all else failed, but Gerald was too hampered by his own integrity to cheat or cut corners. Not that Vivi had volunteered her help, caught up as she was in the drama of her own life.

'Is it true about you and Max?' Gemma challenged her, a few days after her showdown with Nick, unable to trust Harriet's account of events.

'I'm just about to send you Friday's copy. Every single word of it would be blacked if Ferris and Co. were still in charge.' The new presses were manned by electricians – not printers – who had undergone a special induction course in secret, ready for the changeover.

'So it is true,' said Gemma, taking this evasion as an admission. 'How has Nick taken it?'

'Need you ask? He's right behind his dad all the way.'

'I'm not talking about the strike, dammit.'

'I want a really strong illustration. Something that's going to hit them between the eyes . . .'

'Now that you don't need a baby-sitter any more, you've got nothing to say to me, right?'

'The other phone's going. Talk to you later. 'Bye.' She wouldn't talk to her later, of course, for fear of giving too much away. Gemma knew the feeling.

A moment later the light flashed on the modem, and Gemma was able to call up Vivi's Friday column on her screen – an account of her first week at *The Courier*'s new premises, comparing its high-tech orderliness with the rabbit-warren squalor of the old, decaying building, relating the teething problems with the new computerised equipment and describing the gauntlet of angry pickets the staff had to brave each day.

*Much of the violence is orchestrated by outsiders, professional activists and their hangers-on, who swell the so-called picket to 5000 or more. (Overmanned we may have been, but not to that extent.) Print workers, however disgruntled, are not the real architects of the violence that has already resulted in fifty policemen being injured. They're stooges of those who want to turn this into a political issue, and who won't be happy until they provoke a death or a serious casualty, for which, of course, they will blame the police, the government and the evil forces of capitalism. It is thanks to these rent-a-mob heavies that most of us choose to commute by 'scab-wagons' with wire mesh over the windows, which vary their pick-up points each day to avoid the risk of ambush . . .*

Gemma wondered what Daniel would think of it all; wars were his speciality, after all. He was always on the side of the common soldier, never mind what side he was fighting for, and opposed to the politicians who pulled the strings. But he also regarded wars as inevitable, displaying his usual detachment. He would lack Nick's sentimental support for the print, or Vivi's gung-ho opposition to them. She must be in her element at the moment, thought Gemma; Vivi was never happier than when she was fighting someone. What would happen when she tried to fight Max? Did she seriously think she could get the better of a man like that? Or did she know in her heart that she couldn't?

Gerald was away from home yet again, visiting one of CC's ex-editors, who had retired to the West Country. Gemma had offered to go with him, but the timing had clashed with her Friday deadline, as Gerald's trips invariably did. She suspected that this was deliberate, either to avoid her company or to express his ill-concealed disapproval of her continuing to take the Kellerman shilling. No doubt he thought Max was patronising her. If it hadn't been for Daniel, Gemma might have nurtured the same doubts herself.

It wasn't that he heaped her with praise; that wasn't Daniel's way. But he was pleased with her. She could hear it in his voice. Wherever he was working he would somehow get hold of the Tuesday and Friday *Courier*, and pick up on some little detail Gemma had put in for her own gratification and his, something nobody else but Daniel would have noticed. Lately she had become more 'subversive' than ever, her sketches not so much illustrating Vivi's copy as commenting on, even criticising it. To give Vivi her due, she had never objected, not even to a heartless caricature of herself, earlier that week, depicting her as a *tricoteuse* sitting knitting next to a guillotine, smilingly watching the decapitation of the beleaguered print workers, the previously untouchable aristocrats of the newspaper industry.

Gemma could have found other work, but none which would have given her as much freedom. And besides, *The Courier* paid well, providing her with a financial safety net if her marriage – or what passed for a marriage – finally disintegrated. She had begun to almost hope that it would. Did Gerald feel as miserable as she did? How much longer could they both keep up the charade they maintained for the benefit of family and friends? Would Gerald be relieved if he came home one day to find her gone? Or would he feel rejected, humiliated, betrayed? And how was she supposed to know which, if he refused to talk about it?

She spent the rest of the day at her drawing board, producing the 'strong image' Vivi had asked for – a spider's web made of barbed wire, in which were trapped the writhing bodies of winged protesters in their death throes. At the centre of it was Max, his perfect, white transatlantic teeth bared in a menacing smile, his hooded eyes full of benign malice, encompassing his victims, tentacles outstretched, in a deathly embrace.

Perhaps she would send it to Nick afterwards, just to let him know she was on his side. Not that she felt particularly partisan about the dispute – she could see both points of view too clearly for that – but because it infuriated her that Max should be profiting, a second time, from another's loss. Nick, like Gerald, had lost his heart's desire, and Max, yet again, was waiting to clean up. It might not be stealing – Vivi, like CC, had made things easy for him – but it was nonetheless opportunist. But then, spiders were. They didn't give chase. They just laid their traps and waited.

Rather than ring for a messenger, she decided to visit the battle zone for herself. With Gerald having taken the car, she had to go by taxi. The first one she hailed turned out to be driven by a *Courier* compositor taking time off from the picket, who made no bones about telling her what she could do with her fare. The second cabbie refused to take her all the way, fearing for the bodywork of his vehicle. Gemma settled for being dropped as close to the front line as possible.

The area was bleak and desolate, formerly derelict land on which Max's spanking new building looked misplaced and isolated, a fortress in the middle of a desert. The demonstrators were confined by police to the approach road to the complex, well away from the gatehouse which controlled all the comings and goings. An armoured van swept round the corner and out into the main road just as Gemma alighted from the cab, to be hurried on its way by a volley of abuse and missiles hurled from the other side of the steel barricades. She continued her journey on foot, closing her ears to the routine chants of 'scab!' and 'bitch!', not unduly troubled. It occurred to her for the first time how much her ordeal at the Old Bailey must have toughened her up.

'Gemma! Gem! Over here!'

She turned to see Nick yelling at her from the other side of the barrier and pointing to a spot a safe distance away. Gemma retraced her steps and waited for him to join her.

'You should have brought the car,' he said. 'They're throwing things, you might get hurt.' The set of his face had changed; it had always settled, naturally, half way into a smile, but now the curve of his mouth was tilting the other way and his hazel eyes had lost their mischief.

'What are you doing here?'

'Keeping my old man company. He's been more or less camping out this last week. What about you?'

'I'm delivering my illustration for Friday's edition.'

'Well, they're not letting any visitors into the building at the moment. So you'll have to hand it in at the gatehouse.'

'Why?'

'There was a hell of a bang, couple of hours ago, and a window blew out. They had to evacuate the place while the police searched it, there were sniffer dogs, the lot. But they've all gone back indoors now, like the good little conscripts they are.'

'Was anybody hurt?' said Gemma, thinking of Vivi.

'They didn't send for any ambulances,' shrugged Nick, with a show of nonchalance. 'It was probably just a stunt set up by Kellerman to discredit the strikers. I expect tomorrow's *Courier* will be full of the usual propaganda. Look, I've got the car with me. I may as well drive you up to the gatehouse and then I'll take you home.'

'That won't make you very popular with your mates.'

'I wouldn't be very popular with myself if anything happened to you.'

He led her away, jingling his car keys.

'Can I take a look?' he said, indicating her portfolio. Gemma handed it over and watched while he inspected the sketch on the sheet of stiff board inside. 'Bloody hell. Do you think they'll use it?'

'Yes, actually.' Max's ego was big enough to ask for the original, which was why she preferred to give it to Nick instead. 'I'll send it on to you, if you can bear to look at it.'

'Thanks.' He seemed touched. 'As long as you don't mind me using it as a dartboard.'

'I was going to suggest it.'

He rewarded her with that familiar grin, looking momentarily like the Nick of old. 'It'll be the star attraction at the Printer's Pie. And earn you an honorary safe-conduct to cross the picket any time you like.'

A few minutes later, their delivery made, they were on their way home.

'So how's Gerald's book going?'

'Fine, thanks.' Nick would know exactly how to unravel the story of the old man's life, thought Gemma. And if there wasn't much to unravel, that wouldn't stop him whipping up a large meringue out of half an egg white. But there was no point in asking him for any tips. Gerald had always disapproved of what he called 'muck-raking' — admittedly *The Torch*'s speciality and Nick's stock in trade — even though that had never stopped *The Courier*, or even the quality press, reporting *Torch* stories second hand. And besides, what was Gerald doing with this book but muck-raking? Why did he think he had been paid so much money to write it?

Neither of them said much during the drive, both of them studiously avoiding any mention of Vivi. When Nick finally drew up outside the house, Gemma realised that she was unlikely to see him again.

'I'm sorry about what happened,' she said, in case she didn't get another chance. 'It was so absolutely typical of Vivi. She won't even talk to me at the moment, she knows I'll give her an earful . . .'

'Waste of breath,' said Nick, cutting her short. 'It was on the cards, sooner or later. Would have been sooner if it hadn't been for the kid. See you, Gem. Take care.'

He drove off. She would miss him, thought Gemma. Seeing Nick had always cheered her up. She could only hope that Vivi was missing him too, enough to come to her senses before it was too late, if it wasn't too late already. She rang her as soon as she got in, ostensibly to check that the sketch had reached her, but really to get the inside story on the bomb and reassure herself that she was all right, only to be told that Vivi had left the office, she could always try her at home. Gemma did so, but she got the wretched answerphone as usual. To hell with her, she thought, giving in to an impulse and dialling Daniel instead, on the off-chance that he might be in; she could always hang up if a woman answered.

'Daniel Lawrence.' She loved the bored, curt tone he used to answer the phone and the way his voice softened when she announced herself.

'It's Gemma. Is this a bad time?'

'Hang up,' he said, 'and I'll ring you back on exes.'

Which gave them their usual excuse to talk for over an hour.

'They reckon I'll live,' announced Vivi, rejoining Max in the waiting room with a bandaged hand and leg; the egg-sized lump on the back of her head didn't show through the mass of dark curls. 'I can go home now, thank God.' She chose not to mention that they had wanted to keep her in overnight, for observation.

'You can't go home,' said Max, who had rushed her to Guy's in the anonymity of a scab-wagon rather than advertise that there had been a casualty. 'Not till I've rigged up security at your flat. If someone out there is gunning for you personally, you can bet they know where you live. I'd better take you to Harriet's for the night. Or to Gemma's.'

'No. They'll only fuss.'

'You need someone with you, you're still suffering from shock. If you prefer I can check you into a clinic . . .'

'How often do I have to tell you, I'm all right?'

Shock. Okay, so it had been a shock when her desk drawer had blown out. If she'd been sitting at her terminal, rather than

272

returning to it with a cup of coffee, she might have been seriously hurt. As it was all she had was a scalded hand, cuts from flying glass, and concussion from having been thrown backwards by the blast, banging her head on a filing cabinet and briefly knocking herself out. Thanks to the secluded location of her desk, in a corner next to a window, no one else had been in the firing line, thank God. Which made it all the more likely that the attack had been personal, not random.

How often had she lambasted the print in the last few months, only to have her copy blacked? And now they couldn't black it any longer. Now, if they wanted to shut her up, they, or those claiming to act on their behalf, had to take more drastic action. No doubt they were looking forward to hearing that she was *hors de combat*. All the more reason to carry on regardless.

Max took her arm, led her to where his car was waiting and gave his own address to the driver.

'My apartment's like Fort Knox,' he said. 'Death threats by every mail. Too bad I didn't think to protect you as well as I protect myself.'

'I don't need protection.' But she did. In her present feeble state she was capable of going straight round to Nick's, in the hope that he would take one look at her and forgive her everything. And she mustn't let that happen. She hadn't gone through all this agony just to cave in the minute the going got rough.

And yet the temptation was there, every minute; if she'd loved him less she would have given into it. Losing Cass was nothing compared to this. The withdrawal symptoms had been worse than she could possibly have imagined – aching limbs, a permanent splitting headache, and an overwhelming and unprecedented lethargy. Proof, if proof were needed, that love was an addictive and debilitating drug. It was almost a relief to have visible, localised injuries to take her mind off the other pain, the one that had kept her stubbornly virtuous these past few days, too disgusted with herself to give Max his answer.

The commissionaire for Max's luxury block was fronted by another non-uniformed man equipped with a walkie-talkie. He nodded unsmilingly at Max, his mind evidently on the job.

'Ex-SAS,' commented Max. 'He must be bored out of his skull. Let's hope he stays that way.'

A high-speed lift whisked them to the top floor, where he ushered her into a vast, airy apartment decorated in muted shades of grey and furnished in stark modern style. The effect was understated and very, if subtly, expensive.

'I see Harriet enjoyed spending your money for you.'

'Do you want to ring her or shall I?' Vivi had left strict instructions at the office that callers were not to be told of her injuries, not wanting Gemma or her mother to hear the news second hand.

'Can't we leave it till the morning? She'll want to come charging over here. I can't bear it when she goes all maternal on me.'

'No. She has to be told before she finds out some other way.'

Vivi listened sullenly while he did an effortless job of keeping Harriet at arm's length. Evidently she was only too delighted that Max was looking after her in her stead, and only too tactfully reluctant to intrude. Then he tried Gemma, but her phone turned out to be constantly engaged.

'I'll get hold of her later. Now go to bed and get some rest.' He showed her into a guest bedroom, complete with en suite bathroom. 'Is there anything you want me to fetch from your apartment?'

Vivi shook her head, not wanting him to see the unmade bed, the dirty cups, the overflowing ashtrays, the squalid litter of the past few days of apathy and self-pity. 'Girls like me always carry overnight kit in their handbags. Which reminds me.' She popped out that day's Pill provocatively. 'Once bitten, twice shy and all that.'

'Are you hungry at all?' said Max, fetching her a glass of water to wash it down. 'I can send out for something.' Like her he no doubt presided over an empty fridge; she couldn't imagine Max eating except in a restaurant.

'I don't want anything, thanks. Except some sleep.'

She shut the door on him, stripped down to her slip, and gave herself an awkward spongebath, to keep the bandages dry. Teeth chattering, even though it wasn't cold, she crawled under the duvet and slept heavily, thanks to the powerful painkillers they had given her at the hospital, only to wake in the small hours with a blinding headache, gripped by a terrible indistinct anxiety. The craving for human contact was overpowering, at that moment even Harriet would have done, even though Harriet hadn't 'done' for a good, or rather bad, twenty years, ever since she had become a poor substitute for Dad. Suddenly Vivi was seven years old again, a child alone in the dark, with both her beloved brothers away at school and a useless, drunken mother weeping in the room next door, weaker and even more pathetic than herself.

She got up and went out into the hall, trying doors till she found Max's room. After a second's hesitation, she slipped into the wide bed beside him, wanting only warmth and comfort. He woke instantly and switched on the bedside light.

'Something wrong?'

With Nick she could have said 'I just want a cuddle', but Max wasn't the cuddly type. What he felt for her was lust, not affection. She pulled her slip over her head and laid flesh against flesh, harking back nostalgically to the days when her mind and her body had been capable of independent action.

'Are you well enough for this?'

'I'm relying on you to make me feel better.'

'What about the other question I asked you?' he reminded her. 'Does this mean yes?' Even though his penis was standing to attention like a toy soldier, he would kick her out of bed soon enough if she said no.

'If you like.'

'Then say it. Say "Yes, Max, I'll marry you." But remember I'll hold you to it.'

He made it sound like a business deal and so it was.

'Yes, Max, I'll marry you . . .'

No point trying to recapture the dubious magic of their first encounter. She wasn't the same person any more, worse luck. But Max wasn't to know that, and she didn't want him to find out. Nick had accused her of reverting to type, and that was what she did now. She had always been a great one for showing off in bed, until he had cured her of the habit, given her the confidence to abandon her little box of tricks and all the pretence that went with them. No wonder she and Max had hit it off that night. Like her pre-Nick self, he was all technique and no heart, or rather he kept his heart, if he had one, somewhere nobody could touch it, least of all the woman he planned to marry. Vivi understood that. They were very well suited. Or rather they would have been, once.

Superficially, it was a great success. And superficial was how she wanted things to stay. No more sentimentality, no letting her heart rule her head. In future, she would stick to what she was good at. Looking after number one.

'I've traced Mary Matheson,' ventured Gemma. Not that Gerald had asked her to, but she seemed like an obvious person to interview. Matheson was CC's long-time secretary who had retired on his death; it was she who had turned over the infamous diary to the police. 'Her pension cheques are being sent to an address in Bournemouth.'

'Thanks. But frankly I don't think I could bear to speak to the old bag, after what she did to you.'

'Then I'll go and see her myself,' persisted Gemma, determined not to waste another potentially important lead. 'She had no choice but to hand that diary in, and for all we know she feels bad about it and might be glad to help.'

In the end Gerald agreed that it was worth a try, while warning her that it would probably prove a waste of time. Gemma didn't risk ringing for an appointment. Reporters never did if they thought that the person concerned might not want to see them. This way Matheson would have no opportunity to take evasive action.

It was nice to have the car to herself and get out of the house for the day. Ever since Vivi's injury Gerald had forbidden her to visit the *Courier* building in person. Far from giving up the struggle, the protesters were swelling in number, encouraged by the media coverage they were attracting – publicity which served, ironically enough, to boost *Courier* sales. The picket acted like a magnet for disgruntled militants of all persuasions, never mind their lack of success so far. Apart from a delayed first edition, on the night of the bombing, *The Courier* had hit the streets six days a week since the move, and there was talk of Max starting up a Sunday sister paper to maximise the productivity of the new presses, which were shortly to put out the first colour issue amid a fanfare of TV advertising.

The architect of the explosion had not been identified. Bert Ferris was among those subjected to police questioning; he had complained to a TV interviewer that surveillance operatives from

Special Branch were infringing his civil liberties. Meanwhile Max had tightened security further, with extra guards patrolling the complex night and day.

Vivi's column reported high morale among the staff, though her own morale was another matter. Now that she had moved in with Max – not that she had seen much of him lately, given that he had spent the last two weeks in the States – she was back to her old brittle self, the soft edges Nick had exposed invisible from view. Gerald professed himself 'disappointed' in her, Harriet dreamed of wedding bells and a solution to all her financial problems, while Daniel expressed a weary lack of surprise.

'But she loved Nick,' Gemma protested, over the phone. 'If you'd seen them together as often as I have . . .'

'If she loved him, that explains everything.'

Love made you vulnerable, of course. But then, so did a lack of it. A lack of it tempted you to take terrible risks to find it . . .

Matheson came to the door herself, a tall, angular woman with sharp, pinched features, wearing a turban which struck an oddly exotic note against the tweed skirt and grey twinset. Gemma's lowly path had never crossed hers during her brief employment at *The Courier*, but Gerald had warned her at the time to beware of her, she was CC's number one spy.

'You'd better come in,' muttered Matheson, having listened warily to Gemma's preamble. She seemed uncomfortable, but not overtly hostile.

'Lord Collington kept his private life private,' she said guardedly in response to Gemma's opening question. 'He was always very discreet. He had to be.'

'Discreet about what, for example?' prompted Gemma, whereupon Matheson was consumed by a coughing fit so violent that Gemma took the liberty of finding the kitchen and fetching her a glass of water.

'Women, of course,' she resumed, grey-faced, after a few restorative sips. 'That's what you wanted to hear about, isn't it?'

'Well . . . yes,' admitted Gemma, wondering what was coming next.

'He didn't need to be discreet when he was young, of course. In those days, it was all women of his own class, and his wife turned a blind eye. But as he got older, the women didn't. He liked them young. And the young ones wouldn't have looked at him twice if he hadn't been rich, why else would a pretty girl go with an old man?'

She gave Gemma a penetrating, testing look, which Gemma met full on, glad of her experience of cross-examination.

'Then of course some little trollop threatened to make trouble for him, it was a wonder it hadn't happened before. That gave him quite a fright, I can tell you. He had his reputation to think of.'

'Do you remember her name?'

'I never knew their surnames. I just put them through on the phone. She cost him plenty, that one did. Mary, he said to me, you're the only woman I can trust. The only one I've ever respected. He was very unhappily married, you know.' She blew her nose. 'Anyway, he had to be more careful after that. I used to listen in on the line. I heard him making the arrangements.'

'Arrangements?'

'If he wanted a girl, he'd ring a number and they'd send someone round to a flat he'd rented, in a false name, somewhere in Chalk Farm, I don't recall the exact address. That type of woman doesn't talk, you see. Not if she wants to stay in business.'

'You mean, he used an escort agency?' said Gemma, sticking to euphemisms. 'Do you remember which one?'

'West End Contacts, it was called. I never approved of that kind of thing. But I blamed it all on his wife. To her he was just someone to pay the bills. And she had him over a barrel of course, she could have ruined his good name. When she died, at last, I thought perhaps . . .' She tailed off, lips twitching. 'But he just carried on, the same as before. Young girls were what he liked.'

A woman scorned, thought Gemma, with belated insight. All these years Matheson had nursed some foolish dream that once CC was free, he would turn to the only woman he could trust and respect. Never mind that she was in her sixties by that time, hope, or rather self-delusion, sprang eternal.

'That's all I have to tell you,' she sniffed. 'I'd like you to leave now.'

'Can I come and see you again?' Surely she must know other things? She must have been listening in on the line for years.

'If I'm still alive. I'm off on a round-the-world cruise at the end of the week, while I'm still fit enough to travel. May as well enjoy the time I've got left.' She removed her turban, revealing a bald head. 'Chemotherapy. Useless, in my case.'

'I'm sorry,' said Gemma, embarrassed.

'The police asked me if I remembered a phone call from you, the call he mentioned in his diary, about you begging him to come to see you the day he died. I knew you hadn't phoned. But I told the police I couldn't remember. I didn't want to have to give evidence against him. And I hated you for being young and beautiful.' She replaced her headdress. 'So now you know.'

'Thank you for telling me.'

'You can quote me, you can put it all in your book, I won't be around when it comes out. Now please go.'

Gemma sat in the car afterwards and had a little weep, wishing Gerald could have heard that speech for himself. He had always half believed in that diary; perhaps this would finally convince him it was a fabrication.

'So he used call girls,' snapped Gerald, when she read back her shorthand notes. 'So what?'

'But surely this West End Contacts place is a lead worth following up?'

'Like the old girl said, prostitutes don't tell tales.'

'Why shouldn't they, once he's dead?'

'Really, Gemma. I would never have thought you would be so prurient.'

'Prurient? What's this book pandering to if it isn't public prurience?'

'To me she sounds like a pathetic, jealous old woman trying to get her own back on him before she dies.'

'Whose side are you on? Do you realise, she could have testified that I never phoned CC that morning?'

'Which would appear to prove her lack of good faith. I'm not grubbing around interviewing the madam of any bordellos, and I'm certainly not having you do it. God. No wonder you wanted to sell your story to *The Torch*.'

'What's that supposed to mean?'

'The only miracle is that your friend Ferris didn't know all this already. By all accounts he spends his life snooping on people.'

'Why are you being so difficult? You're always complaining

about how well the old man covered his tracks, how no one is willing to talk, and now –'

'Who's writing this book? You or me?'

'If it wasn't for me, no one would want you to write it!'

'Are you saying I'm exploiting you?'

'Of course not. But –'

'Then for God's sake shut up and let me get on with it!'

'No I won't shut up!' Even an argument was better than non-communication. 'Sometimes I think you don't want to find out the truth about him. Because the truth would get rid of all your prejudices about me. You never quite accepted my side of the story, did you? You stuck by me because Harriet and Vivi and Daniel were all on my side. But you, the person who hated CC most of all, you blamed me for what happened. That's the real reason you can't bear to touch me, that's why you can't –'

She didn't manage to finish the sentence, because Gerald grabbed hold of her and shook her into silence before pushing her away from him in disgust, sending her reeling backwards, jarring her spine against the table behind her.

'I'm fed up with you sneering at me!' he blazed. 'I've had enough of you pretending to be so damned understanding when I know you despise me!'

'You're the one who despises me! What's the point of staying together if we just make each other miserable?' But he had already stormed out of the room and out of the house.

Gemma stood shaken for a moment, only now aware of the pain in her back and the bruises coming out on her upper arms. She would never have believed Gerald capable of violence, this was her cue to leave him. Would that be the brave, decisive thing to do? Or would it just be running away? But before she could resolve that well-worn dilemma a conscience-stricken Gerald returned.

'I behaved appallingly,' he said. 'Did I hurt you?'

'Mentally more than physically.'

'I don't know what came over me. I can't apologise enough. I promise you it will never happen again.'

But why had it happened? Why had he reacted so savagely?

'Gerald,' said Gemma, grasping the nettle. 'Answer me honestly. Is there another woman?' The suspicion had been troubling her for some time. If Gerald was as 'normal' as he hotly attested to being, perhaps he had sought and found consolation elsewhere, with a woman who didn't repel him physically as his wife so obviously did.

He coloured guiltily.

'No. No, of course not. Are you trying to make me feel even worse? Please, Gemma, I've said I'm sorry. Can't we be friends?'

'Is that enough for you? To be friends?'

'It always comes back to sex, doesn't it?' Despite his apology his anger was still simmering away below the surface. 'I suppose you want children. Harriet's already started asking nosy questions. I knew minding that niece of Ferris's would make you broody.'

'You don't credit me with much intelligence, do you? I wouldn't dream of bringing a child into a shaky marriage like ours. We can't carry on like this, Gerald. Either we split up, or we have to get help.'

'All right. All right, we'll get help.' It should have been a relief. 'Though how humiliating myself in front of a stranger is supposed to solve anything I really don't know.'

It seemed like a step in the right direction, thought Gemma, without much hope. She would have to give it a chance.


'Who was that?' murmured Vivi sleepily, as Max replaced the telephone. He had returned that day from the States, after nearly two weeks away, and they had spent most of the night making up for lost time.

'There's been trouble on the picket.' He flung on a shirt. 'Another human barricade, to try to stop the distribution lorries getting out. They had to bring in mounted police and tear gas.'

'Where are you going?' There was nothing unusual about the events he described, which had happened almost daily in his absence.

'To the hospital. One of the demonstrators is in intensive care.'

'God. Did he get kicked by a horse, or what?'

'No. Apparently he had a stroke.' He hesitated a moment before adding impassively, 'You're going to have to know this sooner or later. It's Ferris.'

'Nick?' Vivi's heart went into spasm.

'No. His father.' Of course. Of course it was his father. Oh God. Poor Nick . . . 'He's in a coma.'

'I'm coming with you,' said Vivi, getting up.

'No. I don't want you there. The relatives are probably ready to lynch me.' He picked up the phone again and rang for a cab.

'If you won't take me with you, I'll go on my own.'

She remembered the night Nick had wept in her arms. His mother's death had brought them together. And now his father's would drive them even further apart, finally and for ever. Even so, she had to see him, had to let him know she cared . . .

'Have it your own way, then.' Max wasn't upset by the news, Vivi realised, just concerned at the PR implications. On a personal level he didn't care if people hated or blamed him. He was insensitive, self-contained, confident to the point of arrogance, he genuinely was all the things she pretended and longed to be . . .

'Stupid old fool,' muttered Vivi as they got into the cab. 'Why couldn't he have taken a nice fat pay-off and bought himself a pub somewhere? And now they'll make a bloody martyr out of him. Never mind all the fags he smoked, all the beer he swilled, never mind that he lived on chips. His blood pressure must have been through the roof . . .'

Specially during an all-out fight with police in full riot gear. She could see him now, face red with fury, the veins standing out on his temple, a walking time-bomb of rage. And all the while she was ranting away, she was thinking of Nick . . .

A few minutes later she found herself in Guy's for the second time that month. A clutch of Ferris relatives had already assembled in Casualty, but there was no sign of Nick; Jackie must have returned to Corfu by now. Vivi held back while Max introduced himself – not that he needed any introduction – expressed his regrets, and asked if there was anything he could do. Whereupon Nick's Uncle Bill, an emphysemic skeleton of a man, like Ferris senior stripped of all his flesh, leapt at him with an animal roar and began belabouring him with his bony fists, an assault which Max bore without retaliating, until Vivi, with the help of two orderlies, managed to haul the old boy off him, still yelling abuse.

'Why don't you call the police?' screeched one of the women, a fat, middle-aged matron, whom Vivi recognised as Nick's Auntie Jean. 'That's what you're good at, isn't it? Get the police to beat him up, the way they did Bert . . .'

'They didn't beat him up,' came Nick's voice from the doorway, producing a sudden silence. 'I just checked. Not a mark on him. So that lets Kellerman here off the hook nicely, doesn't it? Not that it makes any difference. He died, a couple of minutes ago. He's gone.'

There was a loud wail from Auntie Jean. Vivi felt sick.

'I'm truly sorry,' said Max. The words sounded trite, but then condolences always did. Vivi couldn't think of anything to say, not that she could have said it anyway. The look on Nick's face robbed her of speech. Coming here with Max had only rubbed salt into the wound, she could see that now. Perhaps it was just as well.

'Do me a favour, will you?' said Nick, addressing both of them. His voice was ice cold. 'Don't show up at the funeral, don't send any flowers, and don't you dare offer us any handouts. Now get out and leave us alone.'

All Vivi wanted was to put her arms around him and share his pain. For one insane moment she almost did so, ready to risk a certain rebuff against the minute hope of redemption. As if sensing her weakness Max took her arm and led her away, into the night.

# 16

PREDICTABLY, GERALD NEVER found time to fit in the promised visit to a marriage guidance counsellor; Gemma had had to cancel several appointments at the last minute, thanks to him either 'forgetting' or having more urgent business to attend to. She couldn't, however, find the will to force the issue; perhaps, she thought dismally, she didn't really want to save their marriage, any more than Gerald did. But now that he was making some headway with the book she felt duty bound to stay with him until it was finished.

The breakthrough had occurred thanks to a mixture of pedantic thoroughness and sheer good luck. By dint of checking all the names in the old man's address books against the *Courier*'s cuttings index – the librarian was an old friend – Gerald had uncovered a link with one Jack Brinksley, who had gone to jail in the early fifties for attempted murder, a bungled gangland hit. The unusual surname had enabled him to track Brinksley down to a council flat in Peckham, where he discovered a long-retired spiv, down on his luck and happy to talk to anyone for a suitable consideration.

Brinksley was quick to confirm that he had indeed had dealings with Charlie Collington, who had been a sleeping partner in one of his money-making rackets. By buying up dirt-cheap slum properties, illegally evicting the sitting tenants – the fines were minimal, even then – and selling the land for development, they had turned in a fat profit over a period of several years, a process hidden behind a variety of company names with which CC had no visible connection. The old man had provided the capital, Brinksley the muscle and know-how in return for a share of the profits.

Gerald might have set out to do a hatchet job, but he still had too much integrity to take the story on trust, and went to painstaking lengths to make it stand up; to his relief, all the information that it was possible to verify – names, dates, and so on – turned out to be accurate, giving credence to Brinksley's assertion that he wasn't CC's only criminal contact. He had given Gerald the names of several 'investment advisers' like himself, one of whom, an ageing former black marketeer, claimed that the old man had bankrolled the illegal import and distribution of luxury rationed goods.

Given CC's carefully nurtured image as an arbiter of public morals, it seemed incredible to Gemma that he should have taken such risks with his reputation. On the other hand, he had taken a similar risk with her. And as Gerald pointed out, in those days the ruling classes were still very much a law unto themselves – Nick would no doubt argue they still were – generally regarded as above suspicion and subject to minimal public scrutiny.

'You've certainly got the hang of that machine,' he commented, as Gemma transcribed his latest notes into the PC. 'If it wasn't for you, I'd be drowning in a sea of paper.'

He gave her hand a conciliatory squeeze; once Gemma would have welcomed the gesture, but now such overtures interfered with her dreams of escape. She didn't want affection from him any more. Just respect.

'It's terribly easy,' she shrugged, calling up BRINKSLEY, J, on the screen to demonstrate, or rather to give herself an excuse to retrieve her hand.

'There are some new leads here for you to enter up,' he added, fishing out his notebook. 'I intend to make some more house calls next week.'

'Do be careful. These underworld friends of Brinksley's might not appreciate your interest. Types like that could turn nasty . . .'

'The first thing I tell them is that I always protect my sources. So they've got nothing to fear, and neither have I.'

Gemma was less interested in CC's criminal activities than she was in his sexual history, especially now that she was writing her part of the story in her own words, to spare Gerald the ordeal of asking her questions. It proved easier than telling it verbally to a packed courtroom; at least this time her freedom wasn't at stake. But when she read through the first draft, her account seemed to cry out for some kind of corroborating evidence, to win over the sceptics who still thought that she had got off because Gerald could afford to buy her a fancy lawyer, and not because she was innocent.

Given Gerald's ban on following up the West End Contacts lead, Gemma turned her attention to Maureen Brady, CC's former housekeeper. According to Harriet she and the husband had retired to Liverpool, to live with a son, and hadn't been heard from since, but Harriet couldn't remember the son's first name, or even the husband's, whom she had known as 'Brady'; the wages records for that period showed only his initial, 'J'.

There proved to be countless Bradys in the Liverpool directory – presumably the phone, if there was one, was in the son's name – which left Gemma with no option but to search for Maureens in the electoral registers, either by visiting the British Museum, or by going up to Liverpool; she decided on the latter, intending to follow up any leads on the spot. Fearing that Gerald might pooh-pooh the project as a wild-goose chase – which it probably would be – she made the journey under pretext of visiting an old school friend in Alchester, where she would be staying overnight.

The registers in the main reference library yielded up addresses for a score of Maureen Bradys. Gemma listed the other household occupants alongside each one, intending to check every name and address combination against the telephone book; those she couldn't find a number for she would have to visit. By this time it was already nearly eight o'clock and she still didn't have anywhere to stay.

The first few hotels she enquired at were full. Not only were there various conferences in progress, she discovered, but the press had descended en masse to cover a big murder story, gobbling up the remaining vacancies. She was advised to try bed and breakfasts, but these would be of no use to her; she needed a phone in her room, so she could make her long list of calls in private, which was why she hadn't tried to economise. She was just walking out of the Adelphi, resigned to finding somewhere out of town, when she bumped into Nick coming in.

She hadn't seen him since the day of the bomb blast, two months ago now. Gemma had balked at attending his father's funeral, uncertain of her welcome, and making do with a totally inadequate

286

letter of condolence. The strike had never been settled, nor would it ever be, given that Max had long since laid off those concerned. Having lost the attention of the media, Rent-a-mob had dispersed, while most of the print workers had either defected full time to their second jobs or found alternative employment, leaving a few diehards to man a token picket. Meanwhile other papers, encouraged by *The Courier*'s success, were making plans to move their own operations to new hi-tech sites elsewhere.

Nick smiled in recognition and kissed Gemma on the cheek, never mind that she was still working for his arch-enemy.

'How are you?' she said, seeing through his superficial cheerfulness, a pale imitation of the real thing.

'Covering my last ever job for *The Torch*. What brings you here?'

'I'm doing research for Gerald's book. I didn't know you were on the move.' Vivi must surely have heard the news on the grapevine. But it was typical of her not to say anything. Vivi never mentioned Nick if she could help it.

'Come and have a drink and I'll tell you all about it.'

Gemma waited, watching, while he ordered the drinks at the hotel bar and exchanged banter with a group of fellow-hacks. He sounded just like the laugh-a-minute Nick of old. But his eyes had aged and for the first time she noticed some silver in the bronze of his hair.

'I hear you're due to be a bridesmaid,' he said, rejoining her. Vivi's wedding was supposed to be a closely guarded secret. No guests, except for Gemma, Harriet and Daniel – Gerald had invented a prior engagement – and no honeymoon. Vivi was too busy getting her new consumer page off the ground to take any time off. 'Next Tuesday, isn't it, at Chelsea Register Office?'

To appease Harriet, Max had used her address in Eaton Place, thereby securing a more fashionable venue than Wandsworth or Finsbury town halls, but it was still a poor substitute for the big church wedding at St Bride's which Vivi had ruled out of hand.

'That's right,' admitted Gemma. She had been counting the days. Daniel would be staying two whole weeks.

'They didn't waste much time.' He kept his expression hidden behind a pint of special.

'No,' agreed Gemma. She would have expected Vivi to hold out longer than a couple of months. But despite her usual surface belligerence some of the fight had gone out of Vivi lately. Having made, in Gemma's opinion, the worst mistake of her life she seemed determined to compound it. Or perhaps Max was simply better than she was at getting his own way.

'So which paper are you going to?' asked Gemma, changing the subject for fear of treading on Nick's corns.

'I'm not. I've decided to go freelance. My old man left quite a bit, he'd been salting it away for years. Plus there's the house, of course, all paid up. And the life assurance. So suddenly I'm in the money.'

It was ironic that Ferris senior should have died worth more than CC, though not, on reflection, surprising.

'How's Cass?'

'Still in Corfu. Jackie wants to use her share of the loot to open up a bar out there. A nice quick way to lose it all, I suppose. How about joining us for dinner?'

'I ought to get a move on. I'm still trying to find a room, everywhere's booked up, including this place . . .'

'Don't worry about that. See that bird over there? The redhead in the green jumper? I guarantee you she won't be sleeping in her own room tonight. She makes Vivi look like Mary Whitehouse. I'll wait to see who she pairs off with and then ask her for her key, she owes me a favour.'

'But –'

'That's settled then. Now let me get you another drink.'

The evening soon degenerated into an informal send-off for Nick, with the redhead in the green jumper evidently particularly sorry to see him go. So much so that she did end up sleeping in her own room after all, with Nick slipping Gemma his key, instead of hers.

'What did I tell you?' he hissed, winking, but she could tell that his heart wasn't in it. It was just a soulless exercise in tit-for-tat, to let Vivi know, via Gemma, that he was having a great time without her. A message she would take a grim delight in passing on.

Next morning she got down to work on the telephone in her room.

'Hello, can I speak to Mrs Maureen Brady please?'

'Who's that?' A woman's voice, too young to be Brady's. There was a dog barking loudly in the background.

'My name's Gemma Lawrence.' The patter had become automatic by this time, twenty calls into the day. 'I'm not sure if I have the right Mrs Brady . . .'

'Gemma Lawrence? The one who stabbed Lord Thingummy?'

'Er . . . yes.' It was the first time she'd been asked, proof of the shortness of the public memory. Her fifteen minutes of fame were over. 'I'm looking for the lady who used to work at Collington Hall, in Little Moldingham . . .'

'My ma-in-law. She doesn't live with us no more, thank the Lord. Got her own place off the council.'

Success.

'Where can I get in touch with her?'

'She's staying with her sister, in Ireland, at the minute.'

'Can I telephone her there?'

'Leave hold of that, Prince!' More barking. 'Her sister's not on the phone.'

'What about her Liverpool address and phone number? I could ring her when she gets back.'

'What's it about?'

Briefly, Gemma explained about the book, mentioning that Mrs Brady's 'expenses' would be paid if she could offer any useful information.

'Well, I don't suppose she'd say no to a few quid. But I'd be in trouble if I put you on to her without the old girl's say-so. Her and me never got on, see. Don't know when she'll be back from Ireland, she's waiting for a brother to die. You'd better speak to my husband.'

'Fine. When are you expecting him home?'

'Some time next week. He's a long-distance lorry driver. Would he get these expenses too?'

'I'll discuss that with him when I ring him.' It wouldn't be next week, or even the one after that. Gemma was keeping the period of Daniel's visit as clear as possible, there were various exhibitions they planned to see together. Plenty of time to talk to Brady after Daniel had gone back to Paris.

As soon as she got home she called up BRADY, MAUREEN, on her database, entered up all the information she had gleaned so far, inserted a diary entry to remind her to renew contact, and promptly forgot all about her. A few more days and Daniel would be here, making the ill wind of Vivi's marriage worth while.

Vivi dreamed of spiders again on the eve of her wedding, haunted by Gemma's image of the barbed-wire web. She woke with such a violent headache that she was physically sick.

'Are you all right?' asked Max, noticing her pallor.

She could have said, 'No, I'm not all right. I should never have agreed to marry you. Let's call it off.' But she didn't have the guts. Max was all she had left now. She had meant to marry him in cold blood, for *The Courier*, and now here she was, doing it on the rebound, out of fear of being alone. Pathetic.

'I'm fine,' said Vivi, downing a couple of painkillers by way of breakfast. 'It's just a migraine, that's all.' Or rather another migraine. It had been three days with, one without, for weeks now. Of course you haven't got a brain tumour, she lectured herself. Stop being such a bloody hypochondriac . . .

It was supposed to be bad luck to see the bridegroom on the morning of the wedding, or for him to see the bridal outfit, two of the many pre-nuptial traditions Vivi insisted on flouting, much to Harriet's chagrin. Vivi had let her choose the dress – her head had been particularly bad that day – an exquisite shot silk number with matching jacket in a pale silvery-blue, the nearest Vivi could countenance to white. The ceremony would be over quickly, with no vows to be broken, just a declaration by both parties that they knew of no reason why they should not be married. Nothing to it. Hardly worth getting in a state about.

She was hurt, nonetheless, that Gerald wasn't coming. It wasn't as if she needed him to give her away, the whole idea of a man giving away a woman to another man was against her feminist principles. But he might have made some pretence of wishing her well. At least Daniel had kept his feelings on the subject, whatever they were, to himself, unlike Gemma, who had the nerve to try to talk her out of it, thereby firming up her wavering resolve.

Harriet, dramatic in purple, was waiting for them with Gemma and Daniel outside Chelsea Register Office. She kissed Max effusively on both cheeks and burbled something cringe-making about what a lovely couple they made. Max returned her embrace; as usual he had her eating out of his hand, with Harriet now entitled, as his mother-in-law, to fuss over him to her heart's content. Meanwhile Vivi's headache had grown too large for her skull, hammering loudly in its futile attempts to get out. Gemma smiled at her placatingly, as if to negate her harangue of the other night and forgive the insults Vivi had hurled back at her. Daniel seemed miles away, recalling his own wedding perhaps, an even hastier affair than this to prevent Natasha being deported, with Vivi looking on in slit-eyed mistrust. Well might he be cynical, but then so was she. That was the beauty of it. No illusions.

She began to feel very faint during the short ceremony. Her own fault for not eating anything. She was horribly unfit at the moment, she hadn't been for a run in weeks, the only exercise she got these days was sex. And having been an early bird all her life, it was all she could do to drag herself out of bed in the mornings. She would definitely take herself in hand, starting tomorrow . . .

Max kissed the bride. Vivi smiled brightly for the photographers – one official, and two marauding paparazzi – remembering how pretty Gemma had looked outside the church at Little Moldingham, her tall, blonde perfection masking a pain even greater than Vivi's own. The motor drives whirred, immortalising the moment – Max, grey-haired and distinguished-looking, towering confidently over his bride in her spindly heels, her wan complexion warmed by blusher, her head held high, to minimise the shadow cast by her wretched nose and make her neck look longer, her dark, heavily made up eyes staring straight at the lens, as if they had nothing to hide.

The pictures taken, they drove to Claridges for the wedding breakfast, where the Dom Perignon was already on ice, awaiting their arrival. It tasted of vinegar. Surely Max would send it back? But no one else seemed to notice. Vivi scooped up a forkful of smoked salmon and scrambled eggs but the smell was so peculiar she put it down again. Brain tumours affected your sense of taste and smell . . . Oh God, she was going to throw up again.

'Excuse me,' she mumbled, standing up too fast. And then she was briefly aware of the room pitching back and forward like a drunken ship, and the next thing she knew she was on the floor, spattered with sick and spilt champagne.

'I'm okay,' she protested, as Max and Daniel lifted her between them and deposited her back in her overturned chair.

'Oh darling! Your beautiful dress! It's ruined!' wailed Harriet, with her usual sense of priorities.

'Put your head between your knees,' counselled Gemma, pouring her a glass of water.

'You're going to see a doctor,' decreed Max. 'The rest of you please stay and finish the meal, I'll send the chauffeur back as soon as he's dropped us off, he'll take you home when you're ready. We'll have a celebration dinner together some other time. Can you walk, sweetheart?' It was unlike Max to be openly affectionate; it was one of the things they had in common.

'Of course I can bloody walk. I don't know what happened. I must have a virus or something.'

'She fainted the other day, when we were buying the dress,' put in Harriet. 'I've never known her faint in her life before. I said to her then, remember that bang you had on the head, back in the summer. Concussion can have delayed effects, people sometimes keel over weeks later with blood clots and fractured skulls . . . Ring me later, won't you Max?' she trilled, as Max led Vivi away. 'Let me know what the doctor says . . .'

'Why didn't you tell me you had fainted?' demanded Max, as the car drove off.

'What was there to tell? It was a hot day, the shop was stuffy.'

'Harriet's right. The hospital could have missed something. I want your head X-rayed again.'

'But –' But they might find something.

'I'll ring my doctor as soon as we get in, arrange a thorough physical check-up.'

'Will you stop bossing me about?'

'You're my wife now,' Max reminded her. 'And you'll do as I say.'

This outrageously sexist remark should have been a red rag to a bull. But Vivi couldn't find the energy to answer back. Or perhaps she simply realised that there wasn't any point.


Harriet's party spirits were soon revived by the sight of a couple of acquaintances at a nearby table, whom she promptly invited to join them to celebrate her daughter's wedding. Gemma and Daniel exchanged glances as she ordered two more bottles of champagne, one of which she proceeded to dispose of single-handed, talking non-stop all the while. By the time they managed to drag her away, she was well on her way to being very drunk, falling fast asleep in the car in mid-sentence. On arrival at Eaton Place, Daniel carried her, comatose, into the flat and put her to bed.

'For God's sake let's get out of here,' he hissed. 'Before she wakes up. What time is Gerald expecting you?'

'Not till this evening. He's out all day.' Gemma had pleaded with him not to boycott the ceremony, but for Gerald this marriage was proof that Max had kept him on to curry favour with Vivi, a further blow to his damaged pride. Gemma knew, as Vivi must, that he was brooding on the loss of *The Courier* again. He had been moody and preoccupied all week, in the run-up to the wedding, even over dinner with Daniel last night; afterwards Gemma had heard him pacing about downstairs well into the small hours.

'Then let's kick off with that Schwitters exhibition at the Tate.'

A bright morning had given way to a dark afternoon, the sky black with impending rain. They got the car to drop them at Bamber Court, where Daniel was staying, so that he could change out of his suit, telling the driver not to wait, they would take a cab up to town. But just as they were about to leave there was a roar of thunder as the clouds finally burst open, hurling a rattle of raindrops against the window panes.

'We'll get soaked if we go out now,' said Gemma. 'Shall I make some coffee, while we wait for it to ease off?'

'Might as well, I suppose,' He sounded bored, indifferent, quite unlike the other Daniel, the one she had never seen, only heard on the phone. Likewise his laughter; Gemma had had to picture for herself what that lovely warm sound must look like. Over the last few weeks they had discussed Vivi's break-up with Nick, Gerald's discoveries about the old man, Gemma's latest cartoons and Daniel's current assignments, without reserve and with the fluency of old friends. And now, face to face, they were like strangers.

'Sorry,' said Daniel over coffee, puncturing the silence. 'I'm not being very sociable. But after listening to my mother chanking on, it's nice to have a bit of peace and quiet.'

'She does worry about you, you know.' As always, when Harriet drank, she had fallen to fretting about his safety and nagging him to get a nice safe job at home. 'We all do.'

'Well, don't bother. It's not half as dangerous as she makes out.

If it was, perhaps I'd get more out of it. Any job becomes routine, after a while.' He was invariably off-hand about his work; Gemma had always sensed the deep current of discontent running below the studied, couldn't-care-less sang-froid. 'Still, better to be a successful snapper then a failed artist. God knows I'm supposed to resemble my father enough already.'

It wasn't just the old man who had thought so. Harriet had admitted it herself, with weary resignation. Like Toby, Daniel was a womaniser. Like Toby he was reckless, restless, fickle, afraid of responsibility, reluctant to save money or acquire property, preferring to live out of a suitcase and strictly for today. And like Toby she feared he would die young; with Toby it had been drugs, with Daniel it was danger.

'If the job's becoming routine, why not take a break from it? You could sell your shares, like Gerald did, only they're worth a lot more now. You could afford to take a few years off, paint for the sake of painting, without worrying about making a living . . .'

'The working artist gives advice to the self-indulgent amateur,' mocked Daniel, giving her that infuriating superior smile and lighting up another filthy French cigarette.

'Not you as well,' muttered Gemma, stung by the sarcasm he had spared her on the phone. 'I thought Gerald was the paranoid one, not you. It must run in the family.'

She shouldn't have said that. She didn't mean to say any more than that. But then Daniel said it for her.

'You're not happy together, are you?'

Gemma muzzled the automatic 'Oh course we are!' The atmosphere had been so strained over dinner last night that Daniel must have guessed that all was not well between them. To lie about it would merely be to protest too much.

'Gerald's not happy with me. He's never come to terms with what happened. He thinks I asked for it. God knows I've thought it often enough myself.'

'Have you talked about it?'

'He won't. He won't talk to me, or anyone else. I've tried everything, and nothing works.' And then, on a sudden, reckless impulse, 'I don't know how much longer I can stick it. Or rather, I do. Once we've finished the book, I'm going to leave him.'

There. She had said it, solidified the thought into words.

Daniel's face didn't move a muscle, a sure sign that he was shocked.

'I know I must seem ungrateful,' she went on, before he could say it first. 'He stuck by me all through the trial, I owe him more than I can ever repay. But we don't love each other any more, I don't think we ever did. Gerald was under pressure to get married, and I had a Cinderella complex. It was all subconscious, not deliberate, but it wasn't love.'

Still Daniel didn't respond. I've blown it now, thought Gemma, too late. She had wrecked the next precious fortnight of his company. How could she expect him to want to spend time with her, knowing that she was planning to run out on his brother the way his own wife had run out on him?

'I'd better go,' she said, mortified. 'I never meant to dump on you like this. Please don't say anything to Gerald, or anyone else.'

'It's raining.'

'Then I'll get wet. I'm sorry. Goodbye.'

'Gemma . . .' He stood up, barring her way.

'I shouldn't have told you. I didn't do it for sympathy, I'm the first to admit I've made a complete mess of my life, and Gerald's. You can't possibly hate me as much as I hate myself . . .' Shut up, she thought, biting her lip, before you start crying.

'I don't hate you, Gemma.'

'Well you ought to. Gerald's not to blame. It's all my fault . . .'

'No. It's mine as well. I could have stopped you marrying him. You know what nearly happened, what could have happened.'

It was the first time either of them had acknowledged that silent, poignant moment when they had stood at a fork in the road and gone their separate ways.

'I know what didn't happen,' said Gemma, rallying. 'If you think I'd have let you treat me the way you treat all those other women . . .'

'That was why it didn't happen. But that wasn't the only reason.'

Another silence while she told herself not to jump to conclusions, while he struggled visibly to find the words he needed. When they finally came they were cloaked in the same derisive tone Vivi always used to talk about things that mattered.

'I'm trying to explain this to myself, as well as you. After

Natasha, I suppose I stopped trusting my feelings. Not that I'd ever trusted them much, otherwise the marriage might have worked. I certainly didn't trust them when I met you. So I stuck to thoughts instead, they're safer. I thought, she's not your type, she's a nice, shy, innocent girl, so keep your dirty hands off her. When I realised Gerald was keen on you, I thought good, they're just right for one another. When you got married I thought good, this way I won't be tempted. Then I thought, we're both safe now, nothing can happen over the telephone. But it can. It did. For me, anyway.'

And for her. She had known it, and denied it, just as he had done, for fear that he didn't feel the same way . . .

'I could sense that things weren't right between you. No, I hoped it. And felt shitty about it. And now I'm going to look as if I'm trying to cash in. I ought to try to persuade you not to leave him, he's my brother, and I love him. But not as much as I love you.'

He sounded angry, defensive. He certainly didn't try to cash in. He just stood there sullenly, arms folded, waiting for her to make the next move.

'Well?' he demanded, as if expecting a rebuff. 'Aren't you going to say anything?'

She couldn't say it. So she did it instead. She took three short steps towards him, pulled his face down towards hers and kissed him for the first time, telling him everything he needed to know, silently but deafeningly, loud enough to drown out their troublesome thoughts and let their feelings take over, like a tidal wave laying waste every puny man-made structure in its path.

She had thought, once, that she would never be able to bear a man's touch again. But there was nothing like being deprived of something to make you want it. Perhaps Gerald had done her more good than he knew, condemning her to that cold, lonely bed. And now she was warm, hot, feverish with need. They tore at each other's clothes with clumsy haste, there had been too much foreplay already. Hours and hours of it, voices intertwined, miles and miles of cable between them. And now Gemma couldn't bear to wait a moment longer, crying out with relief once he was safely inside her, closing herself around him tightly, pushing him in as deep as he could go, wanting him to stay there for ever and ever . . .

Suddenly all the pain and waste and wanting seemed worth

while. Because it surely wouldn't have felt like this if it had happened at the beginning. She was ready for this now, just as he was. She looked into his eyes and saw something that hadn't been there before, something she had put there. It was the purest, most peaceful, most precious moment of her life.

'I can't be pregnant,' said Vivi stubbornly. She had disliked Max's smooth-talking doctor on sight. 'I've been on the Pill, I came on as usual . . .'

'That can happen. I would estimate that you're in your third month.'

It was just over two months since she had last slept with Nick. Just over two months, less a week, since she had first slept with Max and stopped monkeying around with her Pill . . .

'Are you sure it isn't less? Or more?'

'We'll do a scan, of course.' And then, misinterpreting her stricken expression, 'I take it you do wish to proceed with the pregnancy?'

Vivi nodded numbly. She couldn't go through with another abortion. Especially if it was Nick's child. Or even if it was Max's. The important thing was, it was hers. Except that she had a husband now, dammit. She would never, ever have married Max if she'd known that she was pregnant. Or Nick either, come to that. She would never voluntarily have given up the single mother's privilege of having exclusive, automatic, indisputable rights over her child . . .

'Well?' said Max, jumping up as she rejoined him. 'What did he say?'

'That there's nothing wrong with me,' said Vivi airily. 'At least, nothing that a bit of hard labour won't cure.' And then, when he appeared not to understand, 'I'm expecting a baby.'

'What?'

'Your baby. I stopped taking the Pill when I moved in with you. I didn't tell you. I didn't even admit it to the doctor. I pretended it was an accident. I was upset about losing Cass, I wanted a child, and I was afraid you wouldn't. If you don't like it that's just too bad.'

The lies came out so pat she almost believed them herself,

perhaps because they were unrehearsed, instinctive. Max wasn't the type of soft-hearted sap to warm to another man's baby. And besides, it might just be his after all. She needed – no, preferred – to believe that. Perhaps that way she would manage not to love it too much.

'You don't have to pretend you're pleased,' she added. He certainly didn't look it. For a moment she thought he had rumbled her.

'I'm not pleased. You lied to me. You said you didn't want children.'

So she had. But she had been lying to herself, not to him.

'I said that because I was scared I wouldn't be able to have any.' And then, turning the tables on him, 'I've worried about that ever since the abortion.'

She could tell that she had made her point; it was one of the few things he seemed to have a conscience about.

'Wait for me in the car. I want to talk to the doctor, make sure he fixes up for you to see the top man.'

'What's wrong with the top woman?' Vivi called after him, but he ignored her.

His absence gave her time to think. What if the scan exposed her for a liar? No chance of keeping it to herself with Max paying the piper. She should have gone to her own female GP in Battersea, at least she wasn't in Max's pocket. But she had felt so bloody ill, so scared that there was something terrible wrong with her, that she had meekly done what she was told.

Why the hell was he taking so long? Was there something the doctor hadn't told her? Had she done some harm to the baby by continuing to take her Pill? And what about all the painkillers she had taken for her migraines? She should have asked . . .

'What's he been telling you?' she demanded, as Max returned. 'Has he been holding out on me about something?'

'We were just discussing the various clinics, obstetricians and so on.'

'I don't approve of private medicine. I don't see why I can't have it on the NHS.'

'Don't argue with me, Vivi. You can salve your social conscience by not taking up a scarce health service bed. This is my child too, remember.'

She had asked for that. His child too. Even though he still doubted it, judging by the grim look on his face. Well, if it was 'his child too', that made it his heir, and it would bloody well get everything his heir was entitled to. She would make sure of that . . .

Oh God, she thought. I'm turning into my mother.

'I hate all this hole-in-the-corner stuff,' said Daniel irritably. 'We have to tell him.'

Why did lovemaking always have to end like this? Why couldn't he forget the world outside and just enjoy being together? The last few days had been all highs and lows, with no comfortable middle ground between. Gemma didn't want to think about Gerald, and Daniel seemed to think about nothing else. This was much more difficult for him, of course, than it was for her. She was merely deceiving a husband who didn't love her any more; he was sleeping with his brother's wife.

Deceiving Gerald was proving almost too easy. He hadn't queried her numerous shopping expeditions, yet another visit to her friend in Alchester, or her ostensibly legitimate outings with his brother; he barely seemed to notice if she was there or not.

'If I tell him about us,' she repeated patiently, 'he'll never believe that I was going to leave him anyway. He'll think it was because of you, it will wreck your relationship with him for evermore.'

'You've always been good at making excuses not to do things,' said Daniel cruelly. 'And look at the trouble that got you into before. If you won't tell him then I will. Frankly, I'd prefer it that way.'

'If you say one single word to him I'll never forgive you! Don't you have any feelings for him at all?'

'Yes. Respect. The way things are at the moment I'm helping you make a fool of him.'

'I can't leave him yet. I owe him, Daniel. He can't finish the book without me . . .'

'And how long is that going to take? He's bound to be late delivering, you know what a nitpicker he is.'

He was right, of course. This could drag on for another year, a year of lies and evasion, overshadowed by the risk of Gerald, or other people, finding out. Except that Daniel wouldn't wait a year.

'If you leave him now,' continued Daniel relentlessly, 'I won't go back to Paris, except to pick up my gear. If you don't, then I can't play the hypocrite any longer, I'd rather clear off until you do.'

She couldn't bear that, not just for her own sake, but for Daniel's. He had talked a lot in the past few days of his disaffection with his work and his increasing sense of isolation. He no longer fitted in with the young reputation-makers and dreaded ending up as yet another ageing, rootless adrenaline-junkie, of which there were all too many in the business, unable to function without an excess of booze and/or cocaine. He could pick up a London-based job easily enough, or go freelance, and once he was safely home, thought Gemma, she would encourage him to make more time for his painting . . .

'Tell him, Gemma,' he repeated. Not the cool, laid-back, anything-goes Daniel, but the passionate, demanding, impatient, touchingly insecure one. The compulsion to please was as powerful as ever, only this time she would be pleasing herself as well. That was what made it so difficult.

'I'll tell him that I'm leaving,' said Gemma finally. 'But not about you. It would hurt him too much. I'll offer to carry on helping him with the book. I'll find a place of my own, I'll be free to live my own life, and then, after a decent interval, we can start officially seeing each other.'

He didn't trust her yet, thought Gemma, seeing the doubt in his eyes. He found it difficult to believe that Gerald would let her go without a fight, feared that the threat of her leaving would 'bring him to his senses', wouldn't rest until she was free. If she'd told him that her marriage had never been consummated, it might have reassured him. But that was one secret she had no right to share. She might be unfaithful, but she wasn't disloyal.

'All right,' he said grudgingly. 'I suppose that's a workable compromise. As long as you get it over with tonight. The longer you put it off the harder it'll be.' And the more he would doubt her resolve.

'Tonight, then.'

'You won't let him talk you out of it?'

'He won't even try, believe me.' Specially if there really was another woman. It might be hard to imagine Gerald having an affair, but he had blushed scarlet that time she had challenged him. Perhaps he too had a chance of happiness and had too much of a conscience to take it . . .

'I'm being a bastard to you, aren't I?' said Daniel, gathering her into his arms again. 'It's just that I've trained myself not to want things too much. That way you don't get disappointed.'

'That's why you stopped painting, isn't it?'

'I'm afraid of failing. Especially failing at this. I walked away from you, once. It would serve me right if you did the same to me.'

'Wishful thinking. You won't get rid of me that easily.'

His face softened. This time it was slow and gentle and lazy, as if there was all the time in the world, as if they belonged to each other properly. She wanted to cultivate that tender, caring, trusting side of him, drive out the cynicism and self-destructiveness. She wanted to do to him what Nick had tried and failed to do to Vivi . . .

As she drove home that evening she rehearsed a little speech in her head about how much she respected and admired Gerald, and how grateful she was to him, and how she would always be fond of him. But as things were they were making each other miserable, it would be best for both of them if they lived apart. It needn't affect the book in the slightest, she badly wanted it to do well and launch him on a successful writing career . . .

The lights were on, he was home. Gemma let herself in, wondering, absurdly, if she should cook dinner first, or afterwards. Normally Gerald kept to his study, emerging only for meals, often working till very late, but today he was sitting in the living room, brooding over a glass of whisky. He looked up at her, his eyes bright and strange, and she thought, my God, he knows. Somehow or other he had found out. And now he would completely misinterpret what she had intended to say . . .

'I've been waiting for you to get home,' he greeted her. He sounded quite sober. 'I have to talk to you.'

Gemma sat down weakly, preparing herself for recriminations. 'I'm listening.'

There was a large buff board-backed envelope on the coffee table. Gerald withdrew a letter-sized envelope from inside it, and handed it to her. It was addressed with a printed label and inside was a strip of computer paper bearing the message:

LAY OFF COLLINGTON. ABANDON FURTHER RESEARCH NOW.
YOU HAVE BEEN WARNED.

'When did you get this?' said Gemma, horrified. She had
worried, ever since the Brinksley connection, that Gerald was
getting out of his depth. Word must have got around the criminal
community that he was poking around in matters that didn't
concern him . . .
'About ten days ago. I ignored it. I thought it was just another
crank. God knows, we've both had our share of hate mail, with me
an unscrupulous money-grubber getting rich out of a murder, and
you the little slag that should have been hanged, and all the rest.'
Gemma had trained herself to tear such letters up without
reading them; amazing how the people who wrote them managed
to track down the home address of their victims. But there hadn't
been any for several weeks, presumably because the hate brigade
had found someone new to harass. And the hate brigade wrote
long rambling missives in erratic handwriting on cheap lined
paper, they didn't issue curt, computer-generated threats in
untraceable dot matrix print.
'Then a couple of days later, I got this.' He handed her another
envelope, similarly addressed, and this time the message read:

YOU WERE WARNED. ABANDON BOOK NOW OR TASTE YOUR OWN
MEDICINE. PEOPLE WHO LIVE IN GLASS HOUSES SHOULDN'T
THROW STONES.

'What's that supposed to mean?'
'Isn't it obvious? If you're going to expose someone else's secrets
you'd better not have any of your own.'
'What secrets?' His mistress, she thought, with something like
hope. What else could it be?
Gerald took another swallow of whisky before reaching again
inside the envelope and drawing out a third missive.

CANCEL CONTRACT IMMEDIATELY. OTHERWISE GENERAL
DISTRIBUTION, INCLUDING YOUR WIFE. NO MORE WARNINGS.

'Distribution of what?'

'I'm going to ring my agent in the morning,' said Gerald heavily, 'and call off the deal. I'll have to pay back the advance, of course. A great big chunk of it went to clear the overdraft, so it'll mean getting rid of the house, finding somewhere cheaper. That's why I couldn't bring myself to lie to you about it. I'm sorry, Gemma, but I can't bear for people to know. Harriet, Vivi, Daniel, Max bloody Kellerman, and God knows who else. I can't bear it.'

Two large teardrops slithered down his cheeks. He seemed unaware of them. Hesitantly, Gemma got up and sat on the arm of his chair, putting a hand on his shoulder.

'To know what?' Surely it couldn't be that bad? Was the woman married? Was she the one he wanted to protect?

'It proves I was on to something, doesn't it?' muttered Gerald, almost defiantly, blowing his nose. 'It proves I was about to find something out, something that implicates the living, somebody who's got a lot to lose. And whoever it is has been watching me. He's had a private detective on my tail ever since I started this book, before I ever stumbled across Brinksley . . .'

Distribution of photographs, thought Gemma with sudden insight. A private detective had pictures of him with his lover. She wanted to say, don't worry, it doesn't matter, I don't mind. But he didn't expect her not to mind. He expected her to be shattered, hurt. He was about to give her the excuse she needed to leave him . . .

'I'll have to fake a burglary,' he went on. 'Make out the computer and the disks and notes have been stolen, that it would take too long to start again. But you've got a right to know the truth. I should have told you long ago, before we were married.'

Before they were married? Surely Gerald hadn't been having an affair all this time?

'I'll go back to when it started.' He took another swallow of Scotch. 'I was about fifteen, there was a mumps epidemic at school, and anyone who hadn't had it, like me, was sent home, because mumps can make you sterile. Daniel was all right, he'd had it as a kid, so he stayed on. Harriet didn't want your father to catch it – this was just before they split up – so I was exiled to Collington Hall till I was out of quarantine.

'The first weekend I was there the old man turned up. Grammie stayed on in London, she never liked that house, any more than I did. But CC couldn't resist the chance to kick me around a bit. That night he started goading me over dinner about had I had a woman yet and I said yes, just to shut him up, but of course he didn't believe me. His brother John had killed himself a couple of years before, we'd been very close, and inevitably CC started asking me if I was a nancy boy like my uncle, and had we had it off together.'

Perhaps it wasn't another woman, thought Gemma. Perhaps it was a man. Perhaps he was about to own up to something he had always denied . . .

'That housekeeper woman, Maureen Brady, had a niece, Rita. She'd come to work at the house as a domestic, straight from school. She was a big, bosomy, brazen kind of girl, every time I so much as looked at her I got an erection, but of course I was too damned shy to do anything about it.

'Once we'd finished dinner, the old man said that it was time I had an early night. I didn't argue, anything to get away from him. He followed me up the stairs and along the corridor, and I thought he was going to bed as well, but he followed me into my room, and there was Rita, lying on my bed, stark naked. And he said, go on, show me what you can do, prove you're not a fairy. Then he locked the door, and pocketed the key and sat down to watch.'

Gemma could just see the lecherous look on the old man's face, a look she knew only too well.

'If he hadn't been there, believe me, it would have been a wet dream come true. But with him as Peeping Tom it was more like a nightmare. He kept saying, what's the matter with you boy, don't you know what to do, do you want me to show you how? And so he did. I couldn't bear to look, but I could hear. It was disgusting. When they'd finished, I thought thank God for that, but that wasn't the end of it. He twisted my arms behind my back, and she unzipped my flies and got to work. She tried everything. And nothing happened. I can't begin to describe the humiliation of it. The old man crowed and crowed, and I'm sure Rita and her aunt had a good laugh about it afterwards, in the kitchen. That's why I didn't want you to contact Brady, in case she mentioned it. That's why I couldn't face going to see her myself. I had to tell you all this, so you'd understand the next bit.'

'I wish you'd told me before,' said Gemma, confused. 'If not at the beginning, after the rape. Then I might at least have felt you believed me. Because, in a way, it happened to you too . . .'

'I always believed you.' He got up and crossed to the other side of the room, keeping his back to her, shoulders hunched. 'When I went up to Oxford it was right at the end of the swinging sixties. All the girls were suddenly on the Pill, you were no one unless you were sleeping with someone. And needless to say I wasn't. I was terrified of failing again, and the girl gossiping about it to her friends, the way women do. So I became one of those sexless bespectacled swots people joke about.

'At the end of my second year, Daniel and I had the house to ourselves for the summer while Harriet and Simon were at the house in Cannes with Vivi. I had a job at *The Courier*, as a general dogsbody, and Daniel's idea of a holiday was laying as many different girls as possible, he was even worse then than he is now –'

Gemma flushed. No, she thought, he's much worse now, he's spent the last week making love to your wife.

'At night I'd lie there, listening to the sound effects next door and getting more and more frustrated, till I couldn't stand it any more. So one night I got up, drove to Shepherd Market, and picked up a prostitute. She didn't know me, I didn't have to worry about her feelings, or her pleasure, or her marking me out of ten to her friends, all I had to do was to pay her, I was the one in control. And everything was perfectly all right, and no woman can possibly understand what a huge relief that was. So naturally I did it again, and again. It became a compulsion. I thought at first it would give me confidence, but I just felt furtive and grubby and inadequate, the kind of loser who can't get it any other way.'

Now she understood his over-reaction to the West End Contacts lead. He wasn't enough of a hypocrite to pillory the old man for doing what he had done himself.

'I'd come home feeling disgusted with myself and jealous as hell of my brother, for being normal. And I thought, I bet if I ever did fall in love with anyone, bloody Daniel would get to her first . . .'

Gemma covered her face with her hands, glad that he had his back to her.

'Soon Harriet was nagging me to find a wife and start a family, because she thought it would improve my chances of inheriting.

But I wasn't prepared to shackle myself to a woman I didn't love, no matter what the old man did or said. Or risk making a fool of myself with some girl who might talk. If you've ever heard Vivi or my mother dissecting a man's performance, you'll know what I mean.'

So much for sex being easier for men, thought Gemma.

'And then I met you,' he said sadly. 'You were unlike every other girl I'd ever met. Old fashioned, shy, sweet-natured, easy to talk to, you can't believe how few women there are like that, nowadays . . .'

Old-fashioned meaning a virgin, thought Gemma. Shy meaning unassertive and lacking in confidence. Sweet-natured meaning over-eager to please. Easy to talk to meaning passive, a good listener, schooled never to interrupt, never to disagree. He had elevated all her shortcomings into virtues.

'I couldn't believe my luck. I thought, if we have any problems once we're married, we'll sort them out then, but I'm damned if I'm risking losing her now. Which is why I was such a perfect gentleman. I stopped seeing those other women, I was happy to wait for you. I've never been much good at expressing my feelings, but I did love you, Gemma, more than you'll ever believe. I still do.'

I still do. The words hit her like bullets. She didn't want him to love her. She would rather he hated her . . . He would hate her, if he knew.

'And then we had that disastrous honeymoon. One minute you seemed shy and innocent, the next you were acting the red-hot vamp. It threw me completely, I panicked. And then once I found out what you'd been through, to protect me, I felt castrated, useless. I never doubted you, Gemma, not for a minute, it was myself I couldn't live with, for having exposed you to that kind of danger. If I'd been honest with you, you wouldn't have been so afraid to be honest with me. And the more you tried to help me, the worse I felt. I was afraid if we went to a counsellor it would all come out, and that you'd despise me more than ever. The only way I could feel half a man was to . . . to carry on the way I'd been doing before I met you.'

So that was the barrier that had stood between them. Not her guilt, not her shame, but his. And now here he was, confessing all to a wife who had fallen in love with his brother, a brother who inspired the same hang-ups in him as Vivi had always done in his wife . . .

'Look in the envelope,' he said.

Gemma pulled out a sheaf of glossy eight-by-ten photographs, bracing herself for something obscene. But they just showed Gerald, sometimes on the street, sometimes leaning out of his car window, talking to various women, whose clothes proclaimed their trade. They were the kind of pictures Nick had claimed that *The Torch* had in its safe, depicting various bigwigs in similarly compromising situations . . . no wonder Gerald had bitten his head off that day.

'I should have done what the old man did. Paid through the nose for discretion. But at the time I thought this way was safer, more anonymous, that's why I never picked up the same girl twice. Which only makes it look worse, of course.'

'Lots of men go to prostitutes . . .' began Gemma.

'I'm not lots of men. I'm an avenging husband writing a much-hyped exposé of the pervert who raped my beloved wife. A husband everybody's heard of, thanks to the trial. If this came out, I'd be a laughing stock, I'd lose all credibility. You think the gutter press would pass up a juicy story like this? You can bet your life the bloody *Torch* is number one on that distribution list.'

'The pictures don't prove anything. You could always say that you were doing research for the book. I could back you up on that . . .'

Gerald let out a bark of mirthless laughter.

'Well he would say that, wouldn't he?' he lisped, in a parody of public reaction. 'Will you stop making excuses for me? I don't want any more to do with the book, it's got the Collington curse on it, same as *The Courier*. I meant to take my revenge on him but he's won again, as usual, he's probably laughing at us at this very minute. Well, what are you waiting for? Why don't you pack your things and leave?'

But it wasn't a question. It was a plea. A plea for her not to desert him now, a cry from the heart, an expression of need. He wasn't offering her her freedom. He was preventing her escape. This was the man she had married for better for worse, a man who still loved her, who had always loved her more than she loved him.

'I've nothing to offer you any more,' he went on, twisting the knife. 'I've failed you. I've failed at every single thing that mattered to me. I wish I had the guts to kill myself, like you tried to do. I've been thinking about it all day.'

'Don't say that!' It was nothing to do with guts, it was to do with despair, she had been there, she knew what it felt like. And the only thing that stood between Gerald and despair was the help and the hope she could give him.

'What have I got to live for?' Gerald challenged her bitterly. 'I've lost everything, including you. Not that I don't deserve it.'

'You haven't lost me.' The words sounded like so many doors slamming.

'I don't want your pity.'

'I'm not offering pity.' There was no room for that if she was to give him back his pride. 'Things have got to change, Gerald. You've got to be open and honest with me. You've got to stop treating me like the little woman and accept me as an equal. If we're going to stay married, it's got to be a real marriage.'

'You mean . . . you're willing to try again? Even after what I've told you?'

'If you are.'

The relief and disbelief on his face tore at her guts.

'Oh God. Oh God, Gemma, you're the only good thing that's ever happened to me. I know I've treated you abominably. But I'll make it up to you, I swear it.'

He knelt down at her feet and put his head in her lap and sobbed his heart out. And so, invisibly, inaudibly, did she.

# 17

*Winter 1985–Spring 1986*

'We can't win whatever we do for Christmas,' Vivi told Max. 'If we invite them here, I'm going to feel like some overfed baron dispensing alms to the poor.'

The poor being Gemma and Gerald, thanks to his decision to abandon the book after the alleged break-in – an event which Vivi didn't quite believe in, though she hadn't the heart to say so. If she was right in her suspicion that either he, or more probably Gemma, had finally cracked up on the job, it wouldn't help to cast doubt on his face-saving cover story. Certainly he seemed a new man now that he was finally done with picking over the old man's corpse, despite the financial losses entailed, but he remained as touchy as ever about any hint of patronage, having refused Max's offer of a well-paid job and/or interest-free 'loan'.

'It'll be even worse if we go to their place,' she added gloomily. The Lawrences were preparing to trade down to a grotty old house in Shepherd's Bush to reduce the size of their mortgage. Gerald had found himself an ill-paid job editing a highbrow political journal; Gemma was supplementing her *Courier* income by illustrating book jackets. And meanwhile Vivi was living in luxury, burdened by the feeling, however illogical, that she had prospered at their expense.

'So let your mother do the honours,' said Max, not getting the point. He had set Harriet up in her own dear little mews in Chelsea, given her a blank cheque to do it up, and settled a generous monthly allowance on her, finally and openly usurping Gerald's role as provider. The two of them got on like a house on fire; Christmas was no time to rub it in.

'No,' said Vivi, shuddering. 'I can't stand the sight of her playing

Lady Bountiful and wrapping up the leftovers for the poor darlings to take back to their hovel.'

'Then let's duck the problem by going away,' said Max, making short work of the discussion. 'I'll have the house on the island made ready, and the plane waiting for us at Miami.' The island was a dot in the Bahamas inhabited exclusively by the rich and famous in search of peace and quiet, and accessible only by boat or private plane, in this case Max's Piper Seneca, which he piloted himself. 'You've been working too hard,' he added. 'It's bad for the baby.'

A baby he no longer had any doubt was his, the scan having borne out her story. Officially Vivi was sailing through her pregnancy (anything to stop Harriet fussing) and fully restored to her usual formidable energy. Unofficially she felt like death, thanks to morning sickness at all hours of the day, continuing vicious migraines for which she no longer dared take painkillers, and recurring bouts of light-headedness. But the top man had reassured her that she was in excellent health – God help everyone else – even if he did regard her compulsion to carry on working as eccentric, used as he was to pandering to the idle wives of the rich.

After his initially cool reaction, Max had warmed to the idea of fatherhood with the enthusiasm he applied to any new venture, confident of success. Witness the major government contract he had landed in the last month – not as big as the Pentagon one but enormous by British standards. In addition, several large multi-national companies were poised to replace their existing systems with Kellerman hardware and software, much to the disgruntlement of their previous suppliers, the big fish who found themselves outswum by the shark they had mistaken for a minnow.

'Put it in your diary,' went on Max. 'Fly out Christmas Eve, come back New Year's Day.'

It wasn't a suggestion, it was a decision. If Nick had ever made decisions for her, she would have jumped at the excuse to pick a quarrel. But there was no point in trying to fight with Max. There would be no sudden counter-explosions, no passionate reconciliations, just demoralising indifference to her latest tantrum. One withering glance was enough to make her feel like a spoilt brat. Which she was, after all. Better an honest-to-goodness sexist bastard than a man who dominated her by stealth, the way Nick had done.

'All right,' shrugged Vivi, glad to be off the who-goes-where hook. It wasn't as if Daniel was coming home. She hadn't heard from him since he had cut short his last visit, leaving a week early without so much as a goodbye. But then, as Harriet said, that was Daniel all over.

Vivi now had her own office and a fancy title, one she was determined to justify. She might have married the boss but nobody could deny that she was good at her job or that she worked twice as hard as anyone else. Besides keeping up the twice-weekly Vivienne Chambers page, she had launched her new consumer project, which was proving a runaway success. It wasn't so much the fly-by-nights Vivi was after; they tended to vaporise before you could touch them, or go bankrupt at the drop of a hat, thus evading all their liabilities. Banks, insurance companies, car manufacturers, local authorities and government departments were her favoured targets, particularly the untouchable top dogs at their helms, guarded by ferocious secretaries and whipping-boy minions. Amazing how long-standing disputes could be miraculously settled overnight under the threat of bad, personalised publicity. Nick would surely have approved, wouldn't he, of bringing all these fat cats to heel? Not that Vivi cared, of course, whether Nick approved or not.

A week before their departure she saw his by-line on a centre-page spread linked to *The Echo*'s Christmas appeal for the homeless – the story of a week spent living in a cardboard box on the streets of London. Not an original theme, but one he had given a new, sharp edge to. Vivi's own seasonal comments on the subject had earned her an invitation to appear on a Channel 4 TV debate on the housing crisis to be broadcast live in front of an invited studio audience.

Max was in Frankfurt overnight, wooing a potential client. Vivi carried on working at her desk until the studio car arrived to collect her, putting off her evening meal until the programme was over. She was much too anxious to eat, as she always was before going on the air, despite her reputation as a natural performer. She spent the drive self-consciously touching up her blusher in an attempt to make herself look radiant, the way pregnant women were supposed to do. Such myths were all part of a gigantic conspiracy, she had concluded, by women against other women.

And now she had become a conspirator herself rather than show herself up. Some feminist you are, she thought, echoing Nick.

There was the usual piss-up going on in the green room when she arrived. She soon found herself pinned up against the wall by a senior social worker, who took her to task over one of her recent tirades about an at-risk baby returned to its mother and then battered to death by her cohabitee, while Vivi listened with uncharacteristic meekness, too winded by the sudden sight of Nick to argue.

He was standing on the other side of the room, at the centre of an animated group, being his usual life and soul of the party. Vivi couldn't help herself from staring. It was like a replay of love at first sight, even though it hadn't been, at the time. As soon as he spotted her, however, the smile faded instantly, freezing her out. Vivi turned away, cheeks burning; it was terribly hot in here, and she had started to feel faint, a warning sign of low blood sugar.

Spying an acquaintance, she passed the troublesome social worker on to him and made her way towards the buffet table. All that extra progesterone was supposed to make you vague and forgetful, otherwise she would surely have realised that Nick might be here, on the strength of his recent piece, and taken evasive action. She had just picked up a mince pie, the nearest item to hand, when she began to black out.

Fearful of falling and hurting the baby, Vivi sat down on the floor, producing an immediate kerfuffle from a girl with a clipboard and sundry nearby guests. She let them find her a chair while she hurriedly swallowed a bite of life-saving carbohydrate, protesting 'I'm okay' with her mouth full. The girl was saying that they had a doctor appearing on the programme, but he hadn't arrived yet . . .

'I don't need a doctor,' said Vivi, cutting her short. 'It's just the heat in here. Just leave me alone and I'll be fine.'

Uncertainly they dispersed, leaving her sitting alone in the draught from the open door, stolidly munching a synthetic mince pie washed down with tepid Perrier that had lost its fizz. She swallowed painfully, all her throat muscles tightening, as she saw Nick heading in her direction. If he was concerned about her fainting fit, he certainly didn't show it.

'Congratulations,' he said, stopping in front of her chair, looking down on her. 'End of May, isn't it?'

'If you say so. Your sources are usually pretty accurate.'

'Is that why you didn't bother to tell me yourself?'

Their exchange was drowned out by a herd of new arrivals, members of the public brought in to ask questions from the floor. Vivi should have been safe from recriminations in a public place like this, but the background hubbub created an unwanted, if dubious, privacy.

'It was none of your business.'

'No matter what you and Kellerman were up to behind my back there's still a fifty-fifty chance that baby's mine.'

'And there's a one hundred per cent chance it's mine,' snapped Vivi. 'Just like Cass is Jackie's,' she added, unable to bite her tongue in time.

'Not Cass,' Nick corrected her. 'Casey. No wonder you took off. I might have wanted to call the baby Wayne or Sharon. As it is you can have a little Sophie or a Benedict. Or is it a straight choice between Max junior and Maxine?'

'It's not your child,' hissed Vivi. 'I know that because it was planned, deliberate. I decided to have a baby, and I decided to have it with Max, not with you.'

Surprisingly he didn't contest this assertion. It was almost as if she had told him what he wanted to hear.

'I wonder why,' was all he said, shrivelling her with his scorn. To him it must seem so simple. There was no more reliable meal ticket than a rich man's child. But if she tried to contest the false impression she herself had chosen to give, she would only end up admitting to something worse.

'I didn't come here to pick a fight with you,' she said, displaying some of the acquired restraint Max had taught her. 'I don't want us to be enemies . . .'

'Next thing you'll be saying you want us to be friends. Which was where we came in, remember? It didn't work then, and it won't work now. I'm not your friend any more, Mrs Kellerman. And you were never mine. You took me for a mug. Let's hope he does the same to you.'

And with that he walked away, leaving her trembling. She had underestimated him both as friend and as enemy. The genial, tolerant, soft-hearted Nick who had come home to her each night wouldn't have lasted five minutes in the Fleet Street jungle.

The hardbitten Nick who had done battle every day on *The Torch* was a different animal altogether, albeit one who kept his killer instincts hidden behind the boyish smile and rough-and-ready charm. When even they were switched off, you knew you were an outcast, beneath his contempt.

'I'm afraid I'm going down with the flu,' Vivi told the girl with the clipboard. 'Can you get someone to drive me home?'

'I do wish Daniel could be here,' lamented Harriet, over the Christmas pudding. 'When he started coming home more often, I began to hope he was missing us all.'

'*Cherchez la femme*,' said Gerald jovially. 'Knowing Daniel, he'd rather spend Christmas in bed with one of his floozies.'

'I wouldn't mind so much if he met a nice French girl and settled down.'

'Not much hope of that. Daniel's never gone in much for nice girls . . .'

'Have some more brandy butter,' interrupted Gemma, offering the bowl to Harriet.

'No thank you darling, too many calories. Anyway, I finally got through to him the other day and he said he'd renewed his contract for another year. And I expect he'll go chasing all the most dangerous jobs as usual . . .'

Because of me, thought Gemma. She could have told him the whole story, to soften the blow, rather than offer the feeble excuse that she wanted to give her marriage another chance. But loyalty to Gerald had prevailed. She hadn't elaborated and Daniel hadn't demanded a fuller explanation. That deep-grained cynicism of his had filled in all the gaps for him. As far as he was concerned, she had never meant to leave Gerald at all. All that promise and passion had been reduced to a tacky piece of adultery, of which she had repented. And so had he.

'You worry about him too much,' said Gerald.

'I'm a mother. I worry about all of you.'

'Well, you can cross us off your worry list. We're doing just fine, aren't we Gemma?'

He was becoming an optimist, thanks to her, even though she wasn't one herself. In a couple of years, he predicted, they would be back on their feet financially, and then they would be able to start a family. A neat, tidy, predictable life had begun, the kind of life she had married him for, the kind of life she had thought she wanted, once.

'Well, anything you need for the new house I can get you at cost,' said Harriet, in interior-decorator mode. She could have made a proper career at it, thought Gemma, if she wasn't such a chronic dilettante. 'I came across this fabulous watered silk wallpaper –'

'We can't afford silk wallpaper at fifty quid a roll,' cut in Gerald, with some of his old asperity.

'It can be my moving-in present . . .'

'Paid for by Max. I'm very glad he's being generous to you, but Gemma and I can manage on our own. If you'd ever seen that bedsitter she had in Balham, you'd know how brilliant she is at doing a place up on a budget.'

Gemma returned his smile, full of false virtue. The more loving Gerald was to her, the more two-faced she felt. He had been so afraid that his confession had disgusted her, that she would find him physically repellent, never guessing that she was harbouring a much greater guilt than his. But she had dismissed the temptation to confess, to emulate his own honesty and courage, as a self-indulgence. As things were, his confidence was growing daily, especially in bed; she couldn't risk setting him back by reviving all his old complexes about Daniel.

Harriet fell fast asleep on the settee in the middle of the Queen's speech.

'You shouldn't have let her drink so much wine,' said Gemma, concerned.

'I wanted to make sure we had some time to ourselves this afternoon. She won't wake up for at least an hour. Come on. Let's go upstairs.'

Gemma never refused him. Her job was to build him up, to repair years of damage, to reassure him constantly that he was a wonderful lover. He was certainly an anxious and conscientious one. Say you enjoyed something – he questioned her continually on the subject – and he would file the information away, remember to press the right buttons every time, unaware that the circuits weren't wired up, a problem which was beyond his control, and hers. Thank God a woman's impotence didn't show.

She let him undress her slowly, let him kiss every inch of her. She did all the things he liked her to do, things he thought he had taught her. Ironic that she should feel like an adulteress with her own husband. If you weren't in the mood, *Cosmopolitan* said, you should turn yourself on with your favourite sexual fantasy, imagine making love to a different man, if necessary. Which was precisely what she couldn't bring herself to do. She felt enough of a fraud already.

'That was quick,' he murmured, pleased with himself, as Gemma feigned her usual ecstasy. 'We've got time for you to come again . . .'

'No really,' protested Gemma, 'I don't need to.'

'No stamina,' teased Gerald, relieved nonetheless. And then, as he hurtled gratefully towards his own climax, 'Oh, Gemma, I do love you . . .'

'I love you too,' murmured Gemma, stroking his hair as he shuddered to a halt. And she did love him, that was the pity of it. It was just the wrong kind of love. She knew now that it always had been . . .

'Phone,' she said, reaching for the receiver on the bedside table, hoping to be spared the usual detailed how-was-it-for-you post-mortem. Perhaps it was Vivi, calling to wish them a merry Christmas. But it was a man asking for Meestair Gérard Lorrance. Gemma handed over the receiver, using the diversion to get dressed.

'Hello? Yes, speaking. What?' Gerald sat bolt upright in bed. 'When did this happen?' His pale blue eyes, always vulnerable without their spectacles, were wide with alarm. Only then did Gemma realise, belatedly, that the caller was ringing from Paris, that something had happened to Daniel . . .

'Is that all you can tell me?' Gerald was saying.

Gemma sat down on the bed. Panic unfurled itself and began snaking its way through her veins like a river of ice-cold acid. She mustn't let it show, she reminded herself, mustn't give herself away.

'Yes. Yes, I'll inform the rest of the family. You will let me know immediately if there's further news? Yes. Thank you. Goodbye.'

He's been seriously injured, thought Gemma, imagining the other end of the conversation. They don't know yet if he's going to make it. And if it wasn't for her, he would be home, safe, with her. She had saved Gerald and destroyed Daniel instead . . .

'That was the agency,' said Gerald, flinging on his clothes. 'They've just had a call from Beirut. Daniel's been kidnapped.'

'Kidnapped?' It was almost a relief, at first.

'The French media have pretty well pulled out of the Lebanon, because several of their people have been taken hostage in the last few months. But because Daniel's got a British passport, they thought he would be safe. And of course he did volunteer to go, which is absolutely typical of him. Christ. How the hell am I going to tell Harriet?'

Harriet would have her hysterics for her, thought Gemma numbly. She just hoped she knew less about the situation in the Lebanon than Gemma herself did; she always read the papers from cover to cover, never knowing what item of news Vivi would choose to write about next. Islamic fundamentalists were dedicated to driving out the Western presence in the Lebanon, and hostage-taking was part of their campaign to effect the release of the so-called Dawa 17, Shia Muslim terrorists who were currently serving long prison sentences in Kuwait. Several Americans were being held, whereabouts unknown, paying the price of Ronald Reagan's foreign policy, as were a number of Frenchmen, thanks to their country's colonial past.

Harriet proved easy to rouse from her post-prandial stupor; it only took the mention of Daniel's name, coupled with the word 'Beirut' to render her instantly alert.

'When?' she demanded. 'How?'

'They don't know much yet. It seems he was on his way back to the Commodore Hotel earlier today when his taxi was stopped by another car blocking the road. Three men jumped out, forced Daniel into it at gunpoint and drove off. There's no way of knowing which group they're from until someone claims responsibility.'

The rival factions in the Lebanon were answerable to no one but themselves, the forces of law and order having long since broken down in a country torn apart by years of war. Daniel had talked of streets suddenly clearing as local people took cover, alerted by a sixth sense for impending trouble, thus avoiding the crossfire between Amal and Hizbollah gunmen, both struggling for control of the city. A sixth sense he claimed to have developed himself, but this time it had let him down . . .

'I knew it,' said Harriet bleakly. 'I told him when I heard about that broken wrist that the next time it would be his neck. And he just laughed at me for being a stupid old woman.' She began weeping jerkily. Gerald sat patting her hand and saying he knew people in the Foreign Office, he would get on to them right away, while Gemma went to make her a cup of sweet tea, her hands shaking so much she spilt the milk all over the worktop. Spilt milk. She mustn't cry . . .

'Most likely they thought that he was a French national,' Gerald was explaining, as she carried in the tray. 'On account of him working for a French news agency and speaking the language fluently. At the moment these Muslim extremists have got no particular axe to grind with Britain. When they find out he's got a UK passport, they'll let him go, same as they did with those two other chaps they mistook for Americans.'

Tactfully, he failed to mention the one British hostage still in captivity, admittedly at the hands of the Palestinians, rather than the Lebanese. His warders had demanded the release of Arab comrades held in British jails, whereupon the Foreign Office had restated government policy about not doing deals with terrorists under any circumstances.

'If only Max was here,' whimpered Harriet

'There's nothing Max can do,' said Gerald touchily. 'I told you, I've got contacts of my own . . .'

Soon Harriet was weeping uncontrollably, saying that she had lost one child already, it wasn't fair, she couldn't bear to lose Daniel too, specially not at Christmas, like before, Christmas was always the worst time of the year for her.

'Better give her a double dose of these,' Gerald told Gemma, finding a bottle of Valium in Harriet's bag. 'You get her up to bed while I make some phone calls.'

Gemma sat patiently by Harriet's bedside reassuring her that all would be well, hiding her own fear. From now on it would fall to her to be the calm, sensible one while Harriet went to pieces and Vivi raised the roof and Gerald moved heaven and earth to try to get his brother back. She couldn't weep or rage without giving rise to suspicion, she was only the sister-in-law, after all.

'I can't get hold of anybody,' muttered Gerald, on her return downstairs. 'This would happen at bloody Christmas, wouldn't it? I just tried to ring Vivi, before she heard it on the news, but Max answered the phone. He's going to try to keep it from her until they get home, in case the shock sends her into labour. Which is sensible, I suppose. At least it gives me time to get things moving without Vivi charging around like a bull in a china shop and sounding off in her column about Foreign Office wankers. Those kind of techniques don't work in Whitehall. We have to take this slowly and carefully . . .' He slumped limply on to the settee, all the worries of the world back on his shoulders. Gemma sat down beside him and put an arm around him.

'Thank God I've got you,' he said. 'I'd never be able to cope with this without you.'

Without me, you wouldn't have had to, thought Gemma.


'Why the hell didn't you tell me before?'

'Keep calm. You'll send your blood pressure up.'

'Will you stop treating me like an incubator? I do have a brain as well as a womb.' But true enough, the news had left her reeling, she felt as if someone had kicked her in the stomach.

'Given that you refuse to make any concessions to being pregnant, I have to make them for you. Where do you think you're going?'

'To see Gerald, find out exactly what's going on.'

'I don't want you getting involved in this, Vivi. The Foreign Office are doing everything possible.'

'Like they're doing for that other poor bastard who got kidnapped? Their idea of doing everything possible is to parrot official policy. Which is like saying, go ahead and kill him, we don't care!'

'Gerald's also been in touch with Terry Waite, he's just come back from the Lebanon –'

'Yes. Empty-handed. You think I'm just going to sit here, relying on other people, while a gang of fanatics hold my brother hostage? I'm going to fly out there and talk to people on the spot. I'll write an open letter to Thatcher in the paper. If it was her son who'd been kidnapped, foreign policy would change overnight.

I'll drum up a huge public campaign, embarrass the government into doing something . . .'

'No you won't. I've spoken to these Foreign Office people myself, and much as it goes against the grain, we have to accept that they understand the situation out there better than we do. And their advice is to keep quiet and let them get on with doing their job, discreetly. If the kidnappers get the idea that Daniel's important, that his case will attract a vast amount of publicity for their cause in the Western press, they'll have every incentive to hang on to him for as long as possible. The more insignificant they think he is, the more likely they are to release him.'

'The more insignificant they think he is, the more worthless he becomes, the more likely they are just to bump him off to save themselves the expense of feeding him! God, I warned him so often to be careful!'

'Then be careful on his behalf. I absolutely forbid you to go to Beirut, or speak to anyone, or write anything on the subject, either in *The Courier* or any other paper.'

'You forbid me? I didn't promise to obey you!'

'No. But in this case, you will. Not just for the sake of Daniel's health but for your own. Or rather for the baby's. Or is it expendable, like the last one?'

Vivi clouted him hard across the face in an attempt to hurt him back. He knew exactly how and where to strike for maximum impact. So much so that she burst into feeble, feminine tears, thereby losing the argument at a stroke.

'If you weren't pregnant,' said Max, 'I'd hit you back. And crying won't cut any ice with me. My name's not Ferris, remember.'

'I hate you!' sobbed Vivi. 'I hate you!'

Which was almost the same thing as love.


In March two British schoolteachers and another Frenchman were abducted. Which made four British hostages in all. Vivi tried to regard this as good news; the more people were abducted, the more pressure there would be on the government to act. As yet no group had claimed responsibility for Daniel, but that wasn't unusual, according to Gerald's sources. He had become a walking encyclopedia on Middle East affairs, approaching the subject with his usual scholastic thoroughness. The original kidnappers, he explained, might still be looking to offload him; entrepreneurial freelance gangs sometimes captured stray Westerners on spec and sold them on to the highest bidder, who might in turn re-sell them at a profit; this pass-the-hostage process could drag on for months.

The other possibility, one which they all refused to entertain, was that Daniel might have been killed, especially if he had been unwise enough to try to resist his captors. Though it would be unlike Daniel to lose his head. He had talked his way out of tight situations before, and like Gerald he had learned stoicism at a particularly tough public school, chosen and paid for by CC, where vicious corporal punishment was administered by licensed sadists at the drop of a hat. Good training for being kicked around by a bunch of thugs while the Foreign Office did – or rather claimed to do – mysterious things behind the scenes. But Max had successfully frightened Vivi into leaving it to Gerald to deal with the Whitehall wallies. Five minutes of their platitudes and she would have blown a gasket, wrecking all the goodwill he had achieved so far.

Meanwhile Harriet had been drinking again. Gemma was particularly vulnerable to her turning up the worse for wear and in search of sympathy. Being Gemma, she hadn't complained, but Vivi could tell that she was feeling the strain. In the end Max had stepped in and threatened to exile Harriet to a drying-out clinic and stop her allowance for the duration – a front for a much gentler policy of making extra time for her in his busy schedule, and appealing to her pride.

'How are Vivi and Gerald supposed to cope if you crack up?' Vivi heard him say, eavesdropping on one of their private sessions. 'It's your role as a mother to set the rest of us an example. You don't want your grandchild to think you're a pathetic old soak, now do you?'

'The same as my children do, you mean?' sniffed Harriet.

'So prove them wrong. Look how strong you were when you were a girl, standing up to your father. You're tougher than you give yourself credit for and now you've got to show that I'm right to have faith in you.'

'Oh Max. You're the only one who does. I'll try not to let you down . . .'

Vivi soon realised, to her inadmissible dismay, that they were becoming closer to each other than either of them were to her. Even more inadmissibly, she was becoming hooked, just as Harriet was, on Max's ruthlessly rationed approval. As always she sought solace in work, supervising the dummy run of a new women's supplement to the forthcoming *Sunday Courier*, which was to spearhead campaigns to improve health screening, fight test discrimination cases in court, lobby for tax relief on child care and interview positive female role models. She planned to work right up till the very last minute and be back at her desk within a few days of giving birth, having hired a first-class nanny – she had vetted dozens – a motherly, fortyish spinster with immaculate credentials who wasn't likely to make eyes at Max or neglect the baby while she entertained her boyfriends. This time she wouldn't repeat all the mistakes she had made with Cass, the same ones her own mother had made with her. She wouldn't be possessive with this child, wouldn't spoil it or become emotionally dependent on it. She had learned her lesson, in more ways than one.

In April, British air bases were used for an American air attack on Libya. Two days later, the two kidnapped British teachers were found murdered in reprisal, together with one of the American hostages, and pictures were released showing that the remaining British hostage, bar Daniel, had been hanged. Vivi's blood pressure rocketed, resulting in an immediate admission to hospital and enforced bed rest to bring it down.

Bed rest didn't preclude phoning the office or writing her column on a laptop, but it still left too much time to think. And trying not to think about Daniel simply lured her into thinking about Nick instead. The 'good operator' who had specialised in sex and scandal was now earning himself a reputation as a serious investigative journalist. The huge network of contacts he had built up on *The Torch* kept him supplied with a constant flow of information; he broke every rule in the NUJ Code of Practice and got away with it, because he was answerable to no one but himself. His most recent story, exposing a child pornography ring, had not only provoked several arrests but instigated a full enquiry into possible police collusion.

The story had gone to *The Echo*, helping it recoup some of the readers it was losing back to *The Courier*. Now that their sales were neck and neck again, it was all the more frustrating not to be able to outbid them. Nick Ferris was the only writer in Fleet Street Vivi couldn't afford to buy.

What she refused to think about was the baby and all the things that could go wrong. Which didn't prevent all the fears she suppressed in the daytime coming out of hiding in her sleep. She dreamed nightly of her dead sister, except that she was the one who had given birth to her and held a tiny, lifeless child in her arms. A child who looked just like Cass, just like Nick. And then it would suddenly turn into Daniel, with his hands tied behind his back and a bullet in his head . . .

She woke to the sound of her own voice screaming, but this time it wasn't a dream; the nightmare had burst into real life. She hadn't expected pain like this, something must be wrong. She rang, panic-stricken, for a nurse, only to be reassured that nothing was amiss, the baby had started a bit early, that was all. Over a month early, in fact . . .

The next spasm, when it came, was even more terrifying than the first, exposing the breathing exercises she had practised with such diligence as a lousy con. They sent for Max straight away, so she had to be brave, she couldn't bring herself to admit to him how bloody scared she was, the way she would have done to Nick. And what about the other fear, the fear that the baby wasn't early at all, that Max would realise she had lied to him?

Vivi had always prided herself on having a high pain threshold. She had never given in to the curse or her migraines, never turned a hair at the dentist's. She had been unwise enough to brag, in her ignorance, that she wasn't going to let them give her any drugs, she wanted to be fully in control of her body, but it wasn't like that at all, her body was in control of her. And just as she was thinking, not long now, this can't possibly last much longer, some cooing nurse suggested to Max that he go off and have something to eat, there was still a fair old way to go.

As soon as he was out of earshot Vivi heard herself begging for something, anything to stop the pain, preferably a general anaesthetic, she couldn't bear it any more, and there was something smug, she fancied, about the way they administered the epidural, the ultimate cop-out, as if thinking, there's another know-all bites the dust.

It was only then, after a lifetime of fighting fear on all fronts, that Vivi owned up to the bitter truth about herself: that she was, and always had been, a coward. Which explained every mistake she had ever made, every self-destructive act she had ever committed. When it starts to hurt, don't let it show, but once it starts to hurt too much, turn tail and run. And nothing on earth hurt as much as love.

But this time, for once, she didn't run away from it. One look at that ugly, crumpled creature and she was instantly besotted. This was the one person in the world she would never use, never damage, never test, never resent, never betray. Her son. Nick's son, she knew that as soon as she saw him. She had always known it.

But Max still didn't, thank God. The baby weighed in at less than six pounds, bearing out the fiction that he was slightly premature. And both his fathers must carry on believing that. She might suffer for it, but not her child. The crime against all three of them would be hers alone.

# PART THREE

*A truth that's told with bad intent*
*Beats all the lies you can invent.*

William Blake

## 18

January–March 1988

The Courier, Leader Page, 21 January 1988

> Two years after Daniel Lawrence's kidnap – 758 days to be
> precise – he is still in captivity. While the French and Germans
> have secured the release of several of their nationals, Britain has
> only deaths on its record, the result of allowing our bases to be
> used for the American bombing raid on Libya in April 1986.
> Daniel Lawrence, John McCarthy and Terry Waite might as
> well be dead too, for all this government seems to care.
>
> But now we have confirmation that Lawrence, at least, is
> alive, thanks to the video released yesterday, showing him
> reading a statement prepared by his captors. They want Britain
> to put pressure on Kuwait – where we enjoy considerable
> influence – to release the Dawa 17, held for acts of terrorism in
> that country. The Dawa 17 are admittedly killers, which gives
> them something in common with the British government (see
> above); both appear to regard innocent lives as expendable.
>
> No deals, we proclaim proudly. It's more important to keep
> the Dawa 17 in prison than to get our hostages out of it. Nor are
> we prepared to negotiate with Iran – as other countries have
> successfully done – to prevail on the kidnap gangs on our
> behalf. The arms-for-hostages Irangate scandal is not a moral
> justification for leaving our people to rot.
>
> Who is really holding Daniel Lawrence hostage? The
> Organisation of Islamic Socialist Justice, which has finally
> admitted responsibility, or the British government, which
> continues to deny it? For two years the hostage families have
> been brainwashed, against their better judgement, into keeping
> a low profile. Publicity, they are told, would put their relatives'

*lives at risk by giving the kidnappers the absurd idea that those lives might actually matter. Well, the fact is that they do matter, to the families if not to Downing Street, whose Foreign Office lackeys have been forced to work with their hands tied behind their backs.*

*Enough is enough. Now it's time for the British public to rise up and tell Mrs Thatcher that people matter more than policies, before more lives are wasted at the altar of political arrogance . . .*

*18 February 1988*
*Dear Daniel*
*We had a meeting of the Campaign Committee today to discuss the poster I mentioned in my last letter. I enclose a rough sketch of the design we decided on.*

Now that they knew who was holding him they were taking it in turns to write, in the faint hope that even one of their letters would find its way through to him, via a tortuous and mysterious chain of intermediaries. Gemma's drawing depicted a hand reaching through the bars of a cage towards another holding a key, tormentingly, just beyond its reach.

*We're having 500,000 copies printed for distribution all over the country, with full-page ads in the national press. We're also having teeshirts and button badges made and we've hired a full-time organiser to co-ordinate everything, a PR company to set up interviews for Vivi, Gerald and Harriet, and a professional lobbyist to put pressure on MPs.*

All of which would have been impossible but for Max shouldering the huge cost of the operation. For once Gerald hadn't objected to his open-handedness; with Daniel's life on the line pride was a luxury he couldn't afford. If it had been up to Vivi they would have started this campaign two years ago. But Max had refused to let her act until the whole family – or rather Gerald, to whom he deferred in all Daniel-related matters – agreed. Gerald had taken Foreign Office warnings very much to heart and

328

infected everyone else, particularly Harriet, with his fear of rocking the boat. But the release of two more French hostages, the previous November, had proved a turning point in his thinking.

'I was born in France,' he had pointed out. 'And if my father hadn't walked out on us when he did, Daniel would have been as well. Plus he was working for a French company when he was kidnapped. If this government can't or won't get him out, then perhaps the French one will . . .'

The release of the video last month, proving that Daniel was alive – he was holding a copy of that day's newspaper – had given Gerald the perfect cue for action. If he made a formal, highly publicised plea to the French Prime Minister, who happened to be standing for President in the forthcoming elections, he would be handing him a golden opportunity to score vote-winning points off his British counterpart, who so disapproved of France's dubious dealings with Iran.

Gemma had watched the video, heart pounding, together with the rest of the family. Daniel's voice was flat, expressionless, and wrongly inflected, as if to let them know that the words he was speaking were not his own. But he looked reasonably healthy, as far as you could tell behind the shaggy beard. Frustratingly little was known about the obscure splinter group holding him, except that they were affiliated to Islamic Jihad, but surely they wouldn't have kept him alive all this time, just to kill him now?

*Please stay alive, Daniel. Don't let that death-wish of yours get the better of you and keep hanging on till we can get you out. If you're allowed to see a television, look out for a video Harriet has made to be shown on Lebanese TV, appealing for your release.*
*All our love*
*Gemma and Gerald.*

She was careful to include the 'and Gerald' even though Gerald wrote separate letters of his own. It helped concentrate the mind. If Daniel were freed tomorrow, she would still be his brother's wife.

It has to be a real marriage, she had told Gerald, when she had made her decision to stay with him. At first she had merely gone through the motions of being a real wife, but in the last two years force of habit had created a reality of its own. What had required a conscious effort had become involuntary, natural, a comfort rather than a duty. And now that they had got the house to rights and cleared their debts, they were planning to start a family, an event which Harriet, already a doting grandmother, was looking forward to with uninhibited delight.

James (Max had named him after his late father), better known as Jamie, had given her an all-consuming, positive interest to counteract her worries about Daniel. She had stopped drinking, given up toy-boys, and even allowed her hair to go grey in deference to her new matriarchal status. To quote Vivi, the old bag seemed to have grown up at last. Certainly she was keen to play an active role in getting Daniel freed. Having lived in France during her first marriage and visited frequently ever since, she spoke excellent French and had persuaded Gerald, an indifferent linguist, to allow her to act as interpreter on his forthcoming mission to Paris.

Vivi helped set things up through a French newspaper proprietor who used his good offices to arrange a meeting with a high-ranking minister. *The Courier* trumpeted the proposed visit under the banner headline LAWRENCE FAMILY GIVE UP ON THATCHER – PIN HOPES ON CHIRAC, producing a sudden personal invitation from the Foreign Secretary for Gerald to come in and discuss 'any problems you might have'. A discussion which didn't stop the trip going ahead as scheduled, with the outward journey fixed for early March, and the return open-ended, depending on the opportunities for publicity.

'You're looking a bit peaky,' Vivi accused Gemma on the way back from the airport; Max was away on business in California. 'You're not in the club already, are you?'

'Actually I've got the curse. And Harriet's asked me once today already.'

'I know the feeling. Still, at least you won't have to look far for a baby-sitter. Not that you'll need one very often. You'll be one of those sickeningly smug full-time mums.'

'I'll still be working, same as you. I'm just lucky to be able to work from home.'

'And I don't need to work at all. Not for the money, anyway.'

She lit her third cigarette of the journey. 'So I've got no excuse not to have another one, have I?'

'Do you need an excuse?'

'If you must know,' shrugged Vivi, tapping the ash off her cigarette, 'I hated being pregnant. I felt like shit the whole nine months, even though there was nothing wrong with me. Then the bloody epidural left me with chronic backache. Serves me right, I suppose, for chickening out of doing it properly. And I had raving post-natal depression for the best part of a year.'

'You never let on,' said Gemma, surprised. Like everyone else she had been well fooled by Vivi's superwoman act.

'No. Well, I was being macho, wasn't I, or whatever the female equivalent is. Sorry, I shouldn't be telling you all this. Don't want to put you off.'

It was unlike Vivi to own up to any weaknesses. And when she did, it tended to be a diversion tactic, to explain away a much bigger, deeper problem.

'Is Max putting pressure on you to have another baby?'

'No. I'm the one who's putting pressure on me. I owe him. Not many wives are given a national newspaper as an anniversary present.'

Gemma knew that Vivi hadn't expected it to happen so soon. Max could have played cat and mouse with her, the way CC had done with Gerald, and perhaps, knowing Vivi, she might have preferred things that way. As it was, the achievement of her life's ambition – albeit one she had suppressed for most of it, out of loyalty to Gerald – had come as an anticlimax. She had displayed no sense of triumph or excitement, just a workaholic determination to justify Max's decision.

'Plus he's picking up the tab for the Free Daniel campaign,' she continued moodily. 'How many other hostage families can afford to buy unlimited publicity? And he's a good father, Jamie adores him. So at the very least, I ought to give him a child of his own, don't you think?'

It was the first time she had admitted, however obliquely, what Gemma had suspected for a long time. Jamie's resemblance to his real father was becoming embarrassingly obvious.

'I know it seems out of character,' she went on, 'me developing scruples all of a sudden, when I tricked Max into thinking Jamie was his and let him settle a million quid on him. After all, if he'd really wanted a child, then he shouldn't have let me have that abortion, now should he?'

'I didn't realise –'

'I hated him for that. But not as much as I still hate myself. Anyway, when he had the documents drawn up to hand over the bloody *Courier*, I must have had a brainstorm or something. I couldn't bring myself to sign them. And as if that wasn't enough I went and told him the truth. A world-class liar like me. Can you believe it?'

Oh yes, thought Gemma, only too well. Vivi had never managed to conquer that troublesome conscience of hers.

'But he just said that he knew, that he'd known for a long time, and it didn't make any difference. So I signed on the dotted line, like the smart cookie I am.'

She seemed perilously near tears; Gemma hoped that she didn't give in to them, because Vivi hated anyone to see her cry, especially her self-contained little sister. If she showed herself up, as it would seem to her, in front of Gemma, she would only resent her for it afterwards.

'Obviously he didn't want to lose Jamie,' said Gemma. 'Or you.'

'Then why give me the paper? Why give me the chance to walk out on him with my swag-bag intact?'

Perhaps he had given her the paper for love, thought Gemma, and wanted her to stay with him for love or not at all. Or was he simply a very accomplished manipulator, using Vivi's guilt to bind her to him? He was such a difficult man to know . . .

'I take it you're not going to walk out on him?'

'It wouldn't be fair on Jamie,' said Vivi shortly. 'Any more than it's fair to deprive him of a brother or sister just because I'm such a frigging coward. Harriet went through it four times, after all. And you'll pop half a dozen like peas, I know you will . . .'

So that was what had triggered all this, thought Gemma. The thought of her becoming a model mother, just as she was supposed to be a model wife. If only she knew . . .

'Do you want to come in?' she said, as the car dropped her off, to give Vivi the excuse she needed to talk some more.

'No thanks. I'm running late for lunch with an advertiser. See you.'

Her tone was abrupt, dismissive; predictably, she was already regretting her outburst, and Gemma could understand why. Why should she confide in a sister who had never confided in her?

She let herself in, stepping over a pile of campaign mail which had arrived by the second post; although they had appointed a paid administrator, Gerald liked to have first sight of everything himself. Anyone who wrote in got a button badge, a pro forma letter to send to their MP, a copy of Gemma's poster, and a monthly campaign newsletter. Gerald's appearance on *Wogan* with Harriet earlier that week had generated a huge response, nearly all of it supportive, apart from the occasional diatribe telling them that Mrs T was quite right not to give in to those dirty Arab bastards, etc.

Gemma sorted the latest batch of correspondence into piles, opening Gerald's, as usual, to identify the ones which needed a personal reply. There was a bumper haul for Harriet, in the wake of the TV programme, including one marked 'Private and Confidential' – no doubt yet another marriage proposal or obscene suggestion. Gemma consigned them to the folder labelled 'Fan mail for Harriet' and put it back in the bulging bottom drawer of Gerald's bureau to await her return.

'The editor wants to see you ASAP, with the lawyers, about the Perriman libel case.'

'Fix up a meeting for this afternoon,' said Vivi, looking at her watch, hoping that it wouldn't drag on too long. She must be home in time for Jamie's bedtime . . .

Much as she loved being with him, work was a drug she couldn't seem to do without, and if she used him as a substitute she would become even more obsessed with him than she was already. She knew what it was like to be brought up by a neurotic, demanding mother and as things were he was a happy little soul, probably because he only saw her at her best in their sacred 'quality time', with Vivi always smiling, patient and cheerful, something she couldn't possibly have kept up all day, every day, like proper mothers had to do. As yet he had no idea that his mummy was a bad-tempered, chain-smoking old ratbag, and that was how Vivi wanted things to stay, not just for him but for the sibling she would give him, give Max, in recompense for all he had given her.

Materially, at least. When it came to his feelings he was as tight-fisted as ever. There was something about him that repelled intimacy, other than the physical kind, the only kind he seemed to need or want. The one place Vivi felt close to him was in bed, but sex wasn't enough any more. She wanted to know him properly, to discover the real person behind the impenetrably self-assured facade, if only so that she, in turn, could reveal more of herself, do voluntarily with Max what she had done with Nick, against her will.

Nick had been an open book, who inspired similar indiscretion; Max remained a stranger who kept her emotionally at arm's length. Which had suited her perfectly at first, because it enabled her to do the same to him. She had felt like a claustrophobic free to breathe again.

But seeing him with Jamie, and Harriet, had revealed another side to Max, warm and spontaneous and accessible. She had found herself wanting him to be like that with her, to give her permission to be like that with him. But she couldn't bring herself to ask for something so nebulous and indefinable and easily denied. Max admitted to no insecurities himself, making it impossible for her to confess her own.

Post-natal depression. That convenient phrase had covered a multitude of sins. And then Daniel's disappearance had thrown up a further smokescreen for her to hide behind. She would feel better once she had Max's baby, if only to replace the last one, the one she had thrown away. Then he might find it in his heart to love her, or at least to let her love him.


Things were going well, Gerald said. They'd had interviews all over the place. The chauvinistic French media loved the all-important 'angle' of the story – an archetypal stiff-upper-lip Englishman like Gerald turning in despair to the country of his birth, asking it to succeed where Britain had so miserably failed. Harriet, who had never been camera-shy, was exploiting her role as the anxious mother to the hilt. Gerald complained that he couldn't keep up with her rapid, colloquial French, but she seemed to be saying the right things, because press coverage had been extremely sympathetic, urging the government to respond.

After ten days of talks, interviews and public appearances, they were due home this evening, having wrung assurances from the relevant minister that 'everything possible would be done'. Meanwhile media attention at home, and the resulting flood of letters to MPs, had already led to embarrassing questions in the House, even though official government policy remained stubbornly unchanged.

'We're going to be late,' grumbled the ever-punctual Vivi on the way to meet the flight. Emergency road works on the westbound section of the motorway had shut it down to a single lane, causing a long tail-back.

'It won't matter,' said Gemma. 'The press conference should keep them busy for at least half an hour.'

'It's the press conference I wanted to be there for. Talking of which, did you hear that Nick Ferris is setting up his own news agency?' It was unlike Vivi to mention him, even with the impersonal addition of his surname.

'Gerald mentioned it. He'd seen a press release.'

'Seems he sent one to every tuppence-ha'penny rag in the country – except *The Courier*, of course. I never thought I'd see the day when he'd join the bosses.'

'Why shouldn't he? You did.'

'Beats me why he wants to give up what he's doing now. God knows he must be creaming it in. You should have got him to ghost-write the book for you, he'd have knocked it out in no time flat and made you a fortune.' And then, catching Gemma on the hop, 'Tell me honestly. There never really was a burglary, was there?'

Gemma felt herself colouring.

'What makes you think that?'

'It was all too pat. Did you throw a massive wobbler on Gerald, or what? You seemed peculiar for ages afterwards.'

This was too much. Typically, Vivi had written her off as feeble and unreliable, blamed her for Gerald losing all that money. As for seeming 'peculiar', she had still been a lot more successful than Vivi at hiding her broken heart . . .

'I told Gerald at the time it was the wrong book,' Vivi went on, taking her silence as confirmation. 'But that doesn't mean he can't start another one. If Daniel comes out of this okay, he could write up the story of the campaign –'

'If he did,' cut in Gemma, still stung at Vivi's wrong assumptions, 'he certainly won't be using the PC this time. At least, not without disconnecting it from the modem first.'

Viv looked at her sharply.

'What's that supposed to mean?'

It couldn't do any harm, thought Gemma, to tell an edited version of the truth. Better than being written off as a wimp.

'Gerald had a load more contacts still to see, shady gangland types, their names and details were all in the index. He was convinced that he was on the brink of discovering something big. And then he started receiving threats. Give up the book or else . . . or else something will happen to your wife. Or words to that effect. We didn't realise then that someone could have hacked in to the database, we never even realised that such things as hackers existed, but it seems obvious, with hindsight.'

It was months later, in the course of Gemma's cover-to-cover newspaper reading, that she had discovered that it was possible to break into any computer linked to a telephone line, given the right equipment and the relevant skills.

'There was a lot of publicity, remember, when Gerald signed the contract, just after the trial,' she added. 'Anyone connected with CC who had anything to hide would have had fair warning.'

'But why didn't Gerald go to the police? Have you still got the names?'

'No. He destroyed everything. He didn't want to take any chances with my safety.'

'God. And it was me that made you put in that phone line in the first place, so I could send you my copy . . .'

'Don't feel responsible,' said Gemma, appeased now that she had cleared her name. 'You weren't to know, any more than we did. It's a fairly recent phenomenon, after all.'

'Max is working on an anti-hacker system at the moment,' mused Vivi, 'to stop people spying on our screens. Talking of which, you ought to be careful what you say on the phone, you never know who might be listening in. GCHQ, in our case, I shouldn't wonder, these past few months. We're a bunch of subversives, after all.'

Subversive. The last person who had called her that was Daniel. The mere word conjured up the sound of his voice. And at this very moment Gerald, the person they had both deceived, was preparing for yet another indefatigable round in the Free Daniel Lawrence campaign . . .

Thanks to the traffic, they were half an hour late. Having checked via the carphone that the plane had landed on time, they went straight to the press room. The volley of flashes that greeted their arrival hurtled Gemma back to the Old Bailey. She held back while Vivi greeted several of the hacks by name and smiled her best PR smile, but nobody smiled back. Where were Gerald and Harriet? Had they missed the flight?

'Miss Chambers?' queried an airline official, approaching. Vivi always used her maiden name. 'Mrs Lawrence? Can you step this way please?'

Gemma never actually remembered being told the news. One minute she didn't know, and the next she did, as if by intuition. She saw the man's mouth moving, but the words were just a jumble of sound, redundant, meaningless. And then she realised, too late, much too late, just how much she must have loved her husband.

Vivi took refuge in practicalities; her first priority was to get Gemma home. She phoned Max, who was in California, from the car, interrupting him in the middle of a meeting, amazing herself by how matter of fact she sounded, while Gemma sat numbly, dumbly, by her side.

'There was an accident on the motorway on the way to Roissy airport.' She felt as if she was phoning in a story. 'A lorry crashed over the central reservation and hit their taxi head on. There was a pile-up, it took rescue teams over an hour to cut them out of the wreckage. They reckon Gerald was killed instantly. Harriet died on the way to hospital.'

She wanted to go back to the office and key it into her terminal, to distance herself from the horror of it all. She wanted Attila to send her out to interview the bereaved family and con them into parting with a snapshot of the deceased, wanted to hide behind the professional role that made it possible to be that insensitive, to feel the adrenaline surge you got when there was a hot news item, however bad that news might be. And tomorrow people would read all about it over their breakfast tables and shake their heads in five-minute sympathy, glad that it hadn't happened to them.

'I'll be on the next flight out,' said Max. 'Ring the doctor, get him to give you both a sedative.'

'I'm all right.' She had to be all right, to look after Gemma. She kept hold of her hand as she spoke. It was ice cold, and her teeth were chattering. Vivi took off her jacket and draped it around her shaking shoulders. Poured a glass of brandy from the hospitality cabinet and forced her to swallow some. Took a big slug herself. Said something ridiculous about not to worry, they would be home soon, as if going home would somehow rewind the spools of time back to the moment they had set off, as if going home could unhappen everything.

Still dazed, Gemma didn't protest when Vivi made her get into bed. The doctor gave her a knock-out injection and offered Vivi the same, which she declined. There were things she had to do. She rang her editor first.

'Slant the story to give the campaign a publicity boost,' she heard herself saying, her voice rock steady. 'You know. Hostage mission ends in tragedy. Hostage crisis claims two more lives. Get a quote from Chirac's office, and from Downing Street. Milk it for all it's worth.'

Then she rang round her fellow-proprietors, asking for similar coverage. She might be the upstart of Fleet Street – the term was now generic rather than geographic, as more and more papers decamped to new-technology sites elsewhere – but no one could deny that she was a real hard-as-nails old pro.

As soon as she had made her calls, the hard-as-nails old pro shut herself in the bedroom, put a pillow over her head and cried herself into a stupor. Poor bloody Harriet. She was just beginning to get her life together at long last. Having the son-in-law of her dreams, and a grandchild to fuss over, and the Daniel campaign to devote her energies to, had given her a sense of purpose and self-worth for the first time in years. And Gerald and Gemma had survived so much together – the loss of *The Courier*, the trial, financial crises, Daniel's kidnap, they would have been one of those couples who stayed together for ever . . .

So many bad things had happened over the last five years. All of them since Max had come on the scene. Not that he was responsible, but every disaster provided a fresh opportunity for him to flourish his cheque book, another chance to play God. Until now. It was an object lesson in the ultimate futility of power, the power she had wanted her share of. You could play God for all you were worth, but in the end God always won.


Vivi was giving Jamie breakfast when Max arrived home, unshaven and hollow-eyed. He had no words or gestures adequate to the occasion, it seemed beyond him to try to comfort her. Drained by a sleepless night, Vivi was short and irritable with him. She couldn't tell him anything that he hadn't already read or heard, except that someone had to go to Paris to identify the bodies.

'I'll do it,' said Max. 'You need to be with your sister. How's she taking it?'

'She hasn't yet. The quack drugged her up to the eyeballs, last time I looked she was still out for the count. I rang her mother.' She adopted a cruel parody of Barbara's South London twang. ' "Poor Gem. She must be ever so upset." Ever so upset. I ask you.'

'Why don't you try to get some rest?'

'I don't want to rest. There's a lot to do. A double funeral to arrange. We'll keep that private. And then a memorial service at St Bride's. I want to give them a proper Fleet Street send-off, with a big piss-up afterwards. Harriet would like that. You know how she loved a good party.'

'You don't have to think about that now. Leave it all to me.'

'Really, Max, I'm disappointed in you. Can't you do better than that? I was relying on you to bring them back to life.'

'Go and see to Gemma,' said Max quietly. 'I have some phone calls to make.'

Vivi found Gemma sitting at the dressing table, fully dressed, combing her hair.

'Would you like some breakfast?' she said, inadequately.

'No thanks. I'll have something later, at home.'

'You can't go home yet. You're staying here, with us.'

'I have to go,' repeated Gemma woodenly. 'I have to be by myself for a bit. You don't need me now, Max is here. Don't worry, I won't try to kill myself. I wouldn't do that to you. Not on top of this.'

I'm just being selfish, thought Vivi, biting back the tears. I want her here for my own benefit, because she's the only one who can understand how it feels. No, not even Gemma understood how it felt. Gemma had nothing to feel guilty about. She had been a much better daughter to Harriet than Vivi had ever been. As for Gerald, Vivi had greedily claimed for herself the one thing he had always wanted, *The Courier*. Only the other day she had been whingeing about the ordeal of having another baby. And now Gemma would never be able to have Gerald's child.

'I don't suppose Gerald had much in the way of life assurance,' said Max, when a red-eyed Vivi returned from taking her home. 'Let her know she won't ever have to worry, will you?'

'Typical,' hissed Vivi.

'What?'

'If there's a problem, throw money at it. That's your answer to everything, isn't it?'

'Money helps. I intend to take over the campaign where Gerald left off. That way at least he and Harriet won't have died in vain.'

'Oh yes. You'll succeed where Gerald failed, the way you always have done.'

'Why are you being like this?'

'I'll bet if it was me who'd been in that car you'd be just as cool, just as objective. You're not human! You're like a bloody computer yourself!'

'You're tired. Why don't you try to get some rest? You haven't slept since it happened.'

'Ever since I met you, it's been one thing after another. It's like you've brought bad luck on this family!'

'I'm sorry you feel that way.'

'Why don't you ever hit back, damn you? Why don't you accuse me of being an ungrateful bitch?'

'I don't want your gratitude,' said Max tightly. 'I've no right to it. I've always acted from selfish motives. Perhaps I have brought bad luck on the family, perhaps I was wrong to marry you. But you know me. When I want something, I have to have it. No matter what.'

'Same as me, you mean?' she goaded, reminding him, to her shame, of the soulless bargain they had struck.

'No, not the same as you. I know what I want. You don't, not

340

really, you never have done. And I exploited that. I always exploit weakness in others. It's the secret of my success. But it hasn't felt like success with you. Even though I've done my best not to make the mistakes Ferris made. You said you didn't want love, remember?'

So she had. And now, perversely, it was all she did want, far more than she had ever wanted *The Courier*. But even more than that, she needed to earn his love, the way she had never been allowed to earn it with Nick.

'That was before I knew you,' she said, embarrassed. 'Except that I still don't know you, you won't let me. You never show your feelings, you won't own up to any weaknesses . . .'

'You're my biggest weakness. And I do have feelings. You can't deny I was fond of Harriet.' To think that she had resented that, once, envying them their easy rapport, their shared laughter. And now she would give anything to see them playing together with Jamie again . . . 'I was fond of Gerald too, even though it wasn't mutual. I'm going to miss them.'

The tremor in his voice was so unexpected, so seductive, that Vivi couldn't let the moment pass. It seemed wrong to want to make love at a time like this, but the urge was all-powerful. She had read somewhere that bereavement heightened the sex urge, or rather the urge to procreate, to replace the lives that had been lost. And he seemed to feel it too, responding to her with all the urgency of their first encounter, rekindling the fire that had long since subsided to a smoulder.

For a moment she was hopeful that this was a new start, that somehow this dreadful tragedy would bring them closer together. But the illusion of intimacy was soon broken. As always, after sex, he was vague, abstracted, remote, already inhabiting some private place she couldn't enter.

'You're shutting me out again,' she accused him. 'And don't tell me it's to do with the accident. You've always held back. It's as if there's something you're not telling me.'

'There are a lot of things I don't tell you. Don't crowd me, Vivi. I don't crowd you.'

True enough. Sometimes their paths didn't cross for a week at a time, thanks to their different, equally demanding schedules. Max had not only kept his promise not to interfere in Vivi's work, but he had never involved her in Kellerman International, she wasn't even a shareholder, let alone on the board, the way wives so often were. What she did know, from reading the business pages rather than talking to Max, was that the stock market crash of the previous October, the so-called 'Black Monday', had wiped millions off the value of Kellerman shares at a time when the company had borrowed extensively to finance a huge expansion programme. And that several big make-or-break contracts were currently in the balance.

'If you lost every penny tomorrow,' she ventured, 'it wouldn't make any difference to me. I'd sell the paper in a minute if it would help you out.'

I must love him, she thought, taken aback by her own spontaneous offer. And now she had as good as told him so. But that wasn't enough. She wanted to prove it to him, to let him know that she wasn't the mercenary, heartless little bitch who had agreed to marry him, that there was nothing she wouldn't do for him if only he would love her back.

'Thank you for offering.' He seemed surprised, touched. 'But it won't come to that.' He began dressing. 'I have things to do. You stay in bed and get some sleep.'

Vivi didn't stay in bed. She got up and got busy. It was the only way to get through it.

## 19

*Spring 1988–Summer 1989*

GERALD HAD BEEN dead a whole month now. And still Gemma couldn't bring herself to cry.

Mum had stayed on for a week after the funeral – minus Fred, who had to hurry back to a golf tournament in Marbella – but her efforts to offer comfort had met with rigid I'm-all-right composure. Mum had wept for a month non-stop when Dad had died, she reminded her dry-eyed daughter, and on and off ever since, not that you could compare twenty-odd years together with only four – her attempt to explain away Gemma's unseemly lack of tears. Mum wasn't to know that she had forfeited her right to grieve. She didn't deserve any sympathy. And so she was careful not to invite any.

There was a tremendous turn-out for the memorial service at St Bride's, a stone's throw from the old *Courier* building. Gemma sat through it with outward calm while hardened hacks wept all around her. Afterwards she stood outside the church, alongside Vivi, shaking hands with the mourners as they emerged, thanking them for coming. She had already told Vivi that she wouldn't be going to the wake, unable to face all that collective pity.

'Gemma. I'm so sorry, love.'

The last face, the last handshake, the last I'm sorry. He must have waited till the end deliberately.

'Nick. Thank you for coming.' She hadn't seen him since their chance encounter in Liverpool, just before Vivi's wedding. 'And for your letter.' It had almost succeeded in making her cry. He had written to Vivi as well, effectively burying the hatchet.

'Gemma, the car's waiting to take you home,' said Vivi. 'Are you sure you don't want to come with us?'

'I can't. Say sorry to people for me, will you?'

'I'll pop in on you later.' She turned to Nick. 'See you at the Savoy, then.'

''Fraid I can't make it.' In other words, thought Gemma, he had no intention of accepting Kellerman hospitality, even now.

'That's a pity,' said Vivi, evidently relieved nonetheless. 'Well, good luck with the agency. Remember *The Courier*'s always in the market for a good story.' And with this businesslike olive branch she walked quickly away.

'Any chance of a lift?' Nick asked Gemma. 'You owe me one, remember?'

Gemma looked blank for a moment.

'Oh yes. That day on the picket.' It seemed like a lifetime ago. 'Where do you want to go?'

'Let's get you home first. Then I'll ask the driver to drop me off. It'll give us a chance to talk.'

Gemma didn't want to talk. She had made that so clear that nobody dared mention Gerald's name in her presence, even Mum had got the message in the end. But it was hard not to respond to Nick's questions, especially as he didn't actually ask any, not directly anyway. Like a water diviner, he could sense the hidden spring bubbling beneath the surface, he knew just where and how deep to dig. Barely aware of being prompted, she found herself describing the traffic jam on the drive to the airport, and being late, and how the crash must have happened before they had even set off, and how the news had been relayed to Vivi's office, only no one there could bring themselves to ring her carphone, leaving it to the airline ground staff to break the news instead. She related the endless if-onlys that had tormented her ever since – if only Gerald and Harriet had come home that morning, as they had originally planned to do. If only they had stayed an extra night and flown home next day. If only they had set off for the airport half a minute earlier, or later, that lorry would have hit another vehicle rather than theirs. And after the if-onlys, the endless unanswered questions. Would they have been aware of the collision? Would they have suffered? Why hadn't she had some kind of premonition, how could she have sat there, talking to Vivi, not knowing, not suspecting, not even worrying? And then the regrets. That she hadn't been more patient with Harriet when she interrupted her work. That she and Gerald had put off having children. Most of all, that she hadn't been with them at the time, that she hadn't been killed as well . . .

When the dam finally burst, with a sudden roar, it did so without warning, knocking her sideways, leaving a big damp patch in the middle of Nick's shirt. She shouldn't have been surprised. Vivi had always said that he could wring blood from a stone.

'You'd better ask me in for a cup of tea, while I dry off,' he said, as the chauffeur drew up outside the small flat-fronted Victorian terraced house, with sparkling windows, gleaming brass knocker and well-scrubbed doorstep. Inside it was similarly spotless. Gemma had taken to cleaning the place from top to bottom every day, in a vain attempt to scrub away her guilt.

'There's no need. I'm not going to try to top myself. Talk about giving a dog a bad name. I've had Vivi watching me like a hawk, ever since it h-happened . . .'

'Milk, two sugars please. Three for you.'

He sent the car away, saying you can bunk off now mate, I'll get the tube home, and followed her inside.

'Nice house,' he said. It hadn't been, but it was now. It was Gemma who had tirelessly painted and dragged the walls, stripped and buffed the cast-iron fireplaces, sanded the floorboards, scoured junk shops, plundered skips, and taught herself carpentry and plumbing from a manual; Gerald had always been clueless about DIY. Upstairs, overlooking the small back garden, was a small bright sunshine yellow room that should have been a nursery. And next to it the narrow all-white bathroom, with Gerald's shaving kit and toothbrush and flannel by the washbasin. And opposite that their cool blue bedroom, where his clothes still hung in the wardrobe, exuding the lingering, evocative scent of pipe tobacco. Gemma had even washed and ironed the dirty laundry in his mangled suitcase and put it back in the drawers.

'Thanks. We'd only just finished doing it up. You know what these old houses are like.'

'Too right I do. They keep you poor. Are you going to be all right for money?'

'Gerald had a policy that paid off the mortgage. And I'm still working.' The all-absorbing interest had become a time-killing chore, but she had to earn a living somehow. Gerald surely wouldn't want her to sponge off Max and Vivi, something he had resolutely declined to do himself. She was glad he hadn't left her enough to keep her in idleness. At least work gave her a reason for getting up in the morning.

Nick carried the tea-tray into the living room, to spare her the embarrassment of it rattling from her shaking hands. It was then that he noticed the framed photograph of Jamie on the mantelpiece; if Gemma had anticipated this visit, she would have thought to hide it. She watched apprehensively as he picked it up for a closer look.

'Tell me I'm imagining things,' he said.

Gemma answered him with an eloquent silence.

'I knew it,' he muttered. 'Or rather, I didn't know, I didn't want to know. I could have hung around outside the house, like some Peeping Tom, waiting for a glimpse of him. But I couldn't face seeing a kid that looked like Kellerman. Or one that looked like me, come to that. Or one that left me guessing. So I kept away. And now . . . does he realise?'

Gemma nodded. 'To be fair to him, it didn't make any difference. He treats him like his own.'

She had always found Max a remote, mysterious, even sinister figure, despite his generosity, his sociable hi-there manner, his unremitting charm. But she had never doubted his love for Jamie.

'I'll bet he does,' seethed Nick, clenching his fists. 'He's always been good at helping himself to other people's property. To think of my kid calling that bastard Daddy . . . I ought to have it out with him. I ought to –'

'You ought to be glad that he's a good father,' said Gemma quietly. 'Which he is, I promise you. Please, Nick, don't make any trouble. Vivi's had enough to cope with lately.'

He ran a hand through his hair, still agitated.

'Bit late now, I suppose, to start staking a claim. My own fault for burying my head in the sand all this time. You know, I was all set to dig up some dirt on him, you can bet your life there's plenty. But in the end I couldn't bring myself to do it. Couldn't hurt him without hurting her, could I? Luckily for him. But that doesn't mean I don't hate his guts as much as ever. Especially now.' And then, gruffly, 'Can I take the photo?'

'Of course.'

'Thanks. I'll return the frame.' He put it in his pocket. 'The rumour is that he's in trouble, you know. Over-expansion.'

'Vivi reckons it's a smear campaign, to undermine shareholders' confidence. You can't have that kind of maverick success without making enemies. A lot of the big boys have got it in for Max, for stealing their business.'

'Well, let's hope one of them sticks the knife in for me. Whoops. Trust me to drop a clanger.' It took Gemma a moment to make the connection. When she did she found herself smiling, despite herself, for the first time in weeks. 'Is she happy with him? There's no right answer to that question, so be honest. I need to know.'

'I don't think Vivi knows how to be happy with anyone. She married Max for *The Courier*, so she says, you can never tell with her, and to get away from you, which I believe, and now she's ended up falling in love with him for her sins. Not that she'd ever admit it, least of all to him. But I've seen her in love before. So I can tell. You did ask me to be honest.'

'In love with him, eh? Poor old Kellerman. I'm starting to feel quite sorry for him.' The attempt at flippancy didn't quite come off; it was as if he had stuffed his anger in his pocket along with the photograph, to be examined in more detail in private.

'How's Casey?' said Gemma, changing the subject.

'Oh, thriving. Jackie's made quite a go of that little bar of hers, ended up dumping Spike for this Greek guy. I met him last year, he seems like a nice bloke. Well off, a widower with two kids. They're talking about getting married.'

'And how's the agency?'

'FPS if you please. Ferris Press Services. I've got a lease on premises in sunny Clerkenwell, we go live at the end of May. Having to get in all the computer gear, of course. Got to, to be competitive. My dad would turn in his grave. Sorry. Put my foot in it again.' He pulled a face and this time Gemma actually laughed, sick joke or not. 'Still, at least I didn't buy Kellerman equipment.'

He drained his cup of tea and stood up to go. 'You going to be okay? Don't want to outstay my welcome.'

'I feel much better now, thanks. It helped to talk.'

'Helped me too. We must do it again. See you, Gem.'

He gave her a peck on the cheek and sauntered off down the

street towards the tube. Gemma had wanted to be alone, so she thought, but now that he had gone the house seemed even emptier than usual. She forced herself to answer some more letters of condolence; she had been touched at the number she had received, not just from people who had known Gerald personally but from members of the public. Vivi had wanted to deal with all the correspondence for her but Gemma welcomed any extra task which might help fill the endless empty acreage of the rest of her life, from the angst-ridden dawn awakening to the moment when she finally dozed off on the settee, rather than climb to that lonely bed above. She could have taken pills to numb her pain but she wanted to feel it, not flee it, it was the only thing she had left.

She worked for a couple of hours at the dining table, rather than at Gerald's desk by the window, which had proved too poignant a reminder of him; she hadn't used it since the day of his death. They had sold most of the antiques he had inherited from his grandmother, to improve their cash flow, but this was one item Gemma had refused to let him part with. A dozen thank-you notes later she went out to catch the last post. On the way back from the letter box, a hundred yards away, her heart began racing, her mouth went dry, and she found it difficult to breathe. By the time she got home, her clothes were sticking to her in damp sweaty patches, even though it was a cool day. She felt sick, giddy.

It wasn't the first time this had happened. She had put it down to stress, told herself that it was normal, quashed the fear that she was having some kind of nervous breakdown. But this attack was much worse than the last one. She struggled to breathe slowly, deeply, waiting for the panic to subside and her pulse rate to return to normal, despising herself for giving in to it, whatever 'it' was.

Next day she drove without mishap to Bermondsey to deliver her latest sketch. But when she went out again later, on foot, to the newsagents, the familiar symptoms returned, forcing her to abandon her outing and run back home as if pursued. From then on she took to shopping by car, but only if she could park nearby. Until she discovered you could get most things delivered, which saved her the ordeal of going out at all. Her work for *The Courier* continued to go badly, leaving her with no creative energy to spare for other commissions. What she eventually handed in, after endless hours of effort, was competent but uninspired, well below her usual standard. If she had been anyone but Vivi's sister, she would surely have been sacked by now. Or at least fallen foul of the author of the comment page (which Vivi, as proprietor, no longer wrote herself, expressing her views through the leader columns instead). But her successor was obviously canny enough not to risk criticising the boss's protégée. Gemma would have resigned, as a point of honour, had it not been for the need to pay the bills. She would have got herself another job, any job, but for her fear of going out.

Vivi came to see her every couple of days – she could just see her writing 'Gemma' into her bulging Filofax – always laden with flowers, fruit, chocolates, books or magazines, as if visiting an invalid in hospital. She would stay at least an hour, valiantly trying to keep up a conversation, and then rush off guiltily to the next item on her agenda. Evidently she was cramming her days even fuller than usual, her way of coping with her loss, but she still made the time to ring as well as visit, sometimes twice or three times a day, on some transparent pretext, just to check that Gemma hadn't slit her wrists.

Poor Vivi. It didn't suit her to be patient and tactful and understanding. Gemma might have felt better if she'd told her to for God's sake pull herself together. But Vivi persisted in asking her to dinner, inventing press tickets for this or that, even suggesting a joint holiday. Invitations which Gemma declined, and not just because she was afraid to leave the house. Vivi had her own life to lead. She had a husband, a child, a newspaper to run, for her there was still life after Gerald. And Vivi had no idea, of course, that what had happened was Gemma's fault . . .

Meanwhile Nick's unheralded I-was-just-passing visits, unlike Vivi's prearranged ones, forced her to get dressed and do her hair and fix her face, just in case he turned up. With Nick there were no awkward silences, the way there were with Vivi. He was never at a loss for words, and his garrulousness was catching. You could say anything to him without worrying afterwards that you had bored him, or made a fool of yourself, even though you probably had.

He wasn't quite the same old Nick she remembered, of course. Some of the swagger had gone, Vivi had stolen that from him for ever, and he continued to brood furiously over Jamie. But he still seemed to bring the sun in with him. He would arrive announcing that he was famished, and wasn't there anything else to eat besides those few poxy biscuits, thereby forcing Gemma to cook or cut sandwiches, forcing her to eat something, because he was there.

'Time I returned the hospitality,' he announced one day. 'I've cadged enough meals off you. What kind of food do you like? French? Italian? Chinese?'

'Chinese,' said Gemma, quick as a flash. 'Our local takeaway delivers.'

'A takeaway? Do me a favour. This is supposed to be my treat. There's a place near me does a terrific Peking duck. Come over to the house first, for a drink, and then we can hoof it. How about tomorrow night?'

She could face driving to Stockwell, just. Even though the front gate had begun to seem like the far side of the moon. But walking all the way to this restaurant and back, however 'near' it was, filled her with dread.

'What's the matter?' And then, misunderstanding her reluctance, 'Honest to God, Gem, this is on the level. I'm not going to try anything on.'

'I never thought you would,' said Gemma, embarrassed.

'And I'm not playing games, to make Vivi jealous, if that's what's worrying you. She knows I come and see you, she knows we're just good mates. I told her, so she wouldn't get the wrong idea.'

Vivi had never mentioned speaking to Nick. Which was telling in itself.

'Did you say anything to her about Jamie?'

'Just that I'd seen the photo. She must have been expecting it, had a little speech all ready, much the same as the one you gave me.'

'And?'

'And I told her I wasn't going to rock the boat.' He shrugged unhappily. 'Okay, so it rots my guts standing by while Kellerman plays father to my child. But I'd rather stay right out of it than confuse the kid. If he's as happy and secure as you keep telling me he is, I suppose that's more important than my ego . . .' He tailed off, aware that he was being over-defensive.

'You don't trust yourself around Vivi, do you?' said Gemma, reading between the lines. 'You're still in love with her.'

'Not enough to make a fool of myself a second time.' And too much, thought Gemma, to try to get his own back on her. 'I've toughened up a lot in the last three years.'

Perhaps, thought Gemma. But Vivi hadn't. Vivi was more vulnerable than ever.

The Courier, 4 *May 1988*
### THREE FRENCH HOSTAGES FREED
*Islamic Jihad yesterday freed three Frenchmen kidnapped in 1985. Diplomats Marcel Carton and Marcel Fontaine, and journalist Jean-Paul Kauffmann were deposited by a car bearing no number plates outside the Summerland Hotel in West Beirut. They were flown to Salonika in Greece late last night and will arrive back in Paris today. They are said to be in good health.*

*The timing of their release, just before the French presidential elections, has fuelled speculation that a secret deal has been done with Iran. The French Interior Minister declined to comment on any such negotiations.*

*Islamic Jihad is known to be affiliated with the Organisation of Islamic Socialist Justice, which is holding British hostage, photographer Daniel Lawrence. Lawrence's late mother and brother recently made an impassioned plea to the French authorities to intercede on his behalf.*

*A Foreign Office spokesman said yesterday, 'I cannot foresee any change in British policy. We have learned that concessions only lead to more hostage-taking.' (See leading article, page 8, and feature, page 11.)*

'I expect Vivi's taken it pretty badly, hasn't she?' said Nick, a week later, over dinner.

It was the second time they had eaten out together, with bad weather saving Gemma's bacon on both occasions. It had been raining when Nick picked her up, necessitating a short drive to her local trattoria rather than a terrifyingly long walk. Otherwise she would have had to invent some excuse to cry off.

'After making that follow-up visit to France, she was banking on Daniel being included in any deals.' As always when discussing Daniel she sounded unemotional, objective. 'But now that Mitterrand's got in for a second term, there's no reason for him to honour any promises Chirac made behind the scenes.'

Releasing the French hostages had been a calculated risk on the part of the Lebanese kidnap gangs and Iran, which pulled their strings. If their man had been elected, they would have stood to gain valuable concessions, and so it made sense to give him a handy pre-election triumph. But now they had lost out. And so had Daniel.

'Still, at least you're making progress at home,' said Nick. Other pressure groups, notably The Friends of John McCarthy, were fighting their own vigorous campaigns, and the hostage situation had now become a major political issue; according to Vivi's sources secret plans were afoot to restore diplomatic relations with Iran. But Gemma found she could no longer pray for Daniel's release with a clear conscience. Not now that Gerald was dead. Gerald dead was a far greater obstacle between them than ever he had been alive. Even to think of getting back together – not that such a thing was likely after all this time – smacked of dancing on his grave.

'So are you ready for the FPS launch next week?' said Gemma, anxious to steer the conversation away from Daniel.

'I don't know about ready. Just because I can drive doesn't mean I can direct traffic. But that's mid-life crisis for you. I suppose I must want to prove something to myself.'

Or to Vivi, thought Gemma. Vivi who had once attacked Nick's lack of ambition in defence of her own excess of it. Vivi knew that she had had it easy, however talented she might be, and clearly got little satisfaction out of having achieved her goals. She was bound to respect Nick, even resent him, for doing things the hard way.

The smaller news agencies worked like bounty hunters, selling stories to the highest bidder. You needed a sixth sense for when a story was about to break, a feel for a hidden, unusual angle, a nose for when you were being conned, a knack for spotting things other people had missed, and the ability to drive a hard bargain. Skills which Nick had already proved he possessed in abundance. But he had no management experience, by his own admission. The windfall his father had left him had given him the freedom to pick and choose his projects and work only when he wanted to. And instead he was investing it in a high-risk venture that could lose him everything.

'Want to see the office?' he suggested, as they stood up to go. 'We could drive over there now, if you like.'

Gemma hesitated, wondering how near they could park, but he had already taken her consent for granted. At least he had left the car right outside the restaurant, which was situated in a narrow one-way street. The rain had stopped, leaving the air clear and fresh and as threatening, to Gemma, as poisonous gas after the comforting indoor fug.

'Look at this,' said Nick, indicating the double-parked vehicle barring his exit. 'Some joker has boxed me in.'

'He's probably in the restaurant,' said Gemma, already retreating. 'We can ask him to move.'

'What the hell. It's turned into a nice evening. We'll walk back to your place and you can drive us over to Clerkenwell. I'll pick up my motor on the way back.'

'But . . . but it must be a good half mile to the house!'

'So? You're not wearing high heels, are you?' Gemma cursed her jeans and trainers. 'Do you good to get some exercise.' He took her arm jauntily. 'What a slob you are, Gem. I can never get you to walk anywhere. Even that pub at the bottom of your road is beyond the pale for you.'

'I've never liked pubs,' said Gemma. 'Too much smoke.'

Whenever he suggested a drink she would offer to open a bottle of wine, or produce a six-pack from the fridge, never mind that Nick derided canned beer as cat's piss.

'And what about that time I offered to help you with the garden? No need, you say, and then you leave me to get on with it, you lazy cow, while you fart about indoors.'

'I've lost interest in gardening.'

'No wonder you're so pale. We ought to drive down to the coast one day and take a nice long walk along the beach, put some colour back in your cheeks.'

Just the thought of all that sky and sea was enough to make her feel giddy. Which ought to have made this little expedition seem easy by comparison. The walk would take less than ten minutes, she told herself, as panic constricted her breath, quickened her heartbeat, desiccated her mouth and drenched the rest of her with sweat.

'Nick . . . please. Can I go in there, and wait for you?'

'What? Where?'

'If I wait inside that cinema, across the road, will you fetch the car and come back for me?'

'What's the matter? Was it something you ate?'

'No. No, I'm not ill. I just feel a bit light-headed.'

'In that case I'm not leaving you on your own. Not at this time of night. Specially in that crummy flea-pit, with a bunch of yobs about to come out any minute. You might pass out.' And with that he squatted down and said, 'Jump aboard.'

'What?'

'Piggy-back. Best I can do. If I lift you any other way I'll slip a disc.'

'You're not going to carry me?'

'Well, if you can't walk, I'll have to, won't I? No chance of hailing a cab round these parts.'

'No . . .' pleaded Gemma, but he had already caught hold of her legs, forcing her to hang on round his neck to retain her balance. 'God, but you weigh a ton,' he groaned, with a mock stagger. 'Warn me if you're going to puke, there's a love, I've just had this jacket dry-cleaned.'

The loss of contact with the ground made her feel dizzy, weightless, like an astronaut walking in space. Every bounce and sway threatened to break her lifeline and hurtle her into the void. She tried counting downwards from twenty and breathing deeply, the way they had taught her to do in hospital, but she reached one much too quickly and the deep breaths came out as short sharp gasps. By the time Nick deposited her on the doorstep, she was panting and shuddering like an exhausted swimmer washed up on the shore, too far gone by now to dissimulate.

'Jesus, Gem. Look at the state of you.'

'It'll pass,' she croaked, fumbling for her keys and staggering into the safety of the hall. 'I'll be okay . . . now I'm indoors.'

'Indoors?'

'It happens . . . when I go outside. I'm sorry. I know it sounds stupid.'

He didn't seem surprised.

'I'd started to wonder,' he said, matter of factly. 'What with all these excuses you've been making. An aunt of mine had the same trouble.'

'Don't tell me to see a doctor,' Gemma pre-empted him. 'He'll either fob me off with pills that make me feel like a zombie or send me to a shrink, and I've had enough of them to last a lifetime. And if you dare tell Vivi . . .'

'Which is exactly what I intend to do,' said Nick. 'I'll have her round here so fast you won't know what's hit you, with a Harley Street quack on each arm. Unless you do what Doctor Ferris here tells you.'

'I already know what he's going to tell me. That it's all in the mind and I've got to get a grip on myself. I've told myself often enough. But it doesn't work.'

'Then perhaps you don't want it to work. You know, in some cultures the widow jumps on the funeral pyre. Or people tear their clothes and mutilate themselves to prove their grief. We all beat ourselves up, one way or another, when someone we love dies. It's normal to feel guilty.'

But not as guilty as she did, thought Gemma. She hadn't realised till now how much perverse comfort she took in her phobia. The last time she had caused a death, she had managed to transfer the blame on to her victim, got out of going to jail. But this time there was no one else to blame, this time she had confined herself to a prison of her own making, for a much greater crime. She felt as if she had wished Gerald dead, even though she never had done, so much so that she no longer had the heart to wish Daniel free . . .

'Well? Is it going to be nice, soft, easy-going me or your bossy-boots of a sister?'

'What is it you want me to do?' said Gemma, cornered. Anything was better than Vivi taking her in hand.

'Not much. We're just going to stand on the doorstep for a bit and admire the view. Tomorrow we'll make it as far as the other side of the road. The day after that, we'll aim for the pillar box. Then we might buy a paper at the corner shop.' He made it sound easy. 'Wait until you're ready, there's no hurry.'

It took her all of five minutes to bring herself to open the door.

She stood there, feeling foolish, for another five, keeping a tight grip on Nick's arm.

'Good girl. Now get some shuteye. See you tomorrow.'

Every day he came back and led her a little bit further towards freedom. Then he made her do the same trips on her own, bringing back various pre-arranged trophies so that she couldn't cheat. It was slow, painful going. It took six weeks to reach the target he had set her and get herself to his office, by public transport – the car was off limits – unaccompanied. Six weeks of so-called progress undermined by the misery of ever-worsening artist's block, misery she took out on Nick, who couldn't even see how bad her work was. There was no point in being second rate at anything, Daniel used to say. And now she was third rate. Her talent was the one thing she had thought no one could take away from her, and now she had lost that too . . .

Nick had borne her rantings with the airy comment that no matter how hard she tried she would never be a patch on her bad-tempered cow of a sister, but never mind, keep on trying. Today he looked up from the untidiest desk she had ever seen, a phone clamped to each ear, and said casually, 'So you made it then', as if he couldn't care less whether she had made it or not, followed by a weary 'How about a cup of tea? I'm parched.'

The office was a mess. There were stacks of files and papers everywhere, drawers gaping open, people wandering in and out demanding Nick's attention, and a small switchboard that winked mournfully to indicate unanswered calls.

'Don't you have anyone to deal with that?' said Gemma, pointing, as she cleared a space for a chipped mug of tea.

'The girl I had walked out yesterday,' said Nick. 'Haven't had time to find anyone else yet. Hello, Ferris Press Services. Where the fuck have you been, sunshine? You were supposed to ring in two hours ago. Hang on a minute. The other phone's going . . .' Gemma picked it up.

'Ferris Press Services,' she said, in her best secretary voice. 'Can I help you?'

She wasn't to know that he had only ever employed a temp to run his office, or that he'd told her not to bother to come in that day. And by the time she found out, it didn't matter any more. She was hooked.

Campaign morale was at rock bottom. Just as things were beginning to look up, an American naval destroyer had accidentally shot down an Iranian airbus, killing three hundred civilians. Six months later, a terrorist bomb had brought a Pan Am jumbo jet down on the Scottish village of Lockerbie, almost certainly an act of retaliation. And now Salman Rushdie had published *The Satanic Verses*, seen by many Muslims as blasphemous, thus bringing fundamentalist wrath not only upon the author but on Britain for giving him state protection against the *fatwa* calling for his death.

All of which had brought relations with the Middle East to a new low. Far from anticipating the release of existing hostages, the Foreign Office was bracing itself for a fresh wave of kidnappings in the wake of the Rushdie affair. Which wasn't the only reason why Vivi was depressed.

'I thought you'd given up smoking?' Max took the offending article from her mouth and stubbed it out. It was all very well for him, thought Vivi. He didn't need nicotine, or booze, or drugs, he had the proverbial nerves of steel.

'Only because of trying to get pregnant. But as it doesn't seem to be working, why bother?'

Having made her decision a year ago now, she hadn't expected to be thwarted. God knows it had happened at the drop of a hat in the past. It might be tactless to confront a widowed, childless Gemma with another nephew or niece, but not as tactless as watching Jamie grow more like Nick every day.

'You've got enough to cope with right now without having another baby,' said Max, returning his attention to the screen on his desk. 'You ought to take some time off. You've been campaigning non-stop for over a year now without a break, as well as putting in too many hours at the paper. Plus you've had to cope with losing your mother and Gerald, and looking after Gemma.'

'I didn't look after her. She wouldn't let me. She still won't.' She had Nick to look after her now, after all.

'You're going to go back to being a secretary?' Vivi had challenged her, aghast, the previous summer.

'Office manager,' Gemma had corrected her. 'I'm sorry to leave you in the lurch, but you'll soon find someone else. I need to be good at something again.'

And so she had proved to be, luckily for Nick. Vivi had never been able to imagine him sitting at a desk giving orders, but thanks to Gemma he didn't need to, he was free to do what he was best at – finding and selling stories – while Gemma kept tabs on the freelances she hired on a daily basis, filtered the constant stream of information that poured into the office and liaised with news desks in need of extra cover. *The Courier* was now a regular client; as Gemma had pointed out to Nick, it wasn't owned by Max any more, and she didn't see why FPS should lose out on valuable business. She seemed to thrive on the long hours and the pressure, earning herself a reputation for toughness and reliability, making a supposedly strong, decisive Vivi feel feeble and fickle.

Ever since the day she had walked out on Nick, she had told herself that she wanted him to find someone new, someone as unlike herself as possible – nice, good-natured, unselfish, the kind of girl who would take good care of him. And ever since Gerald's death, she had hoped that Gemma, a natural-born wife-and-mother if ever there was one, would eventually meet a nice, good-natured, unselfish kind of man, who would take Gerald's place, look after her and give her children. And now they had both met someone she thoroughly approved of. And it hurt.

Oh, nothing had happened yet, but it was bound to, sooner or later. She ought to be pleased for them. She had had her own chance of happiness and blown it, unable to cope with the challenge of loving or being loved. And now that she could cope, or rather now that she wanted to, Max seemed to be drifting further away from her than ever.

She knew he was preoccupied about the company's future. Rumours about it being over-stretched had damaged both consumer and shareholder confidence, just as the rumour-mongers had intended them to do. Lately he had spent more time in planes than he did at home. A source of much anxiety to Vivi as she pictured him in lonely hotel rooms, like the one she herself had seduced him in.

'I'll take a break if you come with me,' she said, in response to his suggestion. 'We could go to Monterey, or the Bahamas, you can take me flying.' Two weeks of uninterrupted leisure together, properly timed, and perhaps she would finally manage to conceive . . .

'How about a simulated flight right now?' she teased, sitting astride him and tugging at his flies.

'Not now, Vivi, I'm working on something.'

'What's the matter with you these days? Don't you want me any more?' And then, before she could stop herself, 'Have you been screwing somebody else?' She hated to admit to being jealous, but at least jealousy was a convenient peg on which to hang all her more profound and indefinable fears.

'I wish I had the energy to spare. I'm beginning to feel like a sperm machine. The whole thing has become too damned clinical.'

'I'm not being clinical now,' lied Vivi. The predictor kit she had bought from the chemists indicated that this was a fertile day. 'It's not even the right time of the month.'

'Then you'll forgive me for being busy right now. I have to have these figures ready for tomorrow.'

'Can't you get someone else to do it?'

'There are some things I prefer to handle myself. Same as you do. Now let me get on with my work, will you?'

'God, but you're cold sometimes.'

'That's one of the reasons you chose me, Vivi, instead of him. You can't have it both ways.'

The shutters had come down abruptly, the way they always did when she made emotional demands on him. She ought to understand that, she had treated Nick the same way, after all. Except that Nick had gradually demolished all her barriers, and Max's were all still intact – no, reinforced – against the onslaught she made on them.

The more she persisted, the more he would withdraw from her. And in the end, if she wasn't careful, she would lose him, just as Nick had lost her, just as Harriet had lost all three husbands. Vivi had lost too many of the people she loved already. Better half a loaf than no bread. A diet which kept her thin. And hungry.


'Have you heard the news?'

'I hear all the news,' said Gemma. She had been dreading Vivi's phone call. Ever since the Israelis had captured Sheik Obeid, a Shia leader, earlier in the week, intending to trade him for Israeli prisoners held in the Lebanon, the hostages' lives had been in the balance. And now one of them, an American, had been executed in retaliation against Obeid's capture. More would die, the kidnap groups threatened, unless he was released.

'Listen, Max is in bloody Australia at the moment. I shall go potty, sitting here on my own, waiting to hear the worst. You wouldn't like to come over tonight, would you?'

Gemma would have preferred to ride out this particular storm in private. But Vivi hadn't asked anything of her since Gerald's death, not even to baby-sit on the nanny's nights off, in a misplaced attempt at tact. How many times had she seen Gerald and Harriet through a Daniel crisis? She couldn't refuse to do the same for Vivi.

Vivi's welcome was rather off-hand; she was evidently embarrassed at having asked a favour. But Jamie, a naturally sociable child, made up for it, dragging Gemma off to his playroom to show her his latest acquisitions while Vivi made herself scarce, not wishing to appear to be flaunting her most prized possession.

'Thanks for coming,' she said lamely, an hour later, once Jamie was in bed. 'What would you like for supper?' She led the way into her gleaming space-age kitchen. The Kellermans were still living in Max's penthouse in the Barbican; although Viv was keen to move to a house, with a big garden for Jamie to play in and space for a dog to run free, so far there hadn't been time in her jam-packed schedule to look for one.

'At least this way I can claim to do my own cooking occasionally,' she said, throwing open an enormous upright freezer stashed with ready-made meals. 'I mean, you can't pig out in Le Gavroche every night, can you, when half the world is starving.'

'Why don't you just enjoy being rich, instead of apologising for it?'

'I can't enjoy it. I suppose it's different if you've earned it from scratch, like Max did. But I cheated, the way I cheat at everything. How about chicken tikka with oriental rice?'

'If you like.'

'I'll do two each, the portions are tiny.' As if either of them were hungry. 'Seven minutes each on full power times four is twenty-eight minutes. God, I'll bet you could knock up a meal from scratch in ten. Let's have a drink while we're waiting for the pinger.'

She dispensed two large gins and tonic, swallowing a couple of painkillers with hers against the headache it would give her. A computer screen built into a shelving unit flashed out the latest agency bulletins from around the world.

'What the hell,' said Vivi, lighting up a cigarette for good measure and opening the window to let the smoke out. 'I came on this morning, so I might as well indulge all my vices. Hope I didn't upset any plans you had for the evening.'

'I should have been working, that's all. Nick's covering for me.'

'He landed on his feet, hiring you, didn't he? I'm always hearing on the grapevine what a hard bitch you are. Take it as a compliment. Dad would never believe that his sweet little girl was out there in the front line, in among the muck and bullets.'

And yet tonight Gemma's role was to be passive and patient, as Dad had trained her to be, when what she really wanted was to give vent to her own fear and frustration . . .

'No, I don't suppose he would,' shrugged Gemma. 'But he wouldn't have any trouble believing in you as the first female proprietor in Fleet Street.'

'He wouldn't approve of it either. He'd say that I'd sold my soul, and he'd be right. You're the one he'd be proud of. The great sufferer and survivor.' Her voice had that old, familiar goading edge.

'Rubbish. He'd say, look at Vivi, she owns her own paper, and what are you? A glorified Girl Friday.'

'How can you think that? I never heard him utter one word of criticism about you, he never stopped singing your praises. Gemma this, Gemma that. It made me want to vomit.'

'Well, that's news to me,' snorted Gemma, unconvinced. Gerald had once told her that Vivi resented her for being Dad's favourite, but she hadn't taken him seriously. 'You were always the great big shining example of everything I could never hope to be. I learned when I was three years old that there was no point trying to compete.'

'Well, you seem to be making up for it now,' accused Vivi, dragging irritably on her cigarette.

'Working for FPS is hardly competing with you.'

'Working for Nick is, though, isn't it?' snapped Vivi, biting her tongue too late.

So she had got the wrong idea, thought Gemma, along with everyone else.

'Trust you to begrudge me the best friend I ever had. I thought Nick had already explained to you that he and I –'

'Are just good mates, I know,' taunted Vivi. 'He used the same technique on me. First he sees you through an emotional crisis and pretends it's all platonic and gets you to trust him, and then wham, he goes in for the kill.'

'That's not fair. He never pretended to feel platonic about you, he was honest with you right from the start.'

'So he's been discussing me with you, has he?'

'Why shouldn't he? I'm your sister! That's the whole problem, isn't it? You'd rather he talked to anyone else but me . . .'

'Frankly yes! Have you ever wondered what it feels like, having a paragon like you show me up all the time? You're beyond reproach, you always have been. Even when you knifed CC, you managed to come up smelling of roses, like the little goody-goody you are . . .'

If only you knew, thought Gemma. It was the first time Vivi had railed at her since Gerald's death, her tension bringing all the old, unresolved hostilities to the surface. She would have liked to reassure her by saying 'There's no need to be jealous. I confused two different kinds of love once before, and I'm not about to make the same mistake again.' Or to tell her that Nick despaired, by his own admission, of ever falling in love with anyone else. As it was she chose to say nothing, rather than too much.

'I'm sorry,' said Vivi crossly, chastened by Gemma's refusal to answer back. 'I didn't mean to have a go at you. If I'm all wound up tonight it's because of Daniel. Let's forget it.'

Forgetting it wasn't a solution, just a compromise. The occasional puff of steam would never be enough to release the pressure, but taking the lid off their real feelings for each other might blow them both away. And they needed each other too much to risk that happening.

Vivi began tapping on her keyboard, switching from one news source to another. Responding to the pinger on the microwave,

Gemma went to retrieve their plastic trays, almost dropping them as she heard Vivi cry out, 'Oh my God! Gemma! Gemma, look!'

FLASH. ORGANISATION OF ISLAMIC SOCIALIST JUSTICE WILL EXECUTE BRITISH HOSTAGE DANIEL LAWRENCE UNLESS SHEIK OBEID FREE BY 12.00 GMT THURSDAY.

Gemma sat screaming silently while Vivi rang *The Courier* to ask for more details, they were to get on to the story at once and fax her whatever they'd got the minute it came in. This was followed by a call to Downing Street, asking to speak to the PM personally, Vivienne Chambers wanted her comments on the situation before she put the finishing touches to tomorrow's leader page . . .

'They said she'll ring me back,' said Vivi, slamming down the phone. 'She'd bloody better. God, if only there was an election coming up . . .'

You're wasting your time, thought Gemma, as Vivi continued to burn up the phone wires. With the best will in the world, it would take a miracle to break the current deadlock. First Gerald and Harriet, now Daniel. And all because of her . . .

Within an hour a similar threat had been issued by another kidnap group against an American hostage, and Vivi was making arrangements to fly to Beirut via Paris, where she had a better chance of getting a visa quickly.

'You're not serious,' objected Gemma, startled out of her phoney calm. 'What good can it do?'

'None, probably. But it's better than sitting here feeling useless. I want to put out an appeal directly on their media.'

'You can send a video.'

'Which might or might not be shown. If I turn up with a fistful of dollars, I should be able to pay a few people off into giving me some live air time.'

'What about Jamie? What if something happens to you?'

'Nothing's going to happen to me. But if it did, he's got Max.' And then, unexpectedly, 'And he's got you.'

'Me? You hardly ever let me see him!'

'Only because I feel so bloody guilty about having a child when you don't.'

'You feel guilty?' exploded Gemma. 'How do you think I'm going to feel if you end up catching a stray bullet?'

Suppose the plane crashed, suppose she had an accident on the way to the airport? It was like seeing Gerald and Harriet off all over again, only this time she had the sense to worry, crushed by a sense of foreboding. Irrational, perhaps, but overpowering nonetheless.

'If I did, which I won't, nobody's going to blame you,' said Vivi, zipping up a hastily packed suitcase. 'You can tell Max that you did your best to stop me and I wouldn't listen. Thank Christ he's twelve thousand miles away. That'll be my cab,' she added, as the entryphone buzzed. 'Got to go.'

'Well, try not blaming me for this,' blurted out Gemma, desperate to stop her. 'If it wasn't for me Daniel's life wouldn't be in danger, and you wouldn't be about to put yours on the line as well.'

'If it wasn't for you? What are you talking about?'

'If it wasn't for me,' continued Gemma rashly, gathering momentum, 'he would never have gone back to Beirut, he'd be here, safe, in London. If it wasn't for me, he'd never have been taken hostage and Gerald and Harriet wouldn't have gone to Paris. I'm responsible for two deaths already, and now they're going to kill Daniel too, thanks to me. I can't bear to have you on my conscience as well!'

Vivi looked at her for a long hard moment, reading her face, replaying her words.

'What are you trying to say? You mean . . . you don't mean . . . you and Daniel?' She didn't seem horrified, just enlightened, as if the missing pieces of a puzzle had suddenly slotted into place. 'Have I got this right? For God's sake, spell it out, will you?'

The sheer irrevocability of spelling it out almost robbed Gemma of speech, reducing her to the agonised whisper of the confessional.

'Gerald and I nearly split up. I promised Daniel I'd leave him, he was going to pack up his job and come home for good. But I couldn't go through with it. So he went back. And a couple of months later he was kidnapped.'

She knew she was risking everything, that she stood to lose Vivi's respect for ever. But it was the only way to shock her into listening, the only possible appeal that could work. Even if it didn't, at least she wouldn't have stood cravenly by and watched her walk away.

'It wasn't like you think,' she added feebly, afraid that Vivi would despise her as another of Daniel's easy conquests, dismiss her whole marriage as a sham.

'I don't know what I think yet. Except that it was bloody typical of you to hold out on me all this time. Is that the reason you've been so off with me ever since Gerald died?' She sounded almost relieved. 'Because you thought I'd hate you for it if I knew? After all the shitty things I've done in my life, how can you be afraid to tell me anything?'

'If you don't hate me for it, then don't go to Beirut.'

It was crude emotional blackmail. It was tantamount to telling Vivi that she loved her and asking for her love in return. Before Vivi could answer the entryphone buzzed again.

'Charge my account for a cancelled journey, will you?' Gemma heard her say into the speaker. And then, 'Your turn. Start talking. And I warn you, it better be worth it.'

The challenge smacked of one of her old childhood dares, spurring Gemma to further recklessness. Vivi had married the wrong man herself, after all, which wasn't to say that she didn't love him. If she didn't understand, no one would. But it wasn't sympathy Gemma wanted. Just an acceptance of who she really was, instead of what she had pretended, for so long, to be. She wasn't betraying Gerald. She was being true, for once, to herself. Vivi listened without interruption, tactfully allowing her to leave the gaps in the story unfilled, prompting her only with her eyes.

'We've made a right bloody mess of our lives between us, haven't we?' she said, as Gemma fell silent, having revealed all her secrets, if not Gerald's; there were some things even Vivi would never know. 'Seems we've got more in common than we thought.' Daniel had said the same thing, once.

They sat looking at each other warily, as anxious and hopeful as two lovers contemplating their first kiss. It was Vivi who made the first move, flinging her arms around her sister in a convulsive, protective, protection-seeking embrace which Gemma returned fiercely, all their formidable mutual defences down at last. They clung to each other, weeping with the sheer relief of it, tacitly renouncing their joint heritage of envy and mistrust and fear, most of all the fear of loving each other . . .

In the long dark night that followed they talked endlessly, like two strangers stuck in a lift, strangers who happened to be sisters.

'I want to see more of Jamie in future,' Gemma found the courage to say. 'And I'm going to bring Nick with me. That way it'll seem quite natural, he can be Auntie Gemma's friend . . .'

'No. I'm afraid it'll hurt him too much.'

'Not as much as it's hurting him at the moment.'

'All right, so I'm afraid it'll hurt me too much. I wish to God you'd marry him and get him off my conscience. As it is . . .'

As it was Gemma had reassured her on one point, only to come up against another, bigger fear.

'You'll have me there as a buffer between you,' she pointed out. 'Or a chaperone, if you like.'

Vivi fell to chewing her nails, a habit she had never quite broken.

'Well . . . just as long as you don't start having any fantasies about us getting back together. I may have married Max for all the wrong reasons, but I'm staying with him for the right ones.' A vow which Gemma was bound to respect, having once made a similar one herself. 'I'm determined to make it work, for Jamie's sake. I'm never going to put him through a divorce, with him thinking it's all his fault, the way kids always do . . .'

Which was how they got round to talking about Dad again, properly for once, pooling their knowledge, piecing it all together like two detectives possessed of different clues, and reaching the conclusion, not before time, that he had never really wanted them to be allies, despite all his cant; it would have made them much too powerful. Better for them to turn against each other than him – proof, in its way, that he had loved them both, however selfishly. How much sibling rivalry, and all the misery that went with it, was the product of cleverly disguised, even subconscious, parental divide and rule?

It had taken them over twenty years to understand, and accept, and forgive. It was the night they finally sloughed off the skin of their childhood and wondered how they had ever fitted inside it.

## 20

VIVI DIDN'T FLATTER herself that her televised appeal to the kidnappers – the video had been broadcast hours before the deadline expired – had made any great difference to Daniel's fate. Far more significant was the swearing in of a new President of Iran, whose political agenda it suited to intervene behind the scenes, thereby securing an indefinite stay of execution and granting Gemma and Vivi their first night's sleep in a week.

By this time Gemma had told Nick what he would otherwise have guessed, given her obvious agitation as the deadline for Sheik Obeid's release grew ever nearer. He had responded by sending her home immediately – or rather by taking her to Vivi's – which was how he came to have his first sight of Jamie.

Since then he had visited several times, always in tandem with Gemma. Max was never present by pre-arrangement; he had no more desire to see Nick than Nick had to see him, and might well have been less co-operative had he not shared the general misconception about Nick's relationship with Gemma – one which Vivi chose to reinforce rather than correct.

With the crisis over, the Kellermans left for a restorative two weeks at the house in Monterey, the dates expressly chosen to coincide with the middle of Vivi's cycle. By the time she got back, Gemma would be installed in a small, modern flat at walking distance from FPS. It had been a wrench to put the house on the market, to dismantle the shrine, to give Gerald's clothes to the charity shop and distribute his books and music collection among friends and colleagues who shared his tastes.

But she would never part with his beloved bureau, which still stood by the window in the living room, just as he had left it. Every time Gemma looked at it she could see his fair head bowed in concentration, hear the scratch of his fountain pen or the rattle of his old typewriter. It seemed like grave-robbing to empty out its drawers, in readiness for the removal men, and it wasn't until her last night in the house that she finally steeled herself to do it.

They were full of old receipts, newspaper cuttings, periodicals and scraps of paper covered in Gerald's illegible scholar's handwriting; he had always been an incorrigible hoarder. She had meant to be strong and throw things away, but she ended up decanting the lot into plastic carrier bags, to be sorted through at some future date, letting the tears fall unchecked as she did so. She had learned to welcome the relief they gave her, to view them as part of the healing process, not a symptom of sudden relapse.

The bottom right-hand drawer was so full it had jammed shut; when Gemma finally managed to free it she discovered a folder full of campaign mail addressed to Harriet, still vainly awaiting her return from Paris. Mortified at her lapse, she began reading through it, to see if any of the letters required a personal reply, however belated. Mostly they were routine expressions of good-will, instigated by Harriet's appearance on *Wogan* just before the trip to France. There was one marked 'Private and Confidential' which Gemma dithered over briefly before tearing it open.

*23 Kelsey House, Sholto Estate, Liverpool 8*
*8 March 1988*

    *Dear Harriet*
    *I always used to call you that as a girl, long before you were Mrs anything, and I'm too old to change now.*
    *I nearly wrote to you before, only I was afraid it would do more harm than good. But when I heard you on TV the other night, talking about your Daniel, I got to thinking how I would feel if it was one of my boys out there. I thought to myself, she could be about to lose another child, and no woman deserves for that to happen twice, even one who brought most of her troubles on herself, like what you did.*
    *I talked to Father Devlin and he said to me Maureen, that woman has a right to know the truth about what happened to her baby, and then it will be up to her to decide what to do about it. I've kept quiet all these years because I didn't want to cause*

*any trouble, but I'm nearly eighty now and it's time I put my
house in order before I die.*

 *If you want to know more, you can come and see me. If you
don't, fair enough. Some things are best left in the past.*
*Yours truly*
*Maureen Brady.*

Maureen Brady, CC's old housekeeper. It was nearly four years
since Gemma had gone up to Liverpool to check the electoral rolls.
She remembered making dozens of phone calls, and finally
locating a daughter-in-law who said the old girl was away in
Ireland. And then never ringing her back, as promised, because
Gerald had got those threats and abandoned the book . . .

She read through the letter a second time. It seemed clear,
however cryptically expressed – presumably Brady was reluctant
to put anything in writing – that Harriet's suspicions of foul play
had been well founded. Had Brady been a witness to the crime?
Could she confirm that CC had been behind it? She had carried on
working for the family for another twenty-five years, presumably
she had been well paid to keep her mouth shut. And now, with a
Catholic's dread of hellfire, she wanted to make her confession.
But it was nearly eighteen months now since she had written, she
could be dead already. Seized by a sense of urgency, Gemma
dialled the telephone number at the top of the letter.

'Hello?'

'Is that Mrs Maureen Brady?'

'Are you from the social?'

'No. Just a friend.'

'She's in the hospital. I'm looking after the place till she gets
back, on account of all the break-ins.'

'Is she very ill?'

'She broke a hip. She's in the Royal, Ward 4B, if you want to
visit.'

'Thank you,' said Gemma. A broken hip in an eighty-year-old
was often the prelude to pneumonia and death. If she waited for
Vivi's return, next week, the old girl might die in the meantime. So
the sooner she went to see her the better.

\*

'Ready? Here we go!'

The sea sparkled far below them. Sky-high on adrenaline, Vivi braced herself for a barrel roll, and gave her usual big-dipper scream as the plane revolved through three hundred and sixty degrees. At least when they were ten thousand feet above ground, Max wouldn't suddenly disappear on some urgent errand.

'We'll have you sky-diving yet,' he teased, bringing the aircraft level again. Vivi would have taken him up on it, if it would have prolonged their holiday, but Max had a full diary to go back to, and so, for that matter, did she. She should have been as keen as he was to get back to the fray. And instead she was fantasising about this going on for ever. It was as if two weeks of leisure, after years of overwork, had triggered the dormant virus of laziness into debilitating life.

She was tired of being a high-powered career woman. Tired of having to justify her too-easy ride to the top by proving that she was the toughest, most dynamic proprietor in Fleet Street. Most of all, she was tired of coming second to Max's ambition to dominate the world market. They could sell up tomorrow and never have to work again, except when they wanted to . . .

'Have you ever thought of retiring early?' she asked him that night, after dinner, sitting on the deck watching the waves hit the shore.

'Retiring? Never. I intend to die with my boots on.'

'Think of it,' wheedled Vivi. 'You could take the plane up every day, go back to the creative side of computing. And I could spend more time with Jamie . . .' And with you, she thought. And with a new baby, with luck. '. . . perhaps even try my hand at a novel.' The traditional refuge of the burnt-out journalist. Well, let people snigger if they liked. She had begun to understand, at last, why Dad had dropped out of the rat race. First sign of old age.

'I like working hard,' said Max. 'Taking time out is meaningless without it. I thought you felt the same way. If you don't, go ahead and retire yourself. No one'll think any the worse of you. You're a woman. But for me, it would be a cop-out. Specially at this stage of the game. People would think I'd lost my nerve.'

'I'm not enough for you, am I?'

'The rest wouldn't be enough without you.'

'What if you had to choose? The business or me?'

'You shouldn't see my business as a rival,' he said, avoiding the question. 'It's what brought us together. If I hadn't been drafted, if the army hadn't sent me to college, I'd still be a bum, I'd have wound up in jail or the gutter, and you wouldn't have wanted to know me. Women like you don't go for losers. I'm not about to become one now.'

'But you wouldn't be. How many millions does it take to convince you of that? How can you be so insecure?'

It wasn't a real question, just a rhetorical one. Max had always shied away from self-analysis. But perhaps the holiday lassitude had infected him as well, because he chose, unexpectedly, to answer it.

'Easy. If you have it dinned into you, from when you're eight years old, that you're nothing, nobody, you never finish with proving to yourself that it's not true. If your mother stands by and lets her new husband beat you, you never forget what it feels like to have it and lose it, to be second best. At first you take it out on yourself, the way kids do. You drop out of school, run away from home, get involved in petty crime, you fail, deliberately, and wallow in nobody giving a shit. And then, if you're lucky, like I was, you get a chance to succeed at something. That's when you discover what real power feels like. And once you taste it, you can never get enough of it.'

It was the longest speech he had ever made on the subject. Max had told her, albeit briefly, about his beloved father, his brutal stepfather, his weak-willed mother. But not about himself. Not about the frightened, angry child adrift in a world full of enemies.

'Did you ever forgive her? Your mother, I mean?' Vivi knew how long it had taken her to forgive Dad, and she had had Gemma, a fellow-victim, to help her.

'I sent her money. But I never spoke to her again, till her second husband finally drank himself to death. Then I set her up in a nice apartment, paid her medical bills, hired her a Mexican maid, generally rubbed her nose in it. That's when she finally said she was sorry, Max, but she'd loved the guy, she couldn't help herself. At first I thought, crap, you can always help yourself. But then I met you.'

'You sound as if you wish you hadn't,' fished Vivi.

'I misunderstood what it would take to make you happy.'

'You mean you don't love me the way I love you.' It came out as an accusation, rather than a declaration, even though love had never been part of their original contract. If it had she would have run a mile. For a moment he looked as if he was about to confirm her worst fears, to do to her what she had done to Nick, and perhaps for the same reasons.

'Of course I love you,' he said. 'More than anything in the world. Of course I love you, Vivi.' And then he proved it, the only way he knew how. And this time it was different, this time he didn't shut her out, and at last she realised what had been wrong. Like her, he still felt bad and worthless inside, like her he thought he didn't deserve to be happy. And what they had both mistaken for sexual chemistry was the recognition of each other's pain.

Tempted though Gemma was to mention Maureen Brady's letter to Nick, in order to pick his investigative brains, she could just imagine Vivi's reaction to her involving him behind her back. She had wondered if she ought to consult her by phone before going up to Liverpool on Sunday, but it seemed crass to blight her long-awaited baby-making holiday with morbid talk of infanticide. However distressing Brady's revelations might be, she owed it to Gerald, and to Harriet, to find out the truth.

She arrived at the hospital outside visiting hours, intentionally so, to ensure she spoke to Brady in private, and spun the ward sister a line about being a goddaughter from London who was only passing through and couldn't wait. The old girl's mind tended to wander, she was warned; she was also nearly blind. Gemma decided to take advantage of this by pretending to be Vivi, in case Brady turned out to be one of CC's faithful band of acolytes who thought that hussy Gemma Lawrence should have gone to the gallows.

'Mrs Brady?' she ventured, approaching a sunken-cheeked, opaque-eyed woman in a corner bed and handing over a large box of soft-centred chocolates as a sweetener. 'I'm Harriet's daughter, Vivienne. I've come about the letter you wrote her, last year. Do you remember?'

Maureen Brady looked at her unseeingly.

'She's dead now,' she said, in a squelchy, toothless voice. 'I heard it on the telly.'

'She died before she read your letter. That's why I'm here. To do what she would have done. To ask you to tell me what really happened to her baby. My sister. Like the priest said you ought to do.'

A long silence while Brady fumbled on the bedside table for her teeth and put them in with bony, claw-like hands, indicating her willingness to talk to her, or rather to start work on the chocolates. Encouraged, Gemma drew up a chair and unravelled the cellophane for her.

'Your ma was nothing but trouble as a girl,' muttered Brady through a mouthful of goo. 'When her father found out she was in the family way, there was a terrible to-do. He pushed her down the stairs on purpose, I saw him do it, to try and get rid of the baby.'

And in the end he had succeeded, thought Gemma. Had the doctor been part of the conspiracy? Had that so-called emergency Caesarean merely been a device to rob Harriet of consciousness and fake a stillbirth? A well of residual hatred rose up inside her as she imagined CC plotting against Harriet, just as he had done against her, against Gerald.

After this promising preamble, however, Brady fell silent, looking vacant and senile again. Lost in memories, perhaps. Or having second thoughts about admitting her part in the cover-up. Or unable to keep track of her own train of thought.

'My mother always knew that her daughter wasn't born dead,' Gemma prompted gently. 'When she came round she could hear crying in the next room. Please don't be afraid to tell me what really happened. I promise I won't get you into any trouble.' And then, when Brady still didn't speak, 'The baby was smothered, wasn't she?'

The response was as instant as a ricochet.

'Smothered?' snorted Brady, coming abruptly out of her stupor, and releasing a shiny thread of chocolate-coloured spittle. 'What for? She never took breath, poor little mite.'

She didn't sound defensive, just emphatic. Predisposed as Gemma was to disbelieve her, she had developed a professional instinct for when people were lying, and Brady's words had the spontaneous ring of truth.

'You're sure about that?'

'I saw the doctor lift that baby out of her,' Brady asserted stoutly, fumbling blindly for another sweet. 'I cleaned her up and wrapped her in a towel and gave her to your ma to grieve over. It was all for the best. She was only a child herself, she didn't have a husband. Like her Aunt Emily said, it was God's will.'

So it had been a wild-goose chase, thought Gemma, disappointed, even though she ought to be relieved. Evidently Brady had simply wanted to set the record straight, reassure Harriet that her fears had been unfounded and absolve herself of any blame.

'Do you know where the baby was buried?' Gemma felt bound to ask, reluctant to leave empty-handed. 'My mother would want me to mark the grave . . .'

'Somewhere in the grounds, I don't know where. My husband dealt with it.'

She sighed and leaned back on the pillows, as if exhausted. And then, just as Gemma was preparing to abandon this as a bad job, she added, 'She did hear a baby crying, though.'

'What?'

'Mrs Ashleigh, her Aunt Emily, she had these friends visiting from London. They couldn't get home because of the snow, so they had to stay overnight. There was no keeping from them what was going on, what with your mother going into labour early and screaming blue murder. All the phones were down, because of the blizzard, so my Joe had to go and fetch the doctor. And then he got stuck in a snowdrift and ended up having to walk it all the way there and back. The poor girl nearly died, so she did, before they arrived . . .'

'You mean these friends of Emily's had their baby with them?' said Gemma, interrupting this digression. Harriet had never mentioned there being guests in the house over Christmas. But of course she had been confined to her room, to keep her condition secret.

'No. The wife couldn't have children, see. On account of a riding accident, when she was young. That's why she begged to take the baby, and Mrs Ashleigh agreed, so next morning they took it back to London with them.'

'But the baby died,' Gemma reminded her, puzzled, thinking that the old girl's mind was wandering.

'Oh yes. But there was nothing wrong with the other one.'

'The other one?'

'When the doctor cut her open he found twins. That accounted for your mother being so big and the little girl being so small.'

Gemma sat speechless for a moment, unable to believe that she had finally struck gold. Brady was in full flow now, chattering on the way old people do when recalling the events of long ago.

'The wife – Peggy, her name was – she said she would register the child as her own so nobody would ever know. Mrs Ashleigh jumped at the offer right enough. She was desperate to avoid a scandal, and what with the other baby being dead, she thought Harriet would be none the wiser.'

It was all too detailed to be the invention of a decaying mind . . . wasn't it?

'But she never bargained on your ma taking it so bad,' went on Brady. 'The state of that poor girl! She kept raving that someone had killed her baby, that they couldn't keep her locked up for ever and she was going to go to the police. The doctor had to give her injections to calm her down. He told Mrs Ashleigh straight that she'd done wrong to give the other child away and if the law came calling, he wouldn't be telling them no lies. Then the mistress starts to panic that there's going to be a big hoo-hah, and it will end up the talk of the county and her brother will blame her for it. So she phones Peggy in London to tell her she's changed her mind and she's sending my Joe and me to fetch the baby back, thinking it would keep Harriet quiet. But when we get there, Peggy and her husband have done a flit without leaving a forwarding address, so that was that.'

Poor Harriet, thought Gemma, deprived of her child. Poor Peggy, determined not to be deprived of hers . . .

'Mrs Ashleigh never told the master what she'd done, for fear he'd spill the beans to Harriet, in one of his tempers. She thought this way he'd go easier on her. And the doctor, well he wasn't going to go looking for trouble, I expect she slipped him something, same as she did me. Anyway, your ma soon perked up once her father said she could go to Paris, all he wanted to was to get rid of her and all she wanted was to get away from him. So it all worked out for the best,' she repeated, as if to convince herself.

Gemma wasn't so sure. It wasn't as if Harriet had given the baby up voluntarily. It had been stolen from her, kidnapped, just as

Daniel had been. If Harriet were here now she would surely leave no stone unturned until she found her long-lost child . . .

'Is there anything you can tell me about this couple?' asked Gemma, getting out her shorthand notebook. 'What was their surname?'

'I just remember Mrs Ashleigh calling her Peggy. She knew her from when she lived in London, before she was widowed. Don't recall the husband's name, good-looking chap he was, but he wasn't a well man, he'd been shot up bad in the war. This Peggy did voluntary work in an army hospital somewhere, that's how she met him . . .'

None of which was any use without a name, thought Gemma, frustrated. Brady didn't know their address in London, not that it would have been much help, after all this time. Her husband could have told her, she said, he was the one with the memory, but he had been dead these past five years now, God rest his soul . . .

'Have you any idea which hospital Peggy worked at?' persisted Gemma. It had probably ceased to exist, but Vivi would want to follow up every clue. She could put half a dozen hacks on the job if necessary, or hire a firm of private investigators . . .

'No. Mrs Ashleigh never mentioned it.' And then, making Gemma sit up, 'I do remember her going up to London, though, for the wedding, on account of it being my Joe's birthday. Twentieth of September. He would have been eighty-four next month . . .'

'What year? What year was their wedding?'

'The year the war ended. 1945.'

There couldn't be many Peggys married on that date in London. And one of them would have registered the birth of a child three years and three months later. Once she made that link she would have a name to go on. It was a start. The smell of a story was potent, seductive, she would never be able to rest now until she cracked it . . .

Having listened to further inconsequential ramblings, Gemma drove back to London. Vivi was due back on Wednesday, which would give her time to go up to St Catherine's House tomorrow and find out as much as possible before her return.

She was waiting outside when they opened next morning, having rung the office to say she would be late; Nick was out of town, chasing a story, sparing her the need to explain herself. It didn't take her long to find what she was looking for. There were only three Peggys, or rather Margarets, married in London on the date in question, a weekday. The third of which jumped off the register and hit her in the middle of the solar plexus. Margaret Sybil Campbell. Who on 20 September 1945 had married a lieutenant in the US Army, one James Edward Kellerman.

Gemma chose to dismiss the name at first as a coincidence. There must be any number of James Kellermans in the world, she reasoned, as she searched, head spinning, for a record of a birth to any of the three couples in December 1948 . . .

There was only one. Max Campbell Kellerman, born on Christmas Day at a home address in Hammersmith. But it couldn't be Vivi's Max. Vivi's Max had had his fortieth birthday in January, on 15 January to be precise. And Max had been born in California. Unless . . . unless he had been registered twice, once in December '48, in England, and again in January '49, on the other side of the Atlantic, where Aunt Emily would never find him . . .

No. It wasn't possible. Long-separated siblings marrying by accident was the stuff of fiction. Desperate for contradictory evidence, Gemma rang the press office of Kellerman International from a phone box, claiming to be a freelance journalist doing research. Was it correct that Mr Kellerman's late mother's name was Margaret Sybil Campbell? Yes, thank you so much for confirming that, didn't want to get it wrong . . .

She stood numbly for a moment while the full implications sank in. Vivi had spent the last eighteen months trying to have a baby by her half-brother. Worse, she might already be pregnant . . .

Thank God she hadn't said anything to Nick. Vivi would have died rather than have him, or anyone else, a party to knowledge like this. Unable to contemplate breaking the news over the phone, Gemma had to carry her burden round with her till Vivi came home, two interminable days later. By that time she had chickened out of telling her face to face. Better to speak to Max. He would take it more calmly, he would be less likely to shoot the messenger. And this way Vivi wouldn't have the ordeal of telling Max herself . . .

Vivi rang Gemma at the office to announce her return.

'Max went straight into work from the airport,' she complained. 'Talk about a junkie twitching for a fix. Still we had a great holiday. Max taught Jamie to swim.' She sounded happy, relaxed. 'I'm jet-lagged to hell,' she added, yawning. 'Didn't get a wink on the plane, and I didn't dare take any sleepers, just in case I've struck lucky . . .'

'The other phone's ringing,' said Gemma. 'Got to go.'


'Gemma,' said Max, standing up to greet her, as his secretary showed her into a large, luxurious office on the top floor of Kellerman Tower. Her unannounced arrival had been ill timed; she had had to wait in reception, plied with espresso coffee and glossy magazines, for over half an hour, because Mr Kellerman was taking an important conference call.

'Sorry I had to keep you waiting.' He gestured her towards a leather armchair, politely concealing his impatience to get on with whatever she had interrupted. She found herself staring at him, as if for the first time, looking for a resemblance to Harriet, to Vivi. But she couldn't find any. He had evidently got the hooded eyes and high cheekbones from his father, the itinerant gypsy stable hand of long ago.

'Has something happened while we were away?' he said pleasantly. 'Something I can help with?'

There was no tactful way of telling him, it all came out in a frantic, apologetic, topsy-turvy rush. He didn't look at her as she poured out her anxious narrative. He got up and walked over to the window, looking down at the traffic far below, almost as if he wasn't listening.

'I'm so sorry,' repeated Gemma, perplexed at his lack of reaction. 'I know this must be a terrible shock, I mean, the odds against something like this happening must be phenomenal, I can hardly believe it myself. The thing is, I thought it would be easier for Vivi if you told her rather than me . . .'

'I'm not going to tell her,' said Max, quietly but harshly. 'And neither are you.' He turned round and repeated the words with his eyes.

'But . . . but she has to know. She's trying for a baby.' And then, when he didn't seem to get the point, 'You're brother and sister. It could be born with all kinds of defects . . .'

'She's not going to have a baby,' said Max. 'I had a vasectomy, so that it couldn't happen.'

'You did what? But . . . why?' The answer, obvious though it was, didn't hit her right away. 'You mean . . . you don't mean . . .'

'I knew,' said Max. 'I knew before I married her.'

Gemma was shocked into silence. Shocked but not altogether surprised. Max wasn't the sort of person things happened to by mistake. He made them happen. He controlled events.

'You bastard,' she said weakly.

'Literally. The first time I met her I didn't realise how much of a bastard I was, I still thought I was who I was supposed to be. But I don't agree about the odds against us meeting. I wouldn't put it down to accident, or coincidence, or bad luck. I would say it was destiny, inevitable, that it was meant to happen, that my whole life had been leading up to that moment.'

Gemma was too stunned to do anything but listen, mesmerised by the sheer arrogance of the man.

'I fell head over heels in love with her on sight,' he went on, 'if that doesn't sound too corny. Something I never thought would happen to me. She was so vulnerable under that hard-boiled front of hers, so complicated, so unhappy. As soon as I got home I told my mother that I'd met the woman I intended to marry. She was terminally ill at the time, I thought it would help her die happy. She wanted to know all about this Vivi, all about her family. That's when she finally got round to telling me who I really was.'

But he hadn't told Vivi, thought Gemma. Because by that time –

'By that time,' said Max, as if reading her mind, 'I'd already managed to get her pregnant. So instead of marrying her, I had to let her have an abortion. That's why I took steps to make sure it could never happen again, why I went back to the States for that so-called business trip just after she moved in with me. But I had a few anxious moments, I admit, till the scan showed that she was further gone than she claimed. Not that the doctors told her that. I didn't want her running back to Ferris.'

'I can't believe this,' said Gemma, finding her voice. 'I can't believe even you could be so cold, so calculating, so –'

'So determined not to lose her? I kept away from her for a year after that first meeting, I made up my mind never to see her again. But that only made me want her even more. And then my mother died, and no one else knew the truth, and I found myself thinking, why not? Why the hell not? Sharing one parent isn't so very different from being first cousins, except in the eyes of the law. And who can tell, these days, who's a sister, who's a brother? What about adultery, and promiscuity, and donor insemination, what about adoption, what about kids like Jamie? It must happen all the time.'

'In ignorance, perhaps. But you knew!'

'Do you think it was easy, knowing? Have you any idea what hell it is, wanting someone as badly as I wanted her? I accept the medical arguments. But not the moral ones. The moral ones are designed to protect children, not adults.'

'Consenting adults are one thing. But you tricked her! If you're so sure of your moral code, why weren't you honest with her?'

'Have you always been honest with the people you love?' he challenged her, reminding her of Gerald, of Daniel. 'It helped that she didn't love me, at first, it made it seem . . . fairer. I got what I wanted, and so did she. The way I saw it, we could always adopt, we still can. Vivi loved Casey, even though she wasn't hers. Same as my father loved me. Same as I love Jamie. Biology's not important. Your parents don't define who you are. Who you are is what you decide to be.'

'God, but you're complacent,' said Gemma. 'Didn't it ever occur to you that somebody might find out, like I did?' And then, with a sudden, belated flash of horrified insight, 'My God. It was you, wasn't it? It was you, hacking into Gerald's computer.'

He shrugged, not denying it.

'That's why you gave it to us, and rigged it up to the phone lines, and taught me all that fancy software. So that you could keep tabs on what we were doing, in case we stumbled across the truth. And once you knew we'd found Brady, you sent Gerald the threats and the photographs. You were ready to destroy him . . .'

'No. I knew it wouldn't come to that. I knew he'd drop the book like a hot brick, and he did. I never intended for him to suffer financially. I offered him a loan, and a job that would have got him back on his feet . . .'

'Only because you had a guilty conscience!'

'Would you prefer it if I didn't have one? Would you rather this Maureen Brady woman had had a tragic accident? I considered the possibility, I admit. But I'd killed too many people in Vietnam to want to do it ever again. Even in self-defence, like you did,' he added cruelly. 'My only crime was to fall in love with the wrong woman. Just like you fell in love with the wrong man. Your husband's brother, your sister's brother. Pretty incestuous, don't you think? So don't be in such a hurry to cast the first stone.'

Gemma felt herself go bright red. Damn Vivi for telling him about Daniel. But he had made his point. She had wanted to be part of Vivi's family all her life, so much so that she had married into it, with just as much self-interest as Max had done, and perhaps just as dishonestly. Guilty or not, he had been good to Harriet, shelled out thousands of pounds for the Daniel campaign, even managed to win round Gerald in the end . . .

'And what about your conscience, Gemma?' he went on, kicking her while she was down. 'If you tell Vivi, she'll either stay with me regardless, and feel screwed up as hell about it, or she'll leave me and feel even worse. And who do you think she'll be angrier with? Me, for loving her too much? Or you, for not loving her enough to keep your mouth shut? I may be the villain of the piece, by your lights, but you'll end up as the scapegoat. Think about it, Gemma.'

Gemma thought about it, Nick's words echoing in her ears: *I was tempted to dig up some dirt on him, but I couldn't bring myself to do it. No hurting him without hurting her . . .*

What was more important? To defend a moral and social taboo? Or to preserve Vivi's peace of mind? Vivi had lost Harriet, lost Gerald, she lived in dread of losing Daniel. Could Gemma condemn her to losing Max as well, Max who had given her the stability she had always lacked? And what about Jamie? Jamie who worshipped his father, just as Vivi had once worshipped hers . . .

'Just as well for you she loves you,' said Gemma bitterly, by way of capitulation.

'Not as much as I love her,' said Max.

## 21

*Spring 1990–Summer 1991*

THE PIECE ON the Romanian orphans was the first Vivi had written, other than leader articles, since she had taken over *The Courier*. The word orphans, however, embraced a multitude of sins; in a country where contraception had been unavailable and abortion illegal, vast numbers of unwanted children had been abandoned by mothers unable to feed or clothe them. Not that the state had fed or clothed them either. Thousands of half-naked, malnourished children, crammed into slum institutions, had been condemned to a sub-human existence, cared for, or rather neglected, by overworked, demoralised, and ill-equipped staff whose job had been to hide the problem, not to solve it.

It was the kind of story Daniel should have been covering and one which Vivi couldn't bear to delegate, the springboard for an intensive fund-raising campaign to provide food, clothing and medical supplies, to transport and support volunteer workers, to refurbish old buildings and erect new ones. Kellerman's set the ball rolling with a hefty donation, inspiring competitive largesse in other companies.

It was exhilarating to see her by-line again, to translate two gruelling, emotionally draining weeks of research into hard-hitting, heart-wrenching prose. Donations were pouring in, as were well-meaning offers of a good home for that pretty blonde one in the end cot, or if she wasn't available, the little dark boy would do. The reality was that the pretty blonde one would be dead in a year of Aids, and that the little dark boy, at five years old, was unable to speak or smile, because no one had ever taught him how, or even to cry, because he had learned all by himself that there wasn't any point.

'I was expecting you to arrive home with half a dozen kids in tow,' said Gemma, when they met for lunch soon after Vivi's return.

'Chance would be a fine thing. You wouldn't believe the red tape involved. Just as well, really. Otherwise people would be taking them in like puppies at Christmas and dumping them just as quickly. Max is all for us adopting one, of course, anything to stop me being broody.'

Hypocrite, thought Gemma, addressing the word to herself as well as Max, still unsure if she had done the right thing by keeping quiet. But with every day that passed it became more difficult, not to say impossible, to renege on her original decision. Max had known that. He had put enough doubt and fear in her mind to give her pause for thought and left the passage of time to do the rest. Speak now or for ever hold thy peace . . .

Gemma held her peace, but she couldn't quite meet Vivi's eye. No sooner had the barriers come down between them than Max had erected a new one; just as well she had had plenty of practice at keeping things to herself. Neither she nor Max had ever mentioned their shared secret again. Like Rochester's mad wife it remained locked away in an attic, shrieking vengeance at both of them, waiting its moment to strike.

'As Max says, how can you justify having one of your own when there are so many unwanted kids out there?' continued Vivi. 'When I think of the kind of life Jamie has, and compare it with what I saw out there . . . Can you believe this is me talking? I sound like some bleeding-heart do-gooder with nothing better to do than put the world to rights. When you think how I used to take posers like that apart in my column . . .'

'So what's its name?' said Gemma, seeing through this self-castigatory digression.

'What name?' said Vivi, keeping up the charade. Typically she had scattered clues everywhere, and now she would pretend to be surprised that Gemma had pieced them together.

'The child you've set your heart on.'

'How did you know, you witch? I haven't even told Max yet.'

'Easy,' said Gemma. 'I can always tell when you're in love.'

*

Vivi hadn't chosen Roxana. Roxana chose her. A hustler at five years old, she saw her chance of a better life and went for it, with scant regard for the more deserving cases all around her.

She was a recent arrival at the orphanage, just outside Bucharest. Her mother had died in the revolution, which set her apart from her fellow-inmates, most of whom had been admitted at birth or soon after. As soon as she set eyes on Vivi she held out her arms to her and demanded to be hugged, giving herself an unfair advantage over those who didn't know that such things as hugs existed. Not content with that, she talked to her, or rather at her, in urgent tones which required no translation.

There was nothing winsome or pathetic about Roxana. She was tough, pushy, streetwise beyond her years. Neither was she a pretty child, given the untreated squint in her eye, the ill-fed pasty complexion and the shock of unkempt, dark, greasy hair. But she had it in her to be beautiful. Vivi felt those determined arms coil tightly around her and knew that she had encountered a will far stronger than her own.

The staff warned Vivi against the little minx. She was disobedient, aggressive, uncowed by punishment, she was a thief and a liar. Twice she had managed to run away, even though she had nowhere to run to, only to be picked up, scavenging in the streets, and returned to her prison. Her mother had been a prostitute – not that prostitutes had officially existed in Ceausescu's model state – and her father could be anyone. The child had bad blood.

But not so bad that it harboured HIV, thank God. Vivi knew she wasn't brave enough to take on a child that was doomed to die. And at least she was a genuine orphan, rather than merely abandoned, which would make getting her out of the country marginally easier . . .

Vivi allowed ample time for that first crazy impulse to cool. She reviled herself as a bored, overprivileged woman seduced by the ultimate power trip, the chance to change a child's life. The only way she could cope with the longing inside her was to label it a vice – greed, vanity, egomania – and pretend she was trying to resist it. She needed a new challenge, that was all. Nothing charitable about that. The more successful *The Courier* and *The Sunday Courier* became, the more superfluous she felt, like a mother fussing over adult offspring that could function perfectly well without her. It was like an obsession that had run its course, leaving her purged and dissatisfied.

Counting her blessings didn't help. Max and Jamie weren't enough to fill the breach. Max had always been self-sufficient and Jamie seemed to thrive on maternal neglect, he had always made things too easy for her, earning her credit where none was due. How would he feel about sharing the nest with a cuckoo who might turn out to be the adoptee from hell? Was his mother being abominably, irresponsibly selfish for a change?

In the end she did something against all her principles, played the little woman and left the decision to Max, Max who prided himself on never playing safe. If he'd said no, of course, she would have fought him all the way, but she knew as soon as he saw Roxana that she was home and dry.

'She reminds me of you,' was all he said, before distributing dollars to all concerned to effect her speedy removal. Unwilling to leave without her this time, Vivi extended her stay until all the necessary documents had been rubber-stamped. At the Romanian end, at least. Officially, she still couldn't import the child into Britain, but just let anyone try to stop her. The immigration authorities at Heathrow wouldn't want to find themselves pilloried as heartless bureaucrats on the front page of *The Courier*. Likewise the social services who would have to approve the adoption, and who would be foolish indeed to obstruct the maternal instincts of the campaigning virago of Fleet Street, a woman even the Prime Minister was said to fear. Roxana, with the instincts of a true survivor, had picked out just the right person to save her.


Perhaps Max was right, thought Gemma, watching Roxana take over her new family as surely as if she had been born to it. Perhaps biology wasn't important. As far as the children were concerned, they were brother and sister. So why shouldn't the same apply in reverse? An argument which didn't quite convince, but it helped.

Vivi had worried herself sick, on the quiet, that they wouldn't take to each other. Certainly they couldn't have been less alike, Roxana headstrong and volatile, Jamie placid and easy-going. But Max had done an excellent job, in Vivi's absence, of preparing

Jamie for the role of teacher and protector, and Roxana seemed to recognise him as a valuable ally, one whom she lost no time in cultivating with ingenuous self-interest. Older and yet less able than Jamie – a precocious child who could already read and write and operate a PC – she was eager to catch up, copying whatever he did with ferocious, impatient application and learning far more English from him than from the bilingual tutor Vivi had hired to prepare her for school in September.

In the months since Roxana's arrival Vivi had loosened her hold on *The Courier*, whittling down the time spent at the office and concentrating her surplus energies on her Romanian orphans campaign. Meanwhile her other all-consuming project – getting Daniel out of the Lebanon – was finally showing signs of fruition.

In April, two American hostages were released, thanks to the intervention of the new Iranian president, and in August the Iraqi invasion of Kuwait resulted in the Dawa 17 escaping from prison. Their release had been central to the kidnappers' demands, and now, fortuitously, they were free. As was Brian Keenan, the Irish hostage, who had been captured not long after Daniel. The subsequent restoration of diplomatic relations with Iran seemed like another good sign. Vivi started talking about 'when Daniel comes home', as if a date had already been fixed, throwing Gemma into a state akin to panic.

'This place will be ideal for him to recuperate in,' Vivi announced over Sunday lunch in the garden of the new Kellerman country home, a lavishly converted oasthouse in Kent. As always when Nick came to visit Jamie, Max was away on business.

'Don't tempt fate,' said Gemma quietly, touching the wood of the table.

'You carry on being superstitious if you like,' said Vivi. 'I'd rather be well prepared. When he gets out he'll need a bolt-hole, away from London, where nobody can find him. You know how Daniel loathes the limelight and suddenly he'll be hot news. That's why we kept it quiet that we'd bought this place. Or rather, Roxana bought it, to celebrate the adoption being signed and sealed. She's a woman of property, aren't you darling? Or she will be, on her twenty-first birthday.'

'Oh to have a squillionaire for a dad,' said Nick. Gemma kicked him under the table.

'Oh to hear the taxman gnashing his teeth,' said Vivi sweetly. 'The best possible reason for giving the stuff away. Talking of which,' she added casually, 'I've been offered a good price for the *Courier* newspapers and I'm tempted to take it. I keep thinking of all the things I could do with the money.'

'I thought you wanted to pass them on to Jamie?' said Gemma, astonished, exchanging glances with Nick. Was this a symptom of Vivi's perennial throwaway discontent or a sign that she had finally got her priorities straight?

'I did, at first. But now I want him to be free of *The Courier* like I am. Or rather, like I soon will be.'

'And there's me thinking you'd found the one true love of your life,' said Nick, choosing his words with provocative care.

'Until I realised that a paper can't love you back,' shrugged Vivi, colouring; quite an admission, from her. 'Which was part of the attraction, at the time. I grew up hating CC for the power it gave him over us, and wanting that power for myself. I thought that once I had *The Courier* I wouldn't need or want anything else. Well, I was wrong. And now I've got a chance to make up for it. Except that I hate to think of myself as some mealy-mouthed philanthropist. It makes me feel such a fogey.'

'Come off it,' said Nick, mocking her discomfiture. 'You'll be ahead of the trend, as usual. We're through with the greed-is-good eighties now, and into the caring nineties, if you believe what the feature writers tell you. A social conscience is the latest designer accessory. Is that enough, love?' He helped Roxana to a second helping of blackberry and apple pie. She still ate with over-anxious haste, never quite believing that there was plenty more where that came from.

'Well, in my case it's cleverly disguised self-indulgence,' insisted Vivi. 'And besides, Max has already seen to it that Jamie and Roxana will be well provided for, whatever happens. He couldn't have pressed ahead with the expansion programme if he'd been worried about the financial risks to the family.'

'What about the financial risks to his shareholders?' said Nick, reminding Gemma of all the times he had said that he wouldn't touch Kellerman shares with a bargepole, that bastard was going to come unstuck one day for sure.

'If people want a nice safe investment with a guaranteed low return, there are plenty of other places they can stash their cash. A lot of people have got rich quick out of Max. They've reaped the benefits of the chances he's taken so they have to take the rough with the smooth. Even when the shares plummeted, back in eighty-seven, hardly anybody sold up in the end. And now they've more than recouped their losses.'

'End of Kellerman propaganda bulletin number ten thousand and three,' muttered Nick, as Vivi went to fetch coffee. Gemma kicked him a second time.

'I heard that,' yelled Vivi from the kitchen.

'You were meant to,' shouted back Nick. Such exchanges had become routine, their way of defusing the still tangible tension between them, with both of them relying on Gemma to act as a lightning conductor.

'You're such a peasant, Ferris,' said Vivi, returning with the percolator. 'If it wasn't for Gemma minding the till, you're the one who'd be in hock by now. I even used to have to fiddle your exes for you. You never could count above ten.'

'One, two, three, four, five, six,' interjected Roxana, showing off as usual. 'Phone!' Both children wriggled down from the table and raced to answer it first.

'That'll be Max ringing from Rome,' said Vivi, looking at her watch, and following the children into the house.

'I do wish you wouldn't make digs about Max,' remonstrated Gemma, knowing that she was wasting her breath. 'At least in front of the kids.'

'They're too young to understand. And Vivi would rather I made digs to her face than behind her back. She was breaking my heart with that stuff about him providing for the family. Even financial illiterates like me know that tying up assets in the wife's and kids' names is your standard beat-the-receivers dodge. When types like him go bust they don't end up poor. You can bet your life he's salted away a fortune in a Swiss bank account. And that it's money the taxman knows nothing about. God, if only I had the guts to turn him over . . .'

He broke off as Vivi rejoined them. She looked dazed.

'That was the Foreign Office,' she said. 'They've just had word. Daniel's been released. They're flying him home tomorrow . . .'

She flung her arms around Gemma and kissed her, then around

Nick, and kissed him, or rather he kissed her, on the mouth, long and hard, in front of a startled Gemma, who ran quickly inside to intercept the children, only to find them already sprawled in front of the television in the playroom. She leaned on the door jamb for a moment, still winded by the news. She might have longed for Daniel's release for his sake, but she had been dreading it for her own. Four, nearly five years was a long time. He would be a different person now, just as she was. She could only hope that would make things easier for both of them.

There was the sound of footsteps running into the house. Gemma caught a glimpse of Vivi disappearing up the stairs, just as Nick came in through the kitchen, rubbing his cheek.

'No need for you to tell me off,' he said. 'She's already slapped my face.'

'I should hope so too.'

'But not before she kissed me back.'

'Nick! You promised me . . .'

'I know, I know. It was a one-off, heat of the moment, I knew it was the only chance I'd get. And meanwhile you're looking cool as ice, as usual.'

'I always look like that when I'm scared.'

'At least you're in with a chance of being happy. I'd give anything to feel the way you're feeling now.' He put his arms around her. 'What a pair we are. Why couldn't we have had the common sense to fall in love with each other?'

'Love's got nothing to do with common sense,' said Gemma. 'Worse luck.'


The Foreign Office had arranged for Daniel to be debriefed at RAF Lyneham. Vivi went to meet him on her own; Max had said it was a family occasion, and that he would return from Rome at the end of the week as scheduled, while Gemma had declined to accompany her, unsure if Daniel would want to see her yet, if at all.

An army of press and TV newsmen was waiting to record the event. Knowing that Daniel was embarrassed by public displays of emotion, Vivi stayed out of sight, watching his arrival on television, knowing that Gemma and Nick would be doing the same at FPS. She had braced herself for an emaciated, haggard shadow of the brother she had known, but evidently his captors had been fattening him up in readiness for his release. There was a lot of grey in his hair and in his beard, but apart from that he looked reassuringly the same. He managed a big smile and a wave, repeated it a second time, to ensure that the snappers got the pictures they needed, shook hands with various officials, and then finally walked off the screen to where Vivi was waiting to greet him, in private.

She simply couldn't speak for several minutes, and neither could he. They stood there, just holding each other, and when she finally drew back to look at him properly, she could see how much he had changed. He might look the same, superficially, but his eyes were immeasurably older. She would never know what he had suffered, however hard he tried, or didn't try, to explain. Only someone else who had been through it could possibly hope to understand. Daniel had always been a difficult person to get close to and now he seemed more unreachable than ever.

'I'm sorry, Vivi,' he said at last. 'I'm sorry you've had all this worry.' The word sorry sounded odd, coming from him; the old Daniel had never apologised for anything. 'Harriet must have been out of her mind.' This was it, the moment she had been dreading. 'Is she here? Where's Gerald?'

Taking hold of both his hands, Vivi told him; she hadn't wanted some well-meaning stranger to do it for her. He didn't ask why Gemma wasn't there, because by that time he didn't need to. And then, for the first time ever, Vivi saw her brother cry.

Gemma didn't see the tears. She just saw the smiling figure that waved for the camera, followed by the slightly hesitant but self-composed one who read out a prepared statement at the press conference. He regretted not being able to bring news of any other hostages, having been held in solitary confinement, but he hoped that they too would soon be returned to their families. He gave his thanks to all those who had campaigned for his release, in public and behind the scenes, and asked the media to grant him the privacy to readjust to freedom.

Vivi phoned that evening to say that she was staying at the base with Daniel until he was ready to leave, when they would take off for Kent by helicopter to avoid the risk of being followed. The doctors were still running tests but they seemed to think he was physically okay, apart from his teeth being in a mess, a lack of co-ordination, and visual irregularities which would correct themselves in time. Mentally it was harder to assess the damage but he had agreed to see a shrink tomorrow. It would probably be easier for him to talk to a stranger, conceded Vivi, than to her. No, he hadn't known about Gerald and Harriet, and yes, he had taken the news pretty badly, but that was a good sign, at least he wasn't bottling up his feelings, the way Daniel usually did. Evidently he hadn't asked to speak to Gemma. Even if he had done, she wouldn't have known what to say to him.

'I'm here if you need me,' Nick reminded her, but facing Daniel again, as she would have to do eventually, was one ordeal Nick couldn't help her with. She had to find the courage to look her past in the face before she could move on to the future.

In the meantime she did her best to concentrate on her work. Nick was busy investigating a tip-off about corruption in local government, centred on a council leader who was alleged to be taking backhanders from a building contractor – a highly saleable story, if he could make it stand up. Gemma found it hard to show her usual level of interest in the case. Or even disappointment when Nick's intended exclusive was blown by the intervention of the police, who arrested the crooked councillor on corruption charges, along with three other senior public officials, two in other local authorities and one in a government ministry. It turned out that the open-handed builder had gone bankrupt, thus laying his financial affairs open to official scrutiny and revealing the existence of a slush fund.

'Looks like he grassed so they'd go easier on him,' said Nick. 'Still, at least it proves that my source was on the level . . .' And then, beating her to the phone, 'FPS. Yes, of course she's here, I keep her chained up, don't I? How's Daniel doing?' Gemma held out her hand for the phone but he ignored her. 'I'll bet he is. Another week of you mother-henning him and the poor bastard'll be on the first plane back to bloody Beirut . . . Right . . . I suppose so. Depends if I can find the key to the padlock. Yes, I'll tell her. 'Bye, love.'

'I'll bet he's what?' said Gemma, frustrated to have been deprived of her daily bulletin.

'Pissed off with being treated like an invalid. He and Vivi left the base this morning and as soon as they got to Kent he sent her packing, she was ringing from home. She wants you to get yourself to an art shop and buy him a load of painting gear. Then you're to take it down to him, now, today, on the double.'

'What? I mean . . . is he expecting me?'

'Search me,' shrugged Nick inscrutably. 'I'm only the messenger boy. She reckons the press won't be watching you, so it's all right for you to go by car. But keep an eye in your rear-view mirror.'

Perplexed, Gemma rang Vivi back, only to get the answering machine. Did Daniel really want to see her, or was this a heavy-handed attempt to throw them together?

'And yes, you can have the rest of the day off,' said Nick, kissing the top of her head. 'So get out from under my feet, will you?'

The Kellerman country seat was set in three acres of land, well off the beaten track. Breathless with apprehension, Gemma rang the doorbell with her chin, her arms full of canvas board, paints, brushes and a collapsible easel, the last of which was her own, a relic of Vivi's Christmas present to her all those years ago. There was no answer. Thinking, or rather hoping by now, that Daniel might have gone out, she walked round to the back of the house, where Vivi kept a spare key hidden in a pot of geraniums, stopping short as she saw him stretched out on the garden swing-seat, asleep.

She approached cautiously, curiously, anxious not to wake him, to stare her fill at him unobserved. He had shaved off the beard he had grown in captivity, revealing skin which was unnaturally pale from lack of sunlight, but it was also unlined, for the same reason; visibly he hadn't aged, apart from the grey in his hair. He looked heart-stoppingly like the Daniel she remembered . . .

And then, dammit, she dropped the easel with a clatter, waking him up.

'I'm sorry,' she muttered, embarrassed, bending to retrieve it. Suddenly everything was spilling from her grasp, the box of paints disgorging its contents all over the lawn.

'What are you doing here?' His voice was harsh.

'Vivi asked me to bring you these.'

'She never said you were coming. I told her that I didn't —'

'That you didn't want to see me?' said Gemma. 'It's all right. I'll just put these things in the house and —'

'I just asked her to bring a sketch pad with her, next time she came,' interrupted Daniel. 'She didn't have to get you to fetch all this stuff.' He squatted down beside her and began picking things up, not looking at her. 'They said drawing would help my manual dexterity, or lack of it, and be good exercise for my eyes. I'm clumsy as a kid at the moment, and I still can't judge distances . . .'

He was speaking too fast. Gemma realised that he was as nervous as she was, if for different reasons. Not for him the fear of reproach and rejection, rather the reverse. Perhaps he was afraid that she had been languishing for him all this time, that now Gerald was gone she would expect him to carry on where they had left off.

'There's some coffee on,' he said, following her into the house. 'I can't get enough of the stuff. Want some?'

'Actually, I ought to be going . . .'

'Don't. I didn't mean to snap. You startled me, that's all. Every time I wake up it takes me a moment to remember where I am. And even then, I feel like Rip Van Winkle.' He filled two mugs from the filter machine, holding on to the jug with two hands. 'Quite a place Vivi's got here.'

'Yes, isn't it.'

'She's bringing the kids out at the weekend. I was expecting to see you then.' In the company of others, thought Gemma, not alone, like now. Damn Vivi for setting her up like this . . . 'Is it still white, no sugar?'

'Yes. Imagine you remembering.'

'There was nothing to do but remember. I've learned my whole life off by heart in the last few years. Quite an education.' He took the two mugs into the conservatory; Gemma sat down beside him, on one of Vivi's cane-backed easy chairs, looking out at the garden, ablaze with the colours of late summer. Daniel squinted at the light painfully for a moment before going in search of his sunglasses. Gemma wished she had thought to bring some too, afraid that her eyes would say more than she meant them to.

'Plenty to paint around here,' she said, inadequately.

'If I can remember how. Vivi said you'd given it up.'

'I got blocked after Gerald died.' There. She had said his name. 'And besides, I don't have much time these days.'

'I hear the agency's doing well.'

'Yes. We've doubled turnover in the last year.'

'Can't imagine you doing a job like that.'

'Oh, you'd be surprised.'

'Not surprised, no. Just lacking in imagination. You were always tough, underneath.' He lit a cigarette with a hand that was visibly unsteady. 'I got your letters. Some of them, anyway, until they stopped giving them to me. Including one from Gerald, praising you to the skies. You were right to stay with him. He loved you all right. Knowing that helped me come to terms.'

'I loved him too,' said Gemma.

'I'm glad. I mean it. I'm glad you were there to see him through it. I should have guessed that something had happened, when they stopped giving me the letters. But I thought they were just being bloody-minded, as usual.'

'You mean they didn't want you to know?'

'Sensitive souls that they were. Perhaps they thought I'd try to end it all. Not that there was any chance of that. That death-wish of mine you were all so worried about turned out to be just an affectation. There's nothing like thinking every day might be your last to give you the will to live. In fact, I was so obsessed with keeping myself alive that it never occurred to me that anyone else might be dead.'

'I feel so responsible for everything . . .' began Gemma.

'You feel responsible? I'm the one who stomped off like a spoilt kid and got myself into trouble. I wondered, afterwards, if I was half hoping to get shot up, just to make you sorry. Too bad I wasn't.'

'Daniel, please . . .'

'And instead, my mother and brother bought it, thanks to me. Not you. Me.'

'You mustn't think like that. They wouldn't want you to think like that . . .'

'You're as bad as Vivi! I've had it up to here with everyone treating me with kid gloves and acting like I'm some kind of conquering hero. I'm about as much of a hero as someone who walks into an open manhole and waits for someone else to haul him out. I wasn't even risking my life to get some great pictures. I'd been to a Christmas piss-up the night before, and knocked back so much booze I passed out on the floor, and next morning I took a taxi back to the hotel, still half cut, and that's when they jumped me. And people expect me to be proud of it. All I did was survive.'

'Surviving isn't easy,' said Gemma. 'You told me that yourself, remember, after I tried to kill myself. And you were right.'

'Stop being so bloody understanding, will you?' he hissed, turning on her with startling venom. Vivi had warned her that Daniel was touchy and prone to sudden mood swings, but his attack on her was unexpected nonetheless. 'I was dreading seeing you again! I knew that you'd be the worst of the lot. You, of all people, ought to have the grace to blame me for being stupid and careless and arrogant and –'

'I do blame you!' Gemma flew at him, goaded into ill-considered retaliation. 'If you went out there to get your own back on me, you bloody well succeeded and I'll never forgive you for it!'

Until now she had borne all the guilt herself, to divert it away from him. She couldn't be angry with Daniel all the while his life was on the line. But now he was safe, and well, and here, and misjudging her as usual, she couldn't resist offloading some of the burden she had carried all this time alone. She railed pitilessly at him, she told him just how much everyone had suffered on his account, she let him know, by the sheer force of her fury, that she had never stopped loving him, until she ran abruptly out of steam, appalled at herself for pouring salt into his still open wounds.

'I don't want you to forgive me,' said Daniel quietly, strangely appeased by this outburst. 'I just want you to forgive yourself. And then, perhaps, I'll manage to do the same. I don't know how long it'll take for that to happen. Years, probably. The rest of my life, perhaps. All I know is that you'll have to do it first. If you can't, what hope is there for me?'

She knew then that they had both travelled too far, and suffered too much, to build on what they had had before. Their only hope was to get to know each other – or rather the people they had become – all over again, from scratch. Last time had been helter-skelter, downhill all the way. This time would have to be a slow, steady climb. Like him, she didn't know if they would manage it or how long it would take. Years, probably. Or, perhaps, if they were very lucky, the rest of their lives.

'But you've only just got home!' protested Vivi, as Max repacked his suitcase. 'You promised me you'd keep this weekend free . . .'

'You'll have Daniel there. And Gemma. And the kids. And Nick.' It was the first time she had ever heard Max use his first name.

'But what is it that's so important all of a sudden? Surely you can send somebody else?'

'I wish I could.'

'Max, what's going on? Is there a problem? Is there something you're not telling me?'

'Don't ask, Vivi. If there's a problem, I'll sort it out in my own way, like I always do.'

He pulled her to him and kissed her. As a rule his parting embraces were brief, perfunctory, Max had always kept passion for the bedroom, but this kiss was long and lingering, tender and intense.

'What did I do right?' said Vivi.

'Everything. I love you, sweetheart.'

Something's wrong, she thought. Max wasn't given to endearments, or routine protestations of affection.

'Let me come with you to the airport at least.'

'No point. I've got work to do on the way.' She followed him into the kitchen, where the children were having breakfast. He scooped Jamie up first, gave him a big hug, and told him to take care of Mummy while he was gone. Then it was Roxana's turn, which took longer, because Roxana hugged like a limpet. Finally Max managed to extricate himself.

''Bye, Vivi,' he said, giving her a big reassuring smile. 'Look after yourself.'

'Ring me when you get to New York or I'll worry!' she shouted after him. But she didn't get the chance to worry. First there was a protracted phone call from the editor of *The Courier*, and then there was a fund-raising lunch and reception to go to before collecting the children, driving to the heliport, and taking off for a weekend in the country. They arrived at six o'clock to find that Daniel had lost all track of time and was still painting busily in the conservatory, oblivious to the clatter in the kitchen next door, where a local lady-what-does was preparing their evening meal.

He shook hands with both children as if they were adults – Daniel had no experience of kids – raising no objection when Roxana got hold of a paintbrush and started adding her own daubings to his work – a dark, brooding abstract, incomprehensible to Vivi's untutored eye, though she could guess what it was about. He had rejected any notion of writing a book about his experiences, preferring to tell his story visually, albeit still under the pretext of occupational therapy rather than self-expression.

He still showed no inclination to talk about his time in captivity, to Vivi, at least; knowing Daniel he never would. But he had asked for the cuttings about other hostages and written to their families, saying that he was at their disposal if they wanted to meet or talk. Rather than dodge the press, he planned to endure a short, sharp period of saturation coverage, knowing from experience that hiding away from the media would merely increase his scarcity value; news editors soon lost interest in those who made themselves freely available for interview. After that, he wanted to get away, somewhere nobody would recognise him. Given that his face had been on posters, all over the country, for the past two and a half years, there was no chance of the anonymity he craved unless he went abroad. He might be grateful to Vivi for the campaign she had waged on his behalf, and to Max for subsidising it, but he didn't thank them for making him into a celebrity, or rather a walking freak show, to use his own dismissive phrase.

'I'm glad you've decided to sell up,' he said over supper.

'So you should be. Your shares are worth a bomb now. And I can get you a much better deal if you throw in yours with mine.'

'I wasn't thinking of that. I always hated *The Courier*. I hated what it did to Harriet, and Gerald, and Gemma. I hated the way it came between you and Nick.'

'It wouldn't have worked between me and Nick.' Even Nick could see that now. 'I'd have made him miserable and hated myself for it, even more than I hated myself already. But now . . . I suppose I'm learning to like myself a little, if that doesn't sound too big-headed. I'm not half as much of a bitch as I used to be, honestly. Max has been good for me.'

Looking back, loving Nick had been too easy. So easy that she had seen it as a sign of weakness, not a source of strength. Loving Max had been hard work, forcing her to use emotional muscles she hadn't known she possessed.

'Perhaps you've been good for him,' said Daniel. 'You seem . . . happier. You wouldn't be if you hadn't made him happier too.'

Happier. Which wasn't quite the same thing as happy. But it was the nearest she, or Max, was likely to get to it. She hadn't expected it, or even wanted it, masochist that she was, but now she had it, she was determined not to lose it. She had made that mistake once before.

'Stupid bugger,' muttered Vivi, switching off Ceefax after lunch on Sunday. Gemma was with the children in the garden; Daniel was painting. She and Nick had tuned into the latest headlines, to find that another senior civil servant had been charged with corruption in the wake of the building contracts scandal. 'If you were in a top job in Whitehall, earning a great big screw with an index-linked pension and a guaranteed knighthood when you retired, would you risk ruining your career and going to jail for taking bribes?'

'I might, if the bribe was big enough and I thought I could get away with it. This kind of thing is going on every day of the week, you can count on it, with Joe Public none the wiser. The ones who've been caught will get the full shock-horror treatment from the media, while the rest carry on pocketing their ill-gotten gains.' He got up and walked over to the french window, looking out at the garden, at Jamie, at Gemma. 'I'm going to miss her like hell when she leaves,' he said sadly.

'Has she said anything?' Vivi hadn't liked to rush things by asking her, or Daniel, what their plans were.

'Not yet. But it's only a matter of time. I can't see Daniel going off on his travels without her. Or her letting him go alone. I'm not talking romance, it's too soon for that. But he's going to need looking after for a good while yet.'

Daniel felt out of his depth, he confessed, in quite ordinary, everyday situations. For years he had been denied the right to make the most basic decisions, and it would be many months before he could negotiate the busy highways of a normal life without fear of getting lost or being run over. In the meantime he would need a guide and mentor. Someone strong and stubborn and capable like Gemma, who knew her way around the darker regions of the soul.

'When I went to collect her today,' Nick went on, 'she had her sketch pad out. First time I've seen that in a while, has to be a good sign. I like to think that things'll work out between them, sentimental berk that I am. Not that love is any guarantee of things working out,' he added, turning round to face her.

'Stop looking at me like that,' said Vivi, colouring. 'And if you ever try it on again, the way you did the other day, you'll get more than a slap in the face. I'm not in the market for an affair.'

'Neither am I,' said Nick tightly. 'Sharing my kid with Kellerman's bad enough without having to share you as well.'

Deep down he was still angry with her; perhaps he always would be. If she wasn't Gemma's sister, he wouldn't be sitting here at this moment, Jamie or no Jamie. Without Gemma their reconciliation would have proved impossible, or untenable. And what would happen if Gemma followed Daniel to some far-flung corner of Italy or Spain, leaving them unsupervised? They would either end up at each other's throats or in each other's arms. And one thing Vivi had sworn to herself was that she would never cheat on Max, never jeopardise her marriage or the children's security, no matter how lonely she was when he was away, no matter how great the temptation. A temptation she had denied until that kiss.

'Well, if you want to carry on sharing him, as opposed to not seeing him at all, you'll respect my marriage.'

'It's myself I'll be respecting, not your marriage. If you divorced Kellerman tomorrow, I'd still feel the same way. Once bitten, twice shy. I kissed you to prove a point. Not because I couldn't help myself. So relax. You're quite safe. And so am I.'

And with that he walked out into the garden, to join Gemma and the children, leaving Vivi to fume. Once upon a time she had blown hot and cold on him, and now he was giving her a taste of her own medicine. His big mistake, looking back, had been to reassure her that he would always be there for her, no matter what.

And now he had learned what Max had known instinctively from the start – that Vivi thrived, however perversely, on uncertainty, not reassurance. Perhaps she had received too many false assurances as a child, perhaps she simply enjoyed an element of suspense, but either way, he had got the message now. That kiss had been an expression of defiance, not of surrender.

The phone rang. Vivi hoped it would be Max; she hadn't heard from him since his departure on Friday morning, apart from a call from his answering service in New York, to tell her that he had arrived safely but would be moving around a lot over the next few days.

But it wasn't Max. It was the children's nanny, who had the weekend off, phoning from the flat in London.

'The police are here,' she announced in a frozen voice. 'They were asking for Mr Kellerman. I had to let them in. They've got a search warrant . . .'

A hundred half-forgotten fragments fused into a moment of indistinct truth. It should have come as no surprise when the doorbell rang before she could frame a response. It was what *The Courier* would have referred to as a synchronised swoop. The two plain-clothes men were very polite, regretting the necessity to disturb her Sunday and brandishing various pieces of paper at her, one of which gave them permission to turn the house upside down, and the other to arrest her husband on charges of conspiracy and corruption.


Vivi refused to answer any of their questions until she had taken legal advice. They, in return, told her little, except that a man currently in police custody had admitted to taking bribes from Max as well as the bankrupt building contractor. A confession he had presumably traded against some promise of leniency. Max must have seen this coming. That explained why he had left so suddenly, why he hadn't given her a contact number, why he hadn't rung her, for fear that they might be listening in. . .

'I never play safe,' Max had told her the very first time she met him. Playing safe would have ensured slow, steady growth. But Max had wanted fast results, meteoric success. And when things had started to go wrong, a few years back, he must have resorted to desperate remedies.

'If I see a weakness,' he had said, 'I exploit it.' By his lights he would have done nothing morally wrong, except capitalise on human frailty and greed. He had started out at too much of a disadvantage to have any qualms about fighting dirty. And taking risks came naturally to him, it was what had given him his edge. He was as much of a danger-addict in his way as Daniel had been. And now, like him, he had taken one risk too many.

The consequences didn't bear thinking about, but Vivi forced herself to do so, wanting to be prepared for the worst. Quite apart from the public humiliation of criminal proceedings – John Poulson, the architect, had gone to prison in the seventies for bribing public servants – the scandal would result in cancelled contracts, a collapse in share prices, the calling in of loans, ruin and disgrace. Max would never be able to bear it. His entire career had been devoted to winning the wealth and power that were fundamental to his self-esteem.

'Why didn't he tell me?' she raged at Gemma, after the police had gone. Daniel had taken the children out for a walk, so that they wouldn't witness the violation of their home; even Jamie's computer had been taken away for examination. 'Why didn't he warn me this might happen?'

'Max would say that what you didn't know couldn't hurt you. That if he'd told you the truth he would have made you an accessory, and this way, at least, your hands stayed clean. He would say that his only crime was in being found out.'

That was exactly what Max would have said, of course. Vivi hadn't credited Gemma with knowing him that well. That explained why he had kept her out of his business dealings, made her financially independent of him by giving her *The Courier*, set up large untouchable trust funds for Jamie and Roxana . . .

'Would you like me to stay tonight?' said Gemma. 'Nick's already left. He thought you wouldn't want him around.'

'Did he say it?' growled Vivi, swallowing an angry sob. She mustn't go to pieces. She mustn't let the kids guess that anything was wrong. 'Did he say, I told you so?'

'He was too shattered to say anything much.'

'What the hell am I going to tell the children?'

'You don't have to tell them anything yet. They're used to Max being away. He'll be in touch, I'm sure, one way or the other.'

'Not if he's got any sense,' said Vivi bleakly. 'You can bet your life the police will intercept any post. And tap every phone line in the place. Here and in London and at the office.'

She tried to imagine Max being extradited from the States, brought home in handcuffs, and knew that he wouldn't let that happen. Perhaps he was already in South America somewhere, negotiating in cash with some other grasping official to buy safe haven for the future. Max surely had money tucked away in all sorts of unlikely places, against just such an eventuality.

'I expect they'll be watching us every minute, to see if we try to join him,' she added. 'I feel like booking a flight to bloody Rio just to give them a run for their money.'

Would he send for her and the children, risk blowing his cover? Or had he kissed her goodbye for the last time, knowing he would never see her again? She remembered the look in his eyes, the hoarseness in his voice, the fervour of his parting embrace, the way he had told Jamie to take care of his mother, and she knew, with a hollow certainty, that he wouldn't ask her to share a life of obscurity and exile, or even risk her offering to do so. He would survive, build a new life, and count on her to do the same . . .

You'll have Daniel there, he had said. And Gemma. And the kids. And Nick. He had been reassuring himself, not her, glad that his former partner in loneliness wasn't alone any more.


Evening Standard, *Monday, 1 October 1990*
*US Federal Agents are continuing their search for missing computer tycoon Max Kellerman, who is wanted by British police in connection with alleged corruption charges. Kellerman was last seen at 3.30 p.m. on Saturday, California time, when he took off from Monterey airport in his privately owned Piper Seneca, supposedly on a short joy-ride which required no flight plan to be filed. It is assumed that Kellerman has since landed in open ground, without reference to air traffic control.*

*Kellerman International has in recent years won major government contracts for computer hardware and software in Europe, the US and Australia, as well as in the UK. It seems*

*likely that investigations will be mounted into all such dealings,
if only to clear those officials involved from suspicion . . .*

'How is she?' said Nick, throwing the paper to one side as
Gemma arrived in the office. He shepherded her into his cubby-
hole and shut the door. 'You haven't left her on her own, have
you?'

'No, Daniel came back to London with us. She's determined to
carry on as normal, she doesn't want anybody thinking she's
hanging her head in shame or pulling strings to keep the press
away. She posed up for the pack and fired off a whole column at
them, saying that if Max is guilty, then so are any number of other
businessmen, and it's sheer hypocrisy to pretend otherwise. She's
sure Max will be following the news and she wants him to know
she's okay.'

'And meanwhile she thinks I'm crowing. And so I should be. I've
spent long enough hoping that something like this would happen.
How am I ever going to face her again without feeling like a bloody
vulture?'

Gemma too felt compromised by the hostile thoughts she had
harboured against Max. She had spent the last year trapped in the
spider's web of his duplicity, longing to be free. But if this was
freedom, it tasted of dust.

'Let's just hope for Vivi's sake they never catch him,' went on
Nick. 'Because if they do they'll make an example of him, like they
did with Poulson, and she'll spend the next ten years visiting him in
jail . . .'

He broke off as there was a tap on his door.

'What is it?' he barked.

'Something you'll want to see. About Kellerman.'

It was there on the screen, flickering at them in green and black:

GUADALAJARA AIR TRAFFIC CONTROL REPORTS MAYDAY
MESSAGE FROM KELLERMAN. FLOATING WING SECTION SIGHTED
BY AIR-SEA RESCUE FIFTY MILES OFF MEXICAN COAST.

Gemma left for Vivi's straight away. Given the time lapse since
Max had taken off from Monterey, he must already have landed
once, safely if illicitly, before continuing his onward journey. To

take on more fuel, perhaps, assuming he could have got hold of any without risk of exposure . . .

The press were still camped in their cars outside Vivi's block of flats; Gemma's arrival produced a simultaneous opening and slamming of doors followed by the whirr of a dozen motor-drives, reminding her of all the times she had sent FPS freelances out to intrude on other people's privacy. Daniel answered the entry-phone and buzzed her up.

'Vivi's in a bad way,' he said, evidently relieved to see her. 'I don't know what to do. All I could think of was to get the nanny to bundle the kids in the car and drive, so that they don't see her like this . . .'

'Like this' was Vivi in an unprecedented frenzy of grief and disbelief. She might have reconciled herself to Max's disappearance, out of sheer beat-the-rap bravado, but she hadn't bargained for losing him altogether. Daniel stood by awkwardly, hands in pockets, his face a mask of controlled distress.

'He radioed to say he'd run out of fuel,' Vivi told Gemma, through a sob. 'He must have underestimated how much he would need, or decided to take a chance. He told them he was going to try to ditch in the sea, but then they lost him . . .'

'They're still searching, remember,' volunteered Daniel un-certainly, looking at Gemma as if to ask, 'Am I saying the right thing?' A question Gemma couldn't answer, except by indicating her own sense of helplessness. 'You said yourself that the plane carried lifejackets, and a raft . . .'

'Don't make me hope! I don't want to hope! I'd rather he was dead, because of what they'll do to him if they find him. I'd rather he was dead because I love him . . .'

She crumpled into Gemma's arms. Her arms, not Daniel's, because she was her sister, because she knew what it was to lose a husband. He gave Gemma that look again, a look which said, thank God you're here.

'He loved you too,' murmured Gemma. 'He loved you too.'

The Sunday Times, 31 *March* 1991
## ANOTHER STONEHOUSE?
*In the six months since Max Kellerman's private plane came down in the Pacific Ocean, controversy still rages as to his fate.*

*There is, however, no doubt that it is his Piper Seneca which now rests at the bottom of the sea – the recovered wing section bore its registration number – or that the aircraft was out of control when it hit the water, breaking up on impact and guaranteeing certain death for anyone aboard . . . if anyone was aboard.*

*Granted, the sea does not always yield up its dead. Nonetheless, the lack of a body has given rise to speculation that the so-called accident was in fact an elaborate hoax to avert continued pursuit by law enforcement agencies. Devotees of this theory believe that Kellerman, an experienced sky-diver, engineered an accurately calculated shortage of fuel, knowing that it would activate the aircraft's alarm system, which he had wired up to trigger off a pre-recorded mayday message. By the time this was transmitted, he would already have parachuted into the sea, many miles short of the crash area – where an accomplice with a boat was waiting to pick him up – leaving the plane to fly itself to destruction on the automatic pilot. A fanciful theory, perhaps, but a technically feasible one, suggesting a carefully plotted escape plan, worked out well in advance.*

*Meanwhile further evidence of bribery continues to emerge, leading to six more arrests so far, which may yet prove to be the tip of an almighty iceberg. Vivienne Chambers, Kellerman's wife/widow, the recently retired proprietor of* Courier News-papers, *fired a parting salvo in her valedictory leader against those who have painted her husband as evil and corrupt. The devil, she claimed, has always been a scapegoat for the human propensity to sin, and if this case exposes the many leeches who profit from high office, then her husband's death, albeit unconfirmed, will not have been in vain . . .*

Officially, Max wasn't dead, making it impossible for Vivi to mourn him properly, not knowing for sure. Even if he was alive and safe somewhere, she knew that he wouldn't implicate her by attempting to make contact, well aware that she would still be under surveillance. She couldn't actually prove that she was being shadowed, or that her phone was being tapped, or her mail tampered with. But it would be naïve to suppose otherwise.

Gemma, too, had reported strange clicks on her line; when they rang each other, they would routinely abuse the unseen listener, and on a prearranged signal, Gemma would distance herself from the receiver to enable Vivi to blow an eardrum-shattering whistle into the phone. Let the victim sue her for damages if he dared.

Outwardly she maintained her customary panache, bloody but unbowed. The sale of *Courier* Newspapers would enable her to build the flamboyantly named Kellerman Clinic in Bucharest, catering for infant victims of Aids. and in seven years, when she legally became a widow, she would inherit whatever had become of Kellerman International, which was currently in the hands of administrators and the subject of a proposed takeover bid. Even on a worst-case estimate, the proceeds would eventually enable her to found enough charitable trusts bearing Max's name to mock and silence his detractors.

She told the children that Daddy had been killed in a plane crash, sparing them the hope that tormented her, so that they could grieve for him and recover. And when she couldn't bring herself to be cheerful and positive, for their sake, when she was having one of her bad days, she relied on Daniel to help her through it. She felt guilty that he had been denied a peaceful period of readjustment, pitched into the middle of a family crisis, in the full glare of the media spotlight. But he had risen to the challenge unselfishly and un-complainingly. As Gemma said, being needed had given him a sense of purpose and helped restore his self-confidence. Even so, Vivi knew she couldn't, or rather mustn't, keep him here much longer.

'I'd rather you moved out,' she told Daniel, over Easter. 'I don't want the kids to get too used to you living here. They'll make a surrogate father out of you, and then they'll miss you when you go. They'll miss you as it is. So clear off and find yourself some sun and get working on your first exhibition.'

'No. If you don't want me here I'll find a flat.'

'Don't make me argue with you. You're not indispensable, and neither is Gemma. So mind you take her with you.'

'No point even asking. She won't leave you, and —'

'You mean you have asked, and she's said no, poor Vivi can't manage without me. God, but she can be a pious cow sometimes. Just leave her to me, I'll soon put her right —'

'I was about to say, and she won't leave Nick either. And I can understand why, the way you've been cold-shouldering him.'

'He's the one who's been cold-shouldering me! He hasn't been near me since it happened.' There had been one short, stilted letter saying he was sorry; obviously he didn't expect her to believe him.

'Have some insight into the way he feels. He doesn't want to look as if he's laying any claims to Jamie. Or taking advantage of Max being ... off the scene. I found myself in much the same position with Gemma. So I know what he's going through.'

'What about the way I feel?' argued Vivi stubbornly. 'I don't see why I should be the one to make the first move ...'

'Then don't make it. It gives Gemma and me an excuse to put things off a bit longer. We're both shit scared that it won't work, being on our own together, so carry on being a coward, with our blessing, so that we can do the same.'

Vivi wondered if Gemma was putting similar pressure on Nick. Half a dozen times she picked up the phone to ring him, but she funked it every time, hoping that he would weaken – or rather prove strong enough – first. But when his call finally came, it was brusque, almost hostile.

'Can you come to the office at eleven tonight?' he said without preamble.

'Tonight? Why?'

'I'll tell you when you get here. Don't be late.'

'Eleven sounds pretty late to me. What's it about?'

'A hot story I need help with. Don't say anything to Gem or Daniel. See you. 'Bye.'

Evidently it was something he didn't want to discuss until all the staff had gone home. Something he preferred to deal with in an office setting, to reassure her that this was strictly business. Except that she wasn't in the business any more ...

Daniel was spending the evening with a fellow-snapper just back from the Gulf War. So there was no need to explain where she was off to at such an unlikely hour. Compulsively early as always, she had parked the car by half past ten. At ten to eleven her curiosity got the better of her.

She rang the bell and waited while Nick came down three flights of stairs to let her in. Really, this office was a dump. And the area was the pits, no wonder he had to lay on mini-cabs for the female staff at night. He ought to improve the agency's image by moving to more prestigious premises, exploit his successful track record to raise capital for a much bigger operation, rather than wait till he could afford to finance it himself; Nick had always had a morbid working-class fear of debt. Would he feel patronised if she offered to become a silent partner? A working relationship might be easier to handle than a personal one. She didn't regret selling *The Courier*, but she was still as much of a news-freak as ever. It would be nice to have a finger in the Fleet Street pie again, if only to stop herself brooding . . .

'Come on up,' said Nick. He looked tired and strained. 'Sorry about the subterfuge. But I knew your phone was bugged, so I couldn't say much.'

'How are you?'

'I'm okay. You?'

'Surviving. I'm sorry I haven't been in touch.'

'Likewise. But I thought you needed a breathing space. Actually, it's just as well we haven't been in contact. Otherwise they might have decided to eavesdrop on me, as well as Gemma. The thing is, I had a call earlier today. From your husband.'

Vivi sat down heavily.

'He didn't identify himself,' went on Nick. 'And he kept it all pretty cryptic, in case anyone was listening in. But it was definitely him. He told me to contact you – not that he mentioned your name – and bring you here tonight.'

'You mean, he's going to phone again?'

'No. He said to have the computer on line, ready for him to send something through.'

Vivi covered her face with her hands, trembling with relief. He was alive. Max was alive . . .

'I guess he's got himself fixed up somewhere,' said Nick, 'and now he's going to ask you to join him. You may as well know I wasn't going to tell you. I was going to let him send his lousy message and think that you'd ignored it. But in the end I couldn't do it to you. And here's me kidding myself I've toughened up.'

'He trusted you to tell me,' said Vivi. 'Max doesn't trust people easily. But when he does, he's usually right.'

'He took me for a mug, you mean. Don't go, Vivi. Not for my sake, for yours and the kids'. You need to be who you really are, God knows it's taken you long enough to find that out. If he loved you he wouldn't ask you to leave everything and everyone you know and spend the rest of your life pretending to be somebody else . . .'

They both jumped up as the light began flashing on the modem. A moment later Nick retrieved and displayed the message.

DARLING VIVI

I WASN'T GOING TO MAKE CONTACT, I THOUGHT IT WOULD BE EASIER FOR YOU. BUT PERHAPS I WAS JUST MAKING THINGS EASIER FOR MYSELF. I'M SAFE AND WELL. YOU WON'T SEE ME AGAIN, AND EVEN IF YOU DID YOU WOULDN'T RECOGNISE ME. TELL GEMMA SHE SAVED MY BACON. THANKS TO HER I REALISED I WASN'T INVINCIBLE AND MADE CONTINGENCY PLANS AGAINST SOMETHING ELSE I'D CONVINCED MYSELF WOULD NEVER HAPPEN. SHE'LL UNDERSTAND WHAT I MEAN. SHE'LL CONFIRM THAT THIS ISN'T A HOAX, THAT IT REALLY CAME FROM ME.

BE HAPPY. TO DEPRIVE YOURSELF OF THAT WOULD BE TO PUNISH ME MORE THAN I DESERVE. THIS IS THE ONE AND ONLY MESSAGE YOU WILL EVER RECEIVE FROM ME. I WILL ALWAYS LOVE YOU.

MAX

'Save it,' said Vivi, her vision fogged by tears. 'Print it . . .'

But as soon as Nick touched the first key, the message disappeared, both from the screen and from the disk.

'He must have programmed it to wipe itself,' he said, perplexed, double-checking the index. 'Just in case I had the police here, tracing the call. Obviously he didn't trust me after all. And he was right. I wasn't going to give you back to him without a fight.'

'Max is the one who's giving me back,' said Vivi quietly. After months of torment she felt at peace. Max was alive and safe and he loved her, he had proved that by setting her free. It would be greedy to ask for more, churlish not to try to do as he had asked her. 'He told me to be happy, didn't he?'

'That's a tall order, for you,' said Nick.

'I'm learning,' said Vivi. 'Slowly. I just need a bit more practice, that's all.'

And a lot more help. Not from good old Nick, poor old Nick, who put up with any amount of shit, who thought he was lucky to have her. Max had seen him off for good. And the Nick who was looking at her now with a new, tough love would learn to thank him for that. Just as she had done.

'I'll miss you,' sniffed Gemma.

'Well, I won't miss you,' said Vivi, blowing her nose. 'I'll be much too busy. Don't worry, I'll look after Nick for you. And try not to fall out with that bad-tempered brother of mine, I don't want to see either of you again for at least six months.'

Daniel kissed Vivi and shook Nick's hand. 'Don't let her work you too hard, will you?'

'Some silent partner she's turned out to be,' complained Nick. 'Yap, yap, yap. She never stops.'

'And he never listens,' countered Vivi. And then, as they heard the final call over the Tannoy, she threw her arms around Gemma in a final farewell embrace.

'One last try,' she said. 'What did Max really mean, about you saving his bacon?'

Gemma looked her sister straight in the eye and held her gaze without wavering.

'That's between him and me,' she said, smiling.